THE LADY AND THE RAKE

"I didn't do anything," Tyler defended.

"You flirted."

"I did nothing of the kind! If you perceived me as flirting, you obviously know nothing about that sort of amusement."

Lady Belinda sniffed. "You continuously flirt, my lord. You have indulged in that occupation for so long that you don't even realize what you are doing."

"Ridiculous!"

"Not so! You do it in the way that you look at one through those absurdly long lashes, and in the manner in which you smile. That charming hint of a dimple and that . . ."

"Since I cannot conceal my physical attributes, perhaps I'd best leave," Tyler interrupted. "Apparently, you object to my presence."

"I thought you were going to help me," Lady Belinda lamented, her mouth forming a perfect pout.

Gazing at her luscious pink lips, Tyler wished he could take her in his arms and kiss her thoroughly.

"Why are you staring at me?" she demanded.

"Truthfully, I was thinking of kissing you."

Lady Belinda tossed her head. "You see? Flirting!"

"No, my dear. I wasn't flirting. I was stating a fact. I would greatly enjoy kissing you and I believe you'd delight in it, too . . .

—from A MATCH FOR LORD FARLEIGH, by Cathleen Clare

Rogues and *Rakes*

Donna Bell
Julie Caille
Cathleen Clare
Monique Ellis
Valerie King
Isobel Linton

ZEBRA BOOKS
KENSINGTON PUBLISHING CORP.

ZEBRA BOOKS are published by

Kensington Publishing Corp.
850 Third Avenue
New York, NY 10022

First Printing: April, 1996

Printed in the United States of America

10 9 8 7 6 5 4 3 2 1

CONTENTS

The Matchmaking Rogue

by
Donna Bell

For my three brothers,
Nick, Steve, and David Day
whose collective wit enhances all
of my male characters.

Merit Emerson let the letter fall to her lap and stared out the window at the peaceful garden where a cool green lawn gave way to geometric flower beds of nasturtiums and pansies arranged *à la française*. Beyond the colorful beds, the lawn was dotted with tall, manicured shrubs. And in one corner, almost hidden by climbing pink roses, was a weathered arbor with a cushioned bench. When she had chosen this house, Merit had planned every inch of the garden, fashioning a haven of serenity amidst the hustle and bustle of the London she had once known.

She glanced down at her old friend's scrawled handwriting and shook her head. Charlotte had no idea what she was asking; Merit had managed to quietly reside in London and still keep out of society for the past seven years. The last thing she wanted was to attend *ton* parties and shepherd a young miss of eighteen.

She had read about the betrothal of Charlotte's sister to the ancient Lord Upton; it had been a nine-day wonder, even reaching her ears. But as she knew from personal experience, it happened all the time.

Merit's father arranged her marriage. And Charlotte's father arranged her first marriage. Charlotte's second marriage, her happy one, had been purely for love and had taken place despite her father and brother.

In a brown study, Merit stared outside again. She smiled and waved to her six-year-old daughter playing in the garden. How could she give up her tranquil life for all that upheaval again? The last thing she wanted was to bring attention to herself! She had no desire to be the *ton*'s idea of a merry widow!

Merit stood up, catching sight of her image in the mirror hanging above the fireplace. She smiled thoughtfully and then sighed. If she had grown fat or ugly, she might consider it. The gentlemen would leave her alone then. But she hadn't; the image staring back was still tall and slim, the long brown hair glossy and full, and the face, with its fine brown eyes and smooth complexion, still undeniably attractive. She had never been beautiful, of course. But she had learned that to the gentlemen, a curvaceous figure and intriguing smile were just as compelling. Added to all that was the considerable fortune her late husband had left her. Oh yes, she thought grimly, the gentlemen would definitely return.

Sitting down again, she reread the letter. No, it was too much to ask. She would simply write to her friend and reassure her that Catherine would no doubt be happy. Hadn't their brother, Lord Blackwell, arranged the marriage?

"Mama, Mama, look what I found!"

"What is it, Maggie?" She held out her hand as her daughter ran into the room, her chubby hands cupped.

Merit peeked inside and saw a butterfly flitting around. "Doesn't it tickle?" she asked.

"Yes, but it's so pretty, Mama."

"They are very beautiful, but they like flying around the garden more than in your hands. Why don't you let it go outside?"

"If I don't, what will happen to it?"

"I imagine it will die."

The little girl's dark brown eyes were thoughtful, and she nodded her head before going back out the French doors, opening her hands, and setting the butterfly free. Laughing, she chased after it, her arms mimicking the wings in flight.

Merit bowed her head, looking down at the letter. Slowly, she rose and went to the delicate writing desk in the corner. Taking pen in hand, she wrote:

Dear Charlotte,
    I will do all I can to ensure your sister's happiness . . .

"Damn it, Catherine! You will stop all your sniveling and whining this instant!"

"But Christian . . ."

The tall, handsome man glared his beautiful sister to silence. "I'll hear no more of your complaints on the subject. Upton and I are agreed. The ceremony will be at St. George's Church on the first of May. Make your arrangements accordingly!"

"Excuse me, my lord, but Lord Gillingham and Mr. Bewick are awaiting you in your study," the butler announced.

Lord Blackwell looked relieved. "Thank you, Reed." He picked up his beaver hat and set it on golden curls. With a final glare at his youngest sister, he said curtly, "Good day, Catherine."

She essayed no reply, only bursting into fresh sobs. Christian hurried away.

Merit sat twisting her handkerchief, looking up at Lord Blackwell's impressive town house. She smoothed her gown and patted her hair but made no move to descend to the pavement.

"Madam? Did you want to get down?" asked the puzzled footman.

Merit took a deep breath and smiled. "Certainly, too late to turn back now," she said, causing her servant to return her smile uncertainly. He helped her to the ground and then ran up the steps in front of her and announced her as the door swung open.

"Mrs. Merit Emerson to see Miss Catherine Richardson."

"I will ascertain if my mistress is at home, madam," intoned the high-browed butler, his nose pointing toward the sky.

Merit's eyes narrowed dangerously. She might not be a "Lady Something," but she was not accustomed to such high-handed tactics.

"Reed, isn't it?" she began in her most supercilious tone. "You will inform Miss Richardson that an old friend of Charlotte's has called."

The butler looked her up and down; though he still didn't

recognize her, he took in the elegant gown as well as the haughty glare and bowed. "Very good, madam. Won't you follow me?" He led her past the main hall and into an airy alcove, holding out a chair for her to sit down. "I'll only be a few minutes, madam," he added more graciously.

Merit inspected the familiar alcove and hallway from her chair; it hadn't changed except that she was no longer viewing it through a green girl's eyes. She recalled visiting Charlotte many times, always in awe of the elegant surroundings. Her own family was just as respectable, even though their home hadn't been as palatial as the Blackwell dynasty's. Now, of course, as the widow of one of the wealthiest and most influential members of Parliament, she could have opted for such an address, but she was more than satisfied with the cozy elegance of her home in Hanover Square.

Merit was startled out of her inspection by the eruption into the hall of three tall, elegant gentlemen. One, a veritable Adonis with golden curls and azure eyes, stopped in front of her chair and leaned forward, looking her up and down. She could smell the alcohol on his breath and instinctively raised her hand to her nose.

With a sneer, he said, "Fifty pounds, madam, that's the most I'll pay."

Merit's mouth flew open and she gasped. All three men laughed and moved as one down the hall and out the front door.

The butler appeared again. "Miss Catherine will see you now, madam. This way, please."

By the time Merit entered the morning room, she had regained her composure, and she was immediately struck by the beauty of its occupant. Now she knew why Catherine was considered the reigning belle of the Season. Her golden hair was short and formed springy ringlets all around her head. The eyes she turned to Merit were the brightest blue she had ever seen.

Admiration changed to sympathy when she realized those bright eyes were heavy with unshed tears.

"My dear child . . ." she began, at which Catherine burst into noisy sobs again.

Merit hurried to the sofa, all her maternal instincts aroused, and gathered the weepy young lady into her arms. While she patted Catherine's shoulder and murmured words of comfort, she heard Lord Blackwell described as, "monster," "too old to understand," and "unfeeling."

When the young lady finally recovered, the experience rendered them instant friends. Catherine, feeling much better for having vented her emotions, found the strength to smile and apologize.

"I am not usually so blue-deviled," she said, extending her hand. "My name is Catherine. I understand from Reed that you are an old friend of Charlotte's, Mrs. Emerson."

"Yes, but please call me Merit or I shall feel ancient and become blue-deviled myself. Charlotte and I were at school together and had our come-outs together—brief as they both were."

Catherine's feeble smile turned into a little sigh. "Just as mine is. Christian—he is my brother and guardian, you must know—says I will be married on the first of May. Whether I like it or not!"

"Have you no say in the matter?"

"None! Between Christian and my betrothed, Lord Upton, I have no say in the matter!" she added petulantly.

"That is monstrous!" exclaimed Merit, remembering how her own miserly father had insisted on her marriage taking place quickly to save him the expense of a long Season.

"I think so, too!"

"Have you spoken to your brother?"

"That is why you discovered me in tears, Merit."

"I see. Well, I shall see what I can do." She related the portion of Charlotte's request that she help Catherine in every way possible, adding, "And so I will!"

Catherine clapped her hands together and smiled, saying, "Then you'll go to the dressmaker with me? My aunt, who usually advises me, has been called away. Some business about chicken pox and those four odious grandsons she has! And just when I need her! Most inconsiderate!"

Merit was taken aback for a moment, but she agreed to the shopping expedition and soon had her neck encircled in a fierce hug.

"You are the best of friends!" exclaimed Catherine, much to Merit's surprise. "When I asked Christian to allow me to hire a companion this morning, he refused. I was near despair, I can tell you. But now, thanks to you, everything is wonderful again!"

"Oh, so that's what he meant," murmured Merit, as both the identity of the blond man—no doubt Lord Blackwell—and the meaning behind his seeming insults were clarified.

"What?" asked Catherine.

"Nothing, nothing."

"I'll tell Reed to have the carriage brought 'round." She pulled the bell rope and gave her instructions to the butler. Then she turned back to Merit and observed, "With my blonde hair and your dark hair, we should take along our footman, Tim."

"Why him in particular?" asked Merit, perplexed by her new friend's train of thought.

"He is redheaded, of course. We shall present such a striking trio!"

"How was your visit, Mama?" asked Maggie, her arms around Merit's neck in a loving embrace.

"It was most interesting, sweetheart. As a matter of fact, I think you and Miss Richardson would get along very well."

"Why, Mama?"

Laughing, Merit gave her daughter a quick hug before she scrambled to the floor. "Because she acts about your age. Where is Lovett?"

"She's talking to Cook. We're going to have a lovely pigeon pie for supper," Maggie said in her most grown-up voice.

"Then you should be happy. Tomorrow, how would you like

to go shopping with me and Miss Richardson at the Pantheon Bazaar?"

"May Lovett come, too?"

"Certainly! And we'll have ices at Gunter's. You'll both like that!"

"Ooh! I'll go tell her!" exclaimed the little girl, scampering away to find her governess.

Not for the first time, Merit wished she had produced a brother or sister for Maggie. She would have loved having another child, but the method of begetting one . . .

Merit picked up the book she was reading and put such unpleasant thoughts far from her mind.

Lord Blackwell put his arms around his mistress and kissed her, giving her bottom a squeeze. They were lying in the cozy bathhouse pool that overlooked a private courtyard. Christian had purchased the house for his mistress—whichever one he fancied at a particular moment. It was located in the middle of quiet Hanover Square.

"Oh!" she squealed. "It is too naughty of you, Blackwell! You promised to take me to your hunting box on the first of May!" She moved a short distance away, presenting her curvaceous backside to him.

"And now you'll have to be patient, Maribella," he said reaching out to stroke her back. "It's for the best, you know. As soon as I can rid myself of this last sister, we shall be able to take trips everywhere."

"To Paris?" she exclaimed, slipping back to his side and pressing against him.

Christian frowned; he disliked being opportuned. It reminded him forcibly of the begging and wheedling his sisters were so adept at. But Maribella, of course, had other methods, much more formidable methods, for getting her way.

He moaned as she reached a particularly vulnerable spot and pulled her out of the water and on top of him again. Her full breasts presented themselves for attention, and he obliged, caus-ing Maribella to return his moan, wriggling against him.

Christian buried his face in her long black hair and forgot about resisting her demands.

Merit couldn't remember the last time she had been so ex-hausted as she swallowed the cold ice. Her feet hurt, her shoul-ders ached, and her throat was sore. It was almost four o'clock, and this was their first break for the day. There had been no luncheon, no tea, except what the modiste had thought to provide.

"I think the blue one, the one with the silver on it would be best," said Maggie. She turned to her mother and asked her opinion.

"Best for what?" Merit asked, returning her attention to her demanding companions.

"For Miss Catherine's engagement ball," said her daughter.

Merit exchanged commiserating glances with Lovett and agreed.

"You really don't think the gold one would be proper?" asked Catherine. "It is so pretty!"

"Now, Catherine, I warned you when you ordered that gown earlier that the style and cloth were more suitable to a matron than an unmarried miss. You don't wish to be thought fast," said Merit for the sixth or seventh time.

"No, I suppose not," said Catherine with a sigh. Then she smiled, saying naively, "I know! After all the guests have gone home, I'll wear it for Upton at our wedding supper."

"By that time, I doubt Lord Upton . . ." Merit let her voice dwindle away as three wide sets of innocent eyes turned on her. She couldn't very well tell the girl that Lord Upton, who was undoubtedly attracted to Catherine's beauty as well as her dowry, would not want to waste his wedding night admiring her daring gold gown. So Merit shrugged and finished with, "I'm certain that will be perfectly acceptable."

"Oh, look, there's Christian," said Catherine, waving at her brother who was walking past with an exquisite beauty on his arm.

Merit grabbed Catherine's arm, looking away hurriedly. But it was too late; Lord Blackwell spoke to his companion and then left her to join them.

"Good afternoon, ladies," he said, his eyes twinkling as he gazed up at Merit's scarlet face.

"We have had the best time, Christian!" exclaimed his sister.

He glanced lazily at the stack of packages surrounding them and drawled, "I must remember to ask Prinny for a loan. Gowns and a companion, too; you're out to ruin me, I vow."

"Oh, silly!" laughed his sister. "Have you met Merit?"

"I'm certain I have not, at least not formally. I would remember someone as lovely as she is," he said, expecting the usual twittering response.

What he received was a hardening of eyes and a jutting of chin—a very lovely chin, he thought, his good humor undisturbed. This new companion his sister had hired was unusually young to be such a dragon. He would simply steer clear of her, not that he was likely to even notice her amongst the chaperons at the balls he attended.

But Catherine was chattering away, and he hadn't been paying attention. He dragged his eyes away from the very pretty dragon and said, "Pardon me, what did you say?"

"I said you have it all wrong, Christian. Merit is one of Charlotte's old friends, not my paid companion. And this is her daughter, Maggie."

"And our friend, Miss Lovett," said Merit, her tone daring him to say anything derogatory about being introduced to Maggie's governess who, having served Merit in that capacity, was like a member of the family.

He bowed low, and said charmingly, "A delight to meet all of you. Miss Maggie, have you enjoyed your day shopping?"

"Yes, my lord, very much," said the little girl formally.

"And you, Miss Lovett? I hope my sister hasn't proven too much of a challenge."

"Certainly not, my lord," said the spinster, blushing at being singled out by such a handsome lord.

"Good. Well, as much as it pains me to leave such prodigious beauty, I fear I must be going. Good day, ladies."

When he had returned to his mistress—for she could be no other—Merit looked at each of the occupants of the carriage in turn as their eyes followed the handsome Lord Blackwell with varying degrees of worship. She almost snorted her disgust.

Later that evening, when Lovett was reading to Maggie and the sun was going down, Merit walked into the cool garden and made her way past the well-ordered flower beds and carved shrubs to the bench in the quiet arbor. The fragrance of the roses enveloped her and soothed her uneasy spirits. She closed her eyes, savoring the tranquil solitude. She knew it was coming to an end. Catherine had promised to remind all the *ton* hostesses of Merit Emerson's existence. The invitations would soon be rolling in, and Catherine would see to it that her new friend would attend every entertainment.

Merit sighed. She was attending the theater on Thursday with Catherine and her betrothed. That would give her the opportunity to observe the two of them.

The quiet was shattered by a shrill laugh, and Merit jumped in surprise. The murmur of voices could be heard beyond the garden wall, and she went toward it. Something was different about the tall stone wall, she thought. Then she realized her neighbors had removed the high, dense shrubs that had lined their side. This was allowing the noise to penetrate her peaceful world.

Another laugh and a squeal punctuated her thoughts. She made a mental note to tell Thomas the gardener to plant something on their side. Some shrubs which would grow quickly, she amended.

Merit returned to the bench and her quiet contemplation. But her peace was short-lived.

"Mama? Are you coming up to kiss me good night?"

"I'm coming," she said, smiling at her daughter. She stood up and called, "Race you up the stairs!"

Laughing and breathless, they tumbled onto the bed in the nursery.

When Maggie was tucked in and kissed good night, she commented astutely, "You don't like Lord Blackwell, do you, Mama?"

"Not particularly," said Merit. "But you are welcome to like him, if you want. He has quite a way with the ladies, I understand."

"Is that bad?"

"No, not bad. But he's not the kind of man I enjoy being around."

"Oh," said the little girl, digesting this with a frown.

"Now, go to sleep."

"I will," she said, snuggling under the covers. "Mama," she said, causing Merit to pause at the door. "I do like Lord Blackwell. Not many gentlemen bother to notice a little girl."

Merit smiled and nodded. "Good night, Maggie."

"Good night."

Merit retired to her bedroom and undressed. She then joined Lovett in the sitting room off her bedchamber where they always had tea in the evenings.

"What are you working on now, Lovett?"

Lovett showed Merit the beginnings of an intricate tapestry laced to a sturdy, wooden frame.

"That will be lovely," said Merit.

"It's for Maggie, for her birthday."

"She'll love the unicorns in it. But what happened to the bolster pillows for the chaise?"

"I finished one, but I decided I'd better get started on this since I can only work on it when Maggie is asleep."

"True, she is always with you. You know, Lovett, I have been thinking. We live so quietly here, Maggie is never with other children."

"Yes, and she should be," replied the proper governess.

"I heard someone laughing in the garden next door. A child, I think. I'll go over and introduce myself tomorrow. Perhaps Maggie can have a playmate."

Merit walked up the steps of the house next door and was surprised to be greeted by a maid instead of a butler. She shrugged and asked to see the mistress of the house, giving her calling card to the wide-eyed servant.

The maid hurried away and returned a moment later to lead Merit toward the back of the house to a pretty pink sitting room. Merit surveyed the decor and concluded that its occupant was probably too taken with the color.

A door opened, and she had a glimpse of an equally pink bedroom. But what struck her was the mistress of this abode. She was dressed in a sheer pink wrapper which hardly covered her charms.

Except for this rather shocking attire, she was a very pretty woman of twenty-five or so who extended her hand and said, "Good morning, Mrs. Emerson. I'm so happy you called." The voice was soft and cultured, but something about the voice and its owner made Merit frown.

She wiped out her doubts with a smile and said, "Thank you for receiving me, Mrs. . . . ?"

"Miss Maribella Smyth," said the pink lady. "It's a pleasure to meet a neighbor."

"Oh, it's Miss Smyth. I thought I heard a child in the garden last night."

"A child?"

Merit hastened to explain that the shrubs being taken out now allowed noise to travel across the garden walls. She finished with, "I assure you, I wasn't eavesdropping. At least, not intentionally. But I did hear a laugh which I took to be a child's. I have a six-year-old daughter, and I was hoping to find a suitable companion . . . for . . . her." Merit glanced toward the bedroom. She was certain she had heard a movement, perhaps even a chuckle.

"No," Miss Smyth was saying, "I'm afraid I don't have any children."

"I see. My mistake." Merit stood up and said, "I appreciate you seeing me, Miss Smyth. I'm sorry to have bothered you."

"No bother at all, Mrs. Emerson. Do call again."

Merit left, and the tall figure of Christian Richardson appeared at the bedroom door.

"We must see about replacing those shrubs," he said, laughing softly.

Thursday was gloomy and threatened rain all day. Merit remained firmly beside the fire all morning, her needlework in her hands, while Lovett and Maggie worked in the schoolroom.

Her butler, a quiet, dignified man, entered the room and cleared his throat.

"Yes, Robert?"

"A young lady has called, madam. A Miss Richardson."

"Oh," said Merit, her voice showing dismay. But there was no hope for it. She had promised Charlotte. "Very well, Robert. Send her in."

"Very good, madam."

He returned with a tearful Catherine who lost no time flying across the room and dropping dramatically on the footstool, placing her weeping face in Merit's skirts.

"What is it, Catherine?" asked Merit, her sympathy and suspicions aroused. "Your brother?"

"It is Upton! He is a beast!"

"What has he done?" Merit asked sharply. When Catherine didn't respond, she lifted the girl's shaking shoulders and handed her a handkerchief. "Now, tell me what has happened."

"He has refused to accompany us to the theater!"

"Why?"

"He said he had to leave town. His sister is ill, and he wants to go see her!"

"That is understandable," said Merit.

"She will still be ill tomorrow! He didn't have to leave today!"

Merit blinked at such selfishness and said sensibly, "Never mind, my dear, we can go to the theater by ourselves. That is perfectly acceptable."

"But I wanted you to meet Upton!" said the petulant Catherine with a pouting lip. Merit marveled that, despite the tears and the pout, Catherine was still amazingly beautiful.

"I can meet him when he returns. Besides, you are going to wear your new gown, aren't you? The pink one, I mean." Catherine nodded, and Merit continued, "I dare say we won't be alone very long. All of your jealous beaux will be only too delighted to find you away from your betrothed."

Cheered by this, Catherine smiled, saying, "I think I'll wear pink rosebuds in my hair. And you, Merit, you must wear something light and becoming, too."

Merit laughed and said, "I don't think I own such a gown anymore. You amaze me with your eye for detail, Catherine. When you make plans to go out, do you always think of it as an artist must when laying out his painting?"

"I suppose I do. I think beauty is something to be appreciated and cultivated. Now, let's go up and see what you have in your wardrobe."

Despite Merit's protests, she found herself seated on the bed with Maggie and Lovett while her abigail and Catherine inspected and rejected gown after gown. Finally, reaching into the depths of the wardrobe, Catherine settled on a gown which Merit had worn only once. It was yellow, with an overskirt of blond lace. She had ordered it one bright spring day two years before and had quickly regretted it. It was much too young and frivolous for a widow of nine-and-twenty.

But Catherine pronounced it perfect and would stand for no

argument. "After tonight," she pronounced knowingly, "you'll have more beaux than I do."

"That's what I'm afraid of," muttered Merit under her breath.

The theater was crowded and loud, and no one seemed to be paying attention to the play. It was always the same, thought Merit. She enjoyed going to the theater, but she always left with a headache after straining so hard to hear the actors. Catherine was as oblivious as everyone else, chatting in a normal voice with three young bucks who had latched onto them in the lobby and followed them to their box.

The gentlemen had been paying assiduous attentions to both Catherine and Merit who, in her yellow gown, looked almost as young as Catherine. But when Merit mentioned her daughter, their compliments became more sensible. This, and the fact that she ignored them in favor of the play, had led them to direct all their flirtatious remarks to Catherine. She didn't seem to mind, thought Merit cynically, as Catherine fluttered her eyelashes and laughed merrily.

One of the young men, a Mr. Wilton, said very little, but his poetic sighs and dark good looks seemed to appeal to Catherine.

At this thought, Merit frowned. Catherine's behavior was proof positive that she was not suited to marry the elderly Lord Upton. She would have to redouble her efforts and make certain Catherine had ample opportunities to flirt and attract a younger suitor. Perhaps if Catherine could offer a suitable substitute for Upton, her brother might agree to end the betrothal.

There was a lull in the level of noise and the silence was rent by a decidedly feminine laugh, a curiously familiar sound to Merit. All eyes turned to the darkened box opposite theirs.

"Isn't that Christian?" whispered Catherine, her eyes round with curiosity.

"I'm sure it is not," said Merit, knowing full well it was not only Christian but the same lightskirt he had been accompanying when they met him shopping.

Her answer seemed to satisfy Catherine who returned to her flirting. But Merit found her own gaze resting more and more often on the darkened box across the theater. Lord Blackwell was sitting well back from the lights and appeared to have his arms around that wanton woman. She had to be his mistress, she thought, with smug superiority. The woman leaned forward slightly, her voluptuous charms on display for all the world to see. Shocked, Merit reverted her attention to the stage.

But the couple in the shadows were like a magnet, and she found her gaze returning again and again. She could just make out the woman's figure and watched, mesmerized by the two arms that encircled and pulled her back from the light.

Suddenly, the audience began to applaud, and Merit observed that the curtains were closed. Everyone was standing up, and she did, too. Looking across to the opposite box one last time, she flushed with embarrassment. There was Lord Blackwell, smiling directly at her, tipping his hat with a knowing expression on his angelic face. Merit whirled around; grabbing Mr. Wilton's arm, she hurried out of the box.

As they had arranged, Merit called on Catherine the next morning at eleven o'clock. Reed escorted her into the morning room and confided, "Miss Catherine went out for an early ride with Mr. Wilton, but I expect her back momentarily. She requested that you wait for her here, madam. May I bring you something?"

"Thank you, Reed, perhaps some coffee," said Merit, beginning to prowl the room as soon as he had closed the door. She hated closed rooms. That was why she had purchased the house where she now lived. The flowery courtyard was quite large for a town house, and every room on the ground floor opened onto it with French doors. This morning room, by contrast, was stuffy and dark.

"Like a caged tigress," said a deep voice from the doorway. "And just as beautiful."

Embarrassed to be caught wandering, Merit turned and marched to the sofa, sitting down and primly folding her hands in her lap.

"Good morning, Lord Blackwell," she said when she was composed again.

"Good morning, Mrs. Emerson," he replied, entering with the silver service and setting it on the table in front of her. He joined her on the sofa, quite deliberately sitting so close that their legs touched.

"I suppose you want me to pour out," she snapped, wishing she didn't sound so childish.

"Only if you wish to. I am quite capable of pouring my own coffee." With this, he proceeded to do so, offering her the sugar and milk. He smiled and poured another cup for himself.

"Did you enjoy the theater last night?" he asked, turning slightly to watch her reaction.

"Very much. And you?"

"Yes, *King Lear* has always been a favorite of mine."

"It was *Othello*," she scoffed.

"I know," he said, his smile lighting his entire face.

Merit blinked in the face of such radiance. "Then why . . ." she stammered before the realization that he was mocking her set in.

"You really are much too attractive to be a chaperon, you know," he said, ignoring her discomfort.

His comment served to rally her thoughts, and she glared at him. "If you think to charm me with empty compliments, Lord Blackwell, you are much mistaken. I am neither a green girl nor a lightskirt!"

"No, I can see you're not. Now, I wonder what you would do if . . ."

But the hand he raised to her coiled chignon never reached its goal as Merit stood up and moved away.

"You, my lord, are no gentleman. I understand your forcing

unwanted marriages on your sisters; that is a common enough deed. But how dare you offer insult to me, your sister's friend!"

He smiled and drawled lazily, "Most ladies don't consider my attentions an insult, Merit."

"Well, I do! And my name is Mrs. Emerson to you!"

"You know, I had a mistress once who was just as feisty as you are—I forget her name at the moment—but after the initial excitement, she grew very tiresome."

Merit gifted him with her most withering look, the look that had kept men from her doorstep for several years. But Christian only grinned and patted the seat by his side.

"Let's cry peace and be friends. I promise to be as proper as a priest from now on. I have need of your advice."

Cautiously, she rejoined him, keeping her skirts well away from his muscular leg. He smiled at this, but made no comment.

"That's better. Now, Catherine has told me in no uncertain terms that she can't possibly be ready to wed by the first of May. Something about her wedding gown, I believe."

"Yes, that's right. It's not supposed to be ready until that Saturday, and if something should be wrong with it, there might not be time to have it fixed."

"I see. Very well, then it shall be on the eighth," he pronounced.

"Can you tell me, my lord, why it is so important that the wedding take place so quickly?"

"Why? I think it's for the best, that's why," he said. At Merit's frown, he added audaciously, "Don't worry, Catherine is not enceinte."

"I never thought she was!" said Merit, blushing to the roots of her dark hair.

Christian grinned mischievously. "Knowing Catherine, I doubt that is even a possibility," he added thoughtfully.

Merit pursed her lips and looked away. "You are trying to provoke me, my lord."

"Undoubtedly," he said. "Now, let me ask you a question."

"What is it?"

"Why are you concerning yourself with Catherine? I know Charlotte wrote to you. She wrote warning me to beware, or some such thing, that my days of tyranny are coming to a close. Exactly what tyranny she was talking about, I'm not sure. But here you are, so I assume you have been sent to give me my comeuppance."

"Since we are being plain with each other," Merit said, looking him bravely in the eye, "Charlotte is concerned that Catherine is being forced to wed too soon, and to a man old enough to be her father, just to suit you. Recalling her own marriage, her first one, she is naturally concerned. And she has asked me to intervene."

"I see. And are you?" he asked, his expression becoming grim.

"I am simply encouraging Catherine to look at other possibilities. I would not dream of inciting an open rebellion. As much as I may deplore it, you are her guardian, and marriage is the only option for a young lady."

"You say that as though it is repugnant."

"Not repugnant, just a necessary evil."

"Is that a personal observation?" he asked.

Merit shook her head. "You won't get me to admit my own marriage—as inconvenient as it was to me at the time—was evil. My husband was many years my senior, but he was not unkind. And because of him, I am now able to live as I choose. Most of all, I have my daughter."

"Then why are you so against Catherine's marriage?"

"I think you are rushing her. Why must the wedding take place so quickly? Is the cost of a Season too much for your purse?"

It was his turn to be indignant, but after a moment, he laughed. "You couldn't be more wrong, my dear. My sisters have cost me a fortune, but I can well afford it. Money has nothing to do with it."

"Then why?"

Catherine ran into the room, breathless. "Merit? I'm so sorry

I'm late! You remember Mr. Wilton from the theater last night, don't you? Oh, Christian, you here, too?"

"Yes, baggage, keeping your guest company. Hello, Wilton. Saw your horse at Newmarket. Nice looking filly."

"Thank you, my lord. Yes, she's my pride and joy," said the young man, his soleful glances for Catherine forgotten in favor of discussing his horse.

After Wilton had departed, Christian took his leave of the ladies as well. He paused at the door and said, "Merit has told me your wedding gown may not be ready in time for the first of May. So we'll make it the eighth."

"Thank you, Christian," she said sunnily.

"You know, Catherine, if you had only explained that to me instead of whining and crying, we could have saved ourselves a scene."

"I'm sorry. I'll try to be better," she said contritely.

"I suppose it's just a bride's nerves," he said, winking at her.

Merit had her first opportunity to observe Catherine with her betrothed at the engagement ball on the following Tuesday. Lord Upton was nearing fifty and had two grown sons. His manner toward Catherine was that of an indulgent uncle. He carried her fan, waved away a second glass of champagne, and chose her other dance partners. Watching them, Merit wanted to scream.

"So, do they pass your inspection, Merit?" asked a quiet voice in her ear.

Without turning, she knew it was Christian. He had taken to calling her by her given name ever since their conversation in the morning room. She had decided to ignore it, hoping he would tire of it once he realized he couldn't anger her with it. Like her plan to rescue Catherine, it didn't seem to be working.

"That is yet to be decided," she said, hoping to provoke him.

"You are much slower at decisions than I would have guessed. Never mind. Will you dance with me?"

"I don't dance," she said simply.

"Nonsense. I saw you over here tapping your foot, and a very pretty foot it is, I might add. Here you are, dressed in the most lovely green gown I have ever seen, and wasting away with the chaperons. Come on, it's a waltz. I promise not to tread on your toes."

So saying, he swept Merit onto the ballroom floor without receiving permission, and she was forced to keep up with his expert lead.

Halfway around the room, he whispered in her ear, "You know, I would willingly postpone Catherine's wedding if *you* asked me." Startled, Merit jerked away from him, missing her step. Christian steadied her with a gentle hand at her waist. "Easy, my dear, you don't want to cause a stir."

"What did you mean by that?" she asked with a raised brow.

"My, my, we do have an inflated idea of ourselves, don't we. I was merely attempting to flirt with you," he added with a condescending smile.

She glared at him but said nothing. She knew she was out of practice with the complex exchanges that men and women engaged in, but his teasing confused her.

"You know, when you purse your lips like that, they really look inviting." He laughed when her dark eyes grew wide. "But I wouldn't want to cause a scandal at Catherine's ball. I'm sorry, my dear; that will have to wait."

"You are being impossible!" she said, unable to keep the tiny note of hurt from her voice.

Perceiving that he had bruised her feelings, remorse washed over Christian. But he hardened his heart against such frailty. He had only been teasing, enjoying a light flirtation. She was the one being impossible.

His voice crisp, he said, "Never mind. The wedding will take place as planned on the eighth of May. Only three weeks away. You must be delighted."

"What do you mean?"

"I have proven to be the ogre you thought me. And the ironic thing is, once Catherine is married, I shall have to set about finding myself a wife. Not at all a pleasant task. Oh, the hunt can be amusing; I have indulged in those often enough without any real intention of succumbing to a passing fancy. I always had a sister to launch and marry off. But now, I have no more excuses. My carefree days of bachelorhood are all but over. Thank you for making me stay on the straight and narrow, for helping guide me back to Tyburn, so to speak."

"I think you are drunk!" she snapped, pushing away from him as the music ended.

"No, my dear Merit, but 'twill be an enviable state once the jaws of parson's mousetrap snap closed." With this, he turned on his heel, leaving her without a partner among the couples promenading.

Merit left the floor, also, hurrying to the ladies' withdrawing room so her anger could cool. She realized she was making too much of her conversation with Lord Blackwell. What did she care what he thought?

As she made her way back to the ballroom, determined to enjoy herself, she passed an open door and was drawn toward it by raucous laughter.

"And then I told her I'd be drunk all the time just to be able to endure marriage!"

It was Lord Blackwell's voice, and he was speaking about her. Merit's eyes blazed with anger. How dare he tell someone else about their conversation!

"But what are you going to do, Christian?" asked another male voice.

Merit peeked inside and saw Lord Gillingham and another man she didn't recognize.

"What do you mean? I'll find a wife, of course. I told myself I had until the girls were all safely wed. That was my reprieve. But now it's over. Can't escape any longer. It's parson's mousetrap for me," Christian added gloomily. "Gad! I dread bedding a cold fish!"

"Well!" said Merit. Then she clapped her hand to her mouth and hurried away.

The three men flew to the doorway and watched, Christian laughing softly as he recognized her shapely figure.

Merit was thoroughly bewildered. She lay wide awake on her bed watching the sun lighten the flowers on the wallpaper. Nothing made any sense anymore. Catherine's fiancé was nice, even if he was too old for her. Catherine, though she had danced with many of the young men, had also seemed to enjoy Upton's company. Perhaps she would be happy married to the man.

And Christian—Lord Blackwell? The man was stark, raving mad. He had to be. When he had thanked her for making him marry. . . . He was obviously touched in the upper works. She had nothing to do with the fact that he felt it was time to set up his nursery. And she really didn't care one way or the other!

She frowned. From what she had seen of him at the theater, in the park, and so on, he didn't appear to be searching for a wife. He appeared besotted by that dreadful, although beautiful, mistress.

The only thing he had said that was true was that he planned to get drunk. After toasting the happy couple, he had downed enough champagne to make a lesser man stagger. But she had seen him leave not long afterward, wearing his cloak.

Merit stretched and sat up. She went to the window and curled up on the velvet cushions that lined the circular window seat. The servants from the various houses were already appearing, sweeping the steps and polishing the doorknobs. Next door, a well-dressed gentleman was leaving for the day. Odd, she thought, to see a gentleman leaving Miss Smyth's house. Perhaps he was her brother.

Merit put her nose to the glass and stared as the man walked to his carriage. He wasn't dressed for the day; he was wearing evening clothes. That was strange, she thought. One didn't expect. . . . She noticed the groom on the back was dressed in navy blue livery. She frowned, and her eyes widened in shock as she recognized the driver—Lord Blackwell!

Forgetting the hour, Merit threw on a wrapper and bounded down the stairs. Robert had the footmen and maids lined up in the hall giving them instructions for the morning.

"Robert!"

"Madam!" he said, his voice squeaking in surprise. He followed her into the front drawing room.

She was standing by the window and motioning him forward.

"Do you know that house next door?"

"The Morrisons', madam?"

"No, the other side of us. Who lives there?"

"I'm not certain, madam. I believe it is a single lady, but I'm not certain of her identity."

"Find out," she said.

"Very good, madam."

"Miss Catherine has asked to see you, my lord," said Reed when Christian entered the small dining room for luncheon.

"Very well. Tell her to come in here. I'm dashed if I'll postpone my meal; I'm famished."

Christian had slept the morning away, his slumber deep and untroubled after a disturbing night with Maribella. They had argued for hours on end. She had begged him to take her to Paris. He had refused, though he didn't really have a reason. The truth of the matter was, he had no desire to go to Paris with Maribella— or anywhere else. Christian frowned. Maribella had lasted only a few months. He realized he was tiring of her, but the thought of searching out another mistress was unappealing.

"Still," he mused aloud, "I suppose it's time." After all, what was the purpose of having a mistress if she made one so angry all thought of passion fled?

"Good afternoon, Christian," said Catherine, slipping into one of the chairs. She waved away the tray the footman presented to her. "Nothing for me," she said airily.

Christian's eyes narrowed at her tone. She was up to something. "What can I do for you, my dear?"

"Oh, nothing," she said, her hands pleating the tablecloth. "I was just wondering if you might accompany me and Upton to Vauxhall Gardens tomorrow night."

"I'd rather not," he answered baldly.

Catherine scowled, but she managed to keep her temper for another assault. "I could go without you, I suppose, since we are betrothed, but people might talk."

"I doubt it. I think it would be perfectly proper if you and your fiancé attended the gardens alone. It's just over two weeks until the nuptials. Tell Upton he has my blessings."

"But that's the problem," she pouted. "Upton won't go unless you go, too. He said it wouldn't be proper."

"Then I suppose you'll have to wait until you are wed because I'm not going to Vauxhall. I find it a dead bore."

"Unless you are accompanied by your mistress," said Catherine, firing the first salvo.

"You, Catherine, speak more like a stablehand than a young lady. Isn't it fortunate that I shall no longer be forced to teach you manners when you are married? That will be Upton's job. And if he has any sense, he'll accomplish it by turning you over his knee!"

"You dreadful boor! How dare you speak to me like that!"

"I dare because you deserve it," he replied, never losing his infuriating smile.

"I hate you, Christian! You are the most unfeeling cad! Perhaps if you spent more time with your own kind than with that woman, you would be more of a gentleman. Your manners are no better than a lightskirt's."

Christian rose and walked to her chair. Leaning over her in a menacing manner, he spoke in clipped words. "As far as I'm concerned, young lady, you and your betrothed can go to the devil. I'll be damned if I'll spend an entire evening in your company. If you were younger, I would wash your mouth out with soap."

He left as she burst into tears.

It was on this scene that Merit descended. Practically bowled over in the hall by Christian who muttered a terse greeting, she hurried to Catherine's side.

After listening to an abbreviated account of their conversation, which she felt certain was prejudiced to show Catherine in the best light, Merit patted Catherine on the shoulder and said, "I shall go with you, Catherine."

After all, she told herself, whatever Catherine had done or said to aggravate her brother, it could not be worse than what Lord Blackwell had done—buying a house in a perfectly respectable neighborhood for his sordid little liaisons. The tale Robert had told her—sketchy as it had been—had left no doubt in her mind that Lord Blackwell was a rake and a libertine. No fewer than three mistresses had been kept in the house over the past six years!

"But you said you didn't enjoy Vauxhall," Catherine protested weakly.

"It's not my favorite place, and since I suffer from mal de mer, I refuse to go by boat. But I will go for your sake, my dear. Now, dry your eyes. You have your fitting for your wedding gown in an hour, and you want to look your best."

When Merit and Catherine arrived at Almack's that night, sans Upton, they were immediately beset by hopeful young gentlemen begging for dances. Catherine's more mature admirers cajoled Merit into dancing as well, pointing out that since she had waltzed with Blackwell, she had to dance with others or it would be thought odd.

After a country dance, a boulanger, and a waltz, Merit was forced to admit to herself that Almack's was much more amusing when one danced than when simply sitting with the chaperons. The compliments she heard were light and seemingly sincere, and she couldn't help but be pleased.

From the side of the dance floor, Christian glared. He had made himself attend Almack's, telling himself that putting off the inevitable was senseless. When Catherine was wed, his own marriage would need to follow within the year, and he needed to start looking over the crop. He'd rather have been gambling at Carlton House with Prinny and Alvanley, and his expression was one of terminal boredom.

Then Merit whirled past in the arms of Lord Featherstone; she laughed at some witticism, causing Christian's stomach to knot. So the woman is a schemer after all, just like each of my sisters, thought Christian. He continued to think in this vein, concluding that it must have something to do with the fairer sex.

Merit Emerson may have begun her crusade because of Charlotte's letter, but somewhere along the way, her motives had undergone a change, Christian thought. She had abandoned her role as chaperon and adviser; instead, she had decided to use her liaison with Catherine to ensnare a second husband for herself.

The music ended, and Merit's partner excused himself and went to fetch something to drink, a cup of Almack's dreadful orangeate.

Christian stalked over to her. "Taking wagers? If you are, I want to bet on Featherstone. He's been single too long; I don't think you'll manage to bring him up to scratch."

Merit was not about to be drawn into a shouting match, so she subdued her anger and smiled sweetly. "You should know about such matters, my lord. After all, you have made a science of changing from one woman to another, haven't you?"

"What's that supposed to mean? Has Catherine—"

"Catherine has said nothing. But your neighbors are not completely oblivious to your exploits right under our noses."

"Neighbors? But you don't . . . Oh, you mean in Hanover Square. Do you live there? I had no idea," he lied. "Pleasant little spot. Perfect for a discreet dalliance. Tell me, is that why you chose it?"

It was all Merit could do to keep her itching palm from striking him. But she didn't. Instead, she turned on her heel and searched out her next partner. She planned to ignore Lord

Blackwell for the remainder of the evening, but he spoiled her plan by striding out the door immediately following their conversation.

With the mail the next morning, there was a letter which had been hand delivered. Not recognizing the scrawl, Merit opened it first. Her dark eyes flew over the words quickly. Shaking her head in wonder, she read it again, this time more thoughtfully.

> My dear Merit,
>   While I know my behavior last night was inexcusable, I still beg your forgiveness. Please believe that when I entered Almack's, I had no intention of picking a fight with you. I was no doubt put off by the fact that you were having such a jolly time with Featherstone.
>   Nevertheless, my behavior was unpardonable. My foul mood was a result of my dislike at the thought of finding a wife. I believe I will find it an onerous job.
>   If you were not such a wise person, perhaps you would marry me and put me out of my misery. You have too much good sense for that, however. So I will simply beg your forgiveness once again. Believe that I am and will always be
>
>   Your Humble Servant,
>   Blackwell

Merit felt tears prickling her eyes, and she dabbed them away with a lacy handkerchief. Now why, she wondered, had he seen fit to write her such a kind letter? She was much better off entertaining thoughts of anger toward Christian than thoughts of . . .

But she didn't dare question herself too closely on that score. Merit folded the letter and placed it carefully to one side before continuing to open the remaining morning mail.

* * *

Dressed in an elegant riding habit, Merit mounted her bay mare Daisy and turned toward the park. It was early yet, and the fashionable Rotten Row would be empty. Beside her, on a black Welch pony, six-year-old Maggie sat ramrod straight on her small sidesaddle. A groom followed at a distance.

"Mama, are you going to be home tonight?"

"No, my love, I'm going to Vauxhall."

"What's that?" asked the inquisitive child.

"It's a very pretty garden with a waterfall. At midnight, there are fireworks."

"Can I go?"

"No, my dear, it would be much too late for you. When you are older, we'll go. Tonight, I'm going with Miss Richardson and her fiancé Lord Upton."

"Is Lord Blackwell going, too?"

"Goodness, no! Why would you ask that?"

"I heard you saying something to Lovett about his lordship going."

Merit laughed, but she didn't explain to the child that when she said he was "going 'round the bend," she meant he was losing his ability to think rationally. Instead, she turned the topic to Maggie's lessons.

After a short ride, they returned home. Turning in to the street, Merit was surprised to see a wagon next door to her house being loaded with all sorts of belongings. The final cargo was a very angry female swinging a bird cage whose occupant was squawking as volubly as its mistress.

"Who is that, Mama?" asked Maggie, pointing at the spectacle.

"No one we know, my love. Come along. Let's ride around to the stables."

Maggie went upstairs, and Robert brought a tray to the salon, his eyes full of intelligence.

Merit could control her curiosity no longer and asked, casually, she hoped, "What is happening over at Lord Blackwell's house?"

Robert almost rubbed his hands at the thought of relating his exciting news, but he said with dignity, "I believe Lord Blackwell has dismissed his, uh, servant, madam. And it is said he is selling out."

"What? Selling the house?"

"Yes, madam. It's all the talk belowstairs. He's, er, occupied it for the past four or five years, at the very least. And there was no warning, they say."

"I suppose it was spur of the moment. He's probably, uh, relocating his . . ." Merit left the sentence hanging as Robert began shaking his head.

"I don't think so, madam. They say he's only visited his, uh, friend once in the past week or so, and that visit was spent shouting at each other all night."

"Really?" said Merit, intrigued. Robert nodded, and Merit recalled herself, dismissing her butler.

So, Christian had given his mistress her walking papers. What, she wondered, had brought that on? Merit's disobedient mind recalled Christian's letter, but she swiftly put it from her mind, picking up her stitching and concentrating on it ferociously.

Merit wore a burgundy silk gown that evening. Around her neck was an ornate gold necklace encrusted with garnets which set off her creamy décolletage to advantage. She had her abigail twist her long dark tresses into a knot on top of her head allowing a few curls to dangle enticingly. She wanted to look her best, she reasoned, or people might think she was a paid companion instead of a friend obliging Catherine with her presence. The abigail produced some rouge for her cheeks and applied some color to her lips as well. The effect on Merit's flawless porcelain complexion, with her dark eyes framed by long black lashes, was startling.

"Is it too much?" she asked, turning to Maggie and Lovett who were seated on the bed watching this ritual with great interest.

"You look beautiful," said Maggie, her eyes wide with wonder.

"Your mother has always been beautiful," said Lovett, growing misty. "I wish you could have seen her at her come-out ball, Maggie. Every man there wanted the honor of dancing with her."

"Now don't exaggerate, Lovett," laughed Merit, pleased by the compliment. Then she asked again, "But you don't think I look too . . . You know, Lovett."

"Not at all, Merit. You look lovely."

"Madam, the carriage is at the door whenever you are ready," said Robert, his old face breaking into an unaccustomed smile when he saw his mistress.

"Come and give me a kiss, Maggie. I'll tell you all about it tomorrow. Good night, everyone. Oh, Lucy, you needn't wait up for me tonight. I can put myself to bed."

Merit was ushered into the salon where Lord Upton was being entertained by Christian. Both men wore evening clothes, and Merit couldn't help but notice how handsome Christian looked. He wore black pantaloons and a black coat, but his cravat was snowy white and his waistcoat was the color of the sky—the color of his eyes. When he smiled at her, her heart did an odd somersault.

"Good evening, Merit. You're looking especially beautiful this evening. A new gown?" asked Christian, taking her arm and leading her to a chair.

"No, my lord, just one that doesn't often get an airing," she said, looking up at him. Her admiration must have been evident because he pressed her hand and his eyes locked with hers.

"Harumph." Lord Upton cleared his throat and brought them back to the present. "Where is Catherine? She should have been down by now."

"Shall I go up and see if I can hurry her?" asked Merit.

"Certainly not. She'll be down in a moment. Would you care for a glass of wine, Merit?"

"Yes, please."

"If she doesn't hurry up, our boat is liable to hire out to someone else," said Upton.

"Our boat?" asked Merit.

"Yes, is something wrong?" asked Christian.

"I thought we were going by carriage," she said, looking from one man to the other for confirmation.

But they both shook their heads, and Christian said, "No, Catherine insisted on going by boat."

"Oh, I see," murmured Merit, downing her wine in a gulp.

"Would you prefer to take the carriage?" asked Christian, concerned.

Merit shook her head. She was being silly, of course. It had been nerves the last time when she had become so ill on that short boat ride. But she was a grown woman now; her nerves were not going to be bothered by such a small thing as a boat ride.

"You and I could go in the carriage, if you wish."

Merit was drawn into those sympathetic blue eyes which reminded her of a clear blue pool of water. Without hesitation, she said, "No, I shall be fine. Really I will."

"Of course she will," said Upton, adding, "Have another glass of this fine wine, my dear. That will pluck up your courage."

"I'm so sorry I'm late, Upton. I couldn't decide whether to wear the pearls or the sapphires," said Catherine, presenting her cheek to her betrothed for a chaste kiss.

"You look breathtaking," he said, forgetting about time.

"We'd best be going," said Christian practically.

"Oh, are you going, too?" asked Merit, suddenly realizing he meant to accompany them.

"Yes," he said, frowning, "unless you would rather I didn't."

"Of course she didn't mean that, silly," said his sister.

She chatted on while they went down to the carriage and took the short ride to the landing where small boats conducted elegant revelers to Vauxhall Gardens. Merit stood quietly, waiting to board. When it was their turn, she hung back for a moment, but Catherine urged her forward.

Merit fixed a smile on her lips and tried to think of everything except her churning stomach and Catherine's selfishness. The wine she had drunk was trying to keep up with the waves on the water, and all the color drained from her face. In the moonlight, she looked like a pale, painted rag doll.

Christian, who had been standoffish since Merit's surprised exclamation about his accompanying them, finally noticed her silence and asked gruffly, "What's the matter? Aren't you feeling well?"

Merit tried to smile, but the look of panic on her face prevented it, and she hurried away finding a secluded spot to lose her wine.

"Here," said a familiar voice at her elbow, holding out his wet handkerchief. "Let me help." Christian turned her around like a little girl and mopped her face with the wet cloth. Then he found her a chair and sat her down with strict orders to stay put.

When Christian returned, he had another cloth and put this on the back of her neck for a moment before using it to bathe her throat and the swell of her breasts. Leaning back, Merit allowed him to minister to her, feeling much better as the evening air cooled her damp skin.

"We're here. I'll help you off the boat and then find a carriage to take you home," he said, supporting her as she rose.

"No," she whispered. "Really, I'll be fine. Just let me get back to shore. I'll be right as rain."

"We'll see about that," he pronounced grimly. "Why didn't you tell Catherine you couldn't tolerate boats?"

"I did," she said weakly. She realized her mistake when she saw his eyes light with fury.

"I'll—"

"No, Christian, please don't. I'll be fine. There's no harm done. If I weren't so silly . . ."

"You were sick, not silly," he began, but at her pleading look, he acquiesced, muttering, "That chit gets away with far too much."

By the time they reached the rotunda, Merit was regaining her color and feeling much more the thing. She laughed more than she had thought possible trying to assuage Christian's worried brow. It worked, and he was soon entertaining them all with the latest on-dits, even the more risqué which he would tell Upton in a loud aside so the ladies could listen and pretend not to be shocked.

Upton began a tale about a blushing bride on her wedding night only to realize his gaffe and fall into an awkward silence. Christian stepped into the breach, suggesting that they all join the dancers.

When Merit was in his arms, he asked, "Are you feeling better?"

"Much, thank you. You were so kind, Christian."

"Ah, to hear my name on your beautiful lips I would do anything," he intoned, bringing the hand which held hers to his chest dramatically.

Merit giggled. Giggled, she thought in astonishment. She had not thought of applying such a term to herself for ages. But he was so absurd, said an indulgent inner voice.

"Have you forgiven me?" he asked, his voice penetrating her subconsciousness.

"For what?"

"For baiting you unmercifully. You did receive my note, didn't you?" he asked, slowing their steps, causing another couple to narrowly avoid a collision.

"Yes, I did. And yes, you are forgiven."

"Good. I find it most uncomfortable having you truly angry with me. Perhaps I think of you as my conscience."

"Perhaps," said Merit, wondering why this made her feel rather wretched again. She decided it would be best to find another topic and blurted out, "I understand you've found a new abode for your mistress."

It was as though the air had turned to ice as he gazed down at her. Merit opened her mouth to correct herself, but what could she say or do? She hung her head and prayed for the music to end.

When they returned to the Blackwell town house, Merit only wanted to get away as quickly as possible. Since her disastrous reference to Christian's mistress, a social taboo even a green girl would not make, he had been cold and closed-mouthed. And I don't blame him one bit! she thought miserably, wishing she were already home and tucked in bed.

"Merit, could you come upstairs with me for a few minutes?" Catherine asked, her voice sounding like a little girl. "Upton, you don't mind, do you? I'll see you for our drive tomorrow."

"Very well, my dear. Sleep well." He kissed her cheek and took his leave.

With a frigid glare at Merit, Christian muttered something about his club and departed, also.

"Good, now we can be private," said Catherine, patting the seat beside her on the sofa.

"I am very tired, Catherine, so if you could come straight to the point?"

"It is about my wedding."

"Yes?"

The girl ducked her head and mumbled, "My wedding night, to be more precise."

"Oh, I see."

"I would ask one of my sisters, but they are all in the country and don't plan to come until the wedding. And after that tale Upton started to tell, plus what I have been gathering from friends, I had begun to wonder . . . to be afraid . . ."

Merit really wished she had been more prepared for this. And she also wished she felt more up to it. But there was no getting around it; the girl needed advice.

"So you want to know exactly what is going to happen to you on your wedding night," said Merit frankly.

"Not too exactly," Catherine said quickly.

"I wish I could tell you that it will be enjoyable, but I don't really think it is. When a man couples with a mistress, they say the mistress enjoys it no end. I have difficulty believing this; I can't get past the idea that she is being paid to act like she is enjoying herself."

"So it is truly terrible," said Catherine miserably.

Merit put her arm around the girl bracingly. "No, Catherine. It is not terrible. It is awkward and embarrassing the first time. After that, it is simply something one does so that one can have children. You may not enjoy it, but you will learn to tolerate it. And if your husband is kind and patient, you may consider yourself lucky."

"But what, precisely, does he do?"

Merit sighed. So she was not going to get off easily. As briefly as possible, she described her own wedding night, from the high-necked gown being torn accidentally by her inebriated new husband to waking in the morning, her motions stiff and the sheets bloody. Catherine, who was as white as the proverbial sheet by this time, thanked Merit and wished her good night.

Merit hugged Catherine's rigid shoulders and let herself out.

When Merit called on Catherine the next day, Reed informed her that though Miss Catherine had gone out, Lord Blackwell wished to speak to her. The butler led her to his study, announced her, and then closed the door.

Unlike the morning room, this chamber was light and airy, having a row of uncurtained windows along the back of the house that overlooked the garden. She was smiling when Christian looked up from his paperwork and saw her.

"Good morning, Mrs. Emerson," he said formally.

"Lord Blackwell," she replied, the joy going out of her spirit and face.

"I wanted to let you know how concerned I am about your suitability as a companion for my sister. You may have been friends with Charlotte, but I'm not certain you are the right person to be guiding my younger sister toward her marriage."

"How dare you!"

"How dare you, madam, terrify my innocent sister about her wifely duties. She came to me this morning all red-eyed, begging me to call off the betrothal because she didn't think she could stand for Upton to use her as a broodmare! I don't know exactly what you have told her, but it was obviously too much!"

His face was just inches from hers, and he was taken aback when Merit snapped, "Hah! I might have expected as much from a hypocrite like you! You keep a string of mistresses whom you must pay to come to your bed, and then you are upset that your sister might have enough knowledge to decide for herself what she wants to do with her body!"

"I don't even have a mistress now, and besides, they have nothing to do with this!"

"They have everything to do with this! Why on earth you and all the other so-called gentlemen want their wives innocent and ignorant and their cyprians experienced and talented is beyond me! Why not teach your wives the ways of love instead of bedding them in record time just often enough to keep them with child. Is there any pleasure in that? Of course not! Instead, she lives first in terrified innocence and then in deadly boredom!"

"But you terrified Catherine with your torn nightgown and bloody sheets!" he shouted.

"Better the truth now than surprise then! At least she will not be as ignorant as most girls when they are sold to the highest bidder!" exclaimed Merit, her breasts heaving, her dark eyes wild with barely suppressed fear.

Christian glared at her, and her knees trembled, but Merit stood her ground. Then, quick as a flash, he kissed her! His arm snaked around her waist, and he pulled her against him while his other hand guided her face closer to his waiting lips. Merit struggled, but it was useless. His warm lips touched hers; and he felt a wave of triumph as she grew silent, then pliant, then responsive.

But Christian's triumph was forgotten as Merit pressed closer, her urgency matching his. He staggered backward, searching for the sofa where they landed with a thump, their passion taking no notice of the change. Then he was on top of her, his hard body pressing her against the leather cushions as he moved against her. Merit whimpered, meeting his thrusts with moans of pleasure as she pulled his lips down to hers. He plucked at her skirts until his hand slipped underneath, his fingers searching out each crevice hungrily. Gasping for air, Merit tore at his shirt, her hand caught between them as she explored his chest.

"Let's go upstairs," he breathed against her cheek.

She nodded, knowing and not caring that she would agree to anything that would allow him to take her. He stood up, and pulled her to her feet. He kissed the tip of her nose and favored her with a smile.

"Marriage didn't teach you that," he said softly.

Merit took a step back.

"What did you say?" she whispered, her passion extinguished by the smug smile on his face.

"If your theory is right, you couldn't have learned that from your husband," said Christian. He took her hand to lead her upstairs.

She shook him off. "You're no different from all the rest. You even sell the women of your family to the highest bidder, yet you think that is not prostitution. I'm sorry, my lord, if I've led you to believe that I would be willing to become your mistress, but I assure you, I won't."

"Merit! Merit! I'm so glad you're here!" said Catherine, sailing into the room. Fortunately, she was too wrapped up in herself to notice their disarray and anger. "Upton is going to take me to Paris for our wedding trip! Isn't he the most wonderful man? And you, dearest brother, are an absolute genius to find him for me! Thank you, thank you, thank you!" She gave him a quick hug and floated out of the room.

Merit watched her go with dawning irony. She had been a fool! She was trying to "save" a girl who was absolutely delighted by her betrothed and forthcoming marriage. Merit turned back to Christian whose smug face made her lose her composure.

Before she knew what she was about she gave his cheek a resounding slap, then gasped and fled.

Christian couldn't remember when he had felt more "I-told-you-so-righteous." As he left his study, he grinned at Reed who perceptively attributed his master's ebullient state to Mrs. Emerson's scarlet-faced departure.

Christian picked up his beaver hat, set it upon his head, and, swinging his ivory handled cane, headed for his club. He would have a tale to tell Gilly and Bewick! Not about Merit's passionate kiss, but about how he had outsmarted her, debated with her and won.

Gilly and Bewick were deep in a game of piquet when he arrived. They greeted Christian and offered him a drink, but they continued their tightly contested rubber. When they had finally finished, Christian sat thoughtfully resting his chin on the carved handle of his cane.

"Now, what has you looking so blue-deviled today?" asked Lord Gillingham.

"Must be a woman," commented Mr. Bewick knowingly. "Probably that sister of yours, or her friend. I noticed what an opinionated thing she is when I met her at your sister's engagement ball. Has she given you trouble?"

"Merit Emerson? Not at all," said Christian, adding warmly, "Merit's the very best of ladies." Now why did I say that? thought Christian. Five minutes ago, I was ready to gloat about my conquest. Now . . .

"Just wondered," Bewick answered slowly, carefully choosing a card. "Didn't mean to give offense."

Christian looked from one to the other, his frown deepening. "Devil take you both," he muttered, rising suddenly and leaving the club.

He made his way to Manton's shooting gallery and cupped a wafer, but this was curiously unfulfilling. Afterward, he tried Jackson's Boxing Salon where he watched for a time before deciding he didn't feel like trying his luck there. Next came a visit to Harriette Wilson's house. The infamous courtesan was out, but her sisters were quite willing to entertain him. He left after tea and half an hour of conversation.

Frustrated at what should have been a day of personal satisfaction, Christian began walking, his steps eventually taking him to Hanover Square and the house which Maribella had so recently, angrily, vacated. He had dismissed the servants and had the knocker removed until the house should sell, but he still had a key and let himself in.

The house had been cleaned from floor to ceiling, and it had a cold, unlived-in feeling. Firewood was still stacked by the bedroom fireplace, and he spent a few minutes laying the fire. The decanters were still full in the cabinet across from the bed, and he filled his glass. He sat down on the side of the cold bed.

How many times had he done this before? Only he hadn't been alone then. There had been two mistresses before Maribella, but that was all. Surely that was not so many for a man of six-and-thirty, he thought.

His thoughts becoming uncomfortable, he got up and went out to the private courtyard with its small pool. He tried to picture Maribella there, but the face he saw was Merit's, her body bathed in sunlight, her dark eyes beckoning.

"Damn!" he muttered and went into the garden for some fresh air.

He strolled toward the high wall which abutted Merit's garden. He listened but heard nothing.

"Mama! Watch me!" called a child.

Christian strained to hear a response but could hear nothing except the child's laughter. Turning on his heel, he went back inside and refilled his glass. He sat down on the pink velvet fainting couch and sipped the golden liquid thoughtfully.

Merit had been completely in the wrong, he assured himself.

All he had done was succumb to those tempting lips. And, now that he recalled, he had warned her once that to purse her lips was inviting a kiss. She had probably been angling for one!

Christian looked down at his glass, surprised to find it empty. He replenished it, taking the decanter and placing it at his elbow.

The room was full of shadows, both real and ghostly, and, fumbling clumsily, Christian lighted the candle at his elbow.

The cool evening air had no effect on Merit's heated body. She told herself it was from shame at having surrendered to the charms of such a notorious rake. But she knew it was much worse than that. She closed her eyes, sighing as she remembered their kisses and embraces. She had never felt so wicked—so deliciously wicked—and alive. And the worst part was, she was very much afraid she had fallen in love with him.

But what had she said to him? Something about selling his sister—all his sisters! And Catherine was obviously delighted by his choice! She could never face him again!

Not that he would ever want to see her, of course. She represented a trap to the elegant Lord Blackwell. She was of no use to him. After all, she was a lady and couldn't be his mistress.

Could she? She shook her head at such an outrageous thought and forced the remembrance of his embrace from her mind.

"Mama! Mama!"

Merit looked up to see Maggie standing at the nursery window.

"I'll be there in a moment," she called.

"What's that smell, Mama?"

Merit took a deep breath and frowned. Her eyes flew to the roof of the house, but she saw no sign of smoke. Still the odor was pronounced. Something was burning.

"Look, Mama," called the child, pointing next door.

Merit picked up her skirts and ran. "Robert! Send for the fire brigade!" She pointed to two footmen and said, "Come with me!"

When they reached the front door without its knocker, Merit groaned. But she pushed on the door and it opened. The hallway had the faint odor of smoke.

"Something's burning," commented Bob, one of the footmen.

"Search the house," commanded Merit.

She hurried through the hallways downstairs, opening doors. The smell of smoke worsened, and she opened the door of a small courtyard, her eyes stinging in the enclosed, smoke-filled area. Her eyes fell on the pool, and she hastily shut the door. He had been there with that woman—the two of them together, her mind screamed.

She opened the next door and found herself looking at the once-pink sitting room where she had been received by Miss Smyth. A crackling sound came from the bedroom, and she rushed forward.

The flames had swallowed the curtains, and the carpet was smoldering. The bed curtains ignited with a loud pop, the filmy fabric bursting into flames that quickly enveloped the entire bed. Merit looked up; the ceiling paint was peeling, and it looked ready to go up in flames at any second.

Then she saw him. "Bob! Amos! Come quick!" Merit shook Christian, trying to wake him, but it was no good. She moved out of the way as the footmen carried him outside. The fire brigade was pulling up and a crowd was gathering. She sent the footmen with Christian on ahead and then directed the men to the back room where they set about putting out the fire.

His sooty figure took up the entire sofa in the salon. Merit listened to his chest and was relieved to hear a steady heart beat. Lovett hurried in with smelling salts and thrust them under his nose. Christian coughed and sat up, pushing the vial away.

"What the devil!" he exclaimed, his words slurred.

"Shh, my lord, don't talk. Just take deep, steady breaths," said Lovett.

He looked past her to Merit who was standing with one hand to her mouth, her dark eyes wide with fright.

"Mer . . ." he began, struggling against Lovett who was pushing him back against the upholstery.

Merit moved closer and perched on the edge of the sofa. She wrinkled her nose at the combined smell of smoke and brandy. Christian reached for her hand.

"What is it, Christian?" she asked softly.

With a drunken smile, Christian sealed his fate. "Mer . . . I love you, Mer . . . Maribella."

"It's not what I want to do, Lovett. I simply must get away!" said Merit, her eyes pleading for understanding.

"I'm sure he didn't mean to call you that. He was obviously not well."

"Well or not, I want nothing to do with a man who can't tell his mistress from . . ." Merit put her brushes in the case forcefully. She was so hurt and angry, she couldn't see straight. But she was a lady and wasn't supposed to express such violent emotions. She had never before wanted to, she reflected wryly—not until she met Lord Blackwell.

"You're distressed now," said Lovett. "Wait until he calls tomorrow."

"He probably won't even call," said Merit, hoping in her heart he would.

Instead, it was Catherine who called, and though Merit wouldn't see her, Maggie did. She told Catherine her mother was too upset to see anyone.

This was not far from the truth. Merit was busy supervising the packing of her bags and sending her regrets for the many invitations on her desk.

By the next morning, she had kissed Maggie and Lovett and said farewell to the household, swearing each one to secrecy as to her whereabouts.

* * *

Christian spent the week following the fire running from one entertainment to another. He spent a great deal of time convincing himself he was happy to not hear from the troublesome Merit Emerson.

Catherine's wedding was closing in, and she was in a constant state of panic. For the most part, Christian avoided and ignored her. Then one morning, hearing her crying, he went into her room.

"What's the matter, Catherine? Has Upton upset you again? Or was it the dressmaker or the pastry chef, or . . ."

"If you ever paid any attention, Christian, you would know what is the matter!" she exclaimed dramatically.

He shook his head and turned to go. His club was much more diverting than being harangued by his little sister.

"She's gone! And I don't know what you did, but it must have been something you said!" wailed Catherine.

"Who's gone?" he demanded.

"Merit, of course! And she swore her servants to silence. I have no idea where she is!"

"That's ridiculous! Did her daughter go, too?"

"No, Maggie is still there, but they won't let me see her now. And I know it's all your fault! She disappeared after speaking to you last week!"

"Nonsense! Why, you've been shopping with her several times since then," said Christian, unwilling to admit any guilt in the matter.

"That shows how much you know. I told you last week that she had gone, but you just told me to run and play or some such thing. You never listen to me!" As if on cue, she burst into tears.

"She'll turn up, Catherine. She wouldn't miss your wedding!" he said, patting her shoulder awkwardly.

Catherine's wedding came and went and there was still no sign of Merit. Christian sent his sister off with her new husband on their wedding trip and prepared to go to the country. The Season and the thought of looking over the year's crop of beauties for a possible wife had lost its appeal.

So, the house was packed up and the servants sent on to Blackhaven Manor, his estate in Devon. Only a skeletal staff would remain behind to keep the house in order.

Christian's valet finished packing the last valise on the phaeton and returned for one last look.

"We're ready, my lord, whenever you are."

"Thank you," he said, not making a move. Then he stood up and the valet breathed a sigh of relief. But it was premature.

"I've got a call to pay before I go to the country. You go ahead with the phaeton. My groom can drive. I'll follow on horseback."

"Very good, my lord."

Christian rode his horse through the quiet morning streets, covering the short distance to Hanover Square in minutes. The door to Merit's house opened as he pulled up and a footman hurried down the steps to hold his horse.

"Is your mistress at home?" he asked.

"I couldn't say," responded the servant.

Christian went up the steps and into the entranceway. "I've come to see Mrs. Emerson," he said, handing a calling card with the corner turned down to the butler.

The butler didn't even glance at it. He gazed at a point somewhere above Christian's left ear and said, "Madam is not at home, my lord."

"Where is she?"

"I couldn't say, my lord."

"Or won't say. What's your name, my good man?"

"Robert, my lord."

"Well, Robert, I have one hundred pounds here for the location of your mistress."

"I'm afraid I can't divulge that information, my lord. And I am not prone to taking bribes. None of us are."

Christian had to admire the man's loyalty, but he knew a

moment's frustration. With a snap of his fingers, he said, "Then let me see the child."

"That would not be possible, my lord."

Christian glared at him, but he knew it was futile. The man would go to his grave before betraying his mistress, and he had obviously been instructed to keep her destination a secret.

"Very well, Robert. If you should hear from your mistress, please tell her I called and would very much like to see her."

"Of course, my lord. Good day," said the butler, showing him the door.

Christian hadn't planned to ambush Merit's daughter, but since he was still sitting on his horse a little way down the street when the door opened again, he couldn't resist following the child and her governess. His desperation must have shown because he soon learned Merit's direction.

Christian whistled as he rode through the streets of London. Kingston was not very far, and his heart was light at the thought of seeing Merit again. As he rode along, he envisioned their meeting.

She will welcome me, he speculated. She has probably been waiting for me to discover her whereabouts and come after her, he decided. Then Christian grinned, amused by his own conceit. In reality, she will probably slap me again, he thought.

It was early afternoon when he entered the gates that introduced the long drive that led up to Lady Peterhaven's sprawling mansion. He had visited it once, many years before when her son had been alive.

He dismounted at the front steps and was ushered indoors by a butler who was twice as haughty as any London servant he had ever met. He was shown into a stuffy salon and told to wait while he located Mrs. Emerson, if she was at home.

Christian prowled around the room, smiling when he realized he was doing exactly what Merit had been doing that afternoon they had shared a pot of coffee.

Twenty minutes passed, and his smile had faded completely. The door opened and Christian looked up anxiously. But it was only the butler.

"I'm sorry, my lord, but Mrs. Emerson is away at the moment."

"Oh, is she?" he said, his temper fired by his wait. His first inclination was to rush past the butler shouting for Merit. He looked around and a movement outside caught his eye.

"Very well," he said, turning on his heel and heading for the front door. When he was outside, he startled the waiting groom by waving him away and heading around the house.

"Merit!" he called, striding toward the disappearing figure. She looked over her shoulder, picked up her skirts and began running.

Christian followed, his long strides quickly closing the gap between them. They were soon out of sight of the house, and when he overtook her, he held her at arm's length while he caught his breath, frowning fiercely down at her all the while.

"Let go of me!" said Merit, kicking at his shin and trying to scramble away.

"Ow!" he yelled as her foot connected. He neatly swept her feet out from under her, and she sat down with a thump. Christian sat down, too, and enveloped her in an iron embrace.

Breathing heavily, he said, "Not . . . until you listen . . . to me . . . , you harridan!"

"Harridan? Harridan, is it? I don't go around calling you by my lover's name!"

"Ex-lover," he corrected. "And you know I was half-conscious and drunk! And what do you mean, 'your lover'?"

"It doesn't matter!" she countered; then, she said haughtily, "At least I am not so dissipated by drink and carousing that I run a short distance across a little lawn and collapse from a lack of breath! When was the last time you had a decent meal or a good night's sleep?" she asked, not waiting for his reply.

"Two weeks ago," he replied, his breath coming more easily. "About the time I realized I couldn't live without you."

Merit ignored his comment and continued, "I would be ashamed to be your age and in such poor health. If I were you . . . Christian, stop that," she said, as he began to nibble at her neck. He stopped for a moment, and she tried again, "As I was saying, Christian . . . You really must try to . . . Oh, umm . . ."

After several moments, Merit snuggled against his chest, all thought of lectures vanished from her mind.

"You'll come back to London with me, won't you?" he said, his hand stroking her back and sending shivers of anticipation coursing through her body.

"Yes," she murmured, kissing his neck.

"We'll be married as soon as possible," he added.

"Yes," she replied again, tugging persistently at his face so that he would kiss her again.

This time he obliged, and they forgot all about planning for the future in the passion of the moment.

Finally, when he could stand it no longer, he sat up and moved away. "I'm not a very nice fellow, Merit. You deserve better, but I promise I'll improve."

"I don't think I could stand it if you improved any more," she said.

"So, does this mean you will marry me?" he asked with a grin.

Merit turned over and raised up on one elbow, her eyes still heavy with desire. "Is that the only way I can have you? And that pool? What about that pool?"

He laughed and motioned for her to come to him. She obliged, curling up in his lap. "You can have me and the pool. And I promise you, my love, I will not treat you like a good and proper wife in bed."

She gazed up at his handsome, beloved face and replied candidly, "I wouldn't let you."

"So you will marry me?"

"Yes, Christian, I will. I love you so much," she said, eyes shining.

"And I love you, Merit," he said before kissing her soundly.

About the Author

Donna Bell lives with her family in Flower Mound, Texas. Her newest Zebra Regency romance, THE BLUESTOCKING'S BEAU, will be published in May 1996. Donna loves hearing from her readers and you may write to her c/o Zebra Books. Please include a self-addressed stamped envelope if you wish a response.

Becky

by
Julie Caille

"Are you aware that Hugh is betrothed?"

Like a disagreeable smell, the question hovered between the two men who sat drinking brandy in The Honorable John Harding's study. Leighton Raikes set down his glass, temporarily deprived of speech by the other man's unwelcome news. In the heavy silence that followed, Leigh rose and went to the window, where he surveyed the rustling beech trees outside. The tranquil Leicestershire setting should have soothed him, but it didn't.

"To whom?" he said at last. Though his voice sounded satisfyingly remote, his fingers—the three that remained upon his war-ravaged right hand—had tightened into a rigid knot.

"A woman named Jennifer Rossendale." A soft clink followed as John poured them each another brandy. "She's Lady Datchet's goddaughter," he added in a troubled tone. "Used to live in Sussex until her parents died. She's been here about a year now."

For a few seconds, Leigh envisioned the sort of female his despised half brother would choose. She'd either be as starchy and backbiting as Hugh's first wife, Phillipa, or she'd be timid, dull, and self-effacing. Whichever the case, she'd be exactly what Hugh deserved.

Leigh watched the carefree flight of a sparrow, his mouth curled with bitterness. No matter how many years passed, no matter how many men he'd seen die or women he'd seduced, the mere mention of Hugh's name carried him back to a time when he'd been young and helpless, filled with incalculable rage and resentment toward the elder sibling who'd treated him like dirt under his feet.

Outwardly calm, he returned to the wingback chair where he'd been sitting until Hugh's name had intruded. "So?" he said. "Shall I pity her? Or him?"

A grimace flickered across John's face. "Not him, that's for certain. She's a fine young woman."

"Then why would she accept Hugh?"

"Well"—John rubbed the bridge of his nose—"she's no schoolgirl. She's seven-and-twenty if she's a day."

"Ah, that explains it. An old maid's desperation." With a sigh, Leigh reached for his glass. "I suppose she'll prove fertile," he added resignedly.

John swore beneath his breath. Several seconds passed before he leaned forward, his face distressed. "Dash it, Leigh, I always thought Hugh would die childless and you'd inherit the place. I thought . . . you'd come home someday."

Home. A word that had come to mean nothing.

"I suppose I did also." Leigh fell silent as the echo of his own words hammered inside his skull. That, indeed, was the truth. Given the thirteen-year age difference between himself and Hugh, he'd thought it would all come to him someday—perhaps not soon, but in due course—the estate, the title, the sense of belonging. It had been the last self-delusion he'd permitted himself, a will-o'-the-wisp fantasy without basis in hard realism.

"We all thought you were dead, you know. That damned letter the army sent. It was three weeks before the second one came, telling us it was all a mistake. God, Leigh, you can't imagine how I felt." Their gazes met in silent acknowledgment of a friendship born during their first days at Cambridge.

Leigh thought of the carnage of Waterloo, of the bodies stacked up like firewood, stripped of their uniforms by the locals. Amidst the horror, his own injuries had seemed almost minor; yet he'd come close to death, so close it still seemed a miracle he'd survived.

But all he said was, "I'll wager it gave Hugh an unpleasant start. I'm sure he'd prefer me to be dead." He crossed his legs at the ankles and sipped his drink. "I intend to pay him a call while I'm here. We can have a comfortable coze. Just like old times."

"Are you certain that's what you want?"

"Quite." Leigh smiled coldly as the wheels in his mind spun off in a new direction. "And I've an urge to see what sort of female this Rossendale chit is."

"She's a lady, Leigh. Don't make trouble."

"Trouble? You wrong me, John. I only want to make her acquaintance. After all, the lady is cutting me off from an inheritance."

"Only if she breeds," the other man reminded him.

"She'll breed. Hugh wants a son. God knows he did his damnedest to get one with Phillipa. After all those miscarriages, it's no wonder the poor thing died."

"Ah, so you've compassion for her now. That's something new."

"War changes a person." Leigh glanced down at his hand, with its missing fourth and fifth finger, and remembered the blast of cannon-shot that had removed them. "It hardens one, and at the same time—" He shook his head. "Sometimes I have the most peculiar notions."

"Such as?"

Leigh studied his glass. "Attacks of conscience, John. Can you imagine?"

"Of course I can. You're not an evil man."

"No. But I am capable of much."

"So are we all," his friend murmured.

Leigh gave a dry laugh. "Just so. Free will, the ability to distinguish good from evil—that's what separates us from the animals. It's so bloody ironic."

"What is?" John sounded bewildered.

"That men could knowingly choose evil. It's a rebellion of sorts, I suppose. Against authority. God."

"What the devil are you talking about?"

"Never mind." Leigh shook his head, unable to explain the strange forces that tore at his insides. He doubted John could understand even if he attempted to explain. Unlike himself, John had never tasted the forbidden pleasures of debauchery and wickedness, nor had he hated with all the immeasurable strength of his being. John was everything that was simple and good. Leigh's opposite.

"Tell me more about this Rossendale woman. What does she look like?"

"She's tall and rather elegant. Brown eyes, I believe. Her hair is a sort of dark red, heavy and smooth and damnably attractive."

"She's a beauty?"

"No, but she's . . . soft and feminine." John frowned. "What have you in mind, Leigh?"

Leigh noted the genuine concern in the other man's voice. "Why, nothing," he answered.

Nothing I'm willing to tell you, my friend.

Jennifer Rossendale set a vase of spring blooms upon the gleaming rosewood lowboy in the foyer of Datchet Manor, then stepped backward to observe the effect. It was not inspiring. Daffodils flopped listlessly among a collection of half-mangled bluebells and sagging sweet peas. All in all, there was little to suggest she had spent the past half hour struggling to achieve something charming.

Her godmother had fallen asleep upon the sofa in the Blue Saloon, leaving her would-be companion to while away the afternoon on her own. Further down the corridor, the ticking of the great clock in the drawing room mingled with the nearer, gentler whooshes of Lady Datchet's snores. Beneath these sounds, silence predominated.

Jennifer headed upstairs, her stomach clenching with the knowledge that tonight she must dine with Lord Charnwood. Most women in her position would have been elated by the prospect of marriage to a viscount, but Jennifer could summon up no great enthusiasm. Yes, she was nearly eight-and-twenty with no other suitors or prospects. And yes, Hugh was something of a catch in terms of worldly considerations. But neither of these particulars outweighed the fact that her heart yearned for something more.

However, she was too old for romance—Lady Datchet had made that perfectly clear. She was too old for dreams, too old for love and laughter. Impoverished unmarried ladies past the first blush of youth had to compromise. They had to accept the fact that their needs, their desires, must always be supplanted by the needs and wishes of others. So Lady Datchet had said.

And Jennifer had tried very hard to adjust. When Lord Charnwood had shown interest in her, she had been gracious and compliant. When he had asked for her hand, she had not hesitated to accept. Since then she had dined with him twice. Each time, she had been a pattern-card of decorum.

Adjust. Be calm. Be modest. Compromise.

But it was horribly difficult because she wasn't at all calm and she didn't want to compromise. She wanted passion. She wanted the kind of soul-searing love that would light up her life with melting rainbows. She wanted a man who could cast aside propriety, a man willing to face down demons in order to make her his own. Most of all, she wanted a friend, a man to whom she could whisper her innermost secrets.

A man with whom she could laugh.

Poppycock, Lady Datchet would have said with a sniff. Men like that didn't exist. Only a ninnyhammer could be so naive.

Depressed, Jennifer sat down at her dressing table and unpinned her hair. She didn't even like Hugh. He was a dreadful, pompous, conceited prig whose patronizing attitudes barely concealed his underlying contempt for the female gender. Even worse, there were times when his eyes glimmered with something strange, something that almost frightened her.

She began to brush her hair, each long stroke an effort to calm her uneasiness. Why had she accepted him? Foolishly, she had managed to convince herself that it didn't matter who she married, that her romantic dreams were no more than formless wisps, silly in the light of reality.

She had to be sensible. It was too late to cry off now that the announcement had been sent to the London papers, not to mention that respectable ladies did not cancel their bridal obligations. Certainly there was no one else, no desperate suitor whose existence could justify such willful folly. No Lochinvars loomed on the horizon, no knights in shining armor galloped her way.

Jennifer stared at her reflection, deep into the depths of her own anxious eyes. *Yes, you are well and truly trapped. And you have no one but yourself to blame.*

Dinner at Charnwood House proved a pleasureless event. Prior to her acceptance of his suit, Hugh had treated Jennifer with civil deference. He had engaged her and Lady Datchet in courteous, if rather dull, conversation, and had even made an attempt to be gallant. But such pleasantries were at an end. The viscount's smiles now seemed thin and cold, and his conversation had tapered to an icy trickle.

Tonight was worse than usual, for Lady Datchet had stayed home due to a slight indisposition. She had insisted Jennifer go without her, declaring it to be quite safe since Charnwood was such a gentleman. After all, they were betrothed, and in any case everyone knew what a stickler he was about morality. Yet her godmother's absence underscored the discomfort Jennifer had begun to feel in her future husband's company.

Feeling cornered, she stared at her plate, wishing Lady Datchet were present, wishing she were anywhere else but here.

I cannot bear this. I cannot, I cannot . . .

A small cough caught her attention, and she glanced up in time to see his lordship's butler whisper in Lord Charnwood's ear.

"What?" With uncharacteristic volume, the single word erupted from her future husband's throat. "Tell him to be gone! Tell him he's not welcome here. Tell him—"

"Don't expect poor Reeves to do your dirty work," interrupted in a cool, masculine voice.

Jennifer looked around, and felt her breath catch in her throat. The man in the doorway was tall and lean and suave, with an elegance of face and form she found singularly paralyzing. He was perfect. He was not handsome, not in the classical sense, for the lineaments of his face were too severe for such a label. Yet in some curious way he surpassed her wildest imaginings.

"What the devil do you want?" Hugh demanded.

"Come, Hugh, don't be churlish. Surely you won't refuse me dinner." The newcomer's voice, though bland, had a distinctly dangerous edge. He strolled toward them across the carpet, his movements lithe, his golden hair glinting in the warm candlelight. As he moved, his saturnine gaze shifted so that he looked directly into Jennifer's eyes.

"My apologies, ma'am," he said with a bow. "If Hugh won't introduce me, I'll introduce myself. I'm Leighton Raikes, Hugh's brother, the black sheep of the family. Hugh and I don't rub along well together, but I expect we could be civil for the length of a meal."

She'd known who he was. Her heart had recognized him the instant she'd set eyes on him, though it had taken her numbed brain a few more seconds to assimilate the truth. However, it was clear that *he* didn't recognize *her.*

"How do you do?" she said, trying to smile. Trying to pretend that her pulse wasn't skittering madly.

"Jennifer, you are not to address this man," Charnwood cut in. "He's no fit companion for any respectable woman, particularly not the woman I intend to wed."

Taken aback, she shifted her gaze. "Nevertheless he is your brother, my lord. May I suggest we invite him to join us? I have no brothers or sisters, but if I did I know I would cherish them no matter what sort of . . . of life they'd led."

"Bravo." Leighton Raikes pulled out the empty chair opposite her own and sat down, his expression rather mocking. "I salute you, Hugh. Your bride-to-be has more mettle than I expected. Your taste has improved."

"Bedamned to you." Hugh surged to his feet, his cheeks mottled with red spots. "How dare you force your way in here—"

"Force?" Leigh whipped the word out, his voice sharp as a blade. "You seem to forget I grew up in this house. The servants were glad enough to see me."

"My servants. My house, my servants. Not yours."

"Ah, yes." Leigh's voice grew light, but the slight twist of his mouth conveyed volumes. "You are the elder offspring, while I am only a spurious afterthought. Thank you for the reminder, dear brother. I was almost in danger of forgetting that all this is yours." His right hand swept up just long enough for Jennifer to glimpse the misshapen stumps of two missing fingers. An involuntary gasp escaped her lips.

"My apologies." Leighton cast her a quick look and put his hand out of sight. "I forget how distasteful that is to see."

Sympathy flashed through her, more so because he seemed to think she was repulsed. However, before she could correct him, Charnwood lashed out, "I don't care what body parts you've lost. If you want a meal, go eat in the kitchen. And then take yourself back to whatever godforsaken place you've crawled out of."

Looking rather white, Leighton rose to his feet. "Thank you for your so-gracious offer, but I think not." A taut smile played on his lips, a smile at odds with the ice blue fury in his eyes. "Later, dear Hugh, when you have recovered your temper, it will no doubt occur to you to wonder why I came. As it happens, I did have a purpose. And that purpose has just been solidified."

"And what might that be?" Charnwood sneered.

"Wouldn't you like to know? Think on it, Hugh. I doubt you'll guess, but I hope it keeps you awake nights." His gaze flicked back to Jennifer, the all-encompassing scope of his scrutiny sending prickles down her spine. "Again, I must apologize. Hugh and I ought to know better than to wash our dirty linen in public. On the other hand, you'll be joining the family soon, so perhaps I'm doing you a kindness. After all, it's always best to know how deep the water is before one dives in."

* * *

The night wind grumbled through the trees as Leigh rode the three miles back to John's estate. He had planned to stay with John's family for several days before returning to the piece of property he had purchased a month back. Located a dozen miles eastward, near Melton Mowbray, it held a small but charming manor house previously owned by a country squire, now deceased. It would serve as both home and hunting box between his seasonal forays to London and Brighton.

For he fully intended to resume his former life, the life he'd lived before he'd enlisted in the army. It had been a wild sort of existence, a frenetic wallowing in hedonism that had begun the day his mother died. It had suited him, that life, and would suit him just as well now that he was older.

With dispassion, he acknowledged that his newest scheme was not a noble one. He told himself he didn't care. The war was over; the time for nobility and sacrifice was past. At last the opportunity to punish Hugh had presented itself, and he meant to use it. The desire for revenge had festered inside him for so long that any scruples he might once have felt no longer held sway.

He smiled in the dark. By God she attracted him, this Jennifer Rossendale. As John had said, she was no beauty, but she had an appeal he found stimulating. Mentally, he catalogued her assets. Her eyes were wide-spaced, her nose straight, her lips full, and her figure neat. Nothing stood out as being in any way extraordinary, and yet the sum total captivated him. Soft and feminine were the words John had used to describe her, but it was more than that. What was it? That elusive something nagged at him, rolling around in his mind despite his efforts to eject it. Even odder, he had a sense of familiarity, as though in some other time, some other life, she had meant something to him.

But he had never met her before. He was sure of it.

Dismissing the absurd thought, he contemplated his intended seduction of Hugh's bride-to-be. How he would accomplish it he had yet to determine, but accomplish it he would. His lips curved as he imagined each act in the scene. At first she would protest a great deal, but eventually he knew she'd give in. And when she yielded, he'd make sure she enjoyed the experience—his code of ethics demanded that. When it was over, she would weep and say he should marry her. He would refuse, and she would despise him. That was to be expected.

He didn't care.

All he wanted was for Hugh to know.

After that, he would play his cards according to the hand fate—and Hugh—dealt him.

The important thing, the tricky thing, would be to protect the woman from scandal. He would not have Jennifer Rossendale's ruin upon his conscience. No one must know but Hugh, whose silence was guaranteed because the truth would make him look ridiculous. Leigh's smile grew. Yes, the more he thought on it, the more convinced he became that the plan would serve.

Revenge was going to be even sweeter than he had dreamed.

Dusting the soil from her hands, Jennifer rose from the grass and went to sit in the romantic little gazebo near the east end of Lady Datchet's garden. Despite her godmother's protestations, Jennifer spent much of her time working in the flower beds when the weather permitted. She enjoyed the rich, pungent aroma of earth and foliage, and savored the inner peace that came with pulling weeds and wielding clippers—or at least she did under normal circumstances. In recent days, however, contentment had eluded her. Ever since the evening she'd met *him*.

All week he'd haunted her. Day and night, she'd thought of him, dreamt of him, had imaginary conversations with him. Even now, her mind's eye could see him so exactly it was frightening.

And exciting.

Yes, it excited her to imagine what it would be like to be wooed by Leighton Raikes. Was it wrong of her? Heaving a sigh, she stretched out upon a marble bench, closed her eyes, and propped her linked hands behind her head. How could it be wrong? Private thoughts did not constitute betrayal. Every woman was entitled to fantasies, was she not?

For a brief moment, her thoughts wandered to Lord Charnwood, from whom she had heard nothing during this past week. Her future husband was suffering from an inflammation of the stomach, a piece of news relayed to her by Lady Datchet, who had it from a friend whose abigail had a sister who worked in the Charnwood kitchens. Duty had prompted Jennifer to send him a note of commiseration, but she'd had no reply.

Feeling drowsy, she rolled to her side and cradled her head on one arm. A light breeze stirred her curls. Birds chirped in the trees. Little by little, her mind slid into that languid state of semi-awareness that exists between sleep and wakefulness, then something brushed across her cheek, something that felt like . . . a finger?

Her eyes shot open.

Her first startled thought was that Lord Charnwood had found his way into the garden, but the long and exceedingly well-shaped legs before her did not belong to the viscount. Nor did the low, lazy voice that said, "If I kiss you, do I get to keep you?"

Astonished, Jennifer sprang to a sitting position. "What are you doing here?"

Leighton Raikes gazed down at her in a pensive fashion, a glimmer of masculine approval in his eyes. "Looking for you," he said blandly. "What else?"

What else indeed?

Swallowing, she started to lift a hand to her hair, but managed to halt the self-conscious gesture. Her gown was old and her hands were dirty, but what did it signify? Her thoughts darted, stumbling over each other in an effort to come up with a logical reason for his presence. Only one came to mind.

He *did* remember her after all.

"Does Lady Datchet know you're here?" Her heart pounded in an unsteady rhythm.

"No, I came in through the woods." He paused, then without

invitation sat down beside her on the bench. "She'd never leave me alone with you. You know that as well as I."

It was probably true. In the past year, Jennifer had heard much about Leighton Raikes from the gossiping old tabbies in the neighborhood. His mother had been the viscount's second wife, and from all accounts her son had been wild and rebellious from the day he was born. Though no one had actually told Jennifer the facts, enough hints had been dropped for her to infer that he'd seduced a parlor maid at the age of seventeen and been thrown out of the ancestral mansion by his furious father.

From that day onward he had lived by his wits, earned a reputation as a gambler and a rogue, and apparently enjoyed it. At some point he had inherited a sum of money from his mother's side of the family, which made it difficult to understand why he had joined the army as an enlisted man when he could have bought himself an officer's commission. His rumored valor as a Rifler in the 95th failed to redeem him in the eyes of the gabblemongers, who delighted in reminding each other that a rotten apple does not miraculously become edible.

But the man sitting beside her did not look like the blackguard he'd been painted to be. At this moment he seemed approachable, a human being with the capacity to feel and to love. He also seemed the answer to her lonely prayers, God's cryptic reply to the coil into which she'd landed herself.

"Why did you touch me?" she asked in a small voice.

"Because I wanted to, Jennifer." He slanted a glance at her. "You're quite lovely, you know."

"No, I don't know. And I have not given you leave to use my Christian name." She waited, wondering when he would stop the charade. Surely he knew who she was.

"No, you haven't. Give it to me now, for I've no interest in being formal with you." His eyes narrowed, though not with recognition. "I won't deceive you, my dear. I want to know you better. Much better. Are you willing?"

His boldness astounded her. Her original impression—that he did not remember her—returned, and that led to another, wholly startling idea. For some unknown reason he found her attractive. Her head spun with the implications.

"I beg your pardon. I don't think I understand," she murmured, knowing quite well that it was not the response she should make. Knowing she ought to slap his face. Knowing she ought to gather her dignity and walk away before it was too late. Instead, she folded her hands and waited.

"I thought we might go riding together one afternoon," he said. "Tomorrow, perhaps? Could you slip away without anyone knowing?"

The outrageous request stole her breath. The gossips were right—he *was* a rogue. No true gentleman would issue such an invitation. And why should he desire to arrange a clandestine meeting with her of all people? She searched her mind, but could think of no reason except the most gloriously, flatteringly obvious. A heady exultation rushed through her as all her feminine yearnings suddenly seemed a trifle less fantastical and absurd.

"I cannot possibly do such a thing," she replied with a stab of regret. "It's preposterous."

"But you want to."

"I do not! Mr. Raikes, I'm about to be married."

"To a man you don't love." He moved closer, his face intent, his words probing the rawest corners of her soul. "You'll have the rest of your life to wonder, you know. What it would have been like to do something reckless and indiscreet. Something that makes you feel alive. I see it in your face. In your eyes."

She looked down at her fingers, her throat tight with the dread that invariably came when she thought of her upcoming marriage. "No," she said, shaking her head. "No, you're wrong."

"You're deceiving yourself. You don't want Charnwood, you made it obvious the other night. Marriage to him is a death sentence." He touched her hand, a seductive whisper of flesh upon flesh that sent a rush of longing through her entire being. "Before you die, you ought to taste life. Do something improper, Jenny. Meet me tomorrow. I'll bring a mount for you, or you can bring

your own. We'll avoid the villages and roads, and ride acros
country. There's no risk involved. No one will see us."

"I shouldn't. I can't."

But the madness had its grip on her now—her mind was al
ready weaving excuses and rationalizations. She loved to ride
and she had been lonely, so lonely. Riding was a harmless an
genteel pursuit. At her age, she no longer required a chaperon—
even Lady Datchet agreed about that. And this man, despite hi
wicked reputation, had been a soldier—and a brave and honor
able one from all accounts. Knowing this, she could not bring
herself to be afraid of him. Moreover, he would soon be he
brother-in-law, and in view of that impending relationship, riding
with him could not be completely improper. Only her fantasies
made it dangerous—and he would never know about those.

"I shouldn't," she repeated waveringly.

"But will you?" His long-lidded blue eyes held hers, and in
their depths she saw the swirling remnants of her hopes and
dreams.

And she was lost.

"Yes," she whispered.

Jennifer directed her mare through the woods, knowing that
in a few moments they would emerge into the open, where Leigh
would be waiting. Two weeks had passed since that day in the
garden, two incredible weeks in which she'd felt more alive than
she had in years. They had met half a dozen times since then,
and each rendezvous grew more exciting, more stimulating.

The night after the first meeting she'd been unable to sleep,
so she'd gone to her window and gazed at the stars. *Let him
recognize me,* she had prayed. *Let him know who I am and be
pleased with the knowledge. Let it make a difference.*

But it hadn't happened.

Why this was so important she was unsure. Perhaps it was
because she could not speak with complete freedom until he
realized and accepted who she was. After all, she knew things

about him, things he might not wish her to know. Not only did
it make it awkward, but she felt almost guilty for deceiving him.
On the other hand, she could not bring herself to feel guilty for
deceiving Lord Charnwood. It was as though the two brothers'
roles in her life were reversed, as though she belonged, not with
the elder, but with the younger of the two men.

Indeed, she felt vastly more comfortable with Leigh than she
ever had with Hugh. Though Leigh had avoided any mention
of his early life, he'd told her about the war, about London and
Brighton, about the Prince Regent's follies, about his friend,
John Harding. He'd teased and flirted with her, and she'd teased
and flirted back, safe in the knowledge that she could do so
because he was Leigh. And because, despite his blemished reputation, he had not even tried to kiss her.

Her pulse quickened as she neared the spot where he would
be. She glanced down at her habit. Although not in the current
mode, it was made of a rich, deep green that complemented her
hair and coloring. Perhaps it was silly, but she wanted to look
pretty for him. She wanted him to want to kiss her, though she
didn't know how she'd react if he did.

She found him leaning against a tree, his horse tethered to a
nearby branch. He straightened as she approached. Was it only
her imagination or did his eyes light up when he saw her?

"You're late, Jenny," he admonished.

"I'm sorry. A caller delayed my godmother's nap."

"Anyone I know?"

"Only the vicar," she said hastily, lest he think it was Charnwood. She hadn't seen Charnwood since the night she'd had
dinner with him. "I'm glad you waited for me."

"So am I." He made no move to remount his horse, but instead came close and reached for her hands. "Come down," he
commanded. "This is a pleasant place. Private, too."

Without hesitation, she slid to the ground. "How is Mr. Harding's little boy? I trust he is feeling better?"

For a handful of seconds Leigh did not answer, but rather
stood gazing down at her with a queer, frowning look. "I think

so," he said at last. "According to John, Marie fusses too much.
The child's fit as a fiddle."

To her surprise, his fingers remained locked around hers, a
departure from his usual conduct. Her heart skipped a beat. "Did
you wish to walk?" she asked, feeling breathless. "Or . . . shall
we sit?"

His eyes narrowed. "If I told you what I really want, you
would slap my face."

"You should not say such things."

"What do you expect?" He sounded provoked, even angry.
"You know the sort of man I am. You can't be that naive."

"I know your reputation. But I also know you're an honorable
man."

"Oh, do you?" Mockery laced his voice. "How? Because I
haven't done this?"

He slipped an arm around her waist, drawing her against his
body with an easy, steely strength. With his free hand, he forced
up her chin. "You foolish girl, I could have you right here if I
chose. I could do whatever I wished and you couldn't prevent
me." He paused, still studying her. "Doesn't that frighten you?"
Her gentle, entertaining companion was gone, and in his place
stood a stranger whose eyes taunted her for her gullibility.

"Do you want it to frighten me?" she countered, painfully
conscious of all the places where their bodies touched. Through
their dual layers of clothing, she could feel the throbbing tempo
of his heart, the tremor of hard muscles in his lean male torso,
even the bulge between his thighs that told of his urge for a
physical union. Dimly, she realized it was not only he who
wielded power, but the thought fled as he replied,

"To be frank, I want it to arouse you. Does it?"

Unwilling to answer, she tried to pull away. "What is it you
want of me? I thought we were friends."

"Friends," he repeated, his voice amazed and rather thick.
"Do you honestly think a man like me and a woman like you
could have such a simple relationship?"

"Why not?" she demanded, though deep inside she knew the answer. "Why not, Mr. Raikes?"

"Because, damn it, *this* gets in the way."

Before she could utter a word, his mouth came down to cover hers, not gently but insistently, in a way that told her he would not be denied. Caught in the silken threads of desire, her shocked mind refused to object. This was what she had wanted for days and it was most certainly what she wanted now. This could well be the only time in her life she would be kissed by a man she desired. If nothing more, he would give her a memory to cherish, something to help her survive the long, cold nights she would spend with Lord Charnwood.

Drowning in sensual delight, she parted her lips, granting him the access he seemed to want. His tongue surged inside, mating with hers, thrusting and exploring with an aggressiveness that filled her with pulsing excitement. The intimacy—and her own abandoned response to it—stunned her. Dear Lord, he was right. If he wanted her, he could have her, for she lacked both the physical and emotional strength to resist.

But he evidently did, for a moment later he released her and stepped away. "You see?" he said in a short tone.

Shaken, she clasped her trembling hands together and lifted her chin to a defiant angle. "What should I see?"

"That you are vulnerable. That you attract me. That I want you, all of you." His eyes held a glinting, indecipherable look. "This is the only warning I'll give. After today, Jenny, I make no promises."

"The wolf cautioning the sheep?" she ventured dryly.

"Just so." His gaze swept over her, pausing to linger on her kiss-swollen lips. For a moment he looked almost fierce, then a reassuring calmness returned to his face. "Do you still wish to ride?"

Common sense told her to run away, but that same common sense had been allowed far too much rein in her life. For once she was going to do as she wanted. In any case, this was Leigh. Leigh would never do anything to hurt her.

"Of course I want to ride. I'm not the pudding-heart you seem to think. Besides"—she gave him a challenging look—"haven't you just assured me I'm safe for today?"

"So I have," he agreed with an ironic bow.

That evening, Leigh sat in John's study long after his host had gone up to bed. John had claimed to be tired, but Leigh hadn't been fooled. He'd noticed the look Marie had given her husband when she'd excused herself an hour earlier. John and Marie were deeply in love, bound by a power that went far beyond the perfunctory relationships with which Leigh was familiar.

His brow furrowed, he strolled to the window, a glass of port cradled in his good hand. Knowing his host and hostess were probably locked in each other's arms made him restless and irritable. A part of him envied them—the part that wasn't consumed with the need for vengeance.

God, how he hated Hugh. Even now it churned with the wine in his belly, a devil's brew of resentment and rage. Leigh shut his eyes, allowing the enmity to wash over him, encouraging it to subjugate his other, less convenient emotions.

Emotions he had no business feeling.

Damn, damn, damn.

Kissing Jennifer hadn't been part of his plan. Nor had he intended to warn her. In fact, he hadn't meant to touch her at all before the night of the abduction. He'd meant to lull her suspicions, to lure her skillfully into his trap.

His fingers stroked the delicate curve of the wineglass. Now that he'd had a tantalizing taste of her passion, now that he'd inhaled the scent of her skin and felt the sweet press of her breasts against his chest . . . he found it difficult to think of anything else.

He couldn't recall ever being so haunted by a woman. He'd always liked women, always found them delightful. But he'd never singled one out like this, never found one he wanted to be with for more than a single night.

He grimaced, knowing he was acting the fool. One night with her would be enough—if that night ever came now that he'd been stupid enough to warn her away.

Whatever had possessed him?

He expelled a harsh breath through his teeth. In part, he supposed it was his sense of fair play. Added to that, he had an abiding aversion to anyone who hurt or abused someone weaker than himself. Not that he would hurt Jennifer in any way. He would take her virtue, but not against her will. If she resisted, he would not force himself upon her. Rape was not his style. But he intended to exert himself to the fullest, to use every means of seduction to ensure she gave in.

Hugh wanted an heir, a son to prevent Leigh from inheriting the title. He could not prevent Hugh from marrying, but by God he could make him squirm. And he meant to use Jennifer to achieve that end.

For a flickering moment self-loathing seized him, but he chased it away. He would not reconsider. He would pay Hugh back for all those years of misery—misery to the child Leigh had once been, misery to the lovely, emotionally fragile woman who had been his mother. Hugh had bullied and tyrannized them both. He had turned their father against his second wife, humiliated and shamed her with his vile lies . . .

Leigh glanced down sharply. Under the furious pressure of his fingers, he had broken the wineglass. Blood trickled from a cut on his palm, mixing with darker red of the port. The physical pain barely registered.

Vengeance will be mine.

Retribution was what counted. Unscrupulous or not, he would carry out his plan to seduce Jennifer.

And when it was over, he would not look back.

The note from Leigh came two days later. Jennifer read and reread it, her brows gathered into a tiny frown.

As always, she'd found the folded and sealed missive tucked

under a loose board in the gazebo. It had been his way of communicating with her, of arranging meetings or altering plans already made. Despite the dangerous currents of their last meeting, she had continued to check beneath the board.

Still frowning, she took a seat on a bench. Always before he had asked her to meet him during the afternoon, when Lady Datchet was napping. Always before he had instructed her to bring her mount, the little brown mare her godmother had provided for her use. This time was different.

A light breeze sifted past Jennifer's face, caressing her curls like gentle fingers. She gazed down at the words he had scrawled. *Don't let anyone see you leave the house. Come on foot to the clearing tonight, when everyone else is asleep. Don't fail me, Jenny. I'll be waiting. I need you.* It was signed with the letter "L."

What did it mean?

Conflicting emotions whirled in her mind—shock, anticipation, wariness, even a spurt of anger. Riding with him was one thing, but did he expect her to creep out in the night like a thief? Did he think he had but to crook his finger and she would come? Was he that sure of her?

She studied the note, trying to read between the lines, searching for clues to his meaning. Come to me. I need you. It was hardly a lover's entreaty. In fact, it was almost curt.

Her attention fixed on the word "need." If he'd said he'd wanted her, that would have had unmistakable connotations. But need? In what way did he need her? Was he in some kind of trouble? It didn't seem likely, but the possibility plagued her, filling her with concern.

No one had ever needed her before.

Her parents, though they had loved her, had only needed each other. She had no siblings, no relatives other than a distant aunt, no one who depended on her for anything. Her one experience with romance, a brief courtship with a country squire, had ended when he'd learned the size of her small inheritance. Even Lady Datchet didn't need her, and neither did Lord Charnwood.

Perhaps such knowledge should have given a sense of freedom, but it didn't. Instead, she felt useless, without purpose. To be needed, to be necessary, to make a difference to someone—more than anything this was what she desired. It was the source of the restless yearning that so often seethed inside her.

She shook her head, rejecting the notion that Leigh could need her. It must be an unfortunate choice of words. And yet . . . what if it wasn't? She cared for him far too much to take that chance.

She would go.

Distant thunder heralded an approaching storm as Jennifer picked her way through the darkness. Trees creaked and swayed in the wind, their long-fingered branches catching at her clothing and hair. She shoved a few errant strands from her eyes, straining to see the path in front of her. Leigh dominated her thoughts.

At last she stumbled into the clearing. Eyes narrowed, she looked around, hoping he had preceded her. To her relief, a tall shadow disconnected from a deeper pool of black and moved toward her. "Jenny," it said. "You came."

"Of course I came." He was only a faint silhouette against the sky, but his hand settled warmly, deliciously, upon her arm. "But what is this about, Leigh? Is something wrong?"

"We can't talk here," he answered.

Taking her hand, he led her through the shadows to his horse. The great thoroughbred shifted restlessly as, with no apparent effort, Leigh tossed her onto its back, then mounted behind her, his arms forming a protective circle around her body.

As the mighty beast leaped forward, Jennifer tried to twist around. "Where are we going?"

"Relax, Jenny. You're quite safe, I promise."

"But I don't—" She broke off as a huge bolt of lightning streaked across the sky. Leigh was right; they could not talk now. Doubtless he was taking her to some place of shelter. Explanations could wait.

Closing her eyes, she allowed herself to lean against the solid wall of his chest. How easy it was to pretend, just for a few moments, that this was where she belonged. How safe and secure he made her feel . . . and how cherished, though the latter was no more than a product of her capricious imagination.

How many minutes passed she had no idea, but at last they came to a halt. A country road lay before them, and on that road, directly in front of them, waited a coach-and-four.

As the first large raindrops began to pelt down, Leigh slid to the ground. "Hurry," he directed, reaching up to assist her, "before we get soaked."

As Jennifer's feet hit the ground, a liveried servant ran over and took the horse's reins, while another let down the carriage steps. Leigh's hand closed on her elbow, propelling her forward until she found herself seated on velvet squabs. He followed her inside and sat opposite. A single lantern lit the interior.

"What in the world . . . ?" Dazed, she pushed a lock of damp hair from her face. "Mr. Raikes, what is the meaning of this?"

"I thought we agreed you would call me Leigh."

"Pray answer my question."

"Very well." His eyes held hers. "I'm abducting you."

"Please give me a serious answer."

"I assure you I'm quite serious. I'm abducting you, Jenny. I warned you, didn't I? You should have heeded me while I was playing fair."

Prickles of unease scampered down Jennifer's spine. There was something odd about him, a glint in his eyes, a slight muzziness to his voice. Suddenly, she understood.

"You've been drinking," she accused.

"True," he responded, his smile slight, "but I'm not foxed, if that's what troubles you."

"Perhaps you mean this for a jest—"

"You underrate yourself, my dear. This is no jest."

"But why?" She stared at him in bewilderment. "Why would you want to . . . to abduct me?" Even the word sounded absurd.

"Because I couldn't be sure you'd come willingly." His blond head cocked to the side. "I thought you might, but I had to be certain."

She examined his face. "I demand that you take me back. I am not at all amused."

"I didn't intend you to be amused. Nor do I intend to return you to Lady Datchet's house before sunrise."

Slowly, his meaning sank in. Dismayed, she regarded him anew, taking in his unyielding expression, the obdurate slant of his mouth, the almost feral stretch of skin over the high, elegant cheekbones. And his eyes. Something smoldered in their depths, something that triggered a strange, alien tingling in the pit of her stomach.

She shook her head. "This is madness. What can you possibly want with me?"

"I want exactly what you think I want."

The words invoked images—vague, sensual images created from her most secret fantasies, from yearnings that had haunted her for days and months and years.

Biting her lip, she glanced toward the window, but could see nothing of what was outside. Surely he wasn't taking her to John Harding's estate. "Where are we going?"

"To my home."

"Your home?" she repeated. "You have a house?"

"Yes, a dozen miles from here. You didn't think I lived with John, did you? By the way, you ought to thank me for this fashionable conveyance. I purchased it just for you."

She leaned forward, looking him in the eye. "You must listen to me. Somehow I . . . I've given you the wrong impression about me. I am not a loose woman."

"Good God, Jenny, I know that. There's never been any doubt in my mind on the matter of your virtue."

"Then take me back," she implored. "You don't have to do this. I won't tell anyone. Please."

"Save your breath, my dear. My mind is made up. Instead of arguing, why don't you come and sit by me? You could rest your head on my shoulder and sleep."

Ignoring the seductive invitation, she sat back and wondered what to do. There seemed to be nothing she *could* do, short of wrenching open the door in order to fling herself out into the pouring rain. And that was as impractical as it was risky.

What stunned her the most was that she wanted to do as he suggested. A part of her actually yearned to go to him, to lean on him, to yield. Even more, that same scandalous part of her ached for him to show her the meaning of passion.

As the miles passed, she struggled to form an escape plan, which proved difficult because she was so very tired. Every few minutes her head drooped, then she'd start and jerk upright, until the next time it happened. Each time she'd dart a quick glance in his direction. He was always watching her, always with that same brooding expression.

At length, lulled by the sway of the coach, everything faded . . . until the vehicle lurched to a stop. Thus roused, her eyes flew open. She was unnerved to find herself snuggled against Leigh, her head on his chest, his arm about her shoulders. Flustered, she pushed away from him and glared.

He had the audacity to laugh. "Don't bristle. I was only being gallant. You'd have fallen to the floor if I hadn't intervened."

"The moment I step out I mean to tell your servants the truth. I'm certain they will take me back, with or without your consent."

"Sorry, love, but they won't. They're actually some of my army mates. They had nowhere else to go, so I hired them. I think you'll find they're loyal to me, even if they did get a soaking tonight."

Deflated, Jennifer allowed him to guide her into the house, for there seemed no point in standing about in the rain. By fashionable standards his home was small, but a part of her weary brain also noted that it was neat, clean, and cheerful. However, she was in no mood to be cheered. She was tired and rumpled and damp, and very cross with Leigh, a fact she demonstrated by refusing to accompany him up the stairs.

Again, he seemed to find her amusing. "Darling, you've no

choice. Either walk or I'll carry you. I assure you I'm quite capable of hoisting you over my shoulder."

She bit her lip, knowing he spoke the truth. She had already felt his strength. "I met you tonight because you said you needed me. I thought you might be in trouble. Instead, you betray my trust in you—"

"I told you not to trust me," he cut in, his voice smooth as velvet. "You chose to ignore my warning. Now you must take the consequences."

"You keep saying you won't hurt me."

"And I won't." He took hold of her arm, compelling her to mount the stairs, and out of pride she did not fight him. "I intend to give you pleasure, Jenny. A great deal of it, I hope."

"The word 'hurt' has more than one meaning. What do you think the rest of my life will be like if you do this? What do you think Lady Datchet will say?"

"If you're home before dawn, she won't find out. Or if she does, I'm quite sure she'll keep her mouth shut. If necessary, I'll pay her a visit and use my own inimitable powers of persuasion to silence her." Steering her into what appeared to be his bedchamber, he shut the door and locked it, then removed his riding coat and threw it onto a chair. "I'm not out to ruin you, Jenny. Quite the contrary, in fact."

Her mouth went dry as she glanced around, but there was no other exit. "I don't understand why you're doing this. You can't pretend you're in love with me."

"Perhaps I am. I certainly like you well enough."

"How flattering." She watched him stroll to a table and pick up a decanter of wine. As he filled two glasses, she added, "You needn't pour one for me. I won't drink it."

He glanced up, a hint of admiration in his eyes. "What a stubborn girl you are. I rather like that, I think."

Unable to stay still, she moved about the room, and in so doing caught a glimpse of her reflection in the mirror over the shaving stand. An idea occurred to her. "Gracious, I look dreadful. The least you could do is go away and give me a chance to tidy up."

"To what purpose?" He ran a practiced eye over her form. "I'll only untidy you again. Take your hair down, if you like. There's a comb on the washstand." He sipped his wine, regarding her over the rim of the glass in a way that made her knees turn to pudding.

"Why are you doing this?" she asked again. "If you don't tell me I shall scream, and you won't find that very pleasant, I assure you."

He shrugged. "I have to live up to my name. Raikes the Rake has a certain ring to it, don't you think?"

"You're being childish."

He set down his glass, his eyes glittering in the candlelight. "And you're being shrewish. The truth is you tempt me." He moved closer, closer, until they stood only inches apart. Her heart pounded as she fought the urge to retreat. After all, there was nowhere to go. "You tempt me with your eyes and your mouth and the curves of your lovely body. Even more. The way you look at me tempts me."

"The way I look at you?" She realized she was actually trembling and he hadn't even touched her.

Yet.

"You look at me as though I matter to you. As though—" He paused, a sensuous flame darkening the blue of his eyes. "As though you need me."

"I don't need you. I don't need anyone. I'm fine just as I am." She drew a breath and played what she hoped was her trump card. "You seem to forget I'm about to be married. To your brother, Leigh."

At once his expression changed, hardened in a manner that made her take an instinctive step backward. "No, I hadn't forgotten that." In a swooping motion, his hands clamped like shackles around her wrists. "Hugh isn't fit to wipe your shoes, Jenny. He's dirt."

"That's your opinion," she said, more from obstinacy than loyalty to Hugh.

"You'd share my opinion if you knew him as I do." The taut, sculpted lines of Leigh's face had grown harsh and cold, yet an instant later, as if forced away by sheer will, his countenance was once again benign. "Don't fight me, Jenny. We've only a few hours. Let's make them count."

"No." The objection was automatic, the response of a lady of birth and breeding.

"Yes," he whispered, kissing her brow. "Say yes, Jenny. Think of it. You and I together on that bed. Sweet, sweet Jenny, let me love you the way you deserve to be loved."

Her muscles turned to molten syrup as he kissed her cheek, her eyelids, the corners of her mouth. Her heart thudded unbearably as his hands glided over her shoulders, caressed her arms. She had to stop him. But how? *Distract him. Say something, anything . . .*

"Why did you go into the army?" she gasped.

"What?" He lifted his head.

"You've told me about the battles, but you never said why you enlisted. I've . . . I've been curious about that."

He stared at her as though she'd lost her mind. "You want to know this now?" When she nodded, he expelled a breath. "I enlisted because . . . I wanted to prove to myself I had courage."

"And did you?"

For a long moment she thought he wouldn't answer. Then he shrugged and said, "Not really. Courage, I discovered, requires the risk of sacrifice. One must have something—or someone—to lose before one can be deemed courageous. I found I had nothing."

"You had your life," she objected, taken aback.

"True, but—" He paused. "It wasn't much of a life. No more questions, my girl. I didn't bring you here to talk."

Again, his arms came around her, his mouth bonding with hers in a kiss so fiery it shot sparks through her bloodstream. She couldn't resist him. She had to resist him. She couldn't. She had to. *Why?*

Confusion coursed through her, along with a rush of rebellion. Why couldn't she do as she wished? Men could do as they liked. Why not women? It wasn't fair. She did want him. Dear Lord, she had wanted him for weeks. For years, even.

Forever.

A hypnotic composure settled around her. Yes, she wanted this. All along she'd been making excuses, rationalizing reasons to meet him. She'd fooled herself into believing all she wanted from him was friendship. But she wanted more.

Much more.

Absorbed in sensation, she arched her head, her eyes drifting shut as his lips scorched the tender flesh of her throat. Vaguely, she knew that he was removing her cloak, taking the pins from her hair, loosening the fastenings of her gown. Not until the cool air touched her bare shoulders did she regain some semblance of sanity.

"No," she murmured, a half-hearted protest. "You must not. I cannot."

"You can. And you will. Because . . ." He lifted her in his arms, his lips curved in a provocative smile as he carried her to the bed. "Because you want to, my love. Because you and I both know this is meant to be."

Setting her down, he unbuttoned his shirt, his eyes holding promises that made her heart race. While he tossed his shirt aside and pulled off his boots, she drank in the sight of his male beauty. He was magnificent. Perfect. She'd known he would be.

What was she doing?

The voice of her conscience intruded, reminding her of the countless lessons in propriety she'd had drummed into her over the years. This man was a self-proclaimed libertine, a philanderer whose advances she ought to be fighting. But like some spineless, docile babe in the woods, she was succumbing to his spell as though she lacked a mind or will of her own.

No.

She might be insane, but she was not spineless or docile. For once in her life she was defying convention, taking a chance, making a choice that felt right.

Showing courage.

He did not snuff the candles, nor did she avert her gaze as he shed the remainder of his clothing. His body was golden in the candlelight, broad shouldered and lean and utterly flawless.

He lay down beside her, his eyes holding hers. "You aren't frightened, are you, Jenny?"

"Not of you," she admitted. "Of myself, perhaps a little."

Without comment, he gathered her close, murmuring sweet phrases, his expert hands stroking her, arousing her as he eased off her dress and stockings and lowered her shift to her waist. "You're so beautiful," he murmured, his voice thick and slurred.

Like candlewax, she was melting, melting under the heat of his kisses, melting as her heart beat in cadence with his. She no longer cared that he had tricked her. All that mattered was the moment, the ecstasy created by his hands, his mouth, and the glorious, inexpressible knowledge that he was *Leigh*.

"Leigh," she said in a low voice.

"Lift your hips, darling." He tugged at her chemise.

"Leigh, I want to tell you something."

He turned his head and kissed her again. "What is it, Jenny?"

"You haven't remembered me yet, have you?"

"Remembered you?" he echoed, nuzzling the sensitive area below her ear.

She hesitated, wanting to tell him, yet unsure that this was the moment. But she wanted him to know. With the passing of each second, it seemed more and more important.

"Do I look at all familiar to you?"

He raised his head, regarding her quizzically. "What are you trying to say?"

"I'm trying to tell you that we knew each other a long time ago. We were friends, Leigh. For one short summer. You were twelve and I was ten."

She saw his expression change to one of astonishment.

"You remember me now, don't you?" she whispered. "I'm Becky."

* * *

Becky.

Stunned, Leigh gaped at her. His gaze traversed her face, seeking a resemblance to the thin little waif he had befriended.

She couldn't be Becky.

But her eyes were the right color. As he studied her he began to see it, the resemblance to the girl he had once known. Her hair had darkened some, but the freckles on her nose were visible, if one looked closely. So was that tiny scar near the edge of her left eyebrow. How in the blazes had he been so blind?

"I just wanted you to know," she explained, her voice tentative. "Before we . . . we . . ." She bit her lip.

He dragged in a breath. His ardor could not have been more effectively squelched if she had drawn out a dagger and stabbed him. Moving jerkily, he sat up, his back to her, his unseeing eyes fixed on scenes from the past.

She touched his arm. "I'm sorry. I didn't mean to shock you."

"But your name is Jennifer."

"My name is Jennifer Rebecca. My father preferred 'Becky.' Since he died, no one has called me that."

The cynical part of his character failed to understand why it should so affect him. So what if she was Becky? Why should it matter? But it disturbed him. Becky had been the only friend in his unhappy childhood, the one person to whom he had bared his soul. They'd met by chance in the woods, and had continued to meet only there. Among enchanted trees and forest glades, they had talked and played and laughed, even exchanged vows of love.

"You never came back. You never even said goodbye." He could hear the accusation creep into his voice, and it annoyed him.

"I had no chance. My mother recovered from her illness and wanted me home. A letter arrived. Lady Datchet had me packed and into the carriage within an hour."

Memories rushed like a torrent through his head, carrying him back to the lonely, endless weeks after Becky's departure. He hadn't known where to find her, hadn't known who to ask.

During their hours together they'd shut out the realities of the outside world. She'd never told him her surname, nor had he thought to inquire until it was too late. Suddenly, he wondered if she remembered his awkward proposal of marriage—or her own earnest acceptance.

He glanced at her. She had covered herself, and her mahogany eyes held a question that filled him with sharp and unwelcome remorse. Moments before he'd been seducing her, using her to achieve his despicable ends. Now, logical or not, he found he could not go through with it.

"I wanted to write to you," she confessed, "but my mother wouldn't allow it. I missed you so much. I cried myself to sleep every night for weeks."

"We were children," he stated, attempting to dismiss both the subject and his guilt. But his guilt did not abate. "Rest a while," he added heavily. "Then I'll . . . take you home."

He started to rise, but she caught at his hand. It was his maimed hand, and he saw her look down at it. Inwardly, he braced himself, but unlike other women she did not shudder and look away. Instead, to his amazement, she pressed her lips to his scars.

"Don't leave," she said. "Don't you understand? A few minutes ago . . . I made my decision. I want to give myself to you." She paused, her face clouded with uncertainty. "Don't you want me any more?"

Bemused, he surveyed her. Her disheveled red hair tumbled over her shoulders, creating a paradox of innocence and seduction. In the muted light, she looked fragile, even ethereal, yet a proud strength shone in her face, a beauty that was far more than skin deep. Desire stirred anew in his blood. He wanted to possess her, and under any other circumstances he would have ignored his conscience and damned the consequences. But he could not.

"Jen—" He stopped, not knowing quite what to call her. He cleared his throat. "It's not that."

"Then what is it?"

His lips twisted in self-derision. "Call it a belated surge of honor."

"Honor?" Delicate color tinted her cheeks. "Where was this honor when I was Jenny?"

"Touché," he acknowledged. "Perhaps I had better be frank. My purpose in bringing you here is even less noble than you think. I wanted to have you before Hugh had you so I could throw it in his face. I wanted to wound him, infuriate him. I wanted to laugh in his face the way he used to laugh in mine. I even thought it might prevent the marriage." He paused, watching her pale. "Haven't you wondered why he wants you? He needs a brood mare, Jenny, not a helpmate. You see, if he dies childless, it all comes to me."

"So that's all I am to you," she said faintly. "A tool."

"Untrue," he corrected. "I care for you. I meant to leave you with good memories. You'll need them if you marry Hugh."

"Why do you want to destroy Hugh? Is it only greed?"

Leigh rose to his feet, then recalled his nakedness and reached for his clothes. The silence lengthened as he dressed. Though the memories were painful, he discovered an inexplicable urge to make her understand. It was the one thing he had never told Becky, the one thing he'd been too ashamed to confide.

"For most of my childhood, Hugh made it his business to torment me," he said, his voice clipped and self-conscious. "Mostly it was verbal, but it was also physical. The abuse I might have forgiven, but it was more than that. He did everything he could to hurt my mother. He turned my father against her with his vicious lies. He convinced him that she was an unfaithful wife and that I was a bastard." He paused, ramming an arm in a sleeve as he struggled to maintain a controlled facade. "Between the two of them, they broke her spirit. She became an invalid, incapable of doing anything for herself. Eventually she just . . . faded away. I was seventeen when she died. I vowed vengeance the day they buried her."

Jennifer regarded him somberly. "So I was the means to achieve that vengeance. Until you learned I was Becky. Why does that change your mind?" Her face intent, she leaned forward, and as she did so the sheet drooped so that he caught a glimpse of her rose-tipped breasts.

Heat streaked through him, nearly annihilating his self-control. "Because, damn it, I loved Becky!"

Again, silence enveloped the room. His admission rebounded in his brain, mocking him with its ramifications.

Very softly, she said, "Would you let Becky marry Hugh?"

He fumbled with his buttons.

"Would you?" she persisted.

His fingers stilled. He forced himself to turn and look at her. He also forced himself to face the truth. "Not if I could stop her," he said in an unsteady voice. "The scandal, Jenny, could you face it? Would you dare cry off?"

"For you, I could face anything." She let the sheet fall to her waist. "Come back to me, Leigh. I need you. Give me a memory to cherish, my darling."

Blood pounded in his brain. "Are you sure?" he said hoarsely. She held out a hand.

A tremor ran through him. God, how he wanted her, how he needed her. She was neither Becky nor Jenny, but an enrapturing, intoxicating coalescence of them both. Sweet, caring Jennifer Rebecca. Quite suddenly, she was everything to him—past and future, hopes and dreams, integrity and self-respect.

Redemption.

With a deep-throated groan, he collapsed on the bed and hauled her into his arms.

Jennifer awoke to the sound of birdsong. The rain had stopped; fresh air wafted through the slightly open casement, teasing her with longings that brought memories of last night crashing to the forefront of her mind.

Leigh. The rapturous moments they'd spent together. Her stealthy return to her own bedchamber in Datchet Manor.

How she wished she could have remained with him. How exquisite it would have been to have awakened in his arms, to have been able to reach over and touch him, caress him, love him. But he had been right to insist she return. As he had pointed out, there would be scandal enough as it was.

Despite her lost hours of sleep, she rose and began to dress, the tenderness between her thighs reminding her of the change that had taken place in her life. Exactly what the future held, she was unsure, but she would face it with fortitude. All she knew was that she loved Leigh, and that meant she could not marry another man.

Once dressed, she sat down and wrote to Lord Charnwood, requesting that he pay her a call at his earliest convenience. Stating only that her need to speak with him was urgent, she folded the letter and leaned back, brows knitted as she rehearsed what to say.

The morning passed slowly. She did not confide in Lady Datchet, who prattled on about local gossip and her various aches and pains until Jennifer's nerves were stretched to their limit. By the time her ladyship's butler announced the arrival of a visitor, much of Jennifer's confidence had dwindled.

"Lord Charnwood." She set aside her needlework, her stomach churning with dread. "How good of you to come."

Charnwood bowed. His bony face looked pale and drawn, and his eyes seemed sunken, lending credence to the rumors she'd heard of his illness. "Miss Rossendale," he said in his deep, rather censorious voice. "I am here in response to your message."

Sensing Lady Datchet's surprise, Jennifer hastened to explain that she needed to speak with his lordship alone. The lady's blue eyes widened a trifle, but good manners deterred her from inquiring the reason. Instead, she delivered an effervescent greeting to the viscount, pressed Jennifer's hand in a meaningful manner, and departed.

Left alone with Lord Charnwood, Jennifer rose to her feet, lacing her fingers together as she began the stilted little speech she had prepared.

"My lord, forgive me for what must seem an abrupt summons, but I have something of consequence to say. A month ago, when

I accepted your declaration, it seemed a most desirable match. Indeed, I truly thought we should suit. However"—she cleared her throat, watching the grimness settle around Charnwood's mouth—"after a great deal of reflection, I realize I was wrong. I regret any pain and embarrassment this may cause, but I fear I must retract my acceptance. I . . . I cannot marry you."

Charnwood's thin fingers curled into fists. "Who is he?"

"I beg your pardon?"

"Don't try to gammon me. Women your age don't throw away offers from viscounts without a bloody good reason. Have you another suitor?"

She shook her head, too astonished to protest.

"Then you've taken a lover."

"Don't be absurd." Heat suffused her cheeks. "What an infamous suggestion. I cannot think why you would say such an insulting thing."

Charnwood walked closer, his expression ugly. "Methinks the lady protests too much." He caught hold of her chin, his fingers ungentle. "I haven't just cut my milk teeth, Miss Rossendale. Another man is the only possible reason for this change of heart. Who *is* he?"

"Let go of me." Numb with shock and rage, she struck his hand away. "Your conduct is not that of a gentleman, Lord Charnwood. I must ask you to leave."

"Not before I learn the man's name. Logic tells me he's a newcomer to the neighborhood, someone who has not—" He broke off, his nostrils flaring like a hound on the scent. "By God, it's Leigh, isn't it? That rutting, worthless swine!"

The offensive epithet infuriated her, shredding the fabric of her self-restraint. "How dare you call him that! He's a better man than you, Lord Charnwood. At least *he* has manners."

"You fool, you're as easily duped as the rest of your sex. He's had you, hasn't he?" His contemptuous gaze stripped her naked. "Well, since you're so enamored of him, perhaps you'd be interested to know that he's a bastard. His mother was a weak, untrustworthy woman, quite unable to control her base appetites." His sneer deepened. "Leigh's true father was a notorious roué who died from drink and excess. Wolves breed true, Miss Rossendale. He won't marry you. Men like him don't marry the women they defile."

Shaking with rage, Jennifer stalked to the door and opened it, her spine ramrod straight. "I refuse to listen to this. If you won't leave, I shall summon a servant to see you out."

"I shall not forgive this insult, Miss Rossendale. You may be very sure of that."

"Are you threatening me, Lord Charnwood?"

"You?" His cold smile chilled her to the marrow. "No, not you, my dear."

"What does that mean?" she said sharply. "What do you intend to do?"

"Why, dispatch my dear brother, of course. To the hell where he belongs."

Jennifer urged her mare faster along the road that led to John Harding's estate. She had to warn Leigh, and this was the only place she knew to look; there was no way she could find the house to which he had taken her last night. Not that she believed him incapable of taking care of himself; after all, the man had survived the war. But Lord Charnwood's evil words had driven a spike of pure terror into her heart.

As she had feared, however, Leigh was no longer a guest in Mr. Harding's home. "He left yesterday morning," Harding informed her. He was a stocky man of about thirty, with intelligent gray eyes set in a strong, placid face. "I'm sorry I can't be of more help, Miss Rossendale. Would you care to leave a message in case he returns?"

"If I may. Pray tell him I have spoken to Lord Charnwood and that he is"—she searched for a discreet euphemism—"not pleased. I fear his lordship's displeasure is directed against Mr. Raikes. You must tell him to take care."

Harding's brows shot up. "Leigh is in danger? Is that what you are trying to say?"

"Yes, but—" She released a breath. "Sir, may I count on your discretion?"

"Of course. Leigh is like a brother to me."

Jennifer accepted this with a nod. "The truth is that Lord Charnwood has threatened Leigh's life."

Harding did not so much as blink at her use of Leigh's given name. "I see," he said gravely. "And you think he is serious?"

"Indeed I do, else I would not be here." Not knowing what else to say, she rose to her feet, and Harding did likewise. "Thank you. I can see that Leigh has a good friend in you."

"I will send a messenger to his home, which is where he indicated he would be."

Jennifer nodded, careful to keep her face neutral. "Thank you."

"Don't worry, Miss Rossendale. Leigh is fully able to deal with his brother."

Jennifer took her leave, but despite Mr. Harding's reassurances she could not be easy in her mind. In all likelihood, Leigh was at home, asleep. It made sense. Yet what if he were not? Was there anywhere else she could look?

Yes, there were two places.

The first was the clearing where they'd met as adults.

The second was a site in the heart of the forest—the place ten-year-old Becky and twelve-year-old Leigh had ruled over their secret kingdom. In all this time, she had not gone back, mostly because she knew it would make her sad.

Yet now that she had found him again, now that she loved him and he loved her, the compulsion to return there was so powerful she could not resist. With any luck, he would have had the same compulsion.

She investigated the clearing first, but as she had half expected, he was not there. One place remained. Nudging her horse onward, she directed the patient brown mare deeper into the dense forest. As she rode, she wondered whether she would be able to find the place again.

Her concern soon faded. Engulfed by a sense of timelessness, she easily recognized the various landmarks, the distinctive rocks that marked the way. On horseback, it took mere minutes to reach that mystical place where ancient granite outcroppings thrust upward to form what, to childish minds, had looked like thrones. And there, exactly as she'd imagined, stood Leigh, his hand resting on the trunk of the great oak where he had once carved their names.

"You came," he said. "I wondered if you would."

Like her, he had ridden; his gray gelding stood tethered to a nearby branch. As she slid from the mare's back, she noticed his unshaven jaw, the dark smudges under his eyes.

"Haven't you slept?" she asked.

"I couldn't. Have you?"

"A little." She gave a shy smile. "It wasn't easy."

"And yet you manage to look beautiful." He clasped her hands, his gaze devouring her with its intensity. "You *are* beautiful, you know. I didn't think so at first, but I was wrong."

"I think that's a compliment," she teased.

"It is," he assured, his smile small but perceptible. Then it faded, and he pulled her roughly into his arms. "Oh, God, Jenny, what have I done to you? I thought I had already sunk to the depths of depravity, but never have I sunk so far as this."

Puzzled, she relinquished the bliss of his embrace, drawing back so she could see his face. "What in the world do you mean, Leigh?"

"I refer to last night. I've taken your virtue, scoundrel that I am."

He looked so serious, so stern, that she wanted to laugh. Instead, she laid her palm against the hard plane of his cheek.

"On the contrary, my darling, I gave myself to you of my own free will. I would not change what happened, not for anything."

He did not acknowledge the verity of her words, but only gazed down at her with an anguished expression. "I took advantage of you. I should marry you. God knows I want to. I want you, Jenny, now more than ever. Make no mistake about that."

Bewildered, she looked at him. "Then ask me. I've spoken to Hugh. I'm no longer betrothed. Last night I . . . I thought . . ." What *had* she thought? That he was asking her to marry him? That they would be together forever?

He shook his head. "If you knew half the things I've done, you'd turn from me in disgust. You don't know me, Jenny. The life I've lived doesn't bear describing."

"What difference does that make? You've fought in a war. Of course you've had to do ugly things. You've been noble and heroic too, and don't you dare deny it." She pressed her fingers to his mouth, cutting off his attempt to retort. "Yes, I know you've sown your oats. Perhaps you've done things you're not proud of. But all that's behind you now. You can start anew."

"It's not that simple. I haven't changed, Jenny. I'm still the same man I was before I found you again. The truth is"—he stared at the ground—"there's as much hate inside me as ever. I don't feel I can give you what you need. What you deserve."

"But I don't—" She broke off at his gesture.

"I hate Hugh," he said. "I'll always hate him. And I'm afraid that hate will destroy whatever good you bring out in me."

"Let go of your hate."

"I can't. It has me, Jenny. It's too strong. It's a festering sore beyond any doctor's remedy."

"Perhaps you're not trying."

"I don't want to try." His voice grew testy. "I only want to hurt him. I want to make him suffer."

She turned cold as she studied him, noting the harsh, uncompromising line of his mouth. "And so," she said slowly, "you would make me suffer, too."

His eyes met hers. "Better now than for a lifetime."

The finality of his tone constricted her heart. She had so many arguments, so many things she wanted to say, but only one formed into a coherent thought. "If I did not know better, I'd think this was your way of avoiding the altar."

"No, Jenny, no." His warm hands cupped her shoulders. "Don't you understand? I'm trying not to be selfish for once. As for last night, I want you to know that I, well, I took care with you. I'm quite sure there won't be a child. If I'm wrong, you'll let me know. You can count on me to do what's right."

No, Leigh, I can't.

She gazed up at him, her throat aching with the knowledge that all her hopes, all her dreams, had just withered and crumbled to dust. For a moment Hugh's words came back to her. *He won't marry you.*

All at once, she recalled what else she had come to say. "Hugh is furious," she said. "I didn't tell him you were involved—he simply guessed." She swallowed hard, clinging to the tattered remnants of her pride. "He means to kill you."

To her dismay, his eyes glinted with anticipation. "He does, eh? Well, we'll just see about that."

"Perhaps you ought to go away," she added as fearsome images danced in her mind—images of Leigh wounded, bleeding, dying. "After all, the man has threatened your life."

"Run away, you mean?" He released her and stepped away, his mouth twisted yet tender. "You don't know me at all if you think I'd do that. Come, I'll escort you home."

The discussion was clearly over. Without further comment, he helped her to remount, tossing her into the saddle with an ease that attested to his strength. Jennifer did not argue as he led the way toward the road. It was a longer route than the one she had used, but it did not signify. It would give her a few more precious minutes to be with him.

Desperately, she racked her brain in an effort to come up with words that would influence him. But nothing came to her. He had made up his mind—and only he could change it.

They came to the road and turned westward toward Datchet Manor. As the horses' hooves clopped against the hard-packed earth, the lump in Jennifer's throat grew larger. Her gaze slid sideways. In profile, he looked formidable, ruthless.

Heartless.

Yet he was not heartless. She knew it. She could have sworn that he loved her, that he yearned for her as she yearned for him.

As her thoughts drifted, she became aware of a third set of hoofbeats pounding toward them from behind. Instinctively, she glanced back over her shoulder. Whoever it was, he would soon overtake them, for he was traveling at a neck-or-nothing speed.

A sudden chill iced down her spine.

"Leigh," she said urgently. "Leigh, it's Hugh."

At first she thought Charnwood must somehow have known they would be there, though how that could be so she could not fathom. A moment later, she realized the obvious answer; the road they traveled led first to Datchet Manor, then onward to Lord Charnwood's lands. In the opposite direction, a mile to the east, lay John Harding's estate. Hugh must have gone to Harding's home to seek Leigh, and, having failed to find him, was now returning.

Leigh halted his mount, rotating the great beast so that he faced Hugh. A grim smile tightened his lips as Hugh reined in a short distance away. Neither man paid any heed to Jennifer.

"I demand satisfaction," Hugh snarled.

"I'm at your service." Leigh's reply was scrupulously pleasant. "Which shall it be, dear brother? Swords or pistols?"

"Pistols. Drake and Fisher will second me."

"Harding will act for me. Your seconds may call on him to arrange the meeting."

Hugh bared his teeth, a loathsome parody of a smile. "I don't know how you survived the war, but you won't survive me. I'll shoot you right through your black heart, you bastard."

"You can try," Leigh said, his voice deadly calm.

Before Jennifer could put voice to her horror, Hugh dug his spur into his horse's side and galloped past them down the road. She nudged her horse nearer to Leigh and clutched at his arm. "My God, what have you done? This is madness! You cannot fight a duel with Hugh!"

Leigh's gaze swung over to her, his eyes blank yet burning with emotion. "Jenny. I forgot you were here." With a frown, he disengaged her fingers, gently, though she noticed he was breathing hard. "I'm afraid this is none of your concern. I'm sorry you had to hear this. Hugh should have known better than to issue his challenge in your presence."

"That's of no moment. What matters is that you come to your senses." She gave him a pleading look, willing him to recognize the wisdom of her words. "Please go after him. Tell him you've changed your mind. Tell him you're too civilized for such folly."

"No, Jenny."

His flat refusal kindled a painful anger inside her. "Leigh, this is wrong and you know it! What if you kill him?"

"I've killed before."

"To kill in a war is one thing. This would be cold-blooded murder. You could be hanged."

"I won't hang." His jaw flexed. "If he dies, I'll leave the country."

"You *want* to kill him," she accused, feeling sick. "And what if he kills you first?"

He gave a savage laugh. "Hugh's no marksman. Why the devil he chose pistols, I can't guess. Perhaps he thinks the loss of my fingers will affect my aim. It won't."

Jennifer stared at him. He'd been a member of the 95th Rifles, one of the best fighting units in the Light Division. She had no doubt he spoke the truth.

Hugh would die.

"I swear to God, Leigh, if you choose this path I'll have nothing more to do with you."

"If I choose this path, there's a damned good chance I'll be free. Then, Jenny, there might be a future for us!"

She shook her head, struggling to keep her chin up, to keep the tremors of despair from her voice. "If Hugh dies, so do our chances. It's your decision. Think what you're throwing away. My love, Leigh. Does that mean nothing to you?"

"I won't throw away my honor." His face was shuttered.

"Honor? This has nothing to do with honor! This is pure selfishness on your part. Self-gratification of the most contemptible kind." She gave a sobbing laugh. "You don't seem to realize that physical courage and moral courage are not at all the same thing. From a moral standpoint," she tossed the quivering words over her shoulder as she wheeled her horse around, "you're a miserable coward, Leighton Raikes."

Tears clogging her throat, she dug her heel into the mare's side. The animal leaped forward, away from him, bearing her back toward Datchet Manor. Back to her staid, dull, lonely existence.

Only once did she look back.

He had not moved.

The morning of the duel dawned clear and cool. Leigh paced up and down in the long, damp grass of the field where it was to take place, his head aching and groggy. Though he knew no fear, depression weighed him down. Nightmares had plagued him for most of the night, destroying any peace he might have found.

"Hugh's late," John murmured. "Mayhap he overslept."

Leigh glanced toward the empty lane. "He'll be here."

Five minutes later, the rumble of a carriage heralded Hugh's arrival. It came into view, drove off the road into the field, and drew to a halt near John Harding's conveyance. Hugh climbed out, followed by two men and a third whom John informed him was the local doctor.

While the seconds inspected and loaded the weapons, Leigh turned his back on the proceedings. Instead of the duel, he found himself thinking about Jennifer's eyes, about the way they smiled when she laughed and sparkled when she grew angry. He thought of the silky curve of her cheek, the gracefulness of her hands, the fullness of her breasts. And he thought about the way she had given herself to him, without reserve, as though she belonged to him and he to her. Even as children, some unique bond had drawn them together. Their recent physical union had only strengthened that bond, made it more solid and substantial. Even sacred.

A hand touched his shoulder. "Are you ready?" John asked.

"Of course." Leigh swiveled, forcing a smile.

And froze.

No sound had warned him of her approach, but there she was atop her brown mare, watching him from the long morning shadows cast by the two carriages. "What the devil is she doing here?"

"I don't know." John shifted uneasily.

Suspicion narrowed Leigh's eyes. John had also tried to talk him out of killing Hugh. "You didn't tell her to come?"

"Certainly not."

"Well, get her out of here," Leigh said curtly. "I don't want her to see this."

John moved away. Leigh didn't look at Jennifer again, but he could feel her eyes. His gut churned. Any moment now she would walk over and try to reason with him again. He braced himself, wondering how he could withstand her pleas. He hated the fact that she was here. He didn't want to deny her anything, yet he must and he would. The knowledge ripped him to shreds.

John returned, his footsteps light in the damp grass. "She refuses to leave." His hand clapped on Leigh's shoulder. "Put her out of your mind, Leigh. It's time."

Leigh turned, his gaze locking, not on Jennifer, but on his brother. Hugh stared back, his eyes black with a hatred that echoed Leigh's own. Painful memories flashed through his head, not individualized, but amassed into one vast, destructive whole. Heat and ice flooded his veins.

"Give me the pistol," he said in a hard voice.

Accepting it, he held it in hand, weighing it, testing its feel. Remembering what it felt like to take aim at another human being. "It's nicely balanced."

"It has a hair trigger," John reminded him nervously. "Confound it, man, button up your coat. The white of your neckcloth

vill give him a target. And be sure to stand sideways. And don't
orget to—"

"I know how to shoot," Leigh cut in.

"Yes." John swiped a hand along the curve of his jaw. For at
least the fourth time, he added, "Just remember, you don't have
o kill him."

Leigh compressed his mouth.

While the seconds measured the paces, his gaze swung back
o Jennifer. She did not flinch from his scrutiny—rather, their
gazes collided in a silent clash of wills. It's your choice, she
seemed to be telling him. I won't try to stop you.

He turned away, more disturbed than if she'd clung to his
arm and wept. It rankled deeply that she'd called him a coward.
Didn't she understand that he finally had something to lose?
Didn't she understand that Hugh had forced this upon him, that
in reality *he* was the offended party? Didn't she understand that
his was the only way he could be free?

His mind in pandemonium, he took his place in the grass.
His mouth felt like cotton wool; blood hammered in his veins.

Physical courage. Moral courage. What if Jennifer was right?
Perhaps taking responsibility for one's actions constituted a different sort of bravery. Perhaps confronting oneself took more
courage than standing in a field with a pistol in one's hand. As
the idea took hold, a shudder ran through him. He couldn't seem
to breathe.

Everything seemed to slow down. One of the seconds held
up a white handkerchief. The handkerchief left the man's fingers, yet took an eternity to flutter to the ground. As it drifted,
a hundred thoughts crystalized in Leigh's brain, one of which
stood out with profound clarity. *At Waterloo, his life had been
spared for a purpose and that purpose was loving Jenny.*

"Fire at will!" someone called.

Acting from instinct, Leigh raised his arm and pointed the
pistol. Hugh did the same, apparently taking careful aim. Then,
without warning, Hugh's arm jerked up, and an explosion tore

through the air above Leigh's head. At the same moment, Hugh
body twisted so that he faced Leigh straight on. Leigh fired.

"Charnwood deloped!"

"He's hit!"

Leigh stood transfixed as Hugh fell to the ground.

At the same moment, the rumble of wheels came to his ear.
An unexpected third conveyance pulled into the field.

"Halt, in the name of the law!" Three men leaped from the
coach and hurried toward them.

Ignoring them, Leigh crossed the grass to where Hugh lay
gasping in pain, one hand clutching his shoulder. The doctor
knelt next to him, attempting to pry Hugh's bloodied fingers
away from the wound.

Two burly officers seized Leigh by either arm, while the third
confiscated the pistol. "Don't try to escape," the man warned.

Hugh shot them a scornful look, his face twisted and gray.
"You idiots, can't you see I'm alive? You may as well let him
go. 'Tis only a damned surface scratch!"

The doctor glanced up. "It's true. This isn't a killing affair,
my lads. There's no need to arrest anyone."

"You make it sound as though you wanted him to kill you."
Jennifer's low accusation split the brief silence. Leigh looked
around in time to see the appalled way she looked at Hugh.
"That's it, isn't it?" she said. "That's why you turned. You de
liberately gave him a clear target. We all saw it."

"By God, she's right," John struck in. "What the devil kind
of rig are you running, Charnwood? Why did you delope?"

"Isn't it obvious?" Hugh's sneer changed to a wince as the
doctor eased his arm out of the sleeve of his coat. "I wanted
my esteemed brother to be arrested for murder. It's why I made
sure *they'd*"—he angled his head toward the three officers—"be
here." The loathing in his choked voice seemed to shock even
the officers, who released Leigh and stepped away.

"You'd go that far to hurt me?" Leigh said incredulously.

"Certainly, since I'm dying anyway. I haven't above a few
months to live." Hugh's laugh was wild. "I could have fathered

son. There was time. Time to cut you out. Now it's too late. 've got no bride . . ."

The doctor confirmed Hugh's claim with a nod. "He has a cancer. There's nothing I can do."

Leigh studied Hugh, aware that for the first time in his life he felt no hate. Like a prisoner released from his bonds, he had an odd sense of lightness, of liberation. Instead of hate, pity filled him—pity for the pathetic creature lying on the ground at his feet. No, he corrected. Not a creature. A man. A human being possessed of a soul.

Hugh groaned and swore as the doctor probed his wound, yet his wrathful gaze remained fixed on Leigh. "Damn it, why didn't you kill me? I gave you the chance."

Leigh dropped down on one knee and looked his brother in the eye. "Because it's time to end this," he said evenly. "I'm sorry you're suffering. This isn't what I wanted."

"So now you're generous," the other man rasped. "Now that you know you'll get the estate. And the title and fortune."

"I never wanted it."

"That's a lie."

"It's the truth. All I ever wanted was acceptance. And kindness and respect for my mother."

Hugh closed his eyes, refusing to speak.

The next few minutes passed in a jumble of confusion, but at last the doctor, along with Drake and Fisher, assisted Hugh back to his coach, which lumbered off in the direction of Charnwood House. The three officers of the law, after a brief consultation amongst themselves, also departed. John wandered back to his carriage, leaving Leigh alone in the field with Jenny.

She stood a few feet away from him, smoothing her skirt, her eyes downcast so that he couldn't read her expression. Tears clung to the tips of her lashes.

"You shouldn't have come," he said gruffly.

"I had to." She lifted her head. "You've forgiven him, haven't you?"

Nonplussed, he looked away, groping for equilibrium. The

spring breeze ruffled his hair as he cleared his throat an squinted into the distance, surveying the surrounding landscar with awakening wonder. Surely the air had never smelled th fresh? Surely the birds had never sung with so much joy? Eve the grass looked greener and the sky bluer.

"I suppose I have," he said in amazement.

Bemused, he transferred his gaze back to Jenny. Sweet, wis Jenny, who had known what was best all along. Reaching ou he pulled her against him, pressing her head into the hollov between his shoulder and his neck. She sighed and hugged him her soft curves molding to the contours of his body.

Filled with reverence, he slid his hand up her arm to her throa lifting her chin so he could drink in the features of her beloved face. It amazed him that he could ever—even for a moment— have believed that a single night with her could be enough.

"I love you, Jennifer Rebecca."

He spoke the words huskily, yet with a hint of trepidation After all, he'd shot Hugh, albeit a superficial wound. Perhaps she did not understand that, had he chosen to kill, he could easily have done so. Perhaps she did not understand that, in the one split second before he'd pulled the trigger, he'd been reborn.

"I love you too, Leigh. And I'm so proud of you."

Her tender avowal eased his mind, creating a bright new hope in his heart. He wanted to laugh, to shout, to fall to his knees with relief, to crush her against him so that every inch of their bodies touched. Choosing the latter, he lowered his head and kissed her, his hand tugging at the ribands of her bonnet until it dropped to the ground, giving him access to her luxurious hair. As his fingers stroked her tresses, plucking out pins, he felt her tremble with the same need that enveloped him. Awash with desire, he showered kisses around the edges of her lips, along the curve of her jaw, against her throat. She was delicious in his arms, lush and inviting as forbidden fruit . . .

"Leigh." The breathless word huffed past his cheek. "Leigh, darling, we've an audience. Not that I wish you to stop, but"— her hands nudged at his chest—"your friend seems most interested in our . . . our demonstrations of affection. So do the coachman and footman, I might add."

One arm still wound about her waist, Leigh swung around. "Devil take you, John! Haven't you a grain of tact in your body? Why the deuce don't you take yourself off?"

John Harding propped a shoulder against the side of the carriage and grinned wickedly. "And leave you to walk home? I wouldn't be so rude. In any case, I'm protecting the lady's reputation."

"Indeed?" Leigh cocked a sardonic eyebrow. "Well, your methods are deplorable. Remind me never to leave my daughter in your custody."

"Come now, you can't expect me to cast a spoke in the wheels of true love. I'm only waiting for a proper declaration. As is the lady, I imagine."

Leigh flushed and glanced back at Jennifer. *"Will* you marry me?" he asked, his voice low and urgent. "I know I'm no prize, but I'm no villain either. I'll be good to you, I swear it." He scanned her face, searching for signs of hesitation. "Say it, Jenny. Say you'll have me or I swear I'll—"

"You'll what, Leigh?" A smile lurked in her lovely eyes.

"I'll abduct you again and keep you with me until you have to marry me."

"I have to marry you now," she said demurely.

"What?" His face tightened. "Did someone see you the other night? What happened? Why didn't you tell me?"

She pressed a finger to his lips. "No one knows I left the house. I have to marry you because we're two parts of a whole. Without you, I know I'll never be completely happy. Besides—"

"Yes?" he prodded.

Mischief and tenderness trembled her voice. "I've been promised to you since I was ten years old. Don't you think it's time we honored that promise?"

"Oh, yes, Jenny. I do indeed."

Despite their grinning audience, he kissed her again.

The warmth of her response assured him that Jennifer Rebecca did not object.

* * *

Seven months later

"Thank goodness you're home." Tossing aside her stitchery, Jennifer hurried across the sitting room to her husband, who had been absent for the better part of two days. "Is he . . . ?"

"Yes." Leigh enfolded her in his arms, a contact she knew dispensed comfort to them both. "It's over at last. Hugh is at peace."

"And you?" She drew back a little, watching the way he rubbed at his temple. Unshaven, with dark shadows under his eyes, he looked as though he had not slept in days.

"I'm fine. Better than before." He paused, then managed a weary smile. "He waited until the end, but he finally said it, Jenny. He forgave me."

"But what did he have to forgive? What did you ever do to him?"

"I stole his bride," he reminded her wryly. "I stole his last chance to have a son, his last chance for immortality."

"Other than that, I mean."

He hugged her closer. "He forgave me for being legitimate."

"I don't understand."

His chest rose and fell beneath her cheek. "It was he who was the bastard. Not me. He told me his mother had an affair with a dispossessed French count. My father never knew. Hugh's lies about my mother were fabricated to protect the memory of his own mother. And to protect himself. He feared that if the true circumstances of his birth were revealed, my father would take steps to disinherit him."

"But your father died while you were at war. And Hugh still behaved abominably toward you."

"Yes, well, you know what I was. He deplored my conduct, and rightly so."

"Wrongly so," she protested, "but never mind that. The important thing is that you forgave one another." She lifted her head. "You're a viscount now, my love."

"And you're a viscountess. How does it feel?"

"I don't know. Will we have to move to Charnwood?"

"I suppose we should. Will you mind?"

She sighed. "A little. I prefer this house."

"And why is that?" Despite his fatigue, his voice held a teasing note.

"Because of the happy memories, of course."

"Ah, so you did enjoy it," he murmured.

"Enjoy what?"

"Being abducted." His lips skimmed her brow. "Being swept off your feet by a handsome rascal. Being seduced."

"I was not seduced," she said with dignity. "You know very well it was my choice."

"So you thought."

"So I know."

He released her in mock surrender. "You win. I can see this is one hand I'd better not play."

"Leighton Raikes, what are you trying to say?"

"My dear heart, I've no idea. I'm only"—his arm slid around her waist—"trying to put certain images into your head."

"Images? What images?"

"Beds," he said. "Sheets and pillows. Warm, naked bodies tangled together in absolute ecstasy—"

She clamped a hand over his mouth and glanced toward the door. "For heaven's sake, Leigh, you are shameless."

". . . because," he continued, prying her fingers loose, "it seems like weeks since I've held you. I need you, Jenny. I need your love and your strength. And I need . . ." He lowered his voice, but his next words still made her blush.

"Oh, very well." Grasping his elbow, she towed him across the carpet. "Come along, you poor neglected man."

She saw his contented smile, and felt an answering surge of gratitude. How lucky they were to have found one another.

Life was very, very good.

About the Author

Julie Caille lives with her family in Texas. Her Zebra Regency romances include CHANGE OF HEART, THE RAKE AND HIS LADY, and THE SCANDALOUS MARQUIS. Julie loves hearing from her readers and you may write to her c/o Zebra Books. Please include a self-addressed stamped envelope if you wish a response.

A Match for Lord Fairleigh

by
Cathleen Clare

The sun was only a promise, slowly illuminating the dark London sky and casting a ghostly glow on the silent streets. Tyler, Lord Fairleigh, still rather disoriented from the night's final bottle of port, leaned against the iron railing of a narrow brick house and tried to regain his wits. Somewhere on the journey home from a most lucrative evening of card play, he had taken a wrong turn, and now found himself in a totally unfamiliar neighborhood of modest, yet respectable, dwellings. Though cursing himself for the utter stupidity of turning down a friend's offer of transportation home, he had to admit that he was lucky. He was quickly sobering in the bone-chilling morning air, and fortunately, he hadn't wandered into an area inhabited by cutthroats and pickpockets. He must be on his guard, however. Districts like this often served as buffer zones between the elegant and the deplorable. With a king's ransom of winnings tucked away in his coat, he would be a profitable target for a member of the city's criminal element.

The earl removed his hat and raked his hand through his dark hair. His valet would look askance at such a careless gesture, but what difference did his appearance make now? Soon, he'd be stretched out in his comfortable bed in Mayfair. It was only a matter of retracing his steps and beginning again, this time with a much clearer head. He might even be fortunate enough to hail a cab. Resolutely, he pushed away from the railing and set out.

"Mister!" Running feet pounded on the bricks behind him. A hand clutched his sleeve and tugged.

Startled, Tyler whirled and stared down at his grubby, young assailant. "What the deuce?"

"You gotta come," the urchin breathlessly told him. "Lady Belinda says you gotta come real fast!"

"Now just a minute, boy." He pulled his stylish Weston coat from the lad's determined grasp and smoothed the fabric. "Who are you, and who is this *lady* who demands my presence?"

"It's Lady Belinda! Everybody knows who she is!" the child piped impatiently. "An' I'm Billy Downing."

Lady Belinda? The earl could not remember a female of that name among the circles of the *ton*. Besides, why would a true lady be summoning him in this place, at this early hour?

"C'mon," the boy begged, now almost tearfully. "It's gonna be too late!"

Half of Tyler's foggy brain, the clearest thinking part, shied away from any excursion of the sort, but the other portion, the raffish side of his intellect, was intrigued. He was certain that Billy Downing would not lead him to a well-bred lady. *Lady Belinda* was probably the pseudonym of a female of an entirely different sort. She might, however, lend a pleasurable grand finale to his stimulating night.

"Mister . . ." Billy Downing pled.

Tyler grinned. "What's the matter? Not make your quota tonight?"

The child stared at him with round-eyed bewilderment.

"Very well, lad," he acquiesced. "Lead the way."

With an audible sigh of relief, the youth spun on his heel and trotted back in the opposite direction. Tyler followed at a more sedate rate of speed, which caused the boy all manner of anxiety. Frequently glancing back, he finally stopped to wait.

"Takin' you long enough," he grumbled.

"You cannot expect me to run, no matter what the lady's charms."

"I don't know nothin' 'bout no charms," Billy said irritably. "All's I know is that I'll get a walloping if I don't get you there quick."

"From Lady Belinda?" Tyler lifted a careless shoulder. "Believe me, lad, there is no point in rushing such matters."

"Well, you oughta know." The boy started off again with a perturbed glance back at him. "An' Lady Belinda wouldn't hit *nobody!* M'dad would do it."

The earl shook his head at the thought of parents who pushed their children into nefarious trades and then reaped the rewards thereof. It was no wonder that London was riddled with crime. Ill-doing was inherited.

As they walked, the orderly neighborhood deteriorated into one of decline. Tall, crumbling, ancient brick structures, divided, no doubt, into as many small flats as their landlords could cram, lined the grimy streets. Twice Tyler was forced to skirt the tossed out contents of someone's chamber pot. He had begun to change his mind about his visitation to Lady Belinda, when Billy Downing came to a halt.

"It's right here, mister."

Hesitating, the earl looked up at the eroding facade. It wasn't *quite* as distasteful as those on either side, but it certainly was not the type of residence he'd ever set foot in. The "lady" must not be very adept at her vocation if she were forced to take rooms in a place like this.

"Come on!" This time, Billy took his hand and pulled.

Again, Tyler jerked free. "On second thought, I don't believe I shall partake. Here. Have this for your troubles." He reached into his pocket and withdrew a shilling.

"That won't help," the boy wailed. "She needs *you!"*

The earl shook his head. "Frankly, my boy, I don't intend to carry on my . . . er . . . business in such filth."

"The place ain't dirty! M'sisters keep it nice 'n' clean. You'll see. C'mon! Lady Belinda really needs you! She can't do it by herself !"

Chuckling to himself, Tyler wavered. The lady must be very desperate for male attention. If she was beautiful, and as insatiable as her little procurer seemed to portray her, he just might set her up in the establishment he kept for such purposes. Since he was in between mistresses at the moment, the house was vacant and ready for a stimulating, new female occupant.

"All right," he agreed. "Show me in."

The lad darted up the stoop and through the scarred door. "It's on the second floor."

A mouse scurried across Tyler's shining Hessians as he started up the steps in Billy's wake. The earl's nose twitched with distaste. He hoped the trollop's sheets were clean.

"In here." Billy thrust open a door.

Entering a dimly lit room, he was conscious of several people sitting in the shadows, but he had no time to consider that, before the child opened another door and literally shoved him inside.

Tyler gaped, rooted to the spot. This room was brightly illuminated so there was little doubt as to what was happening. A moaning woman lay in a rumpled bed, obviously in the throes of childbirth. She was attended by a slender, delicate female, who sat with her back to him, her hand clasped tightly by the soon-to-be mother. She cocked her head sideways, but didn't look at him.

"Thank heavens you've come so quickly!" she cried in cultured accents that equaled his own.

"Me? What need have you of me?" cried the earl, sobering fully.

The young lady whirled and glared accusingly at him. "You're not the doctor!" she shrieked.

Tyler stared speechlessly and shook his head. Suddenly able to move, he leapt backward toward the door, treading squarely on Billy's feet and knocking the lad into the next room.

"Ow!" shrilled the boy. "M'toes!"

The earl caught the doorjamb to regain his balance.

"Stop that caterwauling, Billy Downing," the lady ordered, "and explain to me why you haven't fetched the doctor."

"That's him, ain't it?" Billy cried.

"No, it is not." She shifted her gaze to Tyler, her china blue eyes narrowing with annoyance. "Just what are you doing here? Is this the result of some silly wager?"

Tyler's temper rose. "I was nearly dragged here, that's what, and I don't appreciate it one whit!"

"Well, neither do I! You are supposed to be the doctor. Can you not see what we are facing?"

"Lady, miss, madam, whoever you are! I assure you that I've arrived under no misapprehensions. I thought you were a . . . a . . ." He snapped shut his mouth. Though he might be considered wicked and perfectly scandalous by the *ton,* he'd been born a gentleman and reared to behave like one in the proper company. This young woman was unmistakably a lady, but what was she doing here, playing the part of a midwife?

"It doesn't matter who I am, but I certainly recognize you, sir. You are Lord Fairleigh, the most noxious knave in all the kingdom," she caustically informed him and sniffed the air. "Furthermore, you are thoroughly foxed and of value to no one, not that you are useful in any other state of being, of course!"

The earl's gray eyes turned steely dark. He set his jaw. "Due to your state of distress, madam, I shall overlook those excessive remarks, but I will have you know that I happen to be completely sober."

"Fiddlesticks! I can smell the fumes. Get out of here at once! Billy?" she called. "You must return and fetch the *real* doctor! This man is an impostor."

"Impostor?" Tyler barked. "I never pretended to be a doctor!"

"He was standin' outside the doctor's house, lookin' like he owned it," Billy chirped, entering the fray in defense of himself.

"Must everyone dispute me?" the lady sputtered. "He is not the doctor. If a roach is crawling beside the pastry safe, do you think it's a pastry? This man is nothing but a drunken sot! Go at once, and *this time* rap on the doctor's door!"

The woman in bed heaved a sigh, drawing their attention. "Don't you worry about me, Lady Belinda. I've had many a babe."

"You told me this time seemed different, Mrs. Downing," Lady Belinda reminded, her voice sweetly softening.

The woman's answer came in the form of a groan. As another labor pain assailed her, she clutched her helper's hand, nearly bending the slender extremity in two. Lady Belinda blanched, but did not wince with pain.

"Just fetch the doctor," she said dully, "and this time make no mistakes."

Tyler speedily followed Billy from the room and out the front door. "If you could give me the direction to Bond Street, I would be very grateful."

"It's back the way we came," the boy said and took to his heels.

"Thanks for nothing." Feeling ill-used, Tyler strode after him. When he reached the doctor's house, he saw young Billy again, waiting on the steps. This time the lad was successful, for a man rushed out, carrying his distinguishing black bag. The earl nodded to them as they sped past, and continued on in what he hoped was the correct direction. Apparently now, Lady Belinda and Mrs. Downing would receive the help they needed.

Despite the gravity of the situation, the earl smiled as he thought of the case of mistaken identity. If he told his friends of the experience, they would surely collapse with laughter. To confuse the rakish Lord Fairleigh with an upright physician was perfectly ludicrous, but the boy had been overset and the location had been correct.

His smile faded, however, as he also recalled the epithets Lady Belinda had flung his way. She had called him a useless knave, compared him to a roach, chastened him for drinking, and all the time she'd been doing this, she'd been fully aware of his identity. Tyler knew that his reputation was not the most spotless. He was, in fact, deemed a rake. But he certainly wasn't the only man about town who spent most of his waking hours indulging in the pleasurable side of life. And like others before him, he intended someday to settle enough to take a wife, rear a family, and assume his seat in the House of Lords. That was his duty, but at present, he simply wasn't prepared to perform it. That didn't make him worthless, did it? Just who was this Lady Belinda to berate him so?

Tyler ground his teeth. The devilish little minx! So she knew who he was? He'd find out just who *she* was! Young, gently bred females were certainly not to be found attending childbirths in the seedier parts of town. Lady Belinda was not behaving as she should either.

If anyone was well acquainted with the foibles of the *ton,* it was his mother. She would be cognizant of such an outrageous young lady. Once he became acquainted with Lady Belinda's faults, Tyler would feel much better about his own. Then if he saw that prissy miss again, he'd toss *her* reputation right in her face!

Returning home, Tyler greatly surprised his servants by asking for breakfast to be served in the library, instead of going to bed as was his usual habit. After the tasty repast, he requested his mother's presence as soon as she was up and about, then settled himself on the sofa to nap. It wasn't long before the countess, stunned by her son's departure from the norm, entered the room and shook his shoulder.

"Tyler, my dear, what is wrong? Are you ill?"

"No, Mama, I'm fine." Dragging himself awake, Tyler momentarily wished he had put Lady Belinda from his mind and gone on with his accustomed routine.

She arched an eyebrow. "You don't look it," she observed, pointedly eyeing his rumpled coat and disarrayed neckcloth.

"I know." He grinned sheepishly, sitting up. "But surely you've seen me look worse."

"Ah, yes, such as the time you contracted the fever at Eton, and I went there to fetch you home. A more pitiful sight I have never seen. But I nursed you through it, in the process spoiling you more than ever." Her green eyes sparkled merrily. "That is what is wrong with you today. I overindulged you, Tyler."

"Nonsense, Mama. An only son is supposed to be pam pered."

Now that he was face-to-face with her, he was hesitant to question her about Lady Belinda. Every time he showed undue interest in a female, Lady Fairleigh's hopes of his marriage were raised. As she comfortably seated herself beside him, he decided to stall for time to arrange his probing into a manner which would give her no room for speculation.

"How was your card party last night?" he asked mundanely.

"La, it must have been a success. I thought they'd never leave! Such gossiping . . . I've never heard the like! I was glad when all departed and I could seek my bed."

"Come now, Mama, you know you enjoy having guests and hearing all the latest on-dits. Was I the main subject?"

"Not at all, my dear. I do not believe your name was even mentioned." She patted his cheek and tilted her head suspiciously. "Should it have been?"

"Of course not," he drawled, thinking of the scene the night before. Rising, he crossed the room to the liquor cabinet and poured a partial glass of brandy, bracing himself for the inevitable comment.

"Really, Tyler, must you commence your revelry so early in the day?"

"This isn't revelry, Mama. It's merely a fortifier," he argued.

"Fustian," she scoffed. "Tea would be preferable, particularly for the headache you must be suffering."

"I don't have a headache." He returned to the sofa. "I never do."

"More's the pity." She sighed. "If you were forced to ante up in the morning, you would change your ways."

He swirled liquor in his glass, squinting through the amber fluid. "Perhaps."

"You should take control of your life," she lectured, "or better still, you should find a wife. Really, Tyler, you must cease this procrastination and set up your nursery. Don't you realize how old you are?"

"Oh, yes. My joints creak with every step I take."

She feigned a moue of disgust. "Do not treat me to such balderdash when I am speaking seriously."

"Mama, I am not ready for marriage," he stated, "but actually, I did wish to ask you about a particular lady."

"Hm . . ." She leaned forward, her eyes bright with curiosity. "Who might she be?"

"I know her only as Lady Belinda. I heard no last name."

"Lady Belinda," the countess mused, knitting her brow.

"She is slender and fair, blue-eyed, and quite . . . er . . . commanding," he added.

His mother smiled at that last adjective. "By that, I assume that you failed to intimidate her? She did not hang on your every word, gazing at you with soulful eyes?"

He flushed. "Really, Mama, must you?"

She laughed. "I am pleased that I have retained the ability to cause you discomfort, Tyler. You appear quite charming when you are overset."

"May we return to our original topic?" he prodded. "About the young lady?"

The countess thoughtfully nibbled a nail. "I seem to recall a Lady Belinda, but I cannot place her. She isn't among the latest crop of young hopefuls. I do know that."

"I could have guessed as much. She isn't of an age to be making her first come-out, and furthermore, she must be quite independent. If you remember her from previous seasons, your recollection would be of someone who, though quite attractive, didn't manage to snare a husband."

"Why do you say that?"

"No sane man would allow her to pursue the occupation I found her in." With a snort, he briefly told her of the early morning event. "So you see? She's quite out of the ordinary."

"Alas," his mother mourned. "I thought you, at last, had found someone who might hold your interest."

"Certainly not," he declared.

"No." She shook her head. "A female like that would not be

suitable for the role of Countess of Fairleigh. Your wife must be beyond reproach and—"

"And just as boring as last year's jests," he finished.

"Not necessarily. Tyler, there are many fine young ladies who would make excellent wives!"

He grinned insouciantly. "That's the problem, Mama. I like them all. If a man could have more than one wife, my life would be a different story."

"I surrender!" She threw up her hands and rose. "Mark my words, young man. You will fall in love someday, and when you do, you'll collapse like a ton of bricks. Then I shall laugh and laugh."

"You'll have a long wait," he fired back.

At the door, she paused. "I am sorry I couldn't recall the Lady Belinda. I could ask around a bit and perhaps come up with some information."

"No," he firmly declined. "There's enough talk about me as it is. I certainly don't wish my name to be paired with that hoyden."

"Very well." With a nod, she left the room.

Tossing down his brandy, Tyler, too, left the library. It was past time that he had some decent rest in order to carry out his nightly pursuit of entertainment. But after he had finished his bath and climbed under the sheets, he was unable to sleep. The clip-clop of horses outside the house and the muted voices of servants within unduly disturbed him, but most of all, visions of the mysterious Lady Belinda and her unlikely presence at the Downing flat kept floating through his mind. Finally, he threw back the covers, got up, and rang for his valet. He would visit the scene of the previous night's encounter. If Lady Belinda was still there, he'd find out once and for all who she was and what she was doing. If she was not, he might be able to extract some information about her from the Downings. Either way, he was determined to assuage his rampant curiosity. Dressing quickly, though with his usual, casual elegance, he called for his curricle and set out.

Since he had regained his wits before he had left the Downing flat, he had no difficulty finding it again. In the full light of day, it looked even shabbier than it had in the early morning. His tiger questioningly eyed him when he drew to a halt.

"Wait here," Tyler commanded, tossing him the reins and stepping down.

Once inside the building, he nearly changed his mind about his visit when he glimpsed a rat scurrying past him on the stairway. This was truly an idiotic mission. Even if he found the lady, what reason could he give for searching her out? In fact, why did he want to see her again? It couldn't be because of those flashing blue eyes, that haughty nose, that pink mouth spewing insults? Tyler shrugged. He sought her because she was a mystery, a diversion in his rather jaded life. That was the only reason. With that perspective, he rapped on the door with his walking stick.

Mr. Downing answered the summons. Upon Tyler's polite questioning, he assured him that all had gone well once the doctor arrived. His wife had safely delivered a baby girl! Unfortunately, however, he did not know Lady Belinda's last name or residence. The sweet lady, however, had promised to return that afternoon to visit her patients and should be arriving momentarily. Did the gentleman care to wait?

Tyler did, but he declined Mr. Downing's invitation to make himself comfortable. Presenting the new father with a gold guinea as a baby gift, he left the building and settled himself in his curricle.

In spite of the speedy progression of her closed carriage through the bustling streets of London, Belinda Kincaid was late on her rounds of charity calls. After her wearisome night at the Downing residence, she had overslept her busy schedule by one crucial hour. As a result, she had foregone breakfast, which made her slightly cross, and now she stood in danger of missing luncheon as well. The delicious aromas emanating from the food baskets on the seat across from her were making her ravenous, but she could seek no personal sustenance until she delivered them. The needy families she aided were far more important than her own comfort.

Beside her, Jenny, her abigail, who also served as chaperon and assistant on her charitable missions, eyed her worriedly. "You must take time to dine and rest, my lady," she said for the third time that morning. "I can deliver the morsels."

"The people expect to see me," Belinda objected.

"They'll understand. If you don't take care of yourself, there'll be no one to help them," she said, her voice heavy with disapproval.

"I'll be fine," Belinda claimed, stifling a yawn.

"You take on too much," the maid muttered. "If you don't slow down, I'm going to tell the duke and duchess."

"Much they'd care," the young lady scoffed. Both she and Jenny knew that her parents paid little heed to their daughter's well-being. After the trouble during her Season, they did no more than provide for her physical needs. As far as they were concerned, she was dead to them.

"You need a good man to look after you," Jenny advanced.

"Ha! Haven't I had enough of men? Always thinking with their . . . well, not with their heads. A pox on the entire gender!" Impatiently, she raised the curtain and peered out. "Why haven't we arrived?"

As her driver rounded the corner and approached the Downing residence, Belinda's sigh of relief turned to a groan. "Oh, no," she lamented, spotting the fashionable curricle drawn up in front of the building. "Speaking of dreadful men! Now I shall be forced to deal with the worst of them."

"Who is it, my lady?" Jenny tried to lean past her to look out the window.

Belinda angrily pursed her lips. "It's that disreputable Tyler Fairleigh, the gentleman who bumbled onto the scene last night. Hm! I suppose one must call him 'gentleman.' He *is* an earl. By the standards of this horrid society, that accords him a noble status. Lud, as gossip would have it, his string of discarded mistresses, if placed shoulder to shoulder, would reach round the world."

The abigail giggled.

"It's true, Jenny." Despite her irritation, Belinda had to laugh. "He is a rake of the highest degree, and far too handsome for his own good . . . and for the good of any female, I suppose. His success at seduction is legendary."

"My lady!" the maid gasped. "You should not even know of such things!"

"Yes, yes, I shouldn't speak so frankly, but where he is concerned, one must be aware of the facts. Have a caution when Lord Fairleigh is present! No female is safe from his web."

"Maybe we ought to drive by and come back at another time," Jenny suggested, sobering.

"And allow him to deter me from my purpose? Certainly not! We shall walk right past him without favoring him with the slightest glance, and if he accosts us, I shall dispose of him in a flash," she boasted as the carriage drew to a halt. "Tyler Fairleigh does not frighten me!"

Head high, she stepped from the vehicle and proceeded toward the old brick building, Jenny following with a basket of food and baby supplies. From the corner of her eye, Belinda saw Lord Fairleigh straighten as he took note of their arrival. She quickened her pace, but he agilely leapt down from his curricle and caught up with them.

"Lady Belinda." He bowed smoothly.

She ignored him, hurrying toward the door, but he hastened to block her way.

"Might I have a word with you, my lady?"

"No, you may not," she said shortly, forced to stop before physically running into him. "Please remove yourself from my presence."

"Not one paltry word?" he requested boyishly.

Belinda was forced to look up at him, and she was sorry that she had. Up close, he was so brutally handsome that he literally made her weak in the knees. Then, once she had seen his silvery gray eyes, she was unable to tear her gaze away.

"What do you wish of me, Lord Fairleigh?" she asked over the rushing heartbeat that pounded in her ears.

He smiled enigmatically.

Belinda flushed, realizing the many meanings that could be bestowed on her question, and knowing that he knew every one of them. Flustered with herself for her embarrassing reaction to him, she squared her shoulders and haughtily stuck out her chin. "Please be brief," she stated, "I am performing an errand of mercy."

Lord Fairleigh grinned more broadly. "Indeed. I imagine that a lady such as yourself must be extremely busy."

"Well, yes I am," she declared.

"I would further assume that my demand is trivial compared to . . . say . . . that of the Downing family."

Belinda tossed her head. "Beyond the slightest doubt, my lord. I venture to say that you have no needs at all compared to them."

"But I do have needs," he went on, holding her captive with those unfathomable, dark-lashed eyes.

"Cease this banter, my lord, and get to the point," she ordered. "I have no time for drawing room prattle."

"Very well," he drawled as if *he* had all the time in the world, which he probably did, given his languid lifestyle. "I have come here to ease my abominable curiosity, which was aroused by the past early morning's event."

"That is simple, Lord Fairleigh. A baby was born, not an uncommon occurrence, particularly during the wee hours. Now I wish you good day." Belinda started forward, but the earl did not budge, forcing her to halt once more.

"What intrigued me the most was your presence at the bedside," he mused. "Who are you? Why was a gentlewoman such as yourself attending a childbirth in this part of town? I cannot grasp the reason. The beauteous Lady Belinda should be dancing the night away in a glittering ballroom."

"I've had my fill of society, thank you!" she snapped. "I prefer to spend my life in the useful endeavor of helping those in need. I am sure that such a sentiment is completely foreign to a man of meaningless enterprise."

His lips twitched. "My, but you have a low opinion of me."

Belinda cocked her head sideways. "I detest self-centered indolence and roguish behavior. I do suppose, however, that being a lord of the realm places you above highwaymen, pickpockets, and footpads, though you are just as useless to the world as they."

His jaw hardened and his eyes darkened dangerously. "I should turn you over my knee for that and all of your previous insults."

"Just try it!" she spat. "Now, get out of my way. I have no time for such as you!"

He ignored her, stubbornly standing his ground. "You have prejudged me, little knowing what boons I provide to those less fortunate."

Belinda sniffed disparagingly. "What fine acts of charity do you perform, my lord? I tend to believe that your kind of aid serves only to perpetuate the sin of prostitution."

"I can scarcely believe that I heard such a thing from the lips of a lady! If you were a man, I'd call you out for that remark." Lord Fairleigh audibly ground his teeth. "Since you are not, I shall await your apology."

"Then you'll grow gray in the process! I speak only the truth, and I won't take it back!"

"You know nothing of my acts of charity." He smiled smugly. "I gave your man, Downing, a guinea this morning."

"Bravo!" she hissed. "For a rich man, that is no great deed."

"Perhaps it is not, but I'll wager I could do as much for the poor as you've ever considered!"

Belinda laughed sarcastically. "You? Personally help the needy? What a whisker!"

"Try me," he challenged.

"I am not merely speaking of a donation of money, although

your contribution would be greatly appreciated," she explained, slightly taken aback. "I refer to a gift of your *time.*"

He tightly nodded. "Very well. Name the hour and place."

Stifling a gasp of surprise, Belinda stared him straight in the eye. Was he truly serious? If so, he would be a perfect actor in the scheme that had been dancing through her head. Unfortunately, he probably would not appear, or if he did, he'd refuse to do her bidding. It was, however, worth a try.

"Very well, Lord Fairleigh. I shall take you up on your offer." Rummaging through her reticule, she bought forth a pencil and scrap of paper. Smiling, she scribbled an address and handed it to him. "Present yourself there at eight o'clock sharp tomorrow morning."

"Eight o'clock!"

"My work does not wait for slugabed noblemen," she airily told him. "Now stand aside!"

Reading her note, he unconsciously moved out of her way. Belinda scampered into the building with Jenny hard on her heels.

"My lady, what do you mean to do with him?" the maid wailed as soon as the door was firmly closed.

"Jenny, do you remember that idea I had about rescuing women from houses of ill repute?" Belinda smirked.

The girl nodded.

"Well, Tyler Fairleigh is the perfect instrument for such a gambit."

"Oh, no, my lady! That man is dangerous," she warned.

"Nonsense! If he agrees to it, just think of the many women we'll save!" Her mind reeling with possibilities, Belinda started up the stairs.

"He'll be trouble," Jenny mumbled, dutifully following her mistress. "Just mark my words."

"My lord." Tyler's valet tentatively touched his shoulder. "You asked me to wake you early."

"So I did." The earl's voice was muffled against the pillows. "Are you sure you haven't mistaken the time?"

"No, my lord."

Tyler yawned. The bed felt so soft, the covers so cozy. He didn't want to leave it. Idly he thought of ignoring the challenge. His curiosity simply wasn't worth such a trial. But then he remembered the Lady Belinda and visualized the dazzle of victory in those big blue eyes if he failed to appear. No female would get the best of him, especially a minx such as she! Irritably, he got out of bed, shrugged into his dressing robe, and began his morning ablutions.

"Shall I fetch your breakfast, sir?" Jennings inquired.

"Just tea," Tyler said. "The very thought of the coming day has quite taken my appetite."

The servant departed, returning shortly with the steaming brew. "What attire shall you wear today, my lord?"

He gratefully sipped the bracing hot brew. "You choose. My brain has not yet begun to function."

Tyler wondered if his intellect had gone begging some time before. To be exact, it had happened at the very moment he'd decided to investigate Lady Belinda. Why on earth had he allowed that aggravating wench to entangle him in this bumble-broth? He had better things to do.

Dressing, he considered the situation. No doubt, Lady Belinda intended to send him on various errands of mercy, such as she had been doing yesterday. He would counter that plot by sending a footman in his stead. Then he would provide a generous donation to her charitable efforts and escape her clutches by claiming a necessary trip out of town. Satisfied with his plan, he called for his carriage and set out to meet with the lady.

Tyler was not surprised when Lady Belinda's direction led him to an antiquated building in a poor part of town. His coachman, however, was astonished.

"My lord, are you certain that this is the correct address?" he queried.

He nodded grimly. "Stay here and wait for me."

"Indeed, sir! I wouldn't be thinking of leaving you stranded at a place like this."

Smiling faintly, Tyler walked to the door and rapped peremptorily with his walking stick.

It was opened immediately by a scrawny, brassy haired wench of about the age of twenty. "Laks!" she cried over the din of the interior. "It's a gentleman! And a 'andsome one at that!"

"I am seeking the Lady Belinda," Tyler said stiffly. "She is expecting me."

"Well, I'll be! I didn't know Lady Belinda had herself a beau." She giggled, waving him in. "Wait'll everybody sees you. You're a prime'un if ever I saw it! Almost makes me wish for the old days."

Flushing, Tyler briefly contemplated flight, but was arrested by the scene before him. The large hall and staircase were filled with women and children of all sorts and ages, bustling toward some unknown destination. Some, like the female who answered the door, bore the obvious looks of common trollops. A goodly number of residents were in various stages of pregnancy. A miscellaneous batch of young and old led children about. In the midst of all the commotion stood Lady Belinda, staring at him with the glitter of challenge in her eyes. He met her gaze and unwaveringly held it.

When the commotion died and the hall was cleared, Lady Belinda approached him. "You look rather shocked, Lord Fairleigh."

He eyed her apprehensively. "What kind of a place *is* this?"

"It is my home for impoverished women," she said proudly. "Most of them are unwed mothers, their children, and . . . er . . . certain females who wish to reform their lives. We care for them, teach them trades, and assist them in finding employment. Would you care to tour the facility, my lord?"

"Not particularly," he declined.

She laughed. "Why, Lord Fairleigh, I do believe that you are afraid of being in the midst of so many ladies. You, London's foremost ladies' man!"

He bit back a sharp rejoinder concerning her loose definition of "lady." "I imagine that such an enterprise is quite costly."

"Oh, yes. I and my small staff operate solely on donations and on the proceeds from my own small inheritance. Would you care to become a patron?"

Relief flooded Tyler's veins. Be damned to his curiosity concerning Lady Belinda herself! Perhaps, now that she had achieved satisfaction by his presence, she would agree to his making an enormous contribution and allow him to be on his way.

"I am prepared to present a handsome sum of money for your cause, my lady," he announced. "I shall fill out a bank draft and leave you to your admirable endeavors."

"Thank you, Lord Fairleigh. We shall put it to good use." She tilted her head and coyly looked up at him. "You did, however, promise to participate *personally* in our work."

Tyler was momentarily mesmerized by her pretty, pert face, but it wasn't long before her words sank in. "Lady Belinda, be reasonable. There is little a man can do in a house such as this."

"To the contrary, there is a great deal. Come to my office. We shall discuss it."

Groaning inwardly, he followed her down a long corridor to an unassuming, businesslike room. Lady Belinda sat down behind her desk and waved him to a nearby chair. She folded her hands and stared thoughtfully up at the ceiling as if to plan her speech.

"Lord Fairleigh, do you realize that, every day, young girls arrive from the country to seek employment in the city?"

He shrugged. "So?"

"Most of them are penniless and intimidated." She paused, nibbling her luscious lower lip. "My lord, I must speak frankly. These girls are tricked into taking jobs of prostitution. By the time they realize their fate, it is too late. The brothels hold them as virtual prisoners, and woe betide them if they defy the proprietors."

"That is unfortunate," he said, "but what has it to do with me?"

Lady Belinda took a deep breath, once again meeting his gaze with that look of challenge in her eyes. "As a female, I cannot gain entry into these houses, but you, Lord Fairleigh, with your scandalous reputation, would be right at home in such surroundings."

Tyler's temper flared. "I am becoming very weary of your persistent disparagement of my character!"

"Well, I am correct, am I not?" she countered.

"My lady, I too will speak frankly!" he blared. "Since my salad days, I've never lowered myself to set foot in one of those houses! *I have had no need to do so!*"

"Your tarts are of a different class, eh?" she said blatantly.

Tyler rose. "I have had enough of you and your tongue. I swear you are the most unladylike *lady* I've ever encountered! You must be the bane of your family's existence."

"You're correct in that!" she snapped. "My family has nothing to do with me. But you do, sir, since you made me a promise. Sit down, Lord Fairleigh!"

To his own surprise, he sat. The comment concerning her family had once again pricked his curiosity. Who was Lady Belinda?

"I am sorry that I have insulted you, my lord," she apologized in a very unsorrowful voice. "I fear I am overly zealous about my scheme."

"Perhaps you can tell me what it is without slandering me," he growled.

She nodded. "I shall attempt it. You see, I need a gentleman whose presence would be unremarkable in an establishment of that sort. Being such a disreputable rake—forgive me!—you would be perfect for the job. You will merely enter the establishment and spirit the girl away."

Again, Tyler rose to leave. "This is ridiculous. I won't be a party to it."

"Crying craven, my lord?"

He halted. "The plot is impossible! How do I know which girl to choose? How do I sneak her away?"

"I have my sources," she mysteriously assured him, "and the girl will be familiar with the inner workings of the house. She can assist in her own escape."

Tyler shook his head. "Lady Belinda, there are others who would be far more adept than I, and, contrary to your belief, there are men whose reputations are blacker than mine. They are the ones who would go unnoticed in such establishments."

"But they, Lord Fairleigh, have not volunteered," she reminded. "You have."

He began to refute her, but held his tongue. Perhaps he would help her, just this once. It would be something different to do.

"Please, Lord Fairleigh." There was appeal in her voice, but her magnificent blue eyes were still filled with her proud, now familiar, look of challenge.

"All right," he consented. "When shall we start?"

"Tonight." She gave a little bounce on her chair. "My carriage will await you in front of your house at nine o'clock. Then I shall give you your final instructions."

"You're going?"

"Certainly! Though I must remain in the coach, I wouldn't miss it for anything."

"Very well," he said resignedly and walked toward the door. "Until then."

"Oh, Lord Fairleigh?" she called. "Haven't you forgotten something?"

He turned.

Lady Belinda smiled sweetly. "Your bank draft."

Tyler strode back to the desk. "Tell me, madam, were you never forestalled in your wishes?"

Her face clouded. "Yes, but it's of no matter now, and I refuse to speak of it."

"Your family . . ."

"Lord Fairleigh," she declared, "ours is a professional relationship. I will not discuss my personal life."

"It might be the thing to do. If we are to jaunt about in your carriage; I am not particularly interested in being called out by an irate husband or relative."

"Rest assured, my lord, that I have no husband, and my family cares little what I do," she stated firmly. "And now the bank draft?"

For the rest of the day, Tyler could think of little more than Lady Belinda. Scarcely a particle of his curiosity had been assuaged by his visit to her. Indeed, it had only increased. Who was she? Why did her family not care for her? There was no point in discussing the matter with his mother again. If he continued to display interest in the young lady, she would be sure to dash off to ferret out information. The gossip would be rampant.

He met with a similar fate at his club. To avoid rumor, he was forced to couch his inquiries in such vague terms that no one could possibly come up with an answer. The only source was Lady Belinda herself, and she had as much as told him that she would be silent. There were ways, though, that he could loosen her lips. After all, tonight he would be alone with her in a darkened carriage. Perhaps a bit of romance might be in order. Tyler was an expert at seducing women's bodies. Couldn't he do so with their minds? He would try.

At nine o'clock sharp, a closed, unmarked carriage drew up before Fairleigh House. Tyler, ready and waiting at the drawing room window, hastened out to meet it.

"Good evening, my lady," he crooned to the black clad, heavily veiled creature within. "I do believe that the time spent with you will more than compensate for the unpleasantry of the venture."

"Fustian," said Lady Belinda. "May I introduce you, my lord, to my abigail and assistant, Jenny Combs?"

Tyler's spirits sank. In the darkness, he hadn't noticed the small figure in the seat across from them. There would be no dalliance with Lady Belinda tonight.

As the coach pulled away, the lady came right to the point. "You will be visiting the establishment of a woman who calls herself Mrs. Kelly. There, you will request the company of a girl named Hilda. Do what you must to rescue her. The carriage will wait round the corner."

"Have you no suggestions as to how I'm to perform this feat?"

"That will be up to you and Hilda," she murmured, the veil muffling her voice. "Anything further?"

"It would be much more pleasant if you would remove those trappings from your pretty face," he complained.

Lady Belinda quietly laughed. "This is not a social occasion, my lord. I do not wish to run the slightest risk of being seen. Nor, if you truly think me pretty, do I wish to distract you from your mission."

Tyler slumped against the corner of the coach. "You won't. Though you may be most attractive, your attitude toward me is so caustic that any distraction would be well nigh impossible. I am only interested in completing this mission with alacrity."

"Excellent, my lord! That, too, is my desire."

They remained silent until the carriage drew to a stop. Lifting the shade, Tyler saw a large, well-kept, brightly lit house. Mrs. Kelly's establishment obviously catered to men of means.

"We will await you round the corner," Lady Belinda repeated.

"I remember. I'm not a ninnyhammer," he grumbled as her footman let down the steps and opened the door.

"Good luck, Lord Fairleigh."

He did not reply, merely casting her a look of aggravation as he stepped out. "Be ready to leave in a rush," he ordered the footman.

"Yes, m'lord." The man grinned naughtily. "Enjoy yourself, sir."

Tyler cursed him under his breath and approached the bordello.

The door was opened by two burly servants, who suspiciously gazed at him as they allowed him to enter an ornate hall. Apparently, he passed their inspection for one detached himself and led him into a front room where a highly painted, middle-aged woman sat alone, sipping a glass of wine.

"I am Mrs. Kelly," she greeted. "You are new to my establishment, Lord Fairleigh."

Tyler started. "How do you know my name?"

"It is my business to recognize those gentlemen of your notoriety, my lord." She poured him a glass of port. "Don't be concerned about it. Here, we pride ourselves on anonymity. There is no gossip about our clientele. Won't you sit down?"

He obeyed, sipping the wine and finding it of the highest quality.

"Because I operate a superior operation, I always inspect new clients," the woman continued. "In your case, of course, it isn't really necessary. I know you will not cause us trouble."

Tyler hoped that his face did not reflect his guilt. Causing trouble for Mrs. Kelly was his goal, but in return, she was causing trouble for him. Since she knew who he was, how could he rescue Hilda without being caught?

"I have seen you in the park and wondered if you were as handsome up close as you were from afar." She sighed. "Ah, you are even more so. My girls will fight over you, my lord."

"Actually," Tyler disclosed, "there is one girl in particular, who has been recommended to me . . . by an anonymous source."

"Indeed?"

He nodded. "The girl's name is Hilda."

"Hilda?" she asked with surprise. "No, my lord, I doubt she would suit. Perhaps I could advise another, or you can look over the girls . . ."

"No," he said firmly. "Hilda, it shall be."

"There's no predicting a gentleman's tastes." Mrs. Kelly shook her head. "I did cut her fingernails after the last bout."

Tyler couldn't keep from smiling, wondering which man of the *ton* bore Hilda's marks and if he'd had to explain the scratches to his wife.

"Very well. Come with me," said the madam, rising. "But if any of the others catch your eye, do feel free to change your mind."

"Thank you, Mrs. Kelly."

Tyler followed her from the room and across the hall, entering a large room, complete with comfortable seating, a bar, card tables, and a flock of blowsily dressed females. There was a number of gentlemen present, many of whom Tyler recognized. Several of them were rakes of varying degrees, but a few of Mrs. Kelly's customers were rather upstanding individuals whom no one would believe to be cheating on their wives.

He was both amused and slightly abashed by the experience. Tyler Fairleigh was well known and envied for his beautiful, desirable mistresses. To be seen in a place such as this, however elegant, was a definite comedown, and seen he was. Everyone, especially the female contingent, was ogling him.

"Where is that girl?" Mrs. Kelly muttered, interrupting his musing. "Disobedient wench! Perhaps she is serving a client, but I doubt it."

Tyler sniffed as if irritated by the delay.

"I'll find her immediately, my lord," the madam was quick to say. "Do finish your drink and have another . . . at no charge. I greatly value your patronage."

Tyler inclined his head. Tossing down his drink, he strolled to the bar for another. The homely Sir Kenneth Justice joined him.

"Slumming it, Fairleigh?"

He lifted an eyebrow. "I could ask you the same."

"Madam Kelly's house of pleasure is more than agreeable to me. For a man like you, however . . ." The baronet chuckled. "Rather a setback, isn't it?"

"I wouldn't say that." He picked up his glass. "Perhaps I am merely curious."

"Or desperately in between mistresses?" Sir Kenneth laughed.

Tyler eyed him scorchingly. "I am never desperate."

"No, I don't suppose you are," the man bemoaned. "More's the pity."

There was no further time for conversation. Mrs. Kelly came up behind him, fairly dragging a drooping young girl. "Here she is, my lord. Here's Hilda."

Tyler gaped. No one who witnessed this incident would be able to believe his own eyes. Hilda was awfully bedraggled in her flimsy red dress. Her fair hair was tangled, and from it dangled a wilted red rose. One of her shoes was missing. Worse than any of that, she could be no more than fifteen years old, if she were a day.

"Good God!" erupted Sir Kenneth.

Mrs. Kelly eyed Tyler questioningly.

He downed his drink and leaned his arm on the bar while the attendant quickly refilled his glass. "Uh . . . she will be fine," he declared.

The madam gave the girl a good shake. "You'll entertain his lordship, missy, and you'll do it well."

Hilda took his hand. Briefly a look of defiance flashed through her glazed blue eyes. "You come with me, sir."

Still clutching his port, Tyler went with her from the room and up a flight of stairs to a small, but well-furnished room. She weakly managed to slam the door. "Lord or not, if you want me, you'll have to fight for it," she slurred.

"You've been drugged, haven't you?" he asked.

"What's it to you?"

"It matters considerably. Have you ever heard of Lady Belinda?"

A spark fleetingly glowed in her eyes.

"She has sent me to take you away from here, but you have to help me," he said hurriedly. "Is there a back way out of here?"

"It's locked," she mumbled.

"Can I kick it open?"

She looked long at him and slowly nodded. "I got to sit down."

"All right," Tyler said irritably. "Sit for a moment. That will lull anyone's suspicions. Then we'll leave this place."

Hilda sank down on the edge of the bed, promptly keeled over backward, and passed out.

"Dammit!" He frantically mopped her face with water from a nearby basin and finally poured the entire ewer over her head, but the girl remained slumbering. "Oh, for God's sake!"

His mind reeling, he sat down and finished his port, then shook her wildly, but Hilda was out cold. "Now what am I going to do?"

Tyler let her collapse again on the bed and went to the door, surreptitiously peeking out. When he saw that the hall was empty, he quietly began an exploration.

In addition to the stairs they had previously used, there was another set leading down to the front hall. Carefully skirting them, he continued on, but discovered no back stairway. Without Hilda, that means of escape was impossible. He returned to the room to find her still unconscious.

Roundly cursing Lady Belinda, Mrs. Kelly, Hilda, and all females in general, Tyler swung the girl up over his shoulder, and carried her from the room and down the staircase into the main hall. The two brawny footmen leapt to attention.

"I wish to see Mrs. Kelly," he announced imperiously.

Alarmed, one of them detached himself and ushered him into the madam's presence.

"What the hell?" cried the startled proprietress.

"I am immensely pleased with this girl," Tyler informed her. "I wish to purchase her from you."

Mrs. Kelly's mouth dropped open.

"Name your price!" he demanded. "And be quick about it! My time is valuable."

She pursed her lips. "Ah . . . as you know, Hilda is one of my best. She'll come high, my lord."

"Balderdash! You tried to point me away from her."

"But if she pleases you . . ."

Tyler glared at her.

Mrs. Kelly threw up her hands. "Two guineas and good riddance! She's been naught but trouble."

He awkwardly fished the coins from his purse and gave them to her, turned on his heel, and set off toward the door.

"Strange taste, the nobs," he heard her say as he departed.

The two doormen had the nerve to chuckle as they let him out into the night. Tyler ground his teeth. He had succeeded in Lady Belinda's mission, but at what price? Mrs. Kelly's famed anonymity or not, every man in London would probably hear of this escapade.

He rounded the corner and walked to the carriage. "Here, my lady, is Hilda," he growled and dumped his burden into her lap.

"What have you done to her?" Lady Belinda screeched.

"They drugged her." He settled himself beside the lady's abigail.

"Poor child." Lady Belinda caressed the girl's forehead. "How did you make your escape?"

"I bought her."

"You . . . *what?* "

Tyler winced. "I told Mrs. Kelly that she pleased me."

Lady Belinda laughed softly.

"Don't you dare comment on that," he warned.

"Not even to say that I think you quite wonderful?" she purred.

"Not even that. My reputation is probably ruined because of this hare-brained caper," he sullenly stated.

She giggled merrily. "Oh, this will only enlarge upon it. If word gets out, the gossips will feed on the tale for months."

"I prefer to have myself paired with beautiful *women,*" he snapped, "not with schoolgirlish harpies."

"Goodness, Lord Fairleigh! Hilda must be lovely or Mrs. Kelly would not have captured her."

"Captured? Hilda probably went willingly until she found out what was involved," he scoffed.

"Oh, no, my lord. Mrs. Kelly, and others like her, meet the country stages and virtually trick the young innocents into coming with them. Once in their clutches, the girls are truly enslaved." She wistfully sighed. "I wish I could put a period to the practice!"

"You cannot save the world, Lady Belinda," he replied.

"No, I suppose I must content myself with helping only a small portion of it," she mused as the carriage drew to a stop. "Well, here we are at your home, Lord Fairleigh. I do appreciate what you have done tonight, and I know that Hilda, when she awakens, will bless you with every breath she takes."

"Let us not be effusive, Lady Belinda."

"I am not, as you will discover." She tossed back her heavy veil and presented her hand.

In the glow of the gas street light from the opened coach door, her pretty face seemed ethereally lovely. Tyler was struck momentarily by the vision, then bent over her proffered hand. Instead of merely lowering his lips over the member, however, he turned it and kissed her palm.

"Lord Fairleigh!" she cried, jerking back.

He laughed mischievously. "What do you expect from a black-hearted rake?"

Lady Belinda stiffened. "Depart at once."

Still laughing, he stepped down from the carriage. "You are much more to my taste, madam, than the child on your lap."

"Fiddlesticks! You are incorrigible!"

As the coach moved away, Lady Belinda cracked open the window and leaned out. "Report to my shelter tomorrow morning, Lord Fairleigh," she called, "so that we may plan our next venture."

"Very well." He waved, then froze, his hand still upraised. What had he promised? To do this again? Dammit! His wits must have left him.

He slowly climbed the steps to his house. Tomorrow, Lady Belinda would wait in vain. Tyler, the elegant Lord Fairleigh, would not deign to set foot in anyone's house of pleasure, ever again. Tomorrow night would find him attending the opera, observing the new dancer who'd become the talk of his club. If she proved as pleasing as all had described, it would be she who would fill his nights. Not the wretched Lady Belinda or any of her humiliating, benevolent schemes!

After leaving Lord Fairleigh, Belinda delivered the sleeping Hilda into the capable care of one of her two assistants, who lived at the shelter, and ordered her coachman to take her home. She was bone-weary from her busy activities, but her satisfaction in Hilda's rescue more than compensated her for any degree of exhaustion. She wondered if Lord Fairleigh felt as elated as she did. It was doubtful. He probably considered the mission as merely an unpleasant tangle he'd gotten himself into and not as the salvation of a helpless, innocent girl.

She glanced at Jenny. "What do you think of him?"

There was no need to clarify the pronoun. "Lord Fairleigh's the most handsome man I've ever seen," the maid proclaimed. "He fair takes your breath away."

"But as a person," Belinda prodded. "What do you think of him as a person?"

Jenny shrugged "At first I thought he was dangerous, but now I don't believe he's as wicked as everyone says."

"I must agree, but where there's smoke there's fire. He is a terrible flirt. I wonder if he will continue to help us," she mused.

"You want him to, don't you, my lady? You like him."

"I like what he does for our cause," she answered archly, her palm tingling from the memory of his lips. "Perhaps I enjoy fencing a bit with him. That is all!"

The abigail giggled softly.

"We will speak no more of him," Belinda ordained, and was silent until the carriage drew up at her parents' residence. Light seemed to glow from every window of the house as the footman opened the carriage door and stood aside to assist her. Belinda groaned. Obviously, the duke and duchess were entertaining.

"Go round to the back," she ordered. "I shall enter through the servants' door."

The footman pressed his lips together in conspicuous disapproval, but passed the command to the coachman.

"My situation is awkward for all concerned," Belinda unhappily observed, "but there is no help for it."

"It's not right," Jenny complained.

"I fear my parents had no choice. I count myself fortunate that they did not banish me from under their roof. At least in these circumstances, I can devote all my money to charity. Otherwise, I would have been forced to use it to support myself."

"But they didn't even listen to your side of the story!"

Belinda lifted a shoulder. "The outcome would have been no different. Oh, let us speak no more of it! It's an old story now, and it's much too depressing."

The coachman pulled up in the small alleyway. Belinda and Jenny departed and hurriedly entered the rear door. Safe inside and unseen, Belinda paused.

"I am absolutely starving. I'll go on upstairs, but please, Jenny, won't you fetch me a light repast from the kitchen? Perhaps Cook has saved me a lobster patty!"

"I'm sure she did . . . as always."

Smiling conspiratorially, mistress and maid parted. Belinda climbed the steep back stairs and entered the hall, hastening toward her bedroom. Engulfed in her heavy veil, she nearly walked into her younger sister, who was hurrying in the opposite direction.

"Belinda! Is that you? What are you doing in that horrid attire?" Sarah cried.

"Nothing of interest." She snatched off the head gear and smiled at her sister. "You, in contrast, look perfectly lovely, but why are you not at the party?"

"Lord Arrington stepped on my hem and tore it. I was forced to retire for repairs. Oh, Belinda, I am having the most marvelous time! Lord Compton has asked me for *two* dances. He is surely the handsomest man alive!"

Belinda did not agree, but she wouldn't spoil her sister's elation with a negative comment. The last time she'd seen Lord

Compton, he was a homely, pimply faced boy. That had been several years ago, however. In the interim, he'd probably outgrown his adolescence, but only a miracle could rearrange his features into anything resembling attractiveness.

"I'm happy for you, Sarah," she commended, "if he appeals to you."

"He does, indeed. I never thought such a paragon would even take notice of me! But I must rush." She quickly kissed Belinda's cheek. "I do not wish to miss my dance with Lord Compton!"

"Heavens no," Belinda sarcastically murmured to herself as she entered her chamber. "No one would want to miss a moment with *Lord Ill-favored.*"

Immediately, she silently chided herself. Beauty to one was ugliness to another, but no one at all could dispute the fact that Lord Fairleigh was absolutely gorgeous. If only Sarah could see *her* evening companion!

A sudden tear trickled down Belinda's cheek. She furiously wiped it away. Nowadays, her lack of social activity and marital eligibility seldom overset her. Her charity work was enough. It had to be, for there was no other choice. And Lord Fairleigh? She had tricked him into assisting her. Of his own free will, he wouldn't even have thought of doing it. She'd probably never see him again, unless by chance from a distance.

Angry with herself for giving in to the moment of self-pity, she strode into her dressing room and kicked off her slippers. Hell and damnation! She was saving unfortunate women and children from lives of the utmost misery. This mission was far more important than having a husband, children, and a home of her own!

Belinda managed to unfasten the tapes of her dress and slip out of it, donning her dressing gown. She must concentrate on her work. Just think of what she'd accomplished tonight! With a tremulous smile, she walked through her bedroom, flung open the doors to her balcony, and stepped outside.

The garden had been lit with fairy lanterns, which cast a celestial sheen on the paths and plantings. Strains of music and laughter drifted up from the terrace below. Belinda bitterly turned away. Such an evening had been her downfall. If only she hadn't . . .

"My lady," Jenny called excitedly, coming into the room with a heavily laden tray, "Cook has saved the best of the tasty morsels for you!"

Belinda sighed. "I fear I have lost my appetite."

The abigail's smile faded. "She'll be disappointed."

She nodded. "I know. I'll try a few bites. And so will you! You must be starving after our adventurous evening."

Jenny brightened. "Yes, ma'am, I am."

"Then sit with me and let us see if we can finish off this bounty."

"My lady, I couldn't be so familiar!"

"You can." Belinda took her place at the small table overlooking the garden. "We work together; we shall eat together. After all, Jenny, you are as much my companion as maid."

Uncertainly, the girl joined her. At first, they ate silently. But after partaking in the champagne, the two finished the meal laughing uproariously over how ridiculous Lord Fairleigh had looked when he'd come from Mrs. Kelly's with Hilda tossed over his shoulder like a sack of meal.

"I hope he keeps on helping us!" the abigail laughed.

But instead of Lord Fairleigh's assistance, Belinda visualized his handsome face. "I hope he does, too," she said wistfully.

Jenny's eyes twinkled. "I think he's attracted to you, my lady."

"Certainly not!"

"That's how it looks to me."

"You are wrong," Belinda firmly disagreed. "It's just his way. He's a flirt."

The maid closely watched her. "What if he *is* seriously attracted? Even the blackest of rakes eventually do their duty and wed."

She sighed. "Perhaps Lord Fairleigh will do that someday,

but it would never be to me, even if I would wish to have him. Whether it is true or not, I am considered ruined."

"But for a man of his reputation . . ."

"That doesn't matter. No gentleman of *ton* would marry such a woman as I."

"It's not fair," Jenny muttered.

"Maybe not, but it's true. Let us speak of it no more!" Belinda buttered a zephr-light roll. "We must finish our delicious repast and seek our beds. We have an exciting day ahead of us."

"Yes, my lady." The maid followed suit, but when she tucked Belinda into bed, she murmured, "Maybe a man like Lord Fairleigh, who's had the experience of being talked about, would look behind all the gossip and learn the truth."

Belinda suppressed a bitter reply and closed her eyes. Jenny was just too loyal to understand. Lord Fairleigh, if and when he chose to marry, would select a lady of spotless repute. Even if he was certain of the truth, he wouldn't look twice at a woman like she. He owed that much to his heritage.

Hearing the door close behind her abigail, she rolled over and pressed her face into the pillow to smother a sob. After tonight, she would never again think of the devastating effects of the past, and she wouldn't allow Jenny to speak of such matters. She would concentrate only on the future and on those who wanted and needed her. It *would* be enough. It had to be.

Though rested and terribly fit after his unaccustomed good night's sleep, Tyler seriously questioned his sanity as he strode up the short flight of steps to Lady Belinda's home of good works. He had turned down a trip to the races and an invitation to participate in a high-stakes card game to come to this aggravating place. This wasn't at all in his style. True, he wasn't reporting as early as Lady Belinda might have preferred, yet here he was, trotting along like a puppy dog doing his mistress's will. It was absurd.

A middle-aged woman with steel gray hair answered his rap on the door and stared suspiciously at him.

"Lord Fairleigh to see Lady Belinda," he muttered shortly. Her severe expression eased. "Lord Fairleigh, do come in! I am Mrs. Briggs, Lady Belinda's assistant. My lady hoped you would call."

Call? He seriously doubted that Lady Belinda merely wished for a visit. She probably had some preposterous task for him to perform.

"Wait here," commanded the woman.

Within moments, a smiling Lady Belinda, accompanied by a comely young girl, appeared in the hall. "Lord Fairleigh!" she cried enthusiastically. "How kind of you to come."

"I don't recall that I had a choice." He glanced at the girl accompanying Lady Belinda. She looked somewhat familiar, but that was not unusual. When one perused the features of as many females as Tyler had, they took on a certain sameness.

Lady Belinda smiled with all the satisfaction of a cat lapping cream. "This is Hilda, my lord."

"Hilda?" He couldn't believe his eyes. This pretty young girl, dressed like a school miss, her hair neatly wound in a knot at the nape of her neck, certainly didn't look like the tart he'd thrown over his shoulder last night.

"Hilda," Lady Belinda prompted, "haven't you something to say to Lord Fairleigh?"

"T-thank you, my lord," she murmured, head lowered, but that was all the composure she could muster. "Oh, Lord Fairleigh!" she shrieked, throwing herself into his arms. "You saved me from that hell! How can I ever pay you back?"

"My goodness, Hilda!" her patroness snapped. "Cease that behavior at once! Unhand his lordship!"

The girl heedlessly clung to Tyler's neck. "I'll do anything!" she screeched. "I'll even . . ."

"Stop it!" cried Lady Belinda, grasping Hilda around the waist and trying to pull her away. "We'll have no conduct like this around here!"

Tyler pried himself free and smiled kindly at the girl. "Your happiness is enough for me, Hilda. I want nothing else than to see you make a success of your life."

"Well, that may be, but I know what else men want, and for you, I'd be willing to . . ."

"No, you would not!" Lady Belinda dictated sternly, her face turning scarlet.

Tyler chuckled.

"Shame on you, my lord," she scolded.

"Oh, I see," Hilda said pertly. "You're *her* man."

"He's nobody's man," Lady Belinda pronounced. "Now go back to your classroom, Hilda, and concentrate on your work."

"Yes, ma'am." With a bobbing curtsy, she dashed down the hall.

"I shall not condone such behavior," Lady Belinda threatened, favoring him with an accusatory glare.

"*I* didn't do anything," Tyler defended.

"You flirted."

"I did nothing of the kind! If you perceived me as flirting, you obviously know nothing about that sort of amusement."

She sniffed. "You continuously flirt, my lord. You have indulged in that occupation for so long that you don't even realize what you are doing."

"Ridiculous!"

"Not so! You do it in the way that you look at one through those absurdly long lashes, and in the manner in which you smile. That charming hint of a dimple and that . . ."

"Since I cannot conceal my physical attributes, perhaps I'd best leave," Tyler interrupted. "Apparently, you object to my presence."

"I thought you were going to help me," Lady Belinda lamented, her mouth forming a perfect pout.

Gazing at her luscious pink lips, Tyler wished he could take her in his arms and kiss her thoroughly. It was too bad that she had not made him the same offer as Hilda. Lady or not, he doubted that he could have turned her down.

"Why are you staring at me?" she demanded.

"Truthfully, I was thinking of kissing you." She tossed her head. "You see? Flirting!"

"No, my dear. I wasn't flirting. I was stating a fact. I would greatly enjoy kissing you, and I believe you'd delight in it, too."

Lady Belinda faltered a moment before regaining her air of control. "Balderdash! I have never heard such nonsense!"

"Kissing you wouldn't be nonsense," he predicted. "You have a mouth made for it, and a spirit to match."

"Lord Fairleigh, you forget yourself!" she gasped.

He laughed. "Very well. We'll cease this line of discourse. But I won't apologize for it, because I'm not at all sorry."

Speechless, she managed only to eye him with a mixture of frustration and confusion.

Tyler came to her assistance. "Perhaps you could inform me of my next assignment?"

"I am so glad that you will continue to help us, my lord." She took a deep breath as if to steady herself. "There is an older girl this time, imprisoned in an establishment that is not as fine as Mrs. Kelly's. Perhaps you'd best not dress so stylishly, if that is possible."

"Possible, though distasteful. Same time?"

She nodded.

"All right."

Tyler took his leave of her and proceeded to White's for luncheon. Unfortunately, as soon as he entered the dining room, he spied Sir Kenneth Justice. Before he could retreat, the baronet hailed him.

"Won't you join me, Fairleigh?"

Good manners forbade him to decline immediately. Tyler approached the table, greeted the man, and sat down. He waved away the waiter.

"I am not dining. I was merely looking for someone. I cannot stay long. I trust you are well, Justice?"

"Indeed." Sir Kenneth sliced into his beefsteak. "I am quite fit after a delectably active evening."

Tyler inwardly cringed. Surely the man wasn't going to launch into a discussion of Kelly's brothel. Moreover, had he heard of the escapade with Hilda?

The baronet leaned secretively across the table. "Whoever tipped you off to that hideous wench was doing you a disservice, Fairleigh. Next time, try Gigi."

"I'll think on it," Tyler said coolly.

"Take my advice." Sir Kenneth laughed conspiratorially. "I am familiar with the place and several others. I'm well acquainted with the wares. Some of us can't afford to set up our own little love nests."

"There are factors both for and against."

"I suppose so. But in the final tally, men like ourselves become speedily tired of one woman, eh, Fairleigh?"

Tyler held back a retort. He didn't like Sir Kenneth and didn't wish to be grouped with him in any fashion. *But was the man speaking the truth?* Did Tyler Fairleigh appear to others as Sir Kenneth did to him? A jaded, womanizing rake who would eventually become a lecherous, leering, old man? Surely not!

The baronet shook his head. "Keeping one's own mistress requires such commitment. You may prefer to follow my example. And don't forget. I'm more than happy to make suggestions."

Tyler nodded and rose. "I'll remember."

"Happy to be of service. In fact, if you would care to join me tonight . . ."

"I have other plans," he said shortly, "but thank you, Justice, and good day to you."

Tyler left his club and hurried home in time for luncheon, thoroughly surprising his mother when he entered the dining room.

"My goodness, I thought you were still abed!" she greeted him.

"I was home early last night." He took his place at the head of the table. "Tell me honestly, Mother. Am I beginning to look like a jaded, lecherous, old man?"

"Certainly not!" she cried with shock. "You appear rather young to me."

Tyler sighed and refrained from reminding her of the other two adjectives. Perhaps it was time that he looked about for a wife. The picture Sir Kenneth had painted was all too grim.

When darkness had fallen, Tyler once again joined Lady Belinda in her closed carriage. She was attired as she'd been the previous night in the sad, drooping black of the deepest mourning.

"Can't you wear something more cheerful?" he complained, still somewhat bitter from his noontime reflections.

"I cannot take the risk of someone recognizing me."

"After dark, in a closed carriage?" he scoffed. "There is no chance whatsoever."

She shook her head, veil fluttering. "There is danger in our work. If certain people knew what we were about, they would stop at nothing to put an end to our activities."

"I doubt that Mrs. Kelly has any grievances," he said dryly. "If there is so much danger involved in this business, why are you plunging me into it? I don't wear a veil. I can be recognized."

"Sadly, my lord," she lamented, "you will not last long."

"Then thank you for putting me in this position, Belinda. I've always hoped for an early death."

She inhaled sharply. "You should not do that!"

"Die young for the cause?" he said bitingly. "Perhaps it is preferable to living out my life as a lewd old . . ."

"Not that. I refer to the other. You must not address me with such familiarity," she interrupted.

"Oh, for God's sake!" he grumbled. "Here we are together at night, in a closed carriage, roaming the streets of London. You may consider your abigail to lend propriety, but I scarcely believe that the *ton* would agree. And you're worried about me calling you by your first name? Ha! I would place more importance upon the matter of my premature demise. Explain that to me and call me Tyler while you're doing it, *Belinda*."

"Yes . . . well . . . I suppose we are partners in this enterprise . . . Tyler."

"That's better." It was infinitely pleasant to hear his Christian name on her lips. She had a delightful way of saying it, her voice softening when she did so. "Now about my mortality," he prompted.

"My lord . . . Tyler, I hope that you will continue to help me, but we cannot do so indefinitely. You will become connected with the disappearance of the girls. Since a great deal of money is involved with this business . . ." She ceased her discourse, letting him draw his own conclusions.

If he needed the time to ponder her words, he didn't have it. The coach had stopped. "Any instructions?" he asked.

"The girl's name is Rose. Through my sources, she knows you are coming and will be watching for you."

He stepped from the carriage and was surprised to see a well-known gaming hell he had patronized during his salad days. This would be easy. With all the confusion of drunken revelry, he should be able to spirit Rose away without hindrance.

Tyler decided to feign slight intoxication to fit in with the rest of the crowd. Rumpling his cravat, he entered with a small stagger and quickly procured a glass of blue ruin. Taking a long drink, he surveyed the room.

The clientele was made up of a mixture of the social classes, all rubbing shoulders with each other in the pursuit of enjoyment. Once more, he was astonished to see certain upstanding members of the *ton* whom he would never have suspected to be occupied in such a fashion. Luckily, Sir Kenneth was not present, though he did notice several other fellow club members. Tyler sighed. There was a great deal of *ton* money financing these nefarious enterprises. It was rather embarrassing.

"Lord Fairleigh?" a tall, pock-marked redhead whispered. "I am Rose. Come with me."

He presented his arm and escorted her up the stairs, feeling as if holes were being bored into his back by the gaping of countless onlookers. Good God! If anyone he knew saw him with Rose, they would be astounded. She had a red head, but that was her only similarity to the flower for which she'd been named. The woman, with the exception of her ample endowments, was as ugly in the face as a champion hog. She was unquestionably not in Lord Fairleigh's style!

Rose exhaled loudly as they entered her room. "Hell and damnation! I thought you'd never get here! By damn, I guess it was because I was so nervous. Wait here. I'll be right back." At the door, she stopped and glanced over her shoulder. "Hell, you're the prettiest man I've ever seen. Maybe we oughta have a bit of fun . . . just as a goodbye to the old days."

"No!" Tyler quickly denied. "Lady Belinda is waiting. We must hurry."

"Damn it all!" She smiled a toothless grin. "All right."

Rose left and returned with another female, this one younger and considerably better-looking. "This is Yvette, m'lord. She wants to go, too."

"Both of you?" he exclaimed, his brain working furiously.

"Yes, and . . ."

The door swung open to a third woman. "Laks! I had a sight of trouble gettin' away! Had to pop a fellow in the head." She grinned at Tyler and curtsied awkwardly. "M'lord, I'm Flora."

"*Three* of you?" Tyler cried.

"Why not?" Rose asked pertly. "They say bein' at Lady Belinda's is a whole lot better."

He sat down on the edge of the bed. "How am I going to do this?"

"Don't you know?" Flora queried in awe. "They said you knew all about this business."

"*They* were wrong. Is there a back stair?"

The females nodded. "Goes to the cellar," Yvette offered. "An' there's a door to the alley."

"Then that's the way we'll escape."

Rising, he crossed the room and peeked into the hall. There

was no one about, and the din from below would drown any noise they might make. He motioned to the women.

"Go quickly to the back stairs."

Half running, they hastened past him. Tyler darted after them, fearing that any minute someone might enter the corridor or come up from below and see them. His concern was not unfounded. As they reached the steps, a door banged open and a man cursed raucously.

"Stop her! That wench hit me in the head!"

Tyler didn't look back. "Run for it!"

They dashed down what seemed like thousands of stairs. As they reached the door to the cellar, Tyler heard heavy footsteps on the stairs above. "Someone's coming after us! Hurry!"

Rose fumbled with the knob. "It's locked!"

"Sure it's locked," Yvette announced. "If it hadn't 'ave been, I'd 'ave gone long ago!"

"Stand back." With a mighty kick, which sent wrenching pain from his foot to his hip, Tyler burst through the barrier into the dank darkness and tumbled down another set of steps, landing hard on the cellar's stone floor.

"M'lord! Be ye injured?" Rose shrilled.

"Only a bit, but we haven't time for it." He struggled to his feet and frantically tried to pierce the darkness. "Does anyone know the whereabouts of the outside door?"

"I think I can find it," Yvette volunteered.

"I hope so. Catch hold of each other so we won't get lost and find that door! Hurry!"

Tyler caught Rose's shoulder and used her as a crutch while they groped their way through the gloom, the sounds of their pursuers growing ever closer.

"Here it is!" Yvette slid the bolt and let them out into the alley. "We'll help you, m'lord."

With Rose on his one side and Yvette on the other, Tyler half ran, half hopped through the alley.

"Stop them!" someone shouted from behind. A shot rang out.

"You run. I'll hide," he told his helpers.

"Not on yer life, m'lord, for that's what it'd be!" Rose spit out. "Ain't no time to act like a gentleman."

"They want you. Not me."

"I wouldn't bet on it." Grimly, she pulled him onward. "We ain't leavin' you."

As more shots resounded, Tyler suddenly saw Lady Belinda's carriage turn into the alleyway. "Damn fool woman," he muttered.

"Tyler!" she screamed, leaning out. "We heard gunfire! Oh, what has happened?"

"Stay inside, you idiot!" he barked, relief sweeping over him as the footman leaped down to assist.

"You are hurt!" Belinda wailed and tried to descend, but was halted by the women flocking into the carriage. The footman unceremoniously dumped Tyler onto the floor at her feet.

"I shall never forgive myself," she moaned, trying to kneel down beside him as the coach careened out of the alley and down the street. "Did they shoot you?"

"He probably busted his foot kickin' the door," Flora told her. "Are you Lady Belinda?"

In her agony, Belinda had attention only for him. "Oh, Tyler, I am so sorry," she crooned, gently wiping his forehead with her lavender-scented handkerchief. "Does it hurt?"

The vehicle lurched, toppling her onto his chest. Pain momentarily forgotten as her soft breast pressed against him, Tyler circled her with his arm. "You feel luscious, my minx."

"Cease this at once!" she gasped, unsuccessfully trying to squirm away.

Tyler tightened his grasp. "You owe me this moment of bliss, Belinda," he whispered in the small shell-like ear so near to his mouth.

"I most certainly do not! You came of your own free will," she gibbered. "And if, in the dark recesses of your lecherous mind, I *do* owe you something, I definitely should not be called upon to make payment in the presence of witnesses!"

"This closed carriage is black as pitch."

"They have ears, my lord!"

"Um . . . and so do you." Unable to resist the temptation of the delicate organ, he gently nibbled its lobe.

For the briefest moment, she yielded to his seduction, then wriggling free, she delivered a stunning smack to his cheek. "You licentious knave!" she berated and, probably inadvertently kneeing him in a most sensitive spot, she pounced onto the seat.

Again, Tyler felt pain, not only from his foot, but he couldn't help chuckling. The females he'd rescued tittered. There was no response from the lady's maid, but Belinda was not to be muted.

"There will be nothing said of this event!" she proclaimed.

"Aah," said Rose, "he was only . . ."

"Nothing!" she ordered in a voice that would brook no disobedience.

Silence reigned until they reached Tyler's home and the footman assisted him from the carriage.

"You should summon a doctor, my lord," Lady Belinda muttered, leaning forward to look out at him.

"Thank you for your concern, my lady," he answered, gingerly testing his weight on his aching foot, "but I believe it to be merely a sprain."

"Nevertheless, one cannot be too complacent about such injuries," she said airily. "I would dislike being the cause of your suffering a loss of your swaggering savoir faire."

Tyler grinned. "Oh, madam, you are so priceless."

"And you, sir, are perfectly shocking," she intoned and flounced back against the squabs. "Drive on!"

The footman hesitated. "M'lord, Lady Belinda . . . she ain't what you think. She's an innocent girl what's been robbed of her due."

"What happened to her?" Tyler hastened to ask. "Why isn't she . . ."

But the servant hurried away, leaving him with no answers to the enigma that was Lady Belinda.

Tyler stood on the sidewalk until the coach rounded a corner and disappeared from view. He was somewhat closer to discovering the story, because the footman seemed as if he might be willing to talk. On first chance, he'd query the man. His interest in the matter had not diminished. Indeed, it had increased quite substantially when he'd first held the delectable lady in his arms and absorbed the lushness of her curvaceous body. Belinda, he must admit, was the most fascinating woman he'd ever encountered. He would learn her secret and then what? Shaking his head, Tyler turned and hobbled toward his house, the tenderness of her dainty earlobe still sweet on his lips.

After a night of tossing and turning, with dreams of Tyler's intimate touch reeling through her mind, Belinda arrived unrested at her home for women and was met at the door by a nervous Mrs. Briggs.

"My lady, he's waiting for you. Lord Fairleigh is right in your office."

"So early?" Butterflies flittered in her stomach. Quickly, Belinda fled down the corridor and opened the door. "My lord! What are you doing here?"

Tyler rose, demonstrating that his walking stick was practical as well as stylish. "Good morning, Belinda. What a charming welcome to an injured comrade! I am reporting for work as usual."

"But . . . but . . ." she stammered. "Shouldn't you be resting?"

"Whatever for? Our mission is far more important than my mere sprain. Let us plot our course for this evening. What damsels in distress shall I rescue tonight?"

Belinda sat down at her desk. "Lord Fairleigh . . ."

"Tyler," he interrupted.

"*Tyler.* I do not believe you fit for such active exploits."

"Then we could engage in a purely social evening," he smoothly suggested. "Perhaps you would allow me to escort you to Vauxhall. I promise that I shall behave with circumspection and not . . . er . . . accost you in the manner that I did last night."

Her heart pounded with excitement. Maybe Jenny was right. Maybe this handsome lord was truly attracted to her! Wouldn't it be amusing to go out with him, to be seen with him . . .

Her elation came to a resounding halt. She couldn't go out in public with Tyler. Her reputation, overlooked only by her absence from the *ton's* view, would resurface again. It would no doubt hurt Sarah's chances of making a favorable match, and it would certainly cause her parents to disown her. She couldn't do that to her sister or to her mission in life, not for one evening of happiness.

She lowered her eyes. "Much to my regret, I cannot accept, my lord," she said honestly. "You see, I am not so independent as I may appear."

"While I prefer to enjoy your company alone," he persisted, "I am not averse to a chaperon."

She shook her head. "It is impossible."

"Why, Belinda?"

"I do not wish to discuss it." Bravely, she lifted her gaze to meet his searching gray eyes. "The matter is long past and best forgotten."

"Why won't you tell me?" he asked in a voice soft as silk.

"I said *I do not wish to discuss it!*" She flung up out of her chair and went to the window, her back to him. "My lord, perhaps you had best return to your salubrious pleasures and forget all about me and my mission."

"No, Belinda, I refuse to do that. I intend to continue assisting you in your work, and that is final."

She whirled to face him. "Why?"

"Why?" The question seemed to stun him.

"Yes, why?" she repeated. "Is it a passing amusement in your jaded life? A distraction from the every day routine? Or perhaps it is a method of penance for past sins. Maybe your conscience, if you do possess one, has goaded you to atone for your previous support of such establishments as I wish to extinguish."

A flush suffused his face. "I haven't lent my custom to brothels since my salad days," he declared. "Such a sport is not in my style!"

"Ha! How many mistresses have you housed, my lord?"

"Tyler!" he flared.

"Tyler." She smiled sweetly. "How many?"

"That, madam, is not your affair, and if you were a true lady, Belinda, you wouldn't ask."

"Don't you realize that by keeping mistresses, you do aid in perpetuating prostitution?"

"The women who have been under my protection have practiced their profession by their own free will, and, believe me, they haven't suffered monetarily or in any other way."

"I believe you, Tyler, but what becomes of them once you have wearied of their charms?"

"They move on to other protectors, or they retire," he growled. "How would I know? They certainly aren't penniless when they depart."

Belinda sighed. "I wonder what becomes of them when they are too old to attract."

"Hopefully, they've saved enough money to live comfortably," he fired back. "Should I concern myself with the future of a tradesman with whom I do business? It's much the same."

"Not to me, it isn't."

He shook his head. "You just don't understand. This business isn't called 'the world's oldest profession' for nothing. There's a need and a market for it."

"Men could put a period to it."

Tyler did not bother to answer.

Belinda knew he wouldn't. Her statement had been impossibly naive. She lowered her eyes and flashed him a guilty glance through her lashes.

Catching her at it, he laughed. "That's correct, my dear. Your statement was far off the mark. Men *won't* stop it, and a great many women don't want it stopped. A healthy number of your fair sex are making a large amount of money at it. But I disagree with females being *forced* to participate, so what's my next assignment? I've been waiting in fervent anticipation."

She laughed, too. "Very well, but I refuse to allow you to take a risk. You may assist me in meeting coaches."

"Pray enlighten me on this activity."

Ringing for tea and biscuits, Belinda proceeded to do so.

Sitting comfortably in the carriage beside Belinda, who was disguised once more in her widow's weeds, Tyler, also in costume, watched as coach after coach arrived from the country. The inn she'd chosen was a busy place. By the time they had closely surveyed the disposition of the occupants of one conveyance, another bowled into the yard. Nor were they the only observers of the bustle. According to Belinda, three purveyors of comely flesh were present as well, including Sam Dryden, the proprietor of the establishment Tyler had visited the previous evening.

"Perhaps we should leave," she troubled, "I dislike his seeing you so soon."

Tyler, interested in this new game, demurred. "How could he recognize me? He had so little opportunity to see me."

"I don't know," she quibbled, "but I don't feel good about this."

"Balderdash! Nothing will happen."

She clung to her misgivings. "We should leave. It isn't worth taking the chance."

Tyler gave a shout of laughter. "Not worth it? I never thought to hear you make such a statement!"

"The risk is great. Why can I not make you understand the danger of our mission?"

"Little could happen to me in an inn yard," he scoffed. "Besides, who would distinguish the Earl of Fairleigh in footman's livery?"

"Our plan has a fault," she worried. "A footman would not be seated inside the carriage of a lady."

"Well, I refuse to sit on the box. I won't carry this masquerade that far."

Belinda fidgeted, taking off and putting on her gloves. "Tyler, we simply must leave."

He caught her hand at a moment when it was bare and brought its palm to his lips. "Can it be that you've developed a *tendre* for me?"

"Don't be ridiculous," she spouted, but her voice was unconvincing and she was slow to remove her hand from his grasp.

Tyler moved to lift her heavy veil to better glimpse her expression.

"I can see that I should have brought Jenny," she said archly. "I mistakenly thought I was safe with you . . . in the daylight."

Before he could soothe her ruffles, his attention was drawn to the man she feared. "He's approaching a female."

Belinda leaned forward. "La, she looks like an innocent dairymaid, doesn't she?"

"Indeed. A very *pretty* one."

She stiffened.

"As dairymaids go," he added with a grin. "Don't be jealous, my dear."

"What?" she began, incensed.

Tyler cut her off. "I'm going out there."

"No! Wait!" Belinda clutched his sleeve.

He patted her hand. "Isn't that why we've come?"

She reluctantly dropped her hand. "Do be careful."

"I shall." Tyler stepped from the carriage and made his way across the cobbles, approaching the couple in time to hear his opponent's sleek offer.

"I really need the help," the whoremonger told her, "and you'll find that my rooms, food, and pay are the best in all London. I'll also clothe you and provide you with all your necessities."

"All fustian," Tyler butted in. "My lady has long been seeking such a maid as you, and she'll compensate you far beyond what this fellow can offer."

His adversary eyed him angrily. "Who're you to come pushing in on my business? I was here first."

"Nothing wrong with a bit of competition." Tyler smiled warmly at the girl. "Wouldn't you prefer working for a sweet lady, a *titled* lady, than for this ordinary city dweller? There would be a great many more opportunities for advancement."

"Well, I would like to be a lady's maid," she admitted.

"Then come with me."

She nodded. "Thanks for the offer, sir," she told her first would-be employer, "but I'd rather work for a fine lady."

"Excellent." Tyler started to escort her away, but his challenger caught his shoulder.

"Don't I know you?"

"I don't think so." He tried to turn away, but the man tightened his hold.

"Release me," Tyler growled.

The man narrowed his eyes. "I won't put up with no competition."

"Then maybe you're in the wrong business."

"No, maybe *you* are."

Tyler heard a soft rustle of skirts and veils behind him. Dammit! Why couldn't Belinda stay in the carriage and trust him to handle the problem? Her presence compounded the issue.

"Return to the carriage Ty . . . Tyson," she snapped. "I have no time for your dawdling chitchat!"

"Yes, my lady," he answered meekly.

"Come, child," she directed the girl more softly and spun away.

"Go on. Chase after your lady, if *lady* she be," hissed his rival, "but remember, the same goes for *her*, too. There's those of us won't stand no monkeying with our business."

Tyler returned his hard look and followed Belinda and the dairymaid, flicking an imaginary spot of lint from his shoulder. Only when they reached the carriage did he replace his cold expression with a frown. Belinda was right. This game was dangerous. It was the last time he'd allow her to come.

Inside the carriage, Belinda ignored her quarry and favored Tyler with her full attention. "Our mission is finished. I cannot allow you to continue."

"And *I* won't allow that son of a bitch—begging your pardon—to get the upper hand." He gritted his teeth. "I'll continue, with or without you, Belinda."

"Tyler . . ."

"The stakes have changed," he ground out. "There's more than the mission involved now. It's a matter of personal honor."

"Honor! Why must gentlemen become so aroused by some imaginary slight?"

"It wasn't imaginary, Belinda. It was very real."

She haughtily lifted her chin. "My lord, I *forbid* you to pursue this matter!"

"You have no choice, my sweet," he rejoined. "I intend to meet stages for the rest of my life, if I must, in order to give that bastard—pardon again—a good solid dusting in the dirt!"

"Tyler, I . . ." She sniffled, thrusting a handkerchief up under her veil. "I cannot bear it," she whispered.

"Don't concern yourself about me. I can take care of myself."

"If the parties concerned don't do it for you!" she burst out. "Why must you frighten me so?"

When he didn't answer, the dairymaid looked shyly from one to the other. "My lady, my . . . er . . . lord, please tell me . . . What's goin' on?"

Belinda stared soberly into the mirror, scarcely seeing her pretty image, as Jenny expertly whipped the brush through her long silky locks. Ever since Tyler had encountered Dryden, he had been totally driven to create as much trouble as possible for those businesses who tricked and held girls against their will. Against his wishes, she had accompanied him on most of these missions, but they'd had bitter quarrels about it every day. The time would come when he was recognized as the Earl of Fairleigh and then what would happen? He could be easily tracked and murdered. But Tyler wouldn't listen to her logic. He merely laughed it off lightly and assured her that he could take care of himself. *She* was the one who concerned him because she could not. Belinda was confident in her own disguise. No one could unmask her identity. After all, she mostly remained in the carriage. *He* was the one in jeopardy.

"My lady!" Jenny said loudly, jolting her from her fearful thoughts.

"I'm sorry," she murmured. "I was woolgathering. What did you want?"

"I asked how you wished me to coif your hair." Brush poised, the maid looked into the mirror, meeting her troubled gaze. "It's him, isn't it? You're worried about Lord Fairleigh."

"Yes," she breathed, "I am. I must stop his madness. I fear he's becoming too reckless."

"Y'can't stop him from meeting the coaches. He can do that on his own."

"I know, but the other enterprise . . . I try to withhold information about girls who wish to escape, but he always succeeds in worming it out of me by playing on my guilt." She sighed. "Oh, Jenny, I am so frightened for him. What can I do?"

"You're in love with him, aren't you?"

The room seemed to spin. Belinda's pulse throbbed in her throat. She snappily shook her head to clear the dizziness.

"You are," Jenny answered for her.

"What if I am?" she said sadly.

"If he was contemplating marriage, he might be more careful," the abigail offered.

Belinda groaned. "We've been over this ground before. Let's not discuss it again. Lord Fairleigh cannot wed a woman like me, and that's final."

"If he knew how you felt about him, the distraction . . ." Jenny's voice trailed off as she once more returned to assaulting Belinda's hair.

Distract him, Belinda thought, an idea forming. "Jenny," she said contemplatively. "Just leave my hair down tonight. It makes little difference under my widow's weeds."

The abigail eyed her suspiciously.

"And you needn't accompany me," she declared. "After this long, I believe I can trust Lord Fairleigh. He is such an *honorable* man."

"What're you up to?" Jenny asked flatly.

"Oh . . . nothing. Perhaps I'll do as you suggest and admit that I love him."

"You're playing with fire."

Belinda smirked. "Goodness, Jenny! First you advise me to tell him, and then you are reticent about my doing so."

"You be careful," the maid advised. "That man has a way with women."

She tossed her head. "We'll see. I may do nothing at all. I just haven't quite decided yet!"

"I have asked you to attend me tonight," Lady Fairleigh stated, "because I must repeat to you some ignoble gossip that has gotten well out of hand."

Tyler glanced at the clock and poured himself a glass of brandy. He was a bit early for his meeting with Belinda. He could afford his mother a few extra moments of his time.

"I suppose I am the subject of this tattle." He grinned, knowing that, this time, he was completely guiltless. His activities with Belinda's mission had kept him out of social circulation. Only certain peers knew of his presence in the brothels, and they weren't about to admit to it!

"Fire your guns, Mama," he said cheerfully. "There's not a man on the face of this earth more innocent than I!"

"I know that this must be total foolishness . . . that there must be a sound explanation, but the sources are impeccable," she said uncomfortably. "Therefore, I thought it mandatory to discuss the matter with you."

"Do come out with it, Mama. Then we can share a laugh, and I can be on my way."

The countess did not crack a smile. "You are accused, Tyler, of being in the process of establishing a . . . a . . . *brothel,*" she whispered that last, damning word. "And given your reputation, *people believe it!*"

Tyler struggled to keep his smile from fading and thus making himself look guilty. "How am I accorded to be accomplishing this feat?" He managed a laugh, but it sounded hollow to his ears.

His mother keenly eyed him. "Reliable members of the *ton* have seen you at coaching houses, recruiting and departing with country girls. It is further rumored—though no one would admit to the part of witness—that you have been seen at b-b-brothels, stealing women!"

He sat down opposite her. "My, my, what will society come up with next? Gossip must be thin this year, in order for such a tale to be invented! Needless to say, it isn't true."

"My own dear friend, Lady Compton, was witness to one episode. She vowed she saw you solicit a girl in an inn yard and depart with her!" She severely studied him. "Lady Compton is not a liar!"

"What was Lady Compton doing in such a common locale?" he asked snidely. "Acquiring girls for a similar project?"

"Tyler!"

"Well? It makes as much sense," he fired back. "Really, Mama, I can scarcely believe that you have detained me to confer about such folderol."

"Where there's smoke there's fire." She shifted to a more comfortable position, leaning against the sofa cushions and tucking up her feet.

Tyler easily fathomed the signs. Lady Fairleigh was preparing to wait as long as she must for a reasonable answer. She would not be fobbed off. Unless he satisfied her, she would make him impossibly late. With a solemn nod of assent, he delved into the entire unvarnished story of Lady Belinda's work.

During the tale, the countess's face transformed through a myriad of expressions from shock to humor to approval to censure. She interrupted him only a few times to clarify happenings. When he had finished, she frowned ever so slightly.

"This is serious business, Tyler. I applaud the mission, of course, but I can't help but wish that you hadn't become involved. Insofar as Lady Belinda is concerned . . ." She paused. "You are in love with her, aren't you?"

He caught his breath. "I am not entirely sure of what love is, Mama."

"It certainly goes beyond simple attraction. It concerns friendship and caring . . . One cannot imagine not spending the rest of one's life without the loved one. Do you feel that for Lady Belinda?"

Tyler didn't reply. Sometime in the midst of all this, he'd begun to feel all of those things for Belinda, and more. And he knew very little about her!

"I believe that you do," his mother softly pronounced. "What have you found out about her? Who are her parents? Why is a well-bred young woman engaged in such work?"

He shrugged. "I don't know. Foolish, isn't it? I finally find a lady I might wish to wed, and I know nothing about her."

"I shall ask about."

"No, Mama," he hastily said. "There is something dark in her past. I prefer to speak with her myself."

"But you said that she evades answering."

"Perhaps if she learns how I feel . . ." He set his jaw. "Whatever it is, it doesn't matter. My own past is not so pure."

"You cannot marry a fallen woman!" she cried. "That is probably the secret she's hiding."

"I don't care," Tyler avowed.

Lady Fairleigh sat up straight. "You must! What if you met her former paramour face to face? Oh, how awkward it would be! And I shudder to think what would happen if the *ton* knew the story! My dear son, you have the family name to uphold."

"Thus far, I haven't done a very good job of that."

"Then it is time that you remedied it."

"With Belinda," he said stubbornly. "She is the only woman who has fascinated me enough to contemplate taking such a step. If she, also, must shine up her name, then we shall do so together."

The countess wearily bowed her head. "With Belinda," she reluctantly agreed.

"You'll help us?" he asked urgently.

"To my utmost ability." She drew herself up with an obvious effort at happiness. "If she is the one, I shall lend you my total support."

Now that he had admitted to his true feelings, Tyler experienced a buoyancy he'd never known. "I'll talk with her tonight," he pledged. "By morning, Mama, you'll know if you're getting a new daughter."

Lady Fairleigh tried to smile. "I wish you the best of luck, my darling, but remember . . . There are other fish in the sea."

"Not for me, Mama. I have made my decision to wed her . . . if she will have me."

After a brief stop at her charitable institution, Belinda directed her coachman to Tyler's house. Her guilt was almost palpable. That very evening, they had received another desperate message from a poor, enslaved girl. As a result, her determination to avoid placing Tyler in further jeopardy wavered. Perhaps one more time?

Alone in the darkened coach without Jenny's opinion to seek, Belinda trembled. No, she couldn't put Tyler in danger. The mission was ended. At least, his physical part in it was. Through him, she might find another participant, but he must never again set foot in another one of those detestable establishments. If she could hold her tongue, she wouldn't even tell him of the girl's plight. They had saved any number of girls. For now, that must be enough. Belinda threw back her widow's veil and shook out her hair. Seeing her thus, her raffish Tyler might be so distracted that, even if she blurted out the truth, he wouldn't hear it.

The carriage drew abruptly to a halt. Her mind so occupied and her stomach so quivering with butterflies, she didn't note the sounds or jarring of a commotion on the box until the door was roughly jerked open. A man grabbed her wrist and yanked her toward him.

"C'mon m'lady! Yer comin' with us."

Belinda screamed and pulled back, but her assailant had a stout grip on her.

"Yer comin'!"

"Cease this at once!" she gasped, reaching for her reticule. "I am a poor widow. If it's money you seek, you may take what I have, but leave us in peace!"

"We'll take that, too, but we want you the most." He tore the purse from her hand, tossed it to an unseen accomplice, and dragged her from the vehicle.

"What can you want of me?" Belinda tried to dig her heels into the cobblestones. "I am only a—"

"You've been pokin' yer nose where it don't belong and costin' money for them who needs it," he growled. "This'll teach you to leave the girls alone!"

"Costing money!" Belinda scoffed, managing to draw back her foot and kick him hard in the shins. "There are enough willing girls to satisfy your employer's needs. Let me go, I say!"

The man screeched with pain. Momentarily, he loosened his grip, but before Belinda could react, his partner caught her and bundled her into another coach, leaping in after her. He held her fast while the first man, recovering from her assault, joined them, adeptly tying her hands and feet.

"Now she can't cause us no trouble!"

"Please," Belinda tried to reason. "I can pay you for my freedom. I promise you that I'll meet whatever your employer is giving you."

"Trust you?" Her injured captive let loose a string of expletives. "Dryden'll handle you!"

Dryden? Belinda's fear reached fever pitch. She might have been able to deal with another female, but Dryden? She pictured his pinched, evil face. She'd had a horror of what he might do to Tyler. How had he found out about her?

"That scare you?" The man leered into her face. "He's got big plans for you, lady."

"How did he learn of me?"

"One of the girls." He spat into the floor of the filthy conveyance. "They all know about you. Wasn't hard to work the truth outta one of them, once Dryden got on the right track."

No, Belinda thought sadly. It wouldn't be difficult to coerce one of the willing participants of the enterprise.

Both men looked at each other and laughed. "Dryden's gonna see how *you* like workin' for him. Who knows, m'lady? You might have fun!"

"He cannot force me!" she cried.

"No? We'll see about that. Dryden's got ways."

"What kind of ways?" Belinda probed frantically.

"Jest you wait." Their laughter seemed raucous enough to echo through the entire city.

Tyler waited. And waited. And still the coach did not come.

He wondered if Belinda had changed her mind, but she surely would have let him know, even though she'd been against this further mission. Then again, perhaps she would not. This might be her way of preventing him from further participation. Well, he wouldn't allow her to get away with it. He knew that the time was fast approaching when he'd be unable to enter the houses without courting danger, but he certainly planned to continue to aid his wife in the mission after they were wed. Irritably, he called for his carriage and set out toward her house of charity. When he inquired within, the attendant immediately became distraught.

"My lady has gone to fetch you, my lord. She left nearly an hour ago!" She narrowed her eyes. "You were in the right place, weren't you?"

He nodded, frowning.

"Then—"

Tyler cut her off. "Do you know what streets she may have traveled?"

Her blank look told him all he needed to know. Somewhere between here and Mayfair, something had happened to Belinda. He prayed it was only a broken carriage part or harness, but inside he feared the worst.

So did the attendant, her expression changing to one of horror. "Dryden," she whispered. "My lord, please! You must find her! We need her desperately!"

As do I, Tyler thought, though for an entirely different reason.

"Our poor sweet lady," the woman wept. "When I think of what they might do to her . . . Oh, Lord Fairleigh, you must save her!"

"I shall," he said grimly and left her.

Luckily, it was not difficult to locate Belinda's coach. Tyler spied it pulling slowly from an alley not more than a few blocks from the house. Rapping on the roof of his carriage, he leapt out before it drew to a halt and dashed toward Belinda's servants who slumped groggily on the box.

"M'lord!" they simultaneously cried with relief and continued to speak together with differing words.

"One at a time!" Tyler commanded. "Where is Lady Belinda?"

"Accosted, we was, by ruffians," the footman mumbled, pressing his wadded neckcloth to his temple to staunch a bleeding wound. "Tried to fight 'em off, but they was armed. They took our lady."

"Did you recognize any of them?"

"No, sir." The coachman rubbed a bruised jaw. "Heard the name Dryden though."

"Dryden," Tyler repeated. "You are certain of this?"

"Swear it on my mam's grave."

"Did you see which direction they took?" he queried.

They shook their heads. "Knocked us cold, they did," spat the footman. "We just come to and was going to His Grace."

"His Grace?"

"Duke of Westingham," the coach man said somewhat impatiently. "M'lady's papa."

"Westingham," Tyler breathed. "Good God."

"Don't know as he'd do anything though," sourly added the footman.

"Why not?" Tyler set aside the question that might solve the mystery of Belinda. "Never mind. There isn't time for that. Go home, but say nothing of what has happened to your lady. I'll fetch her home."

They soberly nodded. "Yes, m'lord. We'll try to keep mum, but Jenny'll have to know if she sees us come back."

"Then tell her to hold her tongue." Tyler returned to his own conveyance. "A brief stop at Fairleigh House," he told his minions, "then we'll be going elsewhere. And bring that big brawny stable boy along."

They stared at him with barely concealed surprise.

"Yes, there could be danger." Tyler entered the coach and sat down heavily. Dryden! How had he learned of Belinda's role in the game was anyone's guess. But London's underworld was just as gossipy as the *ton* and sometimes that prattle bore truth.

Tyler's next thought was of the Duke of Westingham. Belinda's father! Far from aiding in solving her mystery, it muddied it even further. The arrogant, old curmudgeon was as straitlaced as he could be. Why was his daughter involved in this work?

He shook his head. There was time enough to unravel the matter. Belinda's safety was foremost now.

Arriving at Fairleigh House, he hastened to his room and summoned his valet. "Quickly fetch me some of the servants' attire. Nothing too fine, but nothing too shabby either. I don't wish to appear penniless."

The man gaped, but hurried to carry out the order.

Dressed in what he considered deplorable attire, Tyler went

to his library and lifted a case of dueling pistols from his desk drawer. Carefully loading each one, he thrust them into his belt. Dryden was dangerous and so were his henchmen. Tyler's disguise could not conceal his famous good looks, if a man gazed straight on at him. The weapons might have to be used. With a deep breath, he left the room.

Still bound tightly, Belinda chafed as her captors unloaded her from the carriage like a sack of meal and carried her through the back door into Dryden's gaming establishment and down a long, dimly lit hall. They set her on her feet in front of a door and rapped loudly.

"Come in!" came a shout from within. "Hell's fire, d'you think I'm deaf?"

The ruffians pushed her inside. She stumbled, blinking at the sudden bright light. "Release me immediately!" she ordered.

Her captors eyed their employer.

"Do it, but keep up your guard," Sam Dryden commanded, then smiled brilliantly. "So, my lady, at last we meet formally."

"Formal? Ha!" raged Belinda, rubbing her raw wrists.

"You're right," he amiably agreed, drumming his fingers on his scarred desk top. "This isn't formal at all. In fact, I foresee our relationship becoming quite *informal.*"

"When pigs fly!" Hands on her hips, Belinda defiantly stared at him. "Just what is the meaning of this?"

Her nemesis chuckled. "You should know."

"Oh? Exactly what should I be aware of?" she snapped, tossing her head. "I have been crudely abducted. That is all I fathom!"

"Cease your bluffing, woman. We both know that you are masterminding the plots to lure away female employees from my business and those of others."

Belinda angrily pursed her lips. "You are daft! I haven't the slightest idea of what you are talking about. You will release me at once and return me to my home."

He flashed her a nasty grin. "No, I don't think I'll do that. I intend for you to spend some time with us, here. You have behaved badly, Lady Belinda. Naughty girls must be punished, and I have always maintained that the punishment should fit the crime."

"I've done you no ill!" she said with bravado, but her stomach twisted nervously.

"Aah." He slowly studied her from head to toe. "Do you realize how much money many *gentlemen* will pay for the services of a virgin, especially for as luscious a little handful as you are, my dear?"

Belinda's pulse leapt to her throat. She changed her tactics. "Is it ransom you want?"

Amusedly, he shook his head and tilted back in his chair, sipping a glass of wine. "No, my lovely, it's *you* I want, but I suppose I must wait my turn. You're more valuable intact."

She forced a laugh. "How do you know I am chaste?"

"Bluffing again!" he chortled. "You may have your so-called charitable eccentricities, but you are also a duke's daughter and well guarded."

"You have it all wrong. I am a *disgraced* duke's daughter, and my parents care little about what I do. I am socially shunned for . . . shall we say, an indiscretion?"

"You're lying," he declared, but his smile faded.

Belinda saw her chance. "As a duke's daughter, wouldn't I have been wed long ago if it were not for an impediment? Would I have been permitted to engage in my charity work? I think not. I am used goods, sir. If you do not believe me, ask any member of the *ton* about Lady Belinda Kincaid!"

"I needn't bother. There are other ways of learning the truth," he leered. Righting his chair, he stood and strode round the desk.

"Don't come near me!" Belinda drew back, but her two captors caught her and held her arms.

"Throw her on the sofa," Dryden commanded. "We'll find out right now."

"No!" Belinda shrieked, struggling. "You're right! I was lying!"

The three men guffawed. Dryden picked up his glass from the desk and held it out to her. "Drink this."

"What is it?" she cried, turning her face away.

"It's wine, you silly bitch. Wine to calm you down so that we can discuss your future."

"You're trying to drug me!"

Dryden rolled his eyes. "Didn't you see me drink from this? Do you think I'd drug myself?"

"I prefer my own glass," she said airily.

"You drink this!" He jerked off her veil, cast it aside, and caught her by the hair, forcing her head backwards and holding the glass against her lips.

Belinda gulped.

"That's it." He freed his grasp. "Now, have it all."

The wine tasted cheap and raw, but it did ease her fear. She welcomed the calming influence. With her head clear of panic, she could logically plan an escape.

"More?" he asked her.

"A bit."

"Do sit down, my lady," he offered and refilled her glass.

Belinda sank to the sofa and sipped the fluid. A great warmth spread through her body. Her head suddenly seemed too heavy for her shoulders to support.

"I am drugged," she mumbled. "How . . ."

"Take her upstairs," Dryden said from what seemed like a great distance away. "Lord Harkins'll be here soon. He'll pay dearly for this one."

Belinda tried to resist them, but her limbs were too limp to cause difficulty. One of Dryden's henchmen carried her up a stairway and deposited her on a bed. She was vaguely aware of a woman undressing her.

"Tyler, help me," she whispered as she slipped into slumber.

* * *

Slouching and hoping he looked disreputable, Tyler entered Dryden's gaming hell, his brawny stableman, now armed with one of his lordship's pistols, at his side. He trusted that Jem would remember his part in the plot he'd concocted. The young man seemed bright enough, but he might not be up to the challenge of instantly changing the plan if things went awry.

"Well, Jem, we've entered unnoticed, now on to more." Tyler leaned against a wall in the deepest shadow he could find. "Fetch some blue ruin and begin to mingle. Find yourself a likely woman and bring her to me."

"Yes, m'lord."

"None of that," Tyler cautioned, looking about to see if any had heard. "Call me Frank."

"Yessir, Lord Frank."

"Lord *nothing!*" He wiped a hand across his perspiring forehead. "Jem, just don't call me anything. Remember? I'm merely your friend."

Jem bobbed his head. " 'Twill be hard, but I'll do it."

Tyler sighed deeply. "Very well, be about it."

Still, the man paused. "Sir, you ain't gonna hurt the girl to make 'er talk, are ye? I don't like men bein' rough with a woman, even if she's a 'ore."

"I doubt that will be necessary," he assured him, knowing full well that he'd do anything he had to do in order to find Belinda.

As the servant ambled away into the crowd, Tyler surveyed the gathering. As usual, there were a number of gentlemen he knew and who would recognize him immediately, disguised or not. Choking back a groan, he spied Sir Kenneth Justice chatting with Howard, Lord Harkins, near a faro table. Tyler turned slightly away from them and shrank against the wall. If either of those two saw him, he'd never come up with a reasonable explanation of his attire.

Consistently noting the two rakes' location, he next saw that blackguard, Dryden, approach them. The three spoke fervently, Harkins visibly revealing excitement. With an irritable shrug, Sir Kenneth strode off. Harkins grinned after him and slowly walked off with Dryden. They halted at the bottom of the stairs, seeming to be in the act of striking a bargain.

Tyler frowned. Something strange was afoot. Dryden apparently had offered the two a treat, but only Harkins had been able to dance to the tune. Could the offering be Belinda? Bile rose up into Tyler's throat. There was only one way to find out, and he must do it quickly. He moved away from the wall.

"Sir Kenneth," he greeted, approaching the baronet.

"Fairleigh!" He squinted. "What the hell are you doing in such apparel?"

"Slumming, as one might say." Tyler winked. "Came incognito to look over Dryden's crop of beauties."

Sir Kenneth raised his quizzing glass and wrinkled his nose. "Good God! You even smell the part!" He eyed him suspiciously. "I'll wager you've come to steal ladybirds. Tell me, old friend, when will you open your stable for business? The whole *ton*'s whispering about it!"

"You'll be the first to know," Tyler promised. "Any good stock present here tonight?"

"You've missed the jewel, but you couldn't have gotten away with her, anyway," groused Sir Kenneth. "She's not even on display. Dryden's peddling her himself. Priced me right out! She's one of a kind, if you know what I mean, but not for long. Harkins'll take care of that. Sweet little maidens are his specialty. He'll pay dearly for them."

"Indeed." Tyler struggled to keep the rage from his voice.

"A man could make a mint supplying Harkins's pleasures."

"I suppose he could." Wishing he could knock Sir Kenneth's teeth down his throat instead of giving him a friendly pat on the shoulder, Tyler took leave of him and passed through the crowd, glancing about for Jem. Certain that Belinda must be "the jewel," he had to make his move now, with or without the assistance of the sturdy servant. He finally spotted him far across the room, but it was too late. Dryden and Harkins were ascending the steps.

"Come on." He caught the arm of a buxom brunette. "Let's go upstairs."

"Lawks! Yer a lusty one!" she giggled. "Won't you even buy a lady a drink, first?"

"You've probably had enough already."

"Not so much that I can't give *you* a good time," she pouted flirtatiously.

"Do you want me or not?" Tyler demanded, hoping she wouldn't turn him down. He needed her presence to act as a cover for his ascent.

"Aw, all right. I don't think you'll be much fun, though, even if you are so handsome it should be against the law." She tucked her arm through his. "Maybe we'll have a drink later."

"Maybe so."

They reached the stairs as Dryden and Harkins gained the upper floor and turned to the left.

"Hurry up." He half-dragged the ladybird up the steps.

"Gawd, yer in a hustle!" she complained.

As they gained the upper floor and he moved to follow the men, the brunette planted her feet. "My room's the other way."

"Dammit." At the sound of her voice, he saw Dryden stop and begin to turn. Quickly, he twirled the tart against the wall, and with the back of his head toward Dryden and Harkins, sought her mouth.

"Lawks!" blurted the girl, before he expertly silenced her.

The kiss, which previously might have been rather enjoyable, had no effect on Tyler. His lady of the night might be unlettered, but her breath was sweet with wine and her skill nearly matched his own. He wouldn't, however, trade it or any like it, for the taste of Belinda's soft lips. If he'd had any doubts about settling down to one woman, this moment had proved it. Only Belinda could ultimately satisfy him now.

As the girl slipped her arms around his neck and melted against him, he heard a door open and shut. He abruptly raised his head and pushed her away. Whirling, he met the shocked gaze of Dryden.

"Fairleigh! Why you . . ." He started forward.

Tyler rapidly closed the distance, grasping the larger man by the shoulders. "Where is she?"

"You're too late." Dryden smiled widely before the earl's fist cut up under his jaw, closing his mouth with an audible clack.

"Bastard!" Dryden, mouth bleeding freely from a bitten tongue, aimed a connecting blow to Tyler's eye.

The two men fell grappling to the floor. It was not a fight of which Gentleman Jackson would have approved. Kicking and gouging had no place in a gentlemen's bout. In fact, Tyler was beginning to wonder if he were going to emerge victorious, when the big man was suddenly removed from him and bashed like a rag doll against the wall.

"Thought you looked a bit poorly, m'lord," Jem remarked, rubbing his knuckles as Dryden slid unconscious to the floor.

"There's still one more." Tyler jumped to his feet and dashed to the door.

"Allow me, sir." Jem took a run and burst through the barrier.

In the act of undressing, Harkins squealed like a frightened pig. "What is the meaning of this?"

"This bird ain't for you," Jem stated.

"I paid good money, you bully boy! I shall . . ." His gaze fell on Tyler. "Fairleigh! What in God's name?"

"Out ye go!" Tyler's servant grasped Lord Harkins by the waistband of his trousers and hoisted him toward the door.

"You know nothing of this," Tyler warned, "or we meet at sunrise."

Harkins, not noted for his courage, gaped.

"Nothing," Tyler underlined.

"No, Fairleigh, nothing." He chewed his lip, casting a baleful eye at the earl. "Could I . . . er . . . fetch my clothes?"

"Later. For now, you'll wait in the hall."

"I'll watch 'em both, m'lord," Jem grinned.

With a nod, Tyler entered the room. "Belinda?"

Curled up under the sheets, she drowsily opened her eyes. "Tyler! I knew you would rescue me." She started to sit up, then thought better of it when the linens slipped, revealing her state of undress. "My clothes!"

"You look even more lovely without them, my love," he said wickedly.

"You are the most . . ."

"I know. I am the most lecherous, wanton beast who ever existed, and who also happens to be very much in love with you."

"You are?" she murmured, eyes wide.

"Yes, madam, and I am going to marry you." Wrapping her up in the bedclothes, he lifted her into his arms.

"I can walk!" she protested. "And I have to find my clothing."

"There isn't time. Neither can you walk, Belinda, because you've been drugged," he asserted. "Must you always dispute me?"

She yawned and dropped her head to his shoulder. "No," she whispered.

Tyler hastened to the door. "Fetch your clothes, Harkins, and bring them to the hall. You can dress here and be on your way. I'll remind you, once more, to hold your tongue. The woman you were to seduce is a lady whom Dryden abducted. That rather makes you an accessory, doesn't it?"

"I won't blab! I just want to leave!"

"Then be about it." He turned to Jem. "Pull Dryden into the room, tie him, and gag him. Rip some of the bedding to do it. And you . . ." He glanced at the ladybird, fished in his pocket, and tossed her a gold guinea. "Tie and gag her, too, Jem. Don't resist him," he cautioned the girl. "If Dryden awakens to find you captive, too, he won't accuse you for cooperating in this matter."

"Humph!" She bit the coin and marched haughtily into the room.

With Tyler's previous experience of escaping Dryden's establishment and Jem's outstanding proficiency of bashing doors, their flight was almost an anticlimax. Belinda slept through it all, arousing only when Tyler loaded her into his carriage.

"Where will you take me?" she asked, sharply shaking her head as if to clear the cobwebs.

"Home."

"Home!" she cried. "I can't go home like this!"

"My home," he told her. "My mother will be there to lend propriety."

"No, I cannot. She will be totally shocked!"

"Probably," he said dryly, "but Mama's quite good at bouncing back. Besides, you are the lady I intend to wed. She'll take you properly under her wing."

"I fear she will not. No, it would be best if you took me to my home for women." She took a deep breath. "I cannot marry you, Tyler, no matter how much I love you."

His heart lurched. "Why? Is there another man in your life?"

"No, my darling, there is only you." With a great sigh, Belinda snuggled against him and instantly fell asleep.

"Belinda!" He started to wake her, then decided to let her slumber. When she was restored to her senses, he could sort out her garbled statements. But there was one thing for certain. Nothing would force him to give her up. Belinda would be his countess.

"Mother, I have brought Belinda home," Tyler said, carefully laying his precious burden onto the sofa.

Lady Fairleigh stared disbelievingly.

"She was kidnapped and drugged by one of those who did not approve of our work," he understated, noting that his mother was dressed in ballroom attire. "You will stay at home this evening to lend propriety?"

She laid down her fan and began peeling off her gloves. "I have already gone and have now just returned."

"What luck!"

"Not really, Tyler. I left the ball because I was greatly disturbed." Spying the butler hovering by, she snapped her fingers. "Pour drinks for Lord Fairleigh and me, then fetch my smelling salts and some strong coffee. I intend to wake up this gel and see that she gets home."

Tyler positioned a pillow under Belinda's head. "I thought she could stay here. You could send a note to her parents, so they wouldn't worry."

"I doubt they'd even miss her, but we cannot risk keeping her here. Tyler, do you know whom we are dealing with?"

"I only just found out. Westingham . . ."

"And do you know what is the situation? Do you know *why* her parents have little to do with her?"

"No," he said flatly, "and I don't give a damn."

"Well, I do. That is why I particularly attended the ball . . . to question several of my friends about Lady Belinda." She sighed sympathetically. "That is also why I returned early. What I learned was altogether shocking. Tyler, you cannot wed this gel."

"I *will* do so. No gossip mongering batch of hags will stop me! Mama, you are . . ."

"She is right," Belinda whispered, tightly clutching her sheet and sitting up. "We cannot wed. I told you so."

"You also told me that you loved me, and God knows I love you!" he fairly shouted, setting his wine aside and kneeling down beside her.

"I do love you, Tyler." She gazed beseechingly at him, "but I would bring ruination upon you and your family, for that is what I am . . . ruined. I am not welcome anywhere. My parents barely tolerate my presence in their house."

"Because of your work!" he cried. "That is immaterial. In time, people will grow to accept it. And you, Mama . . ." He looked over his shoulder at her. "You promised to help. Your influence is enormous."

Clutching her glass, the countess stood woodenly, jaw muscles rippling over clenched teeth.

Belinda met her unhappy gaze, then turned her china blue

eyes on him. "Tyler, you must not hold your mother responsible for what she may have said, previously. She was not aware of the facts."

"Well, what in the hell are they?" he thundered. "I wish someone would tell me!"

Belinda smoothed his cheek. "In my Season, I fear I was terribly gullible and foolish. I thought I was in love with a certain gentleman, but he proved to be a rogue of the worst sort. At a ball, we slipped away into the garden . . ." She paused, inhaling deeply.

Tyler grimaced, looking away from her as he thought of the scoundrel who had touched her, kissed her, and taken what should have been his.

"You see, my lord?" she quietly noted. "You turn away. You do not want me now, even though . . ."

"You're wrong, Belinda," he stated, anxiously taking her hand. "I am not such an innocent either. My escapades far outshine your little transgression. There have been women before you . . . scores of them. Your one affair cannot hold a candle to mine. I wish to wed you, my love, and wed you I will!"

She gasped. "You would want me in spite of what has been said?"

"I cannot imagine living without you." He rose to sit beside her and hold her protectively in his arms. "Let the gossips say what they will."

"They will be wrong," she disclosed. "Nothing happened in that garden, not even a kiss. I suddenly realized what type of man he was, just before we were discovered. Nevertheless, I was compromised, but I *refused to wed him*. My father was livid, and my mother . . ."

The door to the salon burst open. "Causing me trouble again, are you?" Duke Westingham roared, stalking toward his daughter. "With another infamous rake!"

"I *do* beg your pardon." Lady Fairleigh rose imperiously to the challenge. "How dare you break into this drawing room like a common brigand?"

Startled by her presence, the duke faltered. "I heard from the servants that my gel'd been kidnapped, and something about this knave Fairleigh . . ."

"Are you addressing my son, sir?" the countess rallied. "People of gentle breeding refer to him as the Earl of Fairleigh, not as knave or any other disgusting epithet you may wish to hurl."

Belinda pressed her face against Tyler's chest, her shoulders heaving.

"Don't cry, my love." He stroked her hair. "I shall straighten out this matter."

She lifted her head, and he saw that her trembling came from laughter, not tears. "Your mama is a priceless combatant. I doubt I have ever seen Papa bested."

"Yes, she has become convinced to take our part, but I believe I'll assist." He kissed her forehead and stood. "Your Grace . . ."

"Be still, Tyler," Lady Fairleigh commanded. "I am not finished with this improprietous upstart. Our family lineage is much longer than that of this *churl*. We arrived with the Conqueror. The Westinghams, I am sure, were digging roots from the dirt at that time."

"Madam, my ancestors fought in the Wars of the Roses. I possess a castle . . ."

"The Fairleighs were influential in the making of the Magna Carta, and my son owns two castles."

"One is in ruins," Tyler expounded. "Duke Westingham, may I have the honor of . . ."

"In spite of your peasant blood," Lady Fairleigh went on, "my son wishes to wed your daughter."

"He'd better! I've never seen such compromise!"

"They are *in love!*"

Both combatants suddenly halted their discourse and stared at Tyler and Belinda.

Finally, the duke pursed his lips. "I believe I must reveal the unfortunate affair that involved Belinda."

"We already know the full story," the countess replied. "Do you? Do you know what an unscrupulous fellow you tried to force Belinda to marry? He should have been thrown in gaol! Instead, you have treated *her* as the villain. What an old fool you are!"

"Enough!" Tyler stepped between the two. "Let us put that occurrence . . . and family history . . . behind us. Belinda and I wish to be wed. With your permission, Your Grace?"

"Of course! I didn't expect . . . Of course! You have my blessing."

"Then it's settled." Lady Fairleigh clapped her hands with glee. "I shall use my considerable influence to stifle. You will do your part, Your Grace?"

"Well, yes," he muttered reluctantly.

"Then come, let us leave these two lovebirds somewhat alone while we discuss our strategy." The countess drew him across the room to sit by the windows.

"As a duke, my influence is the stronger," Westingham pronounced.

Tyler sat down beside Belinda and took her hands in his. "They'll eventually come to agreement. No doubt, they'll succeed in integrating us into the finest society."

"I truly don't care," she admitted. "We shall remain quite busy without the bother of a lengthy social schedule."

"Indeed," he grinned, "especially when we are alone at night."

"Tyler! You are most shocking!" She giggled, then sobered. "We will continue our work?"

"Of course, my darling."

She smiled dreamily. "With your resources and mine, too, we can do ever so much good. But there is one thing that will not happen again!"

"Oh?" he questioned.

"You will never again set foot in one of those horrible houses of ill repute. I simply could not bear it. I fear I shall be a jealous wife," she warned, "so clear your mind of all ideas of mistresses and the like."

"You, madam, will be enough of a ladybird for me. Besides,

we are quite scandalous already. We should do nothing to disturb our parents' efforts to cleanse our names."

"We shall behave with circumspection," she agreed.

"Except for this. Let us be improper just one more time!" Gathering her into his arms, he brought his mouth down upon hers in a deep, wholehearted kiss.

The atmosphere was suddenly silent, then vociferous protestations broke forth from across the room.

About the Author

Cathleen Clare lives with her family in Ironton, Ohio, and is the author of six Regency romances. Her newest Regency, AN ELUSIVE GROOM, will be published by Zebra Books in April 1996. Cathleen loves hearing from her readers and you may write to her c/o Zebra Books. Please include a self-addressed stamped envelope if you wish a response.

The Schooling of a Rake

by
Monique Ellis

The Genuine Article

Kate Watford sighed, crossed her arms on the sill of the barred schoolroom window, burgundy merino dress tucked around her legs, gray shawl snugging her slender shoulders, her eyes red-rimmed as she stared across the sodden landscape. It had been the most miserable two weeks of her entire eighteen years. Nothing but clouds on her horizon. Now the clouds were thicker and darker than ever, and she couldn't bear it.

Papa had been gone, which was bad enough, leaving her to deal as best she could with Mama and Portia. That was poorly under the best of circumstances. These had been the worst. Housebound by rain three days out of four. Mama vaporish. Portia complaining incessantly that none of her beaux came courting in the wet.

Worse yet, Gram Watford—Kate's customary refuge—had been confined to her bed, feeling every minute of her seventy-six years and totally out of charity with independent chits who considered horses more interesting than men, and boys definitely less objectionable than prissed-up misses who thought being "out" made them only slightly less important than God.

All that was bad enough, though not uncommon when Papa went to London leading a string of well-schooled Twin Oaks hunters to Tatt's for auction.

But why had Mr. Prohl had to come upon her exercising Hades on one of the few fine days? And managed to grab Hades's cheek strap and force them home, reading her a bear-garden jaw across four fields while the great black jibbed and snapped at the bit, eyes rolling, ears flat against his noble skull?

The pompous noddy had refused to believe Papa charged her with exercising the pride of the stables. He hadn't even believed Mick McReedy, Papa's head groom. He hadn't believed anyone.

Instead, the vicar'd prosed on forever about it's not being in God's plan for females to ride powerful stallions, especially astride. He'd even had the temerity to cite Portia as the model on whom Kate should pattern herself while Roger Appleby from Three Mile Farm listened with a hint of approval in his eyes. Roger, who—before Portia grew bumps—thought Kate as perfect as a girl could be, and the best horseman in the neighborhood into the bargain. The snake'd said not the least word in her support until the end, and then only grudgingly after she'd sent a swift kick to his shins. That had seemed the unkindest cut of all, but there was worse.

Kate squirmed on the window seat, ignoring the Bible with its marked passages discarded on the seat beside her as she rested her rounded chin on her arms.

Mr. Prohl was one suitor Portia could do without, not that she intended to have him, or anyone in the neighborhood. Oh, no—Portia considered herself far above what Chilton had to offer. Worthy of a viscount at the very least. Silly Portia!

That Papa was the finest horse breeder in all of England meant precisely nothing. Viscounts didn't propose honorable matrimony to the daughters of horse breeders—not unless the horse breeder had a handle to his name, and did it only for fun. No, all a viscount would propose to the likes of Portia or herself was something quite dishonorable. Kate might not be out, but she wasn't totally ignorant.

She knew about rakes and lightskirts and improper suggestions—not the specifics, naturally, but everything Gram considered essential to her well-being given the sorts who often came to Twin Oaks in search of a hunter or two. London swells and titled gentlemen were what country girls avoided at all costs. If they didn't, they were given what was called a slip on the shoulder, ruined, and became ladybirds. Traffic with aristo-cratic types was as foolish, Gram said, as attempting to ride a half-trained horse, and could be equally disastrous. Maintaining a polite distance was essential.

Pattern herself on Portia, all airs and graces and simpers? Not likely!

But that's what the vicar'd insisted she should do. And es-corted her to the house trailed by Roger, propelled her into the parlor in her mud-spattered brown habit—there *had* been a gen-erous skirt over her breeches, no matter what Mr. Prohl said—and proceeded to lecture Mama on the proper management of daughters, quoting scripture as if he hadn't a word of his own to say, and holding Portia up as a paragon of pulchritude.

Mama had resorted to her vinaigrette while Portia simpered her pleasure—a compliment was a compliment, after all—and batted her lashes at Roger who, like every boy in the neighbor-hood, was dancing attendance on her whenever it didn't interfere with his more serious activities. Portia was all the fashion these days.

And Kate?

She'd been banished to the schoolroom for doing precisely as Papa'd instructed while Mr. Prohl offered to exercise Hades in her stead, and ordered Mama to send a message to the stables saying Kate was permanently banned from the filthy premises. Mama might not dare go so far as to entrust Hades to the in-sufferable vicar—Mick McReedy had the power to override any order of hers when it came to the stud—but she had forbidden Kate the stables. And exiled her to the schoolroom when Kate protested no one else could handle the heavy hunter, and Papa had charged her with his well-being, and the stables were prob-ably far cleaner than the vicar's study.

And still that hadn't been the blackest cloud.

Now Papa had returned. Moments ago. With a stranger. A most elegant stranger. Well-to-pass, from the looks of him. They'd gone directly to the stables. Kate had watched from the schoolroom window, dread gripping her heart. She'd been right.

Hades was being lead out. Kate knew what that meant. Guineas changing hands, and Hades, who was her special pet and the best of their breeding stock, gone.

Oh, Papa might reserve the right to have the great black service the Twin Oaks mares, but it wouldn't be the same. Not the same at all.

The stranger could just take himself and his elegant London togs and his guineas back to London.

Only he wouldn't. He'd purchase Hades, just to boast he owned him. And leave with him. It wasn't fair, not fair at all. If she'd been a boy, she might at least've been able to make herself part of the transaction. But, for a girl? Impossible. Papa had promised Hades for her dowry if she one day wed a man who appreciated him, which was the only sort of husband Kate would ever consider. Only, the string Papa'd taken to London couldn't've brought as much as he anticipated, because now he—

Kate watched the big black toss his head at the stranger's self-assured approach. The rotter knew horses, that was certain, running a firm hand down Hades's arched neck and over his gleaming withers, then examining his teeth.

Bite him, Kate pleaded. *Kick him. Trample him, just like the others.*

But the big black, after a moment's uneasy confrontation, was playing the lamb, ears cocked, elegant head turning in inquiry as his hooves were lifted.

Tears slid down the girl's cheeks unheeded.

"Traitor," she whispered. "Traitor!"

The drizzle dripped from the branches of the rhododendrons and blackened the pair of ancient oaks topping a small rise beyond the stud enclosure.

Damnable weather, Richard Hawks grumbled silently, slapping his gloves against his top boots as he surveyed the neat stable yard with a knowledgeable eye. Chronicle Watford had a fine place in Twin Oaks. The gabblemongers at White's hadn't lied. Still, why he'd permitted himself to be inveigled into visiting this God-forsaken spot during a late cold snap remained one of the great mysteries of life—except it was no mystery, and he was the one who'd done the inveigling. Twin Oaks supposedly boasted, in the parlance of his cronies, a genuine article.

That genuine article stood patiently before him now his examination was over, neck arched, eyes bright with intelligence, breath fluttering his dark velvet nostrils. It even had a name: Hades, by Mephistopheles out of Hera. Quite the classicist, Chronicle Watford was, at least when it came to the naming of horses.

Contrary to Hawks's expectations, the enormous black hunter lived up to his reputation for perfection of line. A truly noble beast. If he moved as well as he stood, this one belonged in his own stables. He certainly didn't belong in the hands of a man who could only marginally be termed a gentleman.

"A fine example of horseflesh," Richard Hawks approved. "I might be interested, depending on the terms. How much?"

"For Hades?" Chronicle Watford's gray eyes twinkled as he scanned first the elegant Corinthian in his exquisite buff leathers and elegant hacking jacket of heathered tweed, then his prize stallion. "More than you can afford, Mr. Hawks."

"I've rather deep pockets," Hawks drawled, "as well you know."

"Not that deep."

"Come, Mr. Watford, coy doesn't suit. How much, if he lives up to his promise?"

"Like your freedom?"

Richard Hawks turned to face the grizzled, bandy-legged horse breeder he'd encountered at Tatt's four days earlier. The man had the look of a gnome about him, and a knowing one at that. Presumptuous bumpkin! Well, it served him right, traveling here on the strength of a rumor. Of course, rumor had proved amazingly accurate. This was a mount for which he'd gladly sell his soul, let alone part with a few guineas.

"I beg your pardon?" Hawks said, brown eyes hardening to agate.

"I inquired as to whether you cared for your freedom, sir, and the chance to live your life with no one to answer to but yourself."

"My tastes are of no concern of yours," Hawks returned as the black butted his shoulder demanding admiration and treats, "only my purse."

"Hades isn't the mount I had in mind for you," Watford protested. "Gentleman of your reputation, Mr. Hawks? You know your horseflesh—any breeder would, even an amateur such as yourself—but it wouldn't do. Wouldn't do at all."

"How much?"

"Hades comes high—higher than you'd be willing to pay, or able to, or than I'd be willing to permit. Too rich for your blood, believe me; besides which, sweetening him up in the stable yard's one thing. Riding him's another. Only two of us can throw a leg over with any assurance of not ending in the mud. Been that way since he was first broken to saddle. Even me he takes exception to on occasion."

Hawks's brows rose in polite disbelief.

Watford's smile was disarming, ingenuous, containing not the slightest trace of servility or anxiety to make a sale. Just—and this amazed Hawk—plain certainty.

"Satan's Folly'd be the mount for you," the man continued. "We call him Folly, as the other's rather a mouthful. A black like Hades, same sire and a fine jumper, never flags in the field. Best of all, Folly's a gentleman, unlike this rogue. By Mephistopheles out of Persephone. You saw this one accidentally, being brought back from shoeing. Forget him. He isn't for sale."

"Every horse has his price, and every man. Saddle this one," Hawks instructed the groom at the horse's head. Then, at the look of affronted shock on Watford's face, he appended more equably, "With your kind permission, naturally, sir. I'd like to try his paces, even if you refuse to sell. He looks a sweet goer. Beautiful conformation."

Chronicle Watford shrugged and nodded.

"For those he takes to, he's a sweet goer indeed. You can make the attempt, I suppose. That's not to say you'll succeed. I'd remove that fine coat, though, unless you're willing to risk it in the muck. Can't do much about your breeches, but then into each life a bit of rain must fall. Could be today's the one for some to fall into yours."

"Oh, come now. Hasn't been a mount could throw me since I was eight, sir."

"Be that as it may, this rogue's temper's uncertain at the best of times. Perhaps I should have the edge taken off him? Bit tired from the trip myself, but there's one who should've been exercising him, and apparently hasn't, who can do the trick in a trice."

Hawks glanced at the head groom. "How fresh is he?"

"Matter of a week, an' a bit more," McReedy mumbled shame-facedly. "Not Miss Kate's fault, sir, nor yet be it mine," he protested at Watford's narrowed glance. "Vicar had words with Mrs. Watford. Caught Miss Kate and Hades out past Three Mile Farm. Brought 'em back by the scruff o' the neck. Treated me to a regular jaw-me-dead for letting her take him out, Mr. Prohl did."

Watford muttered something unintelligible, scowling.

"Miss Kate ain't been permitted nigh nor next the stables since he come preaching propriety," McReedy explained in self-exculpation. "Shut in the schoolroom, with Miss Portia coming the flirt with the vicar every chance she gets, and scoring off young Appleby into the bargain. I seen Miss Kate's face in the window sometimes, like now," he said, nodding toward the house, "but nowheres else."

"A girl rides this horse?" Hawks demanded incredulously. "And you intend she should take the edge off him for me? Then your vicar has the right of it. Why, the lass could kill herself!"

"Mr. Prohl hasn't had the right of anything since his first squall, your worship, begging your pardon," McReedy objected with a grin. "Hades is right choicy about them he permits in the saddle. Miss Kate and the master, and that's about it. Squire's son for a minute or two when the mood strikes. It don't strike often."

Hawks frowned at the groom's presumption. A second glance made him hold his tongue.

"Oh, sometimes his nibs'll let me aboard," McReedy expounded, "but not often an' not for long. Been fractious since Miss Kate been kept t'the house, which is why he ain't been rid. Three bad tumbles is enough for any man—even me. Don't let his sweet air muffle you. Softening you up for the kill, he is, and that's the fact of the matter."

"We'll see about that," Hawks murmured.

"Vicar offered hisself in Miss Kate's stead," the head groom continued, turning to his employer. "Don't fatch yourself, Mr. Watford. Didn't let him nigh Hades, for all I was that tempted. Thing of it is, vicar was sure to bring him in lame or worse."

"Tempted I understand," Chronicle Watford said. "Giving in to temptation, now that I could in no way—"

"I'd sooner let young Appleby have the honor of being tossed," the groom protested, incensed. "At least t'lad has a fine seat and velvet hands, for all there's nowt in his brainbox but egg froth."

"The opportunity to try your stallion's paces?" Hawks broke in on what threatened to become an interminable discussion of neighborhood personalities.

"Certain you want it?" Watford shrugged. "On your head be it, then. You've been warned."

He nodded to McReedy. Hades was saddled, his girth tightened twice after firm kneeings in his belly as a legion of stableboys gathered to watch.

"Nasty temper, I'm thinking," McReedy muttered, "for all he's acting the milk-and-water miss. Resents not seeing Miss Kate."

"My wife has a deal to answer for," Watford agreed. "So does that insufferable man-milliner of a—never mind that. Watch yourself," he cautioned Hawks. "Hades has the very devil in his soul when his dander's up, and it's up today and then some."

"Merely playful," Hawks countered, honor at stake, eyeing the black with anticipation. "He'll soon learn who's master."

"More like you will," McReedy mumbled.

"Open the gates," Hawks snapped, patience tried beyond what was acceptable. "I'll bring him to heel once he's run his enthusiasms out." Playful, he admitted privately, was a gross understatement. "Hold his head while I mount and adjust the stirrups."

What followed was, for the elegant Corinthian, ignominious at best.

Oh, it began well enough. The gates were opened. The countryside stretched ahead, benign in the misty afternoon light. Hades stood meek as a lamb while Richard Hawks mounted, perfectly cut hacking jacket stretched smoothly across his broad shoulders, his only precaution the discarding of his hat. Hades kept his ears forward while the noted sportsman adjusted stirrups and gathered reins. He waited until Hawks was comfortably secure in the saddle, flicked an ear. Then he commenced to play, ignoring the open gate and beckoning lane.

A few gentle cow-hops at first, just to show his mettle, and perhaps give his rider time to learn wisdom and dismount in the normal fashion. What followed was a blur, even for the stable crew accustomed to the black's tricks. In the end Hawks lay flat on his back in the mud, the wind knocked from him, staring disbelievingly at the sky as Hades whickered in mock concern and blew gently in his face.

It might have been a faint cheer Chronicle Watford heard, even so far from the house. If it was, he ignored it except for a twitch at the corner of his lips.

"You lasted two minutes," he approved, pocketing his watch. "That's better'n most."

"You bastard!" Hawks gasped into the hunter's face. "You unmitigated, clever bastard!"

"Beggin' your pardon, sir, but Hades's breeding's probably

better'n your own," McReedy protested, "and a deal more careful."

"You were warned, sir." Watford extended a hand to help the Londoner to his feet. "Perhaps now you'll listen."

"The devil, I will! Hold his head."

"But, sir—your coat."

"To perdition with my coat," Hawks panted. "No beast's ever gotten the better of me. Hold his head."

It took seven lessons to teach Richard Hawks he wouldn't be permitted to remain in the saddle that day. By the end of it Hawks was a muddied mess, sore from head to toe. And, amused. The black had shown infinite concern for his unseated rider each time he landed in the mud. They'd developed quite a bond by the end of it, torturer and tortured. That alone had been unusual, the stable crew'd murmured in surprise. The big stallion was indeed a rogue, just as Watford cautioned.

"I'll master that horse of yours, or die in the attempt," the Corinthian insisted, wincing as he limped to the house at the end of it, escorted by his genial and equally amused host. "With your kind permission I'll remain 'til I do, however long it takes."

"Didn't realize you intended to spend the rest of your days with us. No—no," Watford grinned at Hawks's protestations, "you're welcome to make Twin Oaks your home as long as you wish, but except for Hades you're likely to find our corner of England a bit dull. They all do, and they all give up in the end. You aren't the first to attempt it, you see, and you probably won't be the last to fail. A frivolous ambition, of course—to sit a horse that doesn't want to be sat—but there, I suppose if you fine London gentlemen can't find a challenge in life one way, you'll find it another."

The spacious low-ceilinged entry at Twin Oaks had a welcoming air of country comfort to it that more than made up for any lack of *tonnish* elegance. The dark paneling glowed. Brasses gleamed on the mantel. Bright chintz curtains were drawn against the inclement weather, a fire burning cheerily on the hearth opposite the stairs despite the lateness of the season. Lilacs and pussy willows stuffed in an ancient copper ewer made a showy display, echoing the curtains and spicing the air with spring.

"I will be comfortable in my own home," Watford chuckled as Hawks glanced in surprise from the fire to his host, "but I'll thank you not to comment on it. My wife complains it sets the housekeeping accounts to soaring. Holds to the old school: no coal to be burnt after March. Idiotish! Should be one blazing away in your bedchamber, as well. Have 'em in all the bedchambers, night and day."

"Never took you for a sybarite." A crooked grin cracked Hawks's features as he dropped his portmanteau and cloak bag on the polished stone floor, limped to the fireplace and spread his hands to the welcoming warmth. "Condition I'm in at the moment, I'm deuced glad you are, however."

"A man should have his comfort. But there—if Mrs. Watford wasn't complaining about the accounts, she'd natter about spending the spring in London. I'd much rather she complain about the accounts. With those I can play generous husband. Convince her London is damnably uncomfortable and smells of bad drains and worse? That she'd be cut left and right, as I'm not considered a gentleman except in the country? Worse yet, hint she wouldn't have the slightest notion how to go on? You try it!"

"Don't think I'll make the attempt."

"Quickest way into her bad graces, if you've ever a need of discouraging her pretensions, which you may. That, or playing hail-fellow-well-met with my mother. She's kept to her bed the past week according to McReedy, so you're not likely to see her at first. Unfortunate, for she and Kate're the best of us. Rain and cold set her bones to complaining, which is why I insist on fires and my wife detests 'em—or claims she does. The ladies have to natter on about something or they're not content."

"I've noticed that proclivity myself."

Watford eyed his fashionable London guest, brows furrowing. "So I've heard tell," the stud owner said after a moment's consideration. "Chloe deSaules—she's your latest, according to the gabblers. Oh, yes," he continued at the Corinthian's arctic glance, "we hear of such things, even so far from Town. My mother's followed deSaules's career for years. Quite the famous figure. Thing is—" Watford flushed uncomfortably even as his eyes speared Hawks. "Well, you do have a certain reputation," he almost apologized. "Haven't mentioned it, but I have two daughters. Eldest's not up to snuff, though she thinks she is, and a diamond of the first water into the bargain, which she isn't by any stretch. Bit above common's all. The other?"

Watford broke into a smile so warm, so loving there was no way Hawks could take offense.

"Kate, now, she's not like Portia. More boy than girl at the moment, and curses heaven she isn't one. You want to amuse yourself flirting with Portia, I haven't any objection. Just don't turn her head too far, or I'll never get her married off.

"My Kate's another matter. You leave her be. Still more or less in the schoolroom, thanks to Mrs. Watford insisting Portia be wed before her sister's set free. Even if she wasn't, she's not for the likes of you, but I know how you fine London gentlemen're tempted by a pretty face. I won't see my Kate made a May game of, nor yet caused a moment's uneasiness, you understand me?"

"I do indeed."

"I have your word on it? Don't like to ask, but there, Kate's special, and you do have a reputation. Wouldn't like to see you upholding it at her expense."

"You have my word, sir." Hawks broke into a slow smile. "The child shall come to no harm in my company, nor shall she know a moment's disquiet. Aside from the fact that I've no taste for the infantry, I'd never so abuse your hospitality."

"Good. Wouldn't want to have to take a crop to you. Not the thing with a guest. Even I know that."

"She's the one rides Hades?"

"Astride," Watford confirmed proudly, "which is the only way to handle him, and has the vicar in a snit, for all she wears is a split skirt over some of my old smalls. A priggish old maid, Mr. Prohl, without the least spark of imagination, rather less than that of intelligence, and forever poking his nose where it's not wanted. Very long nose, Mr. Prohl has. Courting Portia, which'll tell the tale once you meet her.

"Well, here's Molly with cans of hot water, and Joey to clean your boots and brush your coat and see what he can do about those leathers. Sorry I can't offer you a valet, but I don't hold with unnecessary servants at the house. Joey'll see to you well enough, for all he's naught but a potboy. Sees to me when I've a need of it."

"I'm sure he will," Hawks agreed, eyeing the scrap of black-eyed humanity staring at him in awe from across the entry.

"You stuck on Hades two whole minutes!" the boy said, assuming he'd had all the introduction required. "Ain't no stranger never done that. But lawks, you do be muddied."

"I am indeed," Hawks agreed, breaking into his lopsided grin. "Think you can set me to rights?"

"Do my best, sir. If I can make pots sparkle like Mrs. Breede in t'kitchens wants, should be able to do the same by you. She's that fussy. Them boots be a mess, though. You looks a proper bog-trotter, an' that's the truth."

"I'm quite aware of it. Hades and I are equally tenacious, even if he's the more successful at the moment. Let's see what we can do about regularizing me, shall we?"

"Molly," Watford broke in, turning to the red-cheeked country girl lugging two copper cans of steaming water, "put Mr. Hawks in the front chamber at the end of the hall, air the bed and see the fire's well built up. Don't want our guest taking a chill. I'd best inform Mrs. Watford we have company. Kate confined to the schoolroom?"

"Since Wednesday last, sir. Even been taking her meals there. Vicar assigned her verses to memorize an' prayers to say on account of her sins. She ain't memorized 'em, and she stays until she does."

"Which sins this time?" Watford sighed.

"Pride, vanity, an' disrespect of himself an' God's will, sir. Happens every time you're gone, beggin' your pardon. There's them of us as wishes you'd speak to Mrs. Watford afore gallivanting again. Terrible, seeing Miss Kate penned like a nasty-tempered sow, which is what Mr. Prohl called her."

"That's over. Tell Kate we've a guest interested in a horse soon's you've got Mr. Hawks settled. I'll be wanting her in the parlor. No need for any fuss, though. Tell her that, too. She's to come as she is."

"A fine London gentleman, and unattached, and wealthy as he can stare, and you not sending word ahead!" Mrs. Watford wailed moments later, surging from the foam of shawls draping her solid form. "And me in rags and Portia no better, and no time to order new gowns or acquire a manservant or a lobster, and Mr. Prohl coming to supper—dinner, I mean—because there's a hole in the roof!"

"A hole in the roof?" Watford eyed the ceiling in dismay. "But I had a new slate one installed last year, same time's I had the stables done."

"Not our roof, Mr. Watford—the vicarage's. Portia, shift the fire screen. That blaze is turning me red as a common farmwife. Have you no consideration, Mr. Watford, building it up like that?"

"Bother the fire, Mama," Portia scolded. "Papa always does that whenever he enters a room. You should be accustomed by now. Papa," she continued, turning to her father in a swirl of lace and ribbons, "is he titled?"

"No, no title."

"Oh." Portia's shoulders drooped. "What's all the fuss, then?"

"Never you mind about titles, my girl," Mrs. Watford snapped. "He's the genuine article from what your papa says, and will get us to London. Summon Mrs. Breede. Dinner, oh dinner, oh whatever shall I do?" she moaned, plump hand rising to her brow as her eyes sought heaven. "Will he expect what they call 'supper' as well, d'you think? I haven't the strength!"

"Man's here about a horse, Mrs. Watford, not about Portia or new gowns, or even the vicar's roof," Chronicle Watford insisted as his elder daughter busied herself with following her mother's breathless commands. "Nor is he here about a lobster. No need for any fuss, just as Portia says, any more than there is when Squire Appleby sends Roger about a horse."

"No need for a fuss?" Mrs. Watford gasped. "Oh, dear Lord in heaven, help me! Naught but boiled mutton and stewed parsnips. I sense a palpitation. I shall take to my bed, that's it. Then he can't blame me. Portia shall play hostess, and he shall sit at her right. Then we'll see what happens!"

"Gentlemen don't tumble for country chits merely because they partner them at dinner."

"This case is different. Portia's not a country chit. She's a rose! Lobster—we must have lobster. And oysters. Nothing less is suitable. A London gentleman!"

"Not the least finicking in his tastes, Mrs. Watford, nor puffed up. Mutton'll suit him fine, just as it'll suit us."

"And Portia in an everyday gown! Good enough for Mr. Prohl, but a London gentleman? Go change your gown, Portia. The jonquil muslin you wore for your come-out. That may be fine enough, but only just. What I'll wear for supper—*dinner*—I've not the slightest notion, come to that, if I don't first transpire of moribundation. You see what comes of burning fires beyond time, Mr. Watford? Not enough brass for a proper lady's wardrobe, Mr. Watford—that's what! How you expect Portia to find a husband worthy of her incinerated in the wilderness I'll never know. And then, when you bring someone suitable, you do it in the worst way! Sending word to Mrs. Breede, and not me—and that only after you'd arrived—indeed! D'you want to ruin all Portia's chances? A rose blooms but once, you know."

"Should've 'incinerated' him at the inn," Mr. Watford muttered. "Should've left him in London, or had him bed down with McReedy. Should've 'moribundated' him with the chickens. Should've *given* him a horse. I'm a fool, that's what I am."

"What did you say, Mr. Watford? My fan, Portia! I feel faint. I've a megrim coming on. I sense it. Behind my eyes. My lavender water. It's on the table, Portia."

The parlor door opened. Kate slipped in, closing it silently.

Papa was by the windows, irritably snapping an old crop against his muddied boots as he stared at the closed draperies. Mama reclined on her sofa with the air of one about to stick her spoon in the wall. And Portia? She was playing nurse, posing in pretty concern as she dabbed lavender water on their mother's temples even though there was no one to admire her. Nothing had changed during her exile.

Kate gave a delicate cough. The three spun to face her.

"What are you doing here?" Mrs. Watford demanded querulously. "As if I didn't have troubles enough!"

"Scrubby hoydens who stink of the stable don't belong in the presence of ladies," Portia sniffed haughtily. "You look a variable dowd in that old dress, Catherine."

"The word's 'veritable,' Portia," Kate said sweetly, "as you'd know if you'd ever troubled to study your lessons. Welcome home, Papa. You wanted me?"

"Indeed I do, my girl," Watford beamed. "Come give me a hug!"

Kate sped across the dark floor to throw her arms around her father's generous figure as her mother and sister looked on with displeasure.

"I'm so glad you're back," she whispered in his ear.

Watford gave her a hearty squeeze. "Had an uncomfortable time of it while I was gone, I hear."

"Yes, Papa, and poor Gram's been confined to her bed so I had no one to speak for me who mattered. I'm sorry about Hades, but there was nothing I could do."

"I know, lass. He missed you sorely—almost as much as I did." Watford brushed a tendril of dark hair from her brilliant blue eyes. "You're pale. I don't like that."

"It's only all the rain, and being forced to keep to the school-room. Nothing to concern yourself about. I saw you return, you know. With a stranger. Who is he? What does he want? Not Hades, surely—not after the way the darling unseated him."

"Thinks he wants Hades, but you're right, Hades doesn't want any of him."

"Good! How did the sale go?"

"Not badly. We'll be able to eat over the summer."

"I'm so glad," she grinned. "I was quite worried, you understand, fearing we might be reduced to poaching in Squire Appleby's preserve."

"Catherine! Such matters are not for ladies to discuss," her mother reproved sharply, "nor are they for jesting. Brass is serious."

"Indeed it is, Mama," Kate returned sunnily over her shoulder, "which is why Papa and I joke about it."

"I shall never understand you," Mrs. Watford grumbled. "Don't encourage her, Mr. Watford. Mr. Prohl says—"

"The devil take Mr. Prohl!"

"Mr. Watford! He's a fine gentleman with a fine university edification, and knows what's proper and what isn't."

"What's his education to do with anything? Made him a fine fool, that's all."

"Besides, if the devil's to take anyone, it's you and those horses. Why you can't raise sheep or corn, but must instead concern yourself with—well, it's not gentleman-like, especially going to Town hawking your wares like any common tradesman."

"They've kept a roof over your head, wife, since the day we were wed. Think where you'd be without 'em."

"I don't like to think at all!"

"That's obvious," he muttered, "and always has been."

"Portia, my salts," Mrs. Watford whimpered with a martyred air. "Your father doesn't understand me at all, not because he can't, but because he doesn't want to."

"Papa, who's the stranger?" Kate interrupted with a pleading glance at her father. The old arguments about the stud and its unsuitability to the pose of leisured country gentleman always ended with her father storming from the house and Mama taking to her bed for a week if they weren't stopped at the outset.

"Hawks," her father grumbled.

"Richard Hawks? The famous Corinthian?"

"The same."

"And Hades tossed him, even so," Kate said with considerable satisfaction. "Beautiful, wonderful Hades! I shall have to take him an apple later."

"You'll not go near those stables!" Mrs. Watford shrilled. "That's been settled! Mr. Prohl is right about Catherine's unnatural proclivities, Mr. Watford, as he'll explain at supper, and quote scripture to prove it."

"Kate will go where and when I tell her," Watford returned, "and Mr. Prohl will keep his nose out of places where it's not wanted or I'll chop it off and have it served him sauced with mushrooms. And you, wife, will follow my instructions where Kate's concerned from now on, not his."

"I shall die!" Mrs. Watford wailed. "I shall never dare set foot beyond my own door again, and I shall take to my bed and transpire!"

"If transpiration's your wish, do so, though why you should desire to break into an honest sweat for the first time in your life I've no notion."

"I shall go into a decline," she continued determinedly, "and you will send me to Italy to recover, and Portia shall accompany me, and she will meet an Italian prince, and—"

"You will take to your bed here," Mr. Watford countered, "and Portia will walk out with the apothecary's son, and—"

"I shall not! And there's no need for Italy, Mama," Portia enthused, eyes glowing. "Richard Hawks? Why, he's the most dreadful rake in all of England! You've heard of him—you know you have. Just think, Mama, what a feather in my cap when he forms a hopeless passion for me. I shall refuse him of course, for I do want a title. I'm pretty enough to capture one, if only

Papa will take us to London. Only think of the Gunning sisters," mentioning the penniless Irish beauties of a previous generation who captured titles and fortunes on the marriage mart. "Once I've brought a famous rake to his knees, all of London will open its doors to me."

"Don't be silly," Kate said with a contemptuous laugh.

"Just you wait and see," Portia returned smugly, tossing her head to set her golden curls bouncing. "I shall have the *ton* at my feet, and a viscount at the very least."

"Mr. Hawks offers for you, you'll have your London visit, that I promise," Watford chuckled. "No need for him to stand the nonsense, and be jilted into the bargain."

"Oh, thank you, Papa!"

"Isn't going to happen, Portia," he returned flatly. "Only reason I said I'd do it."

"Watch me!"

It was an intriguing domestic scene that greeted Hawks when, restored to some semblance of himself, he braved the family parlor.

Portia and Mrs. Watford were resplendent in their best gowns, Mrs. Watford posed on the spindly tête-à-tête she'd added to the family furnishings upon her marriage. Portia struck an attitude on the sofa, head tilted, chin resting on fingertip with an air of perpetual pensiveness: Innocence Contemplating Depravity.

Kate curled in a window seat, ostensibly engrossed in a pamphlet on blood lines. She wasn't precisely hiding, but she wasn't putting herself forward, either. No delicate muslin gown with plunging décolletage for her. No fans or laces or jewelry—not that Mama would permit them in any case for fear she might draw attention from Portia. The high-necked, long-sleeved burgundy merino remained in place, gray shawl snugged about her shoulders. Enduring goose flesh didn't suit Kate, nor catering to the whims of fashionable gentlemen. There were distinct advantages to remaining a schoolroom miss.

She peeped from beneath her lashes as her father ushered the Londoner into the room. Mr. Hawks had cleaned himself up, which was no surprise. That he'd managed it without the aid of the valet he was certain to employ in Town was something of a surprise, and hardly to his detriment.

Good hands, Kate noted approvingly, and powerful thighs for all Hades had tossed him like a two weeks' babe. Excellent shoulders, too—no slope to them, and broad and firmly held. Regular, distinguished features, complete with a high-bridged nose, strong brows, close-cropped dark hair, and a firm, almost pugnacious chin. He looked able to hold his own in any company, which was a good thing given the nature of their household. Mama and Portia were bad enough. With *tonnish* buyers, Gram Watford indulged a bluntness of speech calculated to cow and discomfit. She generally succeeded. At least Gram wasn't present, anticipating the moment when she would put the London swell out of countenance. Still, it might be interesting to see what she made of him, and he of her. They just might, Kate conceded, reach an accommodation. Gram Watford didn't suffer fools gladly. Hawks had precisely the same air.

"Mrs. Watford and Portia," Chronicle Watford said, pointing to his wife and elder daughter, "and over there's my Kate. Up with you, Katie-lass. I've a fine London gentleman for you to meet: Mr. Richard Hawks, who's a member of the Corinthian set and has quite a pretty seat if you don't count Hades."

"Papa!" Portia moaned.

"Mr. Watford!" his wife gasped. "Stable cant in my drawing room? And I'm sure our Portia is of far more interest to a fine London gentleman than a mannerless, ill-favored schoolroom miss! Gold's all the rage, not ebony. This, sir," she said, fluttering her shawls and laces like a would-be Ophelia, and getting hopelessly entangled in the mess, "is Miss Watford, our eldest daughter, who is the sinecure of the countryside and well dowered into the bargain, and has every eligible in traveling distance fighting over her golden curls—not that she'll have a one of 'em, being destined for greater things."

"Oh, Mama, how you do exaggerate," Portia tittered, attitude discarded for the nonce, eyes rapacious as she examined Hawks. "Why, I declare—only slightly over half swoon at my glance. The rest merely flock to my side, leaving the other girls to mope. So pleased to make your acquaintance, Mr. Hawks," she fluttered, coyly extending her hand in the style of *La Belle Assemblee*'s illustrations. "An honor, I'm sure."

"Mrs. Watford," Hawks said, bowing slightly and putting first things first, "my thanks for your hospitality. I apologize for putting your household at sixes and sevens, arriving unannounced as I have."

"Oh, la, sir, 'tis an honor to be discommoded by a fashionable such as yourself. Please discommode us whenever it suits your fancy."

"How kind of you," Hawks murmured. "I shall keep your wishes in mind. Miss Watford. Miss Kate."

Portia's hand wavered, rose to cover a negligent yawn. Kate stifled a giggle, gave a curt nod, and remained as she was. The Reverend Mr. Prohl, who lurked by the mantel clutching a copy of Fordyce's *Sermons,* gave an incensed harrumph.

"Oh, yes, and Mr. Baltassar Prohl, our vicar," Watford gestured in afterthought.

"Mr. Hawks," this worthy effused, stalking forward to shake the Londoner's hand, "God's blessing favors your visit. Nothing would be more suitable than for you to remove the incitement to moral laxity that unholy steed represents. I only hope you will not be so disgusted by our lamentable rusticities as to flee Chilton before your goal's worthy accomplishment, and most humbly caution that should you come calling at the vicarage you'd find the leak in the roof distinctly unpleasant."

"Kindness everywhere," Hawks murmured, giving Prohl the briefest of nods. "I'll be certain to avoid the vicarage, in that case. How d'you do?"

Prohl gulped, eyes darting from the unforthcoming Londoner to his own hand flung out in greeting. Taking a page from Portia's book, he turned the gesture into something vaguely oratorical. "I'm certain such a knowledgeable gentleman as your-self, with your wide experience of the world and how ladies properly conduct themselves, can be of material assistance in a little discussion we're having," he toadied.

"Really?" Hawks's dark brows rose. "You overwhelm me, for I've but limited acquaintance with ladies."

He placed a slight emphasis on the last word, permitting his demur with its double entendre to hang in the air like a flung gauntlet. Kate's laughing eyes flew to the Corinthian. His an-swering wink had her blushing furiously. Naughty of him of course, but it was delightful to see Mr. Prohl discomfited. That the vicar most definitely was. No idea what to say. Not even certain whether it was his duty to reprove the top-lofty Lon-doner, calling attention to the solecism he'd just committed, or whether it would be more circumspect to pretend lack of com-prehension in hopes of later cadging a few pounds in service of his leaking roof.

Silence—and the roof—won the day.

"Mr. Hawks, won't you have a seat?" Mrs. Watford simpered. "Beside Portia, naturally. You'll be most comfortable there, be-ing closest to the fire, which I understand gentlemen value even if ladies do not."

"And spoil the charming picture she presents? That would be most uncharitable of me," he protested as Prohl bristled and inched closer to the sofa and Portia dimpled and batted her lashes and resumed her attitude.

"Why she won't mind in the least, will you, Portia?"

"In a moment perhaps, madam, begging your indulgence." Hawks strode over to the corner where Kate still pretended to read her pamphlet. "Miss Kate?" he said softly.

Interesting eyes, she decided, raised above the commonality of mud puddles by the golden flecks lurking in their depths, and the look of quick intelligence that didn't lurk at all, but proclaimed itself with the insistence of blaring trumpets. A touch of humor lurked in their depths as well. Good thing. He'd need it during the next days.

She set the pamphlet aside, rose and bobbed a parlor maid's curtsy.

"May I be of assistance, sir?"

"You're the lass who rides Hades?"

"I am indeed."

"He's your special pet, I'm informed?"

"We understand each other, sir."

"I'd be most grateful if you'd convince him I'm not an ogre in disguise, and quite worthy to try his paces."

"My power extends only so far. Hades has a head of his own."

"And it is precisely this sort of deplorable pertness;" Prohl scolded, bustling up and giving Kate a hard shake, "which we have been discussing, Mr. Hawks. If a gentleman requests a favor of a lady, it is not within the purview of maidenly decorum for her to refuse, as I'm certain you'll agree."

"Any request?" Kate demanded with a martial glint in her eye as she wrenched her arm from Prohl's viselike grasp and Hawks moved protectively to her side, scowling the officious vicar down.

"It is a female's place to submit in all things," Prohl proclaimed.

"Always? Oh, my," Kate said, eyes all wide innocence, "and I was so foolish as to believe Gram when she said there were certain favors a lady had not only an obligation, but a right to refuse a gentleman." She turned to Hawks. "I am sorry, sir, but what you request is entirely out of the question. Hades, like I, selects his own friends."

"I'll have to see what I can do about gaining both his friendship and yours, then," Hawks said too low for the vicar to overhear.

"You're welcome to make the attempt at least, sir," she murmured in response, eyes demurely downcast, as Hawks chuckled.

Hunter and Hunted

Two days passed: two days of grinding tedium for Hawks, relieved only by encounters with the pompous mendicant vicar, a lively discussion regarding the stud's breeding program with the younger daughter of the house, and countless stratagems to avoid the older girl's pursuit. Only in the stables could he find sanctuary.

They were two days of mortifying failure for Baltassar Prohl, unable to convince Mr. Watford that Kate should be severely punished, both for her effrontery in ignoring the Londoner's rights as a Lord of Creation and for refusing to subscribe to his own moral precepts. By comparison, the *tonnish* Corinthian's failure to open his purse at Prohl's repeated references to the sievelike properties of the vicarage roof was a minor annoyance.

For Mrs. Watford they were days of increasing frustration. Say what she might, imply what she would, she couldn't persuade Hawks it was his duty to wed and produce heirs in his likeness. Worse yet, none of her hints regarding the desirability of fragrant country roses for such pleasurable exercises penetrated his dull mind, however practiced his compliments and punctilious his attentions to both Portia and herself.

Watford watched the farce from the sidelines, involving himself only in so far as he showed Mr. Prohl the door each time he appeared, and curtly instructed the vicar to muck out his own stable for a change.

Kate, released from her prison, resumed exercising Hades with the elation of a Cossack and a Cossack's skill in the saddle.

Her rare encounters with the Londoner were interesting, even amusing. He did indeed have that sense of the ridiculous with which she'd first credited him. So long as the ownership of Hades was not at issue he proved an intelligent and interesting companion, but her days were hardly unalloyed joy.

Roger Appleby, incensed when she declined to present him to the famous Corinthian, abandoned her with many a bitter word to seek Hawks out for himself, accompanied by every neighborhood sprig capable of sitting a horse. Hawks, restricted to Folly, caught occasional glimpses of the young girl flying over fences and leaping ditches on Hades as if she were a centaur, and found himself envying her freedom and privacy. His own excursions about the countryside were plagued by a persistent gaggle of young blades anxious to claim his acquaintance while observing the cut of his coat, the angle of his crop, and the manner in which he doffed his hat when greeting the ladies.

The evening of the second day, tried to the limit and bored beyond endurance following an interminable and ill-prepared meal during which his hostess interrupted every attempt at rational conversation with vapid prattlings regarding fashion and fashionables and her elder daughter made heavy-handed attempts at flirtation, Hawks escaped to the Blind Hunter.

There he arranged for a stableboy to carry a letter to the near-by market town of Styne to catch the royal mail. She might detest the country, but his mention of a garnet parure as recompense should bring Chloe deSaules haring to Chilton. If that didn't, his references to the pulchritudinous Miss Watford would. Chloe disliked competition.

Then Hawks crossed the inn yard, intending to join the fraternity of the taproom, make his arrangements and drown his ennui. If the big black hunter hadn't been such a prize, he'd've made his departure that night. As things stood, he was determined to at least ride Hades, come what might, but he had to soften up the Amazon named Kate first. Cost wasn't at issue. Honor and pride were. He was working on it. At least she no longer scowled when he entered a room, though she clearly

resented his presence much of the time. He'd win a smile from
her one of these days, that he swore. It was, he decided, the
most unusual form of seduction in which he'd ever indulged,
and all for the sake of a big black hunter rather than a few hours
dallying in a woman's bed. A far worthier project, when all was
said and done, and far more challenging.

Hawks ducked his head to avoid the lintel, glanced about him
as he entered. The place was small as taprooms went, but then
Chilton was small as villages went. The usual fire burned on
the hearth, sending the usual sparks up the fieldstone chimney.
A long table in the center of the room was well occupied, as
were settles by the fire. He sniffed appreciatively at the aroma
of roast turkey—the Watford table had offered only inedible
Frenchified messes for three interminable nights—selected a
small table in the corner farthest from the hearth, and signaled
the buxom serving girl.

"Have you rooms to let?" he inquired as soon as she bustled
up.

"Sure and we do, m'lord," she dimpled, batting her lashes,
"but Mr. Watford's that respected for his liberality to them as
comes buying at Twin Oaks. What'd you be wanting a room
for? Miss Portia on the prowl?"

"My motive's for me to know and you to guess," he grinned
good-naturedly. "Send the landlord over when he has a moment,
there's a good girl."

She gave him an assessing look, perched on his knee with a
suggestive swish of striped skirts and a rounding of shoulders to
deepen her considerable cleavage. "No need to be askin' him,"
she whispered, hand smoothing the expanse of heathered tweed
straining across his broad shoulder, "if all's you want's a bit
of—"

"Not tonight, sweetheart," he refused without regret, easing
her from her perch. "Just a chat with himself, if you'd be so
kind."

"Spoilsport," she pouted, clearly disappointed the menu
didn't include herself.

Hawks smiled and shrugged. Country entanglements didn't figure in his plans. Certainly they didn't include bold barmaids encountered in stray corners, any more than they did marriage-minded English roses. Chloe, and the protection her presence would afford, couldn't arrive soon enough.

"And what'll be your pleasure this fine evening, since it ain't t'be your pleasure?" the barmaid demanded saucily, tossing her curls.

"Just a tankard of ale, and whatever you're serving for dinner. I'm sharp set. Must be the country air and country hours." Hawks dropped a coin in her cleavage to soften the blow. "And a word with the landlord, if you please."

He patted her rump to speed her along, then sprawled against the wall, arm thrown carelessly across the table's surface, fingers drumming restlessly as his eyes flicked over the rustic company. The usual squirish types. A worthy farmer or two. A village Methuselah, face crinkled like parchment, hunkered by the fire. Not a soul who wasn't ostensibly paying him no notice while observing his every move and word, eyes bright with curiosity. They knew who he was, all of them. He should've anticipated that.

And a flock of bucolic Adonises—the same sprigs who'd dogged his steps for the past two days. That, too, he should've anticipated. Nothing in the way of entertainment locally with the exception of this inn.

One of the lads—Roger Appleby, if he remembered correctly—rose from the bench where he perched with his chums. Hawks frowned him down, determined not to be importuned yet again concerning the arrangement of his neckcloth. Then, at Appleby's crestfallen expression, he gave an apologetic half smile as the rotund landlord arrived toting a tray.

"You've come about lodgings?" the man said as he uncovered dishes, effectively blocking the view of the rest of the room.

"I have indeed. A favor of sorts, you might say." Hawks came close to flushing at the landlord's skeptical glance—a most unaccustomed experience for him. "I've a young cousin in Town whose health hasn't been of the best lately," he essayed after attempting to clear his throat and failing miserably at it. "A stay here would be highly beneficial, don't you think? Fresh air. Sunshine. All that."

"And you're wanting a room for him?" The landlord's bushy brows soared. "Surprised you don't ask Mr. Watford. Glad to have the lad, I'm sure."

"Lady," Hawks corrected, neckcloth strangling him. "Not quite the thing."

"A cousin, you say?"

Hawks nodded, smooth words and tutored manners for once failing him.

"A French cousin, one might say?"

"No, she's as English as you or I, for all her name's French right enough. Old family. Norman." Hawks coughed at the patent disbelief on the landlord's face, his own reddening. "I'll need a room for Miss deSaules, and an adjoining cubby for her abigail. And a private parlor, if you've such a thing. For a week at the least."

"Don't know as we've anything would suit such a fine lady." The landlord's emphasis on that last word was as subtle, and as telling, as if he'd blared his doubts regarding her exact relationship to Hawks from the village steeple.

"I, ah, vouch for her respectability," Hawks came close to spluttering.

The landlord snorted, an assessing look in his eye. Finally he shrugged.

"The vicar don't hold with goings-on," he said. "Don't hold with 'em a'tall, and goings-on is just what you look like t'me. She's not what you say, Mr. Prohl'll sniff it out, and he'll make your life miserable, which I don't mind in the least, and my own into the bargain, which I do."

"How much?" Hawks demanded, certain this was the stumbling block.

"Fifty pounds, for your convenience."

"That's highway robbery!"

"For the rooms, the food, and my *in*convenience."

"I can stable her in Styne indefinitely for a quarter of that."

"Five miles, Styne is. And that's across fields, not by the road. Think on it. 'Sides, what's fifty pounds to a gentleman like yourself?"

"He's flown," Mrs. Watford complained after having her husband summoned from the stud offices, "and it's all your fault, Mr. Watford!"

The family parlor glowed in the light from the lamps set on the mantel. Portia sulked on a footstool at her mother's feet. Her best gown showed signs of careless wear—a spot of butter sauce from dinner, a touch of damp from when she posed fetchingly in the garden earlier. Kate lounged in her usual window seat well away from the center of controversy, the draperies drawn behind her, the window cracked to let in a whiff of fresh evening air.

"There's nothing here to entertain a gentleman," her mother continued, gesturing at the room, "nothing! And you made not the least effort to render yourself agreeable at table, Mr. Watford. Speaking of naught but horses. Interrupting each time I introduced such convenable topics as doings at Court. I was mortified. And having Catherine join us, when I'd told her specifically to keep out of the way. Why you insult Mr. Hawks with the company of a schoolroom miss and speaking interminably of the stud—which everyone knows isn't done as it's business, and business is not discussed at a gentleman's table—and ruining all our chances, I shall never know!"

"Kate's no schoolgirl," Watford protested from the door. "What do you expect? For her to eat in the kitchen? That's not how a daughter of eighteen's treated among the *ton*. It's certainly not how we treat our girls in the country. He'd wonder at it. For pity's sake, open your eyes!"

"And now he's gone," she moaned.

"Returned to London, has he?"

His wife sniveled in her handkerchief, caught between chagrin and pique. Chronicle Watford shrugged, shut the door with a resigned sigh Kate heard all the way from her window seat, and took a single reluctant step into the room.

"Well, I can't say I'm surprised, not the way you've been shoving Portia at him every chance you've had," Watford grumbled. " 'The roses are so beautiful in the moonlight, Mr. Hawks. Portia, do take Mr. Hawks to see the roses,' and not a rose blooming. D'you think the man's blind?"

"He is, if he can't see Portia's worth. As for London, if only that were all! No, 'tis far worse," his wife fussed, what she believed to be a turban sagging over one eye. "He's at the Blind Hunter, for Portia was watching for him in the garden, holding one of her most striking altitudes. She waved, just as I told her, and called to him—which I did not recommend, calling out not being lady-like—and stumbled to perfection, and Portia says he pretended not to see her and rode off in the direction of the village fast as his horse could carry him. Now she's ruined her gown, and 'tis all for naught. He'll be consorting with all the worst sorts, and not a soul in the neighborhood but will know she can't hold a gentleman's interest of an evening. Those who don't now will by morning. How I shall survive the opprobability I've no notion."

"Said he had an errand to run," Watford protested from by the door, clearly hoping for an early escape. "Left almost as soon as we'd finished our port."

"An errand? At this hour? A likely tale! Besides which, if we had sufficient house servants one could've been sent on his errand, and he'd still be here. Impossible for a girl to interest a man if he's not present to be interested. We must do something, or we'll be ruined."

"Hawks foregoing the purchase of a mount or two won't send us to the poorhouse," Watford countered with a long-suffering air.

"I'm not speaking of shillings! I'm speaking of our position in the neighborhood. How is dear Portia to wed if they think the London gentleman's bored with her, for then they'll decide they're bored with her as well, even Mr. Prohl. You must do something!"

Watford trod heavily across the floor, settled himself in his favorite chair, eyes flying to his younger daughter. Kate gave him a saucy wink, shrugged, and cast her eyes to the ceiling.

"Not sure what you expect," he said after a moment. "Want him chained to the table evenings, Mrs. Watford? Or would you prefer the chimney? Bit unusual, but I suppose it would serve to hold him here. Can't see how that would rouse his interest in Portia, but then I'm a mere man, and agreeable to most any suggestion within reason."

"I shall die!"

"Come, madam—beyond your customary vapors, you'll not suffer the least consequences. Y'never do."

"He ignores Portia!"

"On the contrary. He's shown Portia every courtesy."

"Too much courtesy and too little wooing—that's what he's shown her."

"He isn't interested in her, and that's a fact. He isn't interested in any woman of the respectable sort, and that's another fact. He's so far above our touch it's laughable—a third fact for you. Wish me to continue?"

"Portia is a diamond! Portia is a rose! Portia is—"

"Portia's a foolish chit who gives herself airs, madam, because you've raised unreasonable expectations in her. Nothing more."

"There's no need to be insulting, Papa," his elder daughter broke in. "Besides, why am I totally uninteresting to a gentleman worthy of my notice? Because I've never had a Season, there's a fact for you, Papa. Because I don't have proper gowns—another fact. Look at this old rag! Tattered and stained, that's what it is, and outmoded besides. Not worthy of the charity box. It's your cheese-paring ways and—"

"Enough!" Watford roared, driven beyond endurance. "You, miss, will take yourself to your room and consider the possibility that you're uninteresting because you've not an idea in your head, and no ability to do anything but strike attitudes that bear no resemblance to anything in heaven or earth."

"I won't be treated like a child," Portia pouted. "I'm a diamond, and far beyond the age of being sent to my room like some hoydenish schoolgirl."

"A diamond's precisely what you're not! Glass, more like. Off with you."

Portia tossed her curls, struck her favorite attitude for family quarrels—Martyred Youth Blighted by Uncaring Age—and remained precisely where she was.

"Mr. Watford, we must confer. The one to leave is Catherine," Mrs. Watford proclaimed, waving her hand like a distraught sorceress. "She has no business here."

Nothing loath, Kate jumped to her feet, tucking her book under her arm. Her father waved her back.

"As Hawks is here about a horse, Kate has more to do with him than Portia," Watford insisted. "She stays." He turned to his younger daughter, grinned. "Any suggestions on how to solve the problem, missy?"

"Mama's been speaking of a ball," Kate informed her father reluctantly, "only she says there's no place grand enough to hold one in Chilton, and Styne's too far."

"An evening party with dancing, at the least," Mrs. Watford snapped, throwing her younger daughter a furious glance. "The assembly rooms in Styne would be perfect if only they were closer. Flowers and an orchestra, and champagne as well as fruit cup. Less would offer insult. With a new gown for Portia. Her rags're past praying for—that's a fact for you, Mr. Watford. I'll require a suitable gown as well. That's another."

"Portia gets a new gown, then Kate gets one, too. Summon Miss Timmins."

Kate broke in, "Papa, I don't want a new—"

Her father's eyes sent their own message as he shook his head.

"No time for more, Kate, for which I'm sorry. And you stop hiding her away as if she were something of which to be ashamed, Mrs. Watford," he concluded, rounding on his wife, "because she isn't."

"But the ball would be for Portia and Mr. Hawks. To announce their betrothal. Kate'd have no business there, calling attention to herself and ruining Portia's triumph."

"Hasn't asked her yet, has he? And, he won't. How d'you intend to announce a betrothal that's the farthest thing from the mind of the one who must suggest it?"

"Permit me some new gowns, Papa," Portia declared with a toss of her curls, "and I'll bring him up to snuff quickly enough."

"Men don't marry gowns. Men marry women."

"Which just shows how much you know, Papa. Gentlemen marry faces and gowns and jewels and dowries. I have the face. It's the gowns and jewels I lack. And a suitable dowry. The stud would be just the thing, as Mr. Hawks finds horses of interest. He could make you an allowance. And Kate's black monster, naturally."

Kate sprang to her feet, mouth opening. Watford waved her down once more.

"And you'll go on requiring 'em." Chronicle Watford leaned back in his chair as he considered his wife and daughters. "How old's that gown?" he inquired mildly, gesturing at Kate.

"It's perfectly serviceable," Mrs. Watford protested.

"How old? In its original guise? Seems to me I remember it from—"

"Last season," she mumbled.

"How old?"

"Well, a bit more, perhaps."

"Seems to me it first saw light as part of your bride clothes, Mrs. Watford."

"And what if it did? A nip here and a tuck there, and it does perfectly well for Catherine. A schoolroom miss has no need of—"

"An end to it!" Watford exploded. "You want a dancing party, hold a dancing party. Here, not in some hired hall. You," he continued, turning to Kate, "will be in attendance, and properly garbed, d'you understand? No more castoffs. And some other decent gowns as well, and a new habit or two. Toggery fit for a young lady."

"Papa, please! No!"

"You've reached the age and then some, lass," he said, smiling with regret. "I've been remiss in not insisting sooner, but I've been both lazy and reluctant. Kate will be present," he continued, rising and turning to his wife, "or no evening party. And, she'll be properly garbed, and the gown will be new and suited to her."

"There isn't time. I'd counted on the evening three days hence."

"Oh? And I thought there was time and plenty for a gown for Portia, and another for yourself."

"I've already commanded them," Mrs. Watford whimpered. "Days ago. Portia and I were in the dismals because of the inclement weather, and we had to do something to cheer us. What there won't be is time for Miss Timmins to make something for Catherine—not and do justice to the superior toilettes we've selected."

"Then perhaps, madam, you should consider having rather less superior toilettes that Kate may have one that'll put none of us to the blush, yourself included. I've endured this silliness long enough."

"Mr. Watford, d'you want to see Mr. Hawks slipping through our hands, and Portia fading to a spinster, and—"

Kate eased behind the draperies as the argument raged, Portia adding her insulted mite. She opened the window, slid over the sill and dropped lightly to the ground—her customary escape route when Mama became impossible, Portia demanding, and Papa was about to erupt like a volcano.

The moon shone through the heavy-headed lilacs, dappling her arms and turning the comfortable old gown into a creation of fairy elegance. She buried her nose in the spicy blossoms, breathing deeply.

So, it had come. First Hades, who might throw the importuning Londoner but neglected to trample him, and now Papa. Traitors, both.

She had no desire to be placed on the block. Leave such foolishness to Portia, who actually enjoyed the tedium of having gowns fitted, and men boring on forever about how superior they were to all others in some manner. She'd observed Mr. Prohl at his courting, and she'd observed Roger Appleby and Christopher Clough and Bobby Horning. The moment they were in her sister's vicinity they lost what few wits they possessed—which'd never been many to begin with, but at least they'd never been given to inanities until Portia had, well, sprouted bumps.

Kate ducked between the lilacs and darted down the sloping moonlit track to the stud. From the tack room came the soft sounds of polishing cloth against saddle, the low murmur of voices. The stables were quietly busy. Persephone, in a box stall at the end of the row, was due to foal soon. Perhaps tonight, given the anticipatory murmurs.

She slipped into Hades's stall at his welcoming whicker, retrieved his customary treat from the pocket of her gown.

"So, my lord, it's come," she whispered, holding the apple on the flat of her hand. He lipped it delicately, regarding her through wise dark eyes, then seized it between strong teeth. "Choose well for me, for we'll both be cursed with the same tyrant, whoever he may be. The lads in the neighborhood are fine and well for a spree. But over the breakfast cups? Every day? I thank you, no! Even Roger would be impossible, and he's the best of the lot." The big black's only response was a steady munching of the apple. "And make me a widow early," she pleaded. "Preferably on my wedding day. A well-aimed kick to the beggar's brainbox should do it."

She buried her face in the black's coarse mane, one arm flung across his withers, the other circling his strong neck. So it was

Hawks found her half an hour later, face tear-stained, eyes defiant, manner unwelcoming. Remembering a young cousin he'd discovered in similar straits years before, Hawks had the sense to remark on none of it. Instead he made an inconsequential remark regarding the fineness of the night and the quiet activity down the way as he backed Folly into his stall. He continued his soothing prattle in much the same manner Mick McReedy was murmuring to the laboring mare, uncinched the girth, looped the stirrups, and lifted the saddle from the young gelding's back, then whisked off the blanket.

"Yes, it's a fine night," Kate agreed, surreptitiously wiping her eyes on her sleeve.

"And with many flowers blooming, given the warm weather we're having. You sound as if you've a touch of rose fever," Hawks commented, keeping his back to the girl and reaching for the brushes on a ledge. "Lilacs do for me every spring, for all it's not something I customarily admit to. Would you care for a handkerchief?"

"Yes, please," Kate sniffed.

He knew. Unlike the boys, he wasn't saying a word. She liked that. If only he didn't want to purchase Hades, he might be almost nice.

A white square was extended over the wooden partition. She put it to good use.

"Easy now, girl," Mick's voice floated from up the way as a high squeal shattered the peaceful night. "Steady on."

"I take it one of the mares is foaling," Hawks said.

"Persephone." Kate gave her nose a final blow, stuffed the handkerchief in her pocket. "I'd go help, but they'd chase me away."

"Probably think it's no place for a young girl."

"They don't, and Papa agrees. I don't see why, but there it is: I'm to stay out of the way at such times. Idiotish!"

Hades gave a concerned whicker, butted Kate with his head. She scratched between his ears, then clambered into Folly's stall, took down another set of brushes.

"You don't have to do this, you know," she said. "One of the stableboys'd—"

"Knowing how it is at home, I suspect I'd earn the undying enmity of whichever one was set the task," Hawks chuckled. "They've other concerns at the moment."

"Kind of you." Kate brought the brushes down the gelding's arching neck one after the other, matching Hawks's rhythm. "Most buyers don't understand such niceties."

"But then perhaps most buyers didn't grow up in their father's stables."

"You did?" The surprise was as clear in her voice as it was in her eyes as she peered at the London swell over the tall gelding's back.

"To my mother's mortification and my father's amusement. One doesn't develop a serious interest in horseflesh late. It's inborn, I think, as with yourself."

"My mother and sister don't care for horses any more than your mother."

"I know. Constantly giving you scolds, if my experience is anything to go by."

Kate nodded, knelt in the clean straw to give the gelding's right fore a good going over. "There's something I feel I should warn you of," she said hesitantly.

"Yes?" he prodded.

"Mama intends you to offer for Portia. She's planning a dancing party, and wishes to announce your betrothal at it. Perhaps you'd best leave. Immediately. Before any harm's done. From what I've been told, rakes don't want wives, and I have it on the best authority that's what you are."

"No, they don't," Hawks agreed on a choking cough.

"Didn't think so. We won't sell you Hades, so you're wasting your time."

"I'll risk it. Your father may change his mind."

"Hades is mine, and I'm the one who's not selling." She stood, picked a few wisps of straw from her skirt, began work on the placid gelding's broad back. "If you don't want a wife, you'd really best leave as soon as possible. Tomorrow at the latest. Then there won't be a dancing party, and I shan't have to wear a new gown and pretend to be a lady, which I'm not looking forward to in the least."

"Sell me Hades," he grinned, "and I'll depart on the instant."

"This very moment? That would be wonderful," she sighed, "but I've told you: Hades isn't on the block, any more than I am."

Kate attacked Folly's dusty hind quarters. The sweep of the brushes was soothing, almost soporific. Her mind wandered, going over the past few days and the multitude of inconsistencies she'd observed in the fashionable Londoner. Perhaps they stemmed from the frivolity of his life in the capital, its lack of true meaning or purpose. That wouldn't surprise her.

"What's it really like, being a rake?" she asked suddenly. "I suppose you have to have a ladybird under your protection? And say flowery things, the way you do to Mama and Portia. And squire her about all the time, so people'll see you with her and know you're a rake."

"Well, not quite all the time. It rather depends on the occasion and the venue."

"Yes, I suppose it must. You can take one driving or to the opera, but you can't take her to call on your mother. I do know that much. D'you find it amusing, being a rake and able to do just as you please without regard to others?"

"I suppose so."

"You sound doubtful. If it's not amusing, why be one?"

"It's better than the alternative."

"Which alternative?"

"Being leg-shackled." Then, driven beyond what his risibilities could tolerate, Hawks burst into a low rumble of laughter. "This conversation would have your father taking a whip to me and your mother a switch to you if they learned of it," he cautioned. "As for the indefatigable Mr. Prohl—"

"Fiddlesticks! Mama considers me past praying for, and Papa considers me perfect. As for Prosy Prohl, if you believe that mawworm concerns me, you must adjust your thinking. But, you'd best be careful concerning Portia. Of course she claims she'd only use you to get to London, where she'd snaffle a more eligible suitor. A titled one, don't you see? Portia insists on a title. You don't have one. That should keep you safe in the end, for she intends to jilt you, but you've very deep pockets, don't you?"

"They're not to let, at least."

"Just so. She might change her mind, and then where would you be?"

"Where would I be, indeed," he murmured.

"You'll have to offer for her if you don't leave soon," Kate continued blithely. "Mama will contrive it somehow. You see, if you don't offer for Portia her stock will fall and she won't be able to snaffle anyone at all, not even Mr. Prohl. That would be most unpleasant, for Portia would be in a pet and Mama in a taking. It was bad enough last week with all the rain and Papa gone. You'd best leave while you can. Then we can all be comfortable again, or as comfortable as it's possible to be between Mama's vapors and Portia's airs and Mr. Prohl's sermonizing."

"And what of you? You mentioned not wanting the party."

"Papa's all about in his head. He says I must learn to play the fine lady, and that the party to announce your betrothal's just the time for it, though he doesn't believe there'll be a betrothal any more than I do. Fustian! I'm better as I am."

"And how is that?" Hawks asked, finding himself genuinely intrigued.

"I've my own friends. The boys in the neighborhood," she specified at his soaring brows. "We ride together, and we hunt, and we have glorious sprees. I'm to inherit the stud, you see, for Papa won't entrust it to anyone Portia's likely to marry, and I haven't the slightest need of a husband to run it. That won't be for years, and Mama'll want to live with Portia and her husband when it happens, for she doesn't care for me in the least. I'm not a credit to her, being dark and gauche and a thorough gawk."

"My dear child, you don't understand what you're saying."

"Oh, yes, I do. I'll hire Roger Appleby for show, but Mick and I'll be the ones running things. Roger's a second son. He won't care to hang on his brother's sleeve, for Eustace is a prosy stoat, just like Mr. Prohl. Roger's spoken of trying his luck in the colonies, but I don't think he'd like it and the army is out of the question. He has the bottom for it, but he can't remember a thing from one minute to the next."

"Unsuited to the army indeed," Hawks murmured.

"But my pretending to be a lady's a waste of time. You do understand, don't you? Men don't see me that way. That's why we must get you gone before Papa insists on more foolishness. I'll be glad to help you pack," she ended on a hopeful note. "I'll even compose a note to Mama, explaining you were summoned to your favorite aunt's deathbed. Then you can sign it, and no one'll be the wiser."

"So kind of you to offer, but I fear I must decline."

"Taken a fancy to Portia, like all the rest?" she said with ill-disguised disgust.

"No, but as you said, one of the advantages of a rake's life is the freedom to please oneself without regard to others. Irresponsible of me and inconvenient for you, but there it is: I'm more determined than ever to add Hades to my stable."

Kate whirled on him in fury. "I've tried to be accommodating, just as Gram said I must. I've tried to be courteous. I've explained everything. And you don't care! You, sir, are a bounder and a cad and a man-milliner and a Caption Sharp and a—"

She broke off in horror, realizing her voice had been rising.

"Save the third set for me," he countered softly, "as I'll be expected to open the thing with your sister, and the second must go to your mother. We'll give your new gown a fine twirl, and open all their eyes to things even you don't know you are."

With that he unlatched the stall door, attempting to bow her through it.

"I don't dance," she spat.

"Yes, you do. You just don't realize it yet."

* * *

"Mr. Hawks is insufferable," Kate wailed, storming into her grandmother's bedchamber, the aroma of the stables drifting from her skirts, "as I've told you and told you!"

"You managed to speak with him, then?" old Mrs. Watford asked, shifting on her mountain of pillows as her head turned to the door. "And he wouldn't listen?"

"He's deaf! Or else there's nothing but fluff between his ears. Just now, down at the stables. I'd escaped there, for Mama was nattering at Papa again, and it was most wearying. I caught him returning from the Blind Hunter, and I did just as you said, Gram, for all the good it did any of us, may he rot in hell forever!"

"Being as he's a man, he probably will," the old lady chuckled. "Bound that direction at any rate, if all I've read of him's true. No need to foul your pretty mouth cursing him on his way. What if our good Mr. Prohl were to hear you?"

"He'd reinstitute the stocks, I suppose, but he'd have to catch me first."

"That he would. With every landowner in the area having a rick where you could hide, not much chance of that."

She winced, shifting her shoulders slightly. Kate dashed across the room, placed a contrite kiss on her grandmother's wrinkled cheek, adjusted two of the pillows and poured a glass of raspberry cordial, held it to her lips. The old lady drained it, then waved Kate away with an impatient gesture of her gnarled hand.

"Well?" she demanded. "And just what did you say, missy? Didn't make a mull of it, did you?"

"Not in the least. I was most explicit. He'd have to've been a dunce not to understand." Kate set the glass down, scowling. "I taxed him with being least wanted and a great inconvenience, and about to cause even greater inconvenience to everyone, himself included. But, did he listen? He did not! Not to a single word I said."

"No, I suppose he didn't," the old lady sighed. "If he had, you wouldn't've come bellowing like a bull in springtime. We'll have to think of something else."

"Treating Portia as if she were Queen of England, or a princess at the very least," Kate grumbled, going to the fireplace. "Bowing at every turn, and paying her flowery compliments. Praising her wit and grace, if you please!"

She piled more sea coal on the grate and poked it vigorously as her grandmother watched with twinkling eyes. Then she turned back, still gripping the poker.

"And Portia hasn't the sense to realize it doesn't mean a thing. It's just his way. And," she concluded triumphantly, brandishing the poker, "he wants Hades, and insists he will have him!"

"Oh, he does, does he?"

"And he won't leave." Kate shoved the poker in its rack. "He's courting disaster with an obstinacy that makes one wonder if he has all his wits. I told him about Portia's determination to bring him to his knees, and Mama arranging it somehow, just as you told me to, and still he won't leave!"

Kate plumped herself in the chair by old Mrs. Watford's bed, seized the lady's thin, vein-ridged hands.

"Gram, Portia sees herself betrothed by the end of the week, and then off to London for the rest of the Season so she can have her choice of titles, for she intends to jilt him, don't you see? And so does Mama!"

"Course they do. Pair of ninnyhammers, both of 'em. Nothing new in that."

"They refuse to listen to reason, and Portia's making a cake of herself, fawning over him like a dog over a bone one moment and pretending he doesn't exist the next, for she says that's the best way to attach him. And rapping his knuckles with her fan at every opportunity, and he's letting her do it. And sneering at her for all her fine airs, I'm sure of it. His face goes perfectly blank when she strikes an attitude, and then he becomes more punctilious than ever. He's laughing at us. And he's bored. Bored to tears, but he'd die before he'd let us see it."

"Above his company, is he?"

"Oh, I suppose he's nice enough to Papa and me," Kate admitted, remembering her tears and the sodden handkerchief in her pocket, "but he's making sport of Mama and Portia. It's all in his excess of civility, don't you see?"

"Not a very pleasant gentleman," the old lady frowned.

"Gentleman? He's no gentleman! I made him admit he's a rake," Kate explained at her grandmother's soaring brows, "and we all know what they are, and he concedes he enjoys it. Being a rake, I mean, not being taxed with it."

Old Mrs. Watford broke into a peal laughter. "Well, if he insists on making a cake of himself, no reason why he shouldn't enjoy the process. Paying for the privilege, after all," she chortled, "and I do understand that privilege comes high."

"And Mama's even worse, simpering like a miss in her first Season. Worst of all, Hades almost likes him! And, Papa? Papa's not the least use. He insists I have a new gown and attend Mama's silly dancing party and pretend to be a lady. And he's demanded the third set of me. Not requested it—demanded it. Mr. Hawks, not Papa."

"I can see I'm going to have to stir my stumps come tomorrow," old Mrs. Watford complained. "Knew you wouldn't manage on your own."

"I did what you said, Gram," Kate protested, "and I said everything we'd discussed, and a few other things besides which the man was in great want of hearing."

"And made mice feet of it. Always did tell Chronicle he shouldn't marry your mam. But there, he saw a pretty face, and didn't notice the fiddlestick running on behind it. Made a toothsome bride, I'll grant you that. Curves in all the right places, and golden curls to rival the sun and eyes like a summer sky, that's how he put it. Now there's nothing left but the prattling and the airs and the vapors. Ah, well," the old lady sighed, "it got me you, which is nothing short of a miracle considering the dam, if not the sire, and a blessing into the bargain. I suppose that must be reward enough."

"But Gram, what am I to do? Papa insists I have an evening gown, and dance, and flutter my lashes and simper and giggle, and play the coquette with Roger and Bobby and Christopher just as Portia does, and catch me a husband, and I don't *want*—"

"Chronicle won't've been insisting anything of the sort, my girl. I know my son better than that. The gown? Maybe, and high time. The rest? I cut my wisdoms years ago. Don't turn vaporish on me, or I wash my hands of you. Do as I say, and we'll both come through this alive, and your Mr. Hawks will continue to escape Portia."

"He's not my Mr. Hawks!"

"Hades's, then."

In the event, it took five days to put Mrs. Watford's dancing party together.

Or, more accurately, Felicity Timmins declared she couldn't produce a passable gown for Kate in three days—not and complete the toilettes Mrs. Watford had commissioned for Portia and herself. As Watford informed Miss Timmins that she could dun him 'til doomsday if Kate wasn't properly rigged out, five days it was.

During those five days Richard Hawks haunted the stables, determined to acquire the magnificent black hunter, riding out each morning on the gentlemanly Folly, stopping by the Blind Hunter for a bite when mood or hunger struck, and confining his social activities to the inn's habitués and Chronicle Watford's stablehands as a measure of self-protection. He appeared only at the breakfast table each morning, and made certain his appearance was so early there was no danger of encountering Portia or Mrs. Watford.

The senior Mrs. Watford, however, proved both a surprise and a delight when she descended on the first of those early morning breakfasts, leaning heavily on her younger granddaughter's arm and assisting her unsteady progress with a walking stick. Her pithy comments and wry wit were refreshing after the constant saccharine doses dished up by her daughter-in-law and eldest granddaughter. It was clear from whom Kate derived her personality. Just so would the girl be in sixty years, Hawks concluded—quick and birdlike, and preternaturally astute. In the interim she'd've led her husband a merry dance, whoever the poor sod proved to be. That, however, was none of his concern.

That Hawks was being diligently observed and generally found lacking by the arthritic old lady surprised him not in the least. Neither, though he was at a loss to determine its origin, did the amusement lurking at the back of her bright, darting eyes.

As for Kate, invariably an early riser, he ignored her presence with all the punctilious attention to minor courtesies due the infantry, and was as insulting as possible to her youthful sensibilities in the process—the one road he was certain would lead to being in her black books, especially if he maintained constant pressure on her father regarding ownership of the rogue stallion. Kate, for some reason, terrified him. He wanted nothing to do with her. The few minutes spent in her company while currying Folly had been unsettling enough.

Consequently he saw to it her plate was filled and her cup never empty as he commiserated with her father on the bane headstrong girls often proved to their parents.

He expounded at great length upon the inappropriateness of fragile females riding powerful hunters, citing numerous instances in which said fragile females had come to grief.

He commented favorably on Portia's pretty submission to society's view of a woman's role in what was, after all, a man's world. He even went so far as to commend her unknown governess, and swore if he were ever blessed with daughters he hoped to find them an instructress of equal skill. Miraculously, he barely flushed when old Mrs. Watford pointed out he'd best note the sort of female such a superior governess produced, as only Kate had paid the least attention to the long-departed Maude Whipple.

Kate in her turn tossed her head and played an equally deep game of ostensibly ignoring the famous rake-hell Corinthian while hanging on his every word, unerringly discerning each insult he intended and many he did not.

Hawks took advantage of invitations in the neighborhood the first three evenings, departing early and returning late. He could not, he informed his hostess, impose so unpardonably upon her as to expect a London dinner, complete with several courses and appropriate removes, whilst the household was caught up in frenetic preparations for the dancing party in his honor. The last two, with what he insisted to both himself and his *chère amie* was relieved delight, he spent with Chloe deSaules in the private parlor of the Blind Hunter, and later in her bedchamber.

If Chloe seemed far more grasping and far less entertaining in this provincial backwater, if her beauty struck him as florid and her flirtatiousness wearisome, he assumed the fault lay in himself. He reminded himself grimly she'd been the darling of earls and marquesses, and even a pair of royals, that he'd considered her well worth the price six months before, and behaved as she expected him to. If his exercising of his privileges as her protector was less enthusiastic than customary, neither was so foolish as to complain of it.

The morning of Mrs. Watford's dancing party he returned to Twin Oaks barely in time to stable Folly, rumple his bed, shave, change to fresh daytime wear and join the breakfasters before his customary early ride, much the worse for the brandy he'd ingested the night before in an effort to dull his perceptions. Even dawn hadn't provided relief, for Chloe had protested his abandoning her with a persistence he found infinitely grating. He'd snarled something ill-tempered regarding her playing least-in-sight during the day and taken himself off, her practiced pouts having no more effect on him than a mosquito's irritating buzz. Summoning her had been a mistake, no matter how great his boredom in this godforsaken spot. If he wasn't clever enough to avoid parson's mousetrap with the vacuous Portia, he deserved his fate.

After one highly amused glance, old Mrs. Watford recommended a repairing lease to Town. He flushed, began to wish he hadn't troubled to return at all, though what he'd've done with himself instead he had no idea. Hidden in the stables, perhaps.

Hawks settled himself at table, noted Chronicle Watford's absence without commenting on it, and confined himself to scalding black coffee.

"Off your feed?" old Mrs. Watford chuckled with a knowing air. "Too bad your man isn't with you. Chances are he'd have a sovereign remedy for what ails you."

"Grandmama!" Kate protested.

"If it waddles like a gander, honks like a gander, and nips like a gander, chances are what you're seeing's a gander," the old lady retorted. "No reason to call it a swan. Our guest's been making indentures. Time you learned to recognize the signs."

Kate flushed, threw the bleary-eyed Londoner a look of contempt leavened by not a little mortification. His answering wry grin and wink startled her.

"All this gander requires is his usual morning ride to put him to rights. You'll be exercising Hades, Miss Kate? Why not join me," he said, startled by his suggestion even as the words tumbled from his lips. "I'd enjoy the company." The amazing thing was, he spoke the truth. He would enjoy her company.

Her face fell. "Can't," she mumbled. "The Gown."

"The gown?"

"For tonight," she sighed, meeting his puzzled glance. "It's all your fault. Mama wouldn't't've had a dancing party saving your presence, and if she hadn't insisted on a dancing party Papa wouldn't't've insisted I have a new gown and I could've gone riding with you as you wish, only because you're here that's impossible. It's all a muddle, don't you see? Besides, I'm not certain I'd join you even if I could. I don't enjoy being housebound for the sake of a dress. I also don't appreciate those who cause me to endure such silliness."

"Come anyway," he cajoled, determined since he'd condescended to make the offer the country girl would accept it. "I'll even make it right with your mother."

"You wouldn't be able to keep my pace," Kate retorted scornfully, winced at the swift flick of her grandmother's cane across her shins.

"You could moderate your speed to accommodate my more feeble mount and decrepit condition."

"Hades and I moderate our pace for no one."

"My," the London swell returned, not quite certain why he was needling the chit, "proud of our delicate little kitten claws, aren't we! Quite unsheathed them, we have."

"Besides, I'm not certain you should ride today," Kate continued sweetly, a wicked glint in her eyes. "Don't look as if you could handle even such a mollycoddler as Folly. I shouldn't like to see our elevated guest come to grief, nor his mount either. Wouldn't enhance the stud's reputation. Perhaps you should take yourself to Three Mile Farm, see what Roger has available in the way of plow horses."

"See here, miss," Hawks blustered, "I—"

The old lady's delighted chuckle caused Hawks to flush furiously and bury his nose in his cup.

"You might let our guest exercise Hades for you," Mrs. Watford tossed into the sudden silence.

"You're mad!" Kate spluttered, whirling on her grandmother.

Hawks's eyes whipped from the old lady to her granddaughter.

"Not yet," she retorted. "This one needs the cobwebs swept from his brain. So do you. Likely the same's true of your precious pet. A word to him, and he'd let Mr. Hawks stay the course."

"No," Kate said firmly, pushing her plate aside and her chair out. "I'd die first. Do you wish me to see you to your rooms before I report to Miss Timmins?"

The old lady cocked her head, then shook it.

"No," she said, "I believe I'll keep our guest company. He needs more to set him to rights than that devil's brew. You run along."

* * *

The final fitting of the infamous gown was as tedious as Kate anticipated.

Perched on a stool, bullied this way and that by the perfectionist Miss Timmins, Kate stoically bore the process with the air of a young martyr, refusing to so much as glance in the glass. Had she done so, the results might've surprised her.

True, Felicity Timmins was naught but a country seamstress, but she had an unerring eye for line which rivaled that of her famous London counterparts. Left to her own devices, the result was not one of the overstated messes so popular with Mrs. Watford and Portia. It was instead a simple and charming gown for a young girl, clinging where it ought and revealing no more than it should. The most delicate of lace frosted the modest neckline. Miniature silk forget-me-nots emphasized the clear lapis of her eyes. It was, if Kate had bothered to inspect herself, a gown that worked an unexpected transformation on her. Kate didn't bother.

Following Watford's instructions, Miss Timmins had also set her assistants to fashioning a habit of cherry red poplin. That Kate examined with grudging interest, stretching her arms, bending at the waist, twisting this way and that, and generally assuring herself it permitted the freedom of movement she demanded.

She'd just donned the old burgundy merino when her mother and Portia swept into the seamstress's domain, still in their wrappers and rather disheveled, demanding to know the status of their attire for the evening. Miss Timmins bustled forward, a froth of spangled heliotrope gauze stitched with crystal beads and liberally decorated with cabbage roses and feathers draped over her arm. Kate slipped from the room, darted down the stairs and out the back door without their being any the wiser.

From the front of the house came thumps that told of rooms and entry being stripped of their furnishings to make way for dancing. Mr. Hawks and Gram had been chased from their morning conference, whatever it might've entailed.

Kate glanced down at her old dress with a sigh.

She'd been banned from the stables for the day. Not by Mama, which would've been understandable, and who could be ignored.

Not even by Gram, which she could've accepted.

By Papa, who claimed he wasn't about to have her pretend to take a tumble, and so have an excuse not to attend that evening.

He'd issued the edict just before he fled the house, unwilling to subject himself to the dither of Mama's discommodation of all their lives for the sake of impressing an unimpressible and uncaring London swell. She almost wished she hadn't warned Hawks regarding Portia's plans for his future. With Portia wed, life might've returned to normal once she was off on her honeymoon.

Kate narrowed her eyes, watching from behind the clump of lilacs beneath the parlor window. Down in the main paddock, Papa and Mick McReedy were conferring. Abovestairs, Mama and Portia and Miss Timmins were conferring. Everywhere, people were conferring. Probably even down at the Blind Hunter people were conferring. About tonight's entertainment. About Mr. Hawks, and the probability of Portia's snaring him in the end. About the preposterous position into which Kate was being forced. Kate Watford, playing the lady? She'd be a laughingstock.

Ghosts of voices floated from the sun-struck paddock. Papa was exercising Hades now, graced with a large audience. Mr. Hawks appeared at the paddock gate, dressed for riding and trailed by Roger Appleby, Chris Clough, and Bobby Horning. The boys perched on the fence as Hawks let himself in, their carefree laughter reaching Kate beneath the lilacs. A tiny knot formed in her chest, grew as she watched Papa dismount and good-humoredly turn Hades over to the Londoner.

Apparently Hawks had provided himself with an apple, or perhaps a lump of sugar or one of Hades's adored carrots. The great black was butting the man's shoulder, demanding his treat. From the parlor came her mother's voice, querulously inquiring the whereabouts of her younger daughter. Joey claimed not to know. Then Portia's breathy syllables instructed Mama but to open the windows and search among the lilacs.

With a curse Kate tore around the corner of the house and ducked into the passageway to the creamery. The chill from the underground spring suited her mood to perfection. With a despairing sniffle, she perched on the stone ledge surrounding the trapped spring.

Boys—she'd known it for years—had all the fun. It wasn't fair. It simply wasn't fair—to be cooped in the house all day, expected to cackle and cluck and fluff her feathers, as witless and useless as a peahen. But, Hawks had come, and now suddenly Papa'd noticed she'd grown bumps just like Portia's, for all he'd said nothing about them, and this was the result.

That evening, clad in her new muslin gown, her hair twisted in a knot sprinkled with silk forget-me-nots, her feet crammed in Portia's third-best sandals, Kate dutifully performed each dance under her grandmother's and father's proud eyes and her mother's censorious glances, trying to find something to say to her partners that had nothing to do with the stud and the breeding of horses, and finding herself incurably tongue-tied.

Supper came and went.

The dancing resumed. Kate, hoping to join her former playmates after catching a breath of air, overheard their argument as to which one of them was to be cursed with the duty of partnering her next, and which the pleasure of leading Portia out. And which, honor of honors, might attempt to cajole the elegant London visitor into a hand of cards or a cup of wine punch.

Head high, face pale, features frozen, Kate returned to the fray.

At last it was over. Kate, humiliated beyond endurance and close to tears, slipped upstairs to her bedchamber. She left doing the pretty by the neighbors to the others. No one would notice her absence—not between the London swell and her posturing sister. And, the ubiquitous Mr. Prohl. Except for the dance he'd sat out with her, the vicar had kept a constant proprietary eye on Portia, appropriating her company at every opportunity, and doing his best to discourage not only the neighborhood swains, but Hawks himself.

The only moments of pleasure Kate had experienced the entire evening were during the single country dance with Hawks—the third set, with hours left to survive before she could make her escape. Only then had she felt less awkward, as if she belonged taking the floor rather than blooming on the wall. As for the horrid half hour she'd spent in Mr. Prohl's company, forced to endure yet another tirade concerning maidenly deportment, the less said the better.

At least there'd been no betrothal announcement, for Hawks had proved most cleverly elusive. Not once had he agreed to take Portia for a cooling stroll in the rose garden, no matter how Mama insisted Portia was overheated and about to faint, and no matter how long Portia held her breath in an attempt to turn Mama's claims to reality. Instead Mr. Prohl had wrenched Portia's fan from her clenched fingers and vigorously plied it while calling for burnt feathers.

Hawks never requested a second dance with Portia.

He hadn't even taken her in to supper, as Mama attempted to contrive. That honor he'd reserved for Gram, sitting out the supper set and chatting companionably while Kate's former playmates hung on his every word.

Even Roger had danced attendance. Roger, who only weeks before had attempted to shield Kate from the vicar's lectures, claiming she was the very best sort of jolly good fellow and the greatest gun in the district. And now? Now Roger had no use for her at all. None. And abandoned her to the vicar, and claimed he was doing her a favor. And refused to agree Hawks was a useless bit of dandified monkey-bait, unable to sit a horse worth sitting. She'd trained Hades to permit none on his back but herself, Roger said. She'd made certain of Hawks's failure. She'd made certain all of them failed—not, Roger insisted with down-turned mouth, a very gentlemanly thing to do.

No, her only friend during those mortifying hours had been

Hawks. He alone attempted to stem Mr. Prohl's pompous homilies, staying close by during that interminable half hour, and ignoring the vicar's hints that he take himself elsewhere. Hawks had even protested the worst of Prolh's excesses. Hawks alone told her she appeared to advantage in her simple gown while his eyes conveyed the same message. He alone made her feel pretty and graceful, and well worth partnering. With him alone she had felt free to laugh, and to speak naturally of things of true interest.

Only buttering her up, mostly likely, in an attempt to acquire Hades. It was a lowering thought.

As she unpinned her hair, Kate made another determination: If boys had more fun than girls, then men had the most fun of all, for they had the most freedom. No one scolded them or made them play propriety, or claimed they were ungentlemanly when they were merely seeing to their own interests.

And, the man with the most freedom that night had been the London rake.

The Schooling of a Rake

Kate's eyes flicked defiantly over what she could see of her new habit as Hades ambled through a small clearing, the sun warming the cherry red poplin of her jacket and gilding the lace jabot at her neck. It was, to say the least, a splendid costume. Brass buttons glittered. Epaulettes gleamed. The black plumes gracing her shako nodded in the gentle breeze.

Certainly Gram had approved, though what Mama would say to this eye-catching ensemble Kate had no notion. Or, perhaps too good a notion.

Mama would not approve. Neither would Portia: not of the divided skirts with their sweeping train; not of the matching trousers doubled in leather she sported beneath them; not of the form-fitting jacket that revealed curves previously flattened by the old brown habit.

And Mr. Prohl? Were he to happen on her he'd claim she presented the appearance of a Haymarket trollop. And prose on interminably about it. True, red was unconventional for an unmarried girl, even for a riding habit where the usual dictates of insipidity didn't hold. That was precisely why, when given the option, she'd selected the red fabric. As for continuing to ride astride, Baltassar Prohl's comments were beyond bearing. He'd even taxed her with it last night. In Roger's hearing. And Roger, traitor that he was, had promptly agreed! Hire him to help at the stud when the time came? The wisdom of that plan was increasingly doubtful.

The world was crumbling around her ears, bit by shattered

bit. Even Gram, loyal though she was, claimed Papa had the right of it when he insisted Kate transform herself from carefree girl to boring young lady.

"I will not become a missish cipher," Kate muttered for the thousandth time. "I will not! As for Mr. Prohl and his pusillanimous propriety, both may go hang. I'm not so lily-livered as to submit to his dictates. Or, Roger's. Ever."

She let Hades chose his own path, ducking branches, swaying lightly in the saddle.

They'd had a glorious gallop—almost glorious enough to atone for the miseries of the evening before. It was a perfect morning, with puffs of cloud scudding before the brisk breeze in a sky so clear, so blue it was almost painful to the eye. Everywhere trees were hazed delicate rose, and the air held the heady scent of spring full-blown.

Hades whickered, picking his way around thick brambles sporting fresh shoots. Last fall's crisped leaves rustled beneath an answering whicker. Kate frowned as they twined through underbrush and skirted an ancient chestnut. They rounded a great moss-covered boulder and broke onto one of the stud paths.

And there, where she neither expected nor wanted him, was the source of all her distress: Hawks himself, as clear eyed and firm visaged and elegant as if his sojourn at Twin Oaks had not caused her agonies of mortification, and everyone else the greatest inconvenience.

As if he had not spent half the night dancing with every married and unmarried lady in the neighborhood, having his toes crushed and his consequence deferred to in the most toadying manner for his pains

Or, spent the remainder of the night heaven knew where indulging in heaven knew what dissipations.

Certainly he hadn't been at Twin Oaks, asleep in his bed as he should've been. She'd heard his goodnights to her parents shortly after the last carriage clattered down the lane, his more effusive comments to Grandmama, whom he'd actually escorted to her door. The bounder was punctilious—she'd grant him that.

And, not quite half an hour later, she'd heard his precise, almost military tread descending the stairs and echoing across the entry flags where earlier dancers cavorted. She'd watched him slip from the house and down the hill to the stables, dressed for riding. A short time later she'd seen him clearly in the cool moonlight, mounted on Folly and heading in the direction of Chilton as if pursued by the fiends of hell.

And now he was returning from his amusements, and seemed not in the least disturbed by her catching him at it. Had it been she indulging in such pranks—!

Of course, such freedom was highly enviable. Perhaps it had something to do with his being a rake, and the woman with odd-colored hair staying at the Blind Hunter—his convenient, rumor whispered—though she wasn't certain just how. The flesh pots of Sodom and Gomorrah—as Mr. Prohl characterized London's attractions—were too distant, and Chilton had no fleshpots. Mr. Prohl saw to that on a daily basis, poking his long nose where it was least wanted with a tenacity bordering on the prurient. But, it wasn't just that Hawks was a man, of that she was certain. Had Papa or Roger indulged in such late night-ramblings, they would've been taken severely to task by those who felt they had a right, which would include most in their households.

Kate scowled as the Corinthian doffed his hat. Better to scowl than break into the involuntary smile struggling to quirk her lips. She was actually glad to see him, reprobate though he was. Most puzzling.

"I'd been wondering if I'd find you out and about," he said. "You're not the sort to laze half the day away because of one evening's entertainments."

"No, I'm not. Apparently you're not, either." Kate was infinitely proud of the touch of chilly reproof she managed to inject in her tone.

"I'd fritter half my life away if I were," he chuckled, clearly undisturbed by the implied criticism.

"There are some," she muttered, "who would claim you do so in any case."

"I beg your pardon?"

"I said 'Some would claim it's a beautiful day in any case.' "

"Ah, so that was it," he rejoined, regarding her with amusement. "That's a new habit, isn't it?"

"It's not proper to comment on a lady's togs."

"Really? And here I thought that's what ladies like best—to be complimented on their appearance."

"Not this one."

"You didn't mind last night. Still, it's quite attractive." His eyes held definite approval as he examined her. "Such bows to the military are the latest stare. You're fortunate Miss Timmins is willing to remain in Chilton. Perhaps I should attempt setting her up in a shop of her own in Town. It's the dream of every seamstress, or so I've been informed, and she's quite talented. What do you think?"

"I think you should forego putting your nose where it's least wanted. London doesn't need another seamstress, no matter how talented, already having so many. Miss Timmins, however, is the only seamstress Chilton boasts."

"I suppose there's something in that, but then there're Miss Timmins's desires to consider, don't you think?"

"I think now Mama and Portia have had their dancing party and you remain safely unbetrothed, you should consider a rapid return to London," she informed him repressively. "You've been fortunate so far. If Portia decides you're the *parti* she wants, being more prepossessing than anything that's presented itself up to now, she's capable of forcing your hand, complete to tearing her corsage and crying rape, which Gram tells me is how offers are wrung from unwilling victims."

"Why d'you think I prop a chair beneath my doorhandle each night and never indulge in moonlit strolls among the roses?"

"Oh? And I thought you were spending your nights elsewhere—for safety, of course. That was you riding toward the village last night, was it not? And every other night since, well, I don't know how long?"

Hawks had the grace to flush furiously.

"The only reason for your continued presence is Hades," she said with a touch of acid. "You aren't going to have him, so your time here is wasted, and you must find our ways countrified at best. Don't you think you should return to more accustomed haunts and pursuits now you've proved you can disrupt everyone's lives?"

"I certainly find the country manners of a certain young lady surprisingly forthright," he murmured, "if not refreshingly so."

"Your friends are certain to be lamenting your absence. And the ladies of the *ton,* naturally." She shot him a narrow look. Hawks flushed more furiously even as he attempted to demur. "I'd wager you're quite the favorite with them," Kate continued, overriding his protestations, "seeing how everyone here comes fawning it over you, and you seem to accept their deference as natural. Why, Roger's behavior is scandalous, and Gram's isn't far behind given the way you've been emptying the butter boat over her."

"How inhospitable of you! And how uncharitable."

Kate attempted to frown him down, screwing her face into what she hoped was a close approximation of Mr. Prohl's most overbearing fleshpots glower. Hawks's eyes merely twinkled in response.

"Do you plan to go further," he asked, "or are you returning to the stables?"

She eyed the dark patches on Folly's shoulders, the film of dust on his saddle and Hawks's boots. Wherever he'd been, whatever he'd been doing since shortly after Mama's dancing party, it was clear he'd indulged in a lengthy early morning ride in addition. The man was no milksop, whatever she might say to the contrary.

"Go back so soon? Hardly!" She forced a derisive laugh, swept a wayward tendril of glossy hair from her eyes. "No, I intend going somewhat farther. Folly appears done in, however. So do you. Extended periods in the saddle aren't for park saunters and mounts who can't stay the course. Enjoy your trip back to the stables."

Hades wheeled under the light pressure of her knees, took off down the winding trail at a steady canter. Behind her came the drum of pursuing hooves.

"Blast!" she muttered, giving the black his head.

They tore across fallow fields, jumped low stone walls, and splashed through a brook. They pelted past isolated farms, through woods and dales. Nothing discouraged her unwanted cicisbeo.

Finally, with Hades's sides pumping like a smith's bellows, she gave it up, reigned the big stallion in at the top of a sun-swept hill, turning in the saddle to watch as the Londoner and his mount approached. Folly had kept the pace well for once. He was coming along, barely lathered and no more winded than her own mount. Of course, she'd already taken the edge off Hades or she'd have left the pair in the last county, swallowing great draughts of dust and humiliation.

Reluctantly she turned Hades around, wiped her glowing face on the lacy jabot, then pulled off the shako and waved it in the manner of a fan.

It was time to go back, given the sun showed it was close on ten o'clock. Papa had requested she bring the stud records up to date. She'd begun the task while he was gone, but Mr. Prohl had made its completion impossible, and now the sales at Tatt's needed entering as well. Customarily she saw to such chores immediately upon her father's return, but their London guest had interfered with the smooth running of the stud and her own routines, as well as the life of the neighborhood.

"Trying to lose me, minx?" Hawks said, pulling Folly up before her. "It won't work, you know. Better men than you've attempted it."

"I was merely enjoying the day," she countered innocently, hanging her shako from the pommel by its strap, removing her gloves and loosening her damp hair to let the breeze cool it, unaware of the deliciously wanton figure she presented.

"Of course. Do you hunt, little Artemis?"

"When I can." She shook out the heavy mane, then lifted it from the back of her neck. "It's not considered quite the thing here, for a female to join the hunt. Whenever I do, Mr. Prohl devotes an entire sermon to it. That can become wearying."

"How excessively backward," he chuckled.

"Isn't it?" She peered at him doubtfully, shrugged, pulled on her gloves and gestured, indicating they'd best be returning. They walked their mounts down the hill, shifting easily in the creaking saddles, automatically maintaining balance over the uneven ground. "I suppose you're bamming me," she said, "or else looking down your highly aristocratic nose at our rusticities. Still, in this instance we are backward. I understand there're ladies who've been known to ride with even the Quorn."

"Females, at least."

"But they aren't ladies? Yet they seize their freedom with both hands, just as they seize the reins of their mounts, and guide both over the most daunting of obstacles with perfect safety. To me, that makes them the very best sort of ladies."

"Sometimes," Hawks choked, "it's better not to inquire too closely into particulars."

"Which is precisely how Grandmama phrases it when I raise uncomfortable issues. Has she been importuning you to regularize me? Was that the reason for your conference yesterday morning? Because it won't work." Kate shifted in the saddle under the Londoner's assessing eyes. "I don't intend to leave well enough alone. Why should I?" Her eyes examined the horizon with apparent unconcern "Have you ever noticed it's the boys who have the most fun when one is growing up?"

"Well—"

"And when one is grown, it's the gentlemen. It's not fair, Mr. Hawks, for you to keep the best of the challenges to yourselves. Not fair in the least."

"No, I suppose it isn't. Thank the Lord I've no sisters such as yourself."

"Be even more thankful you haven't a wife or daughters.

Papa claims they're the very devil, but that's only when Mama flies into the boughs because of something I've done and Papa must make peace, or when Mama and Gram are brangling."

"They pull caps?"

"You've spent some time with Gram. Can you imagine her and Mama not coming to cuffs, if only verbal ones?"

"No, I suppose that's natural."

"Oil and vinegar," Kate said sagely, "just the same as Mama and I. Gram is forever saying she can't understand how Papa came to marry Mama, except the rest of the time she says it was perfectly natural as Mama had large endowments and masses of golden curls just like Portia, and that's all a gentleman notices at such times. Mama had very large endowments, according to Gram, and enormous blue eyes, and she fawned over Papa just as Portia fawns over you, if you will believe it. And so Papa married her."

"I, however, have no intention of wedding Portia, whatever her, ah, endowments."

"Of course you haven't. Even a looby could tell that, but there'll be the devil to pay when you leave all the same. Portia intends to spend the Season in London as your fiancée, you see. I've told her she'll catch cold at that, but she won't listen." Kate's eyes flew back to the elegant Londoner. "Does Portia plague you dreadfully?"

"In a minor way."

"Only minor?"

"Without meaning to sound puffed up, I'm rather accustomed to ignoring such plaguings."

"Yes, I suppose you would be. You're not totally repulsive," she conceded, "so it's natural enough. Do you enjoy it? Ladies fawning over you, I mean."

"Not in the usual way," he chuckled. "Why d'you ask?"

"I just wondered. So, there are no blots on your escutcheon, whatever such blots may consist of, and no clouds on your horizon," she continued thoughtfully. "Even Papa and Roger have clouds on their horizons, so you are more fortunate than they."

"I suppose I am."

"The only difference between you and Papa and Roger, other than that you live in London, is that you're a rake and they're not. Therefore, if men are the more fortunate of the two sexes, then rakes are the most fortunate of gentlemen, for they've naught to restrain them given they've no serious clouds upon their horizons. *Quod erat demonstrandum,* as Miss Whipple was wont to say when lecturing me upon one or another of my faults. Geometric logic of the purist sort, complete with theorem and postulates, as I'm certain you'll agree. Miss Whipple was something of a geometrician."

Hawks repressed an explosion of mirth, discarded the notion of a stern lecture, and held his peace.

"What, precisely, makes you a rake," Kate continued, "other than you've no one to answer to but yourself?"

"People saying I'm one, I suppose," Hawks conceded after a moment's thought, the seriousness of his tone belied by his dancing eyes.

"You must've done something to encourage the notion. How did you go about it? Could you teach me?"

"My dear girl!"

"No, I mean it," she said, bringing Hades to a halt and turning to face him. "Would it take very long? Why can't a lady be a rake? I'd like a cloudless horizon or two for myself, you see, and my horizon has some very black clouds on it."

"And what might they be?"

"Portia marrying Mr. Prohl, for one, and attempting to ride roughshod over me for the rest of my life."

She set Hades in motion, frowning as she considered the problem. Beside her Folly ambled contentedly, Hawks restraining the gelding's attempts to nibble the tender young grass and new-sprung dandelions with practiced ease.

"I'm not going to marry, for someone will be needed to take

over the stud when Papa—well, it will happen you know," she apologized, "however little I may like to think about it, but even Papa wants me to wed. The way he's given Roger the freedom of the stud, even suggested I permit him to exercise Hades, it's clear what he has in mind, but you can see that wouldn't do. Roger stumbles all over himself paying court to Portia.

"Second of all, marry Roger Appleby? The stud will need a better head than he can offer, and that head will be mine. But before I shoulder all my responsibilities," Kate concluded, eyes seeking Hawks's wistfully, "I'd like to have just a touch of fun. I'm prepared to pay you."

"Pay me?" Hawks spluttered. "I do understand your problem. I even empathize a bit. Life can be most unjust—you have the right of it there. But pay me? For what?"

"For teaching me to be a rake, or at least as much of a rake as a lady can be."

"Good God! You don't know what you're asking."

"I'm quite frugal, not being partial to baubles like Portia is, and so I have almost all my pin money for the last three quarters. It's a considerable sum: ten pounds a quarter, for Papa's most generous."

"Most generous indeed," Hawks choked.

"I'm able to pay you twenty-five pounds. That's an astronomical sum, given Miss Whipple didn't earn near as much, and that was for an entire year's instruction, not just a few days."

"I see. A handsome sum indeed when one considers it's your entire fortune, but I think not."

"It's honest money. I keep the stud books."

"I'm certain it is, but—"

"So, you're like all the rest," she accused, a catch in her voice, "unwilling to share knowledge with one of the female persuasion."

"My dear girl, you don't understand."

"Oh, yes, I do. I took your measure when Hades did. I'd started to doubt our conclusions, but unfortunately we were both right the first time. You may think you're up to anything, but you're up to nothing—at least, nothing of value."

"See here, that's not quite fair."

"Well," she goaded, darting a narrow glance at him, "what am I to think? I'll find someone else to help me if you're too lily-livered," she concluded, playing her trump, "for there're always gentlemen visiting the stud, and many are almost as famous as you."

"Infamous, don't you mean?"

"I do know the difference between the words."

"You mustn't ask anyone else," he said, frowning.

"Why not?"

"Because some rotter might be unprincipled enough to agree."

"Hades almost likes you, which is why I'd thought I could trust you to give me honest value for shillings expended."

"See here, you can't—" He paused, ran his eyes over her, noting the alluring curves under the snug habit, the jaunty new hat now dangling from the saddle. Some bounder was sure to give in to her request. What would happen to the enticingly unconventional girl then didn't bear contemplation. He saw her candid features topping Chloe's experienced body, her eyes turning hard and knowing and avaricious, her innocently seductive movements becoming deliberately wanton. He shuddered, took a deep breath. With him, at least, she'd be safe. Then, reluctantly, he smiled.

"All right, I'll do it," he agreed, "but I'm not interested in your shillings."

"What, then?"

"Hades."

"You're mad!"

"Not in the least. You convince him not to throw me, or even attempt it, and for each hour in the saddle I'll give you an hour's instruction."

"Only if you cease your attempts to purchase him."

"Done."

Kate pulled off her right glove, spat on her hand, extended it. After one incredulous look, Hawks copied her actions and they shook on the bargain.

"I've just spent the most unaccountable morning."

Hawks pulled the door of his paramour's bedchamber at the Blind Hunter closed, tossed his crop, hat, and gloves on the dressing table atop the welter of scent bottles and cosmetic pots reflected in the cloudy mirror. A tray holding breakfast remains teetered carelessly on the corner. Chloe's abigail hunched by the firmly shut window, straining her eyes to repair one of her mistress's wispy nightrails with invisible stitches. The door of the corner armoire gaped, silken gowns and lacy peignoirs spewing to the floor. The place was a pigsty, airless and over-heated and cloyingly sweet thanks to an already wilting bouquet of lilies crammed in a battered pewter pitcher on the night table. Clearly he hadn't been expected to return so soon.

"And so have I been spending an unaccountable morning," Chloe yawned from where she reclined on the bed, posed like a veil-draped odalisque.

He turned at her words, brows rising. "Indeed?"

"Unaccountably boring, Hawks. How fitting—that we should accidentally have passed our time in precisely the same manner."

Chloe deSaules gave a trill of laughter, a practiced arpeggio that began in the stratosphere and tumbled down the scale, each false note grating more acidly on Hawks's sensibilities than the one before. Her eyes flew warily to the armoire. Hawks frowned.

"Will you not do that?" he grumbled. "I've told you time out of mind I don't find such artificial mirth pleasing."

"When do we return to Town?" she pouted. "I pine for company and music and lights, and a place that doesn't die when the sun sets."

"My company is insufficient?"

"You're never here, save for a few hours in the evening."

"There's no difference between Chilton and London in that respect."

"At least there I've my friends. Here there's no one."

"Not even whoever brought you those?" Hawks cast a derisive glance first at the armoire, then the flowers. "I'll wager I can guess who it is."

"One of dozens," she protested airily "I'm not even certain of his name myself, so how could you know it? I'm *bored*, Hawks."

"I pay you well to be bored," he snapped. "Leave us, Tillie," he added more gently to the cowering abigail, whose eyes were now darting uneasily from the armoire to the bed. "You can see to Chloe's fripperies later. Take that repulsive tray with you, and bring a pot of fresh coffee while you're about it. And see what the kitchen can provide in the way of a nuncheon, if you please. I'm famished."

He opened the door, gestured for the girl to leave. She threw Hawks a timorous smile, her mistress a doubtful glance, seized the tray and slipped from the room. Hawks examined the jumble that was his *chère amie*'s temporary abode with a jaundiced eye. Definitely, Chloe was losing her appeal. And her touch. Carelessness, to him, had always signaled the decay of a relationship. Best to end it quickly.

"Where'd that come from?" he said, pointing to the overblown bouquet.

"A tribute from an admirer," Chloe sulked, arranging herself more attractively on the pillows and casually revealing a firm breast with a taut brown nipple as she peeped at Hawks from beneath her lashes, "as well you realize."

"Really?" he drawled. "This far from civilization? You amaze me!" He'd been convinced she was playing him false for some time, but to manage it this far from Town showed a devotion to the exercise that was insulting to say the least. "And who, may I ask, is your bucolic admirer?"

"A charming young man. All young men who admire me are

charming, don't you think?" she said, turning the sulk into a languid, come-hither smile.

He ignored the too obvious demand for yet another compliment, sat in the wing chair he'd ordered brought in the day she arrived, stretched his legs encased in their dusty topboots to their full extent and helped himself to a glass of claret from the decanter on the flanking carriage table.

"Don't be a bore, Chloe," he cautioned, holding the glass to the light. Were those lip prints? He frowned, set the glass back on the tray. "I don't care for bores, especially when I've just spent a most entertaining morning in the company of one who is anything but a bore, desperately trying to keep the pace."

"Oh? And who might that be? The incomparable Miss Watford, of whom I've heard so many intriguing reports? Rather beneath your touch, I'd've thought, even for a country dalliance," Chloe retorted dismissively.

"No—her younger sister."

"Oh, dear! Must you now resort to robbing the cradle? How lowering! I've never heard tell you cared for hoydenish schoolroom chits."

"I don't, in the general way. Kate Watford is, well," he grinned, ignoring Chloe's unwise barbs, "an unaccountable girl. We rode for hours."

"You poor dear! You must've been bored to tears, too." Her eyes flew to the armoire, then back to her protector. "Come here," she cajoled throatily, extending her arms, "and let me entertain you. Such fortitude deserves recompense."

"There was no fortitude required. I bamboozled the girl into promising me Hades, not that she realizes it yet, while being most engagingly entertained."

"The hunter you're after? Wonderful! Now we can leave. Immediately. Order up the carriage, Hawks, and go pack. I'll have Tillie toss my things in my trunk, and we'll shake the dust of this benighted place from our feet within the hour."

"I think not, unless the carriage be for your exclusive use."

"You have your blasted horse! Whatever else can you want here?"

The trace of a smile hovered over Hawks's lips as he rose and strode to the windows overlooking the inn yard's bustle.

"You might be surprised," he murmured. "So, for that matter, might I. Very surprised. Life can be amazingly entertaining, d'you know that? Filled with the most delightful and unanticipated pleasures. Besides, I don't have the horse yet."

"You don't intend to give some farmyard miss a slip on the shoulder, surely?"

"No. Hardly that."

"What, then?"

"There's only one way for me to acquire that hunter," he said absently watching the comings and goings. "I was told so my first day here. Interestingly, the price isn't nearly so high or unreasonable as I'd first thought. In fact, it's rather a bargain, what with one thing and another."

"I don't understand you," Chloe protested.

"I know you don't. I don't quite understand myself, come to that. Let's merely agree Chilton and change are synonymous, and I've been beaten at my own game."

He glanced across the village square to the church and vicar's residence directly opposite. The indefatigable Mr. Prohl was at his gate, talking to an overwrought woman whom Hawks recognized from the night before. She gestured wildly toward the inn with one hand as she gripped Prohl with the other, attempting to pull him forward. Hawks sighed, turned to his soon-to-be former mistress.

"We've had a fine time of it, we two," he said more kindly than he intended. "Let's not spoil it now."

"What!?"

"You heard me, my dear. The game's over."

"You're giving me my *congé?*" Chloe deSaules demanded incredulously. "Here, in the middle of nowhere? For a horse?"

"If you wish to consider it so."

"No one gives me my *congé*. No one ever has. No one ever will."

"Nevertheless, it's time for a parting of the ways. Come, my dear, don't make this worse than need be. We'll pretend it's you who've tired of me."

"I can see what it is. You're ready for Bedlam. That, or you've already compromised some little milkmaid. You've been entrapped, that's what it is," the woman crowed scornfully. "The great Richard Hawks, diddled by one of the middling sort? How the *ton* will laugh!"

"I can't for the life of me understand what Cumberland and Clarence ever saw in you," Hawks murmured. "For that matter, I can't understand what I saw in you."

"An accommodating woman," she spat, "available and not too expensive and infinitely convenient when you were in the mood."

"On one point, at least, I beg to differ. You've been very expensive."

"Not near as expensive as I should've been," she retorted, eyes narrowed. "I'll have the carriage, if you please. Signed and witnessed. And the team. They should bring a pretty penny."

"I'm afraid not," Hawks demurred. "I've a fondness for them, having trained all six from colts. A draft on my bank will have to suffice."

"The carriage and horses, or I'm not leaving."

"Really? And I thought I was being overgenerous, as it happens."

"I will not be subjected to the indignity of the common stage!"

Hawks stalked to the armoire, fumbled among the gowns, grabbed a firmly muscled masculine arm and tugged. There was a muttered curse. Then arm, shoulder and leg appeared, followed reluctantly by the rest of a red-faced Roger Appleby, a feathery peignoir snagged in his coattails, his neckcloth in glorious disarray.

"No carriage I think, my dear," Hawks said. "No team, and

only funds sufficient to see you back to Town. The common stage'll do for a common whore. I'll send you the traditional parting token when I return, but nothing more. As I said, I was being generous before. Far more generous than these circumstances warrant."

"See here, you can't talk to a beautiful lady like that," Roger spluttered.

"Lady? D'you see a lady here, my lad? I don't."

Roger's shoulders hunched as he wrenched away from Hawks, fists doubling.

"Your mother's coming across the square with Mr. Prohl," Hawks continued with indifference. "If I were you, I shouldn't like 'em to find me here. Of course, for myself I don't mind in the least, being past redemption."

"Oh, Lord!" Roger dashed to the window, face paling. "Why didn't you say so?" He whirled to the bed, anguish contorting his immature features. "I'll be back, ma'am. You shan't be left unprotected, I swear it, but I've got to play least in sight just now, don't you see? My mother'd have me transported if she caught me here."

"My poor Roger," Chloe deSaules whispered huskily with the faintest of French accents, throwing Hawks a look of fury. She eased gracefully from her bed making certain her charms were well displayed to the almost incoherent young Appleby. "But, of course you must depart, *mon chéri,* and that the most rapidly possible."

"Make yourself scarce, jackanapes," Hawks grinned sympathetically, "and don't worry about Miss deSaules. I'll see she gets back to London right enough, though I shan't be accompanying her."

"What's all this about Hades and Kate? It was Kate of whom you were speaking, wasn't it? I'll not have you—"

"Later, you graceless whelp, later." From below came sounds of violent altercation, Baltassar Prohl's high-pitched voice soaring above the others. "Oh, Lord, that's torn it," Hawks scowled. "Back among the petticoats with you, my lad," he ordered, whirling Roger around. He shoved the quaking young man in the armoire, pulled the gowns in front of him and slammed the door, latching it firmly. "You, on the bed." He sent Chloe tumbling among the pillows, threw himself over her just as the bedchamber door crashed open. "Not one word out of you, my dear," he murmured under cover of the ensuing chaos, "or I shan't even pay your way to London, let alone cough up that parting trinket."

"I don't know what to make of him, and that's the truth," Kate admitted to Roger Appleby the next morning. Her eyes flew uneasily from the young man prowling the room to her grandmother. "He's infinitely kind, and infinitely entertaining when he wants to be. We've become friends, and allies of a sort. We both value Hades, you see. But, Mr. Hawks's actions so often seem at variance with his words, and both at variance with the image he presents the world."

"Precisely!" Roger proclaimed on a note of triumph, whirling to face Kate. "That's just what I've been trying to tell you. But, oh no, you've become as taken with the bounder as everyone else. Friends, indeed! That loose screw wouldn't know how to be a friend to a woman. Has quite different ideas about their purpose on this planet, let me tell you. You'd best have a care."

" 'Out of the mouths of babes,' " old Mrs. Watford murmured.

"One would think you're setting your cap at him," Roger stormed on, oblivious to any but his own words, "riding out mornings and permitting him to tool you about in his curricle afternoons. I'd never've thought that of you," he concluded in disgust.

"I do think you're exaggerating the problem," Mrs. Watford threw in, eyes twinkling merrily, "and I certainly don't believe Kate must needs cut the gentleman's acquaintance just to accommodate your sense of propriety, Roger, especially as he's a guest in this house. My son knew what Richard Hawks was when he brought him here. Don't refine too much upon yesterday's occurrences."

"What occurrences?" Kate demanded trapped between confusion and insult.

"Never you mind," the old lady and young man chorused.

They were closeted in Mrs. Watford's bedchamber, the door shut against intrusion. Kate had returned from exercising Hades to find her neighbor pacing the alley between the stalls, pounding mangers with his fist, striking posts with his crop, and generally making a noisy nuisance of himself. He'd descended on her like a hawk on a field mouse the moment she led Hades in, mouthing idiocies and insisting a conference between the two of them was essential if her safety and reputation were not to be compromised. Knowing how Roger could rarely entertain more than a single notion at a time, and that notion generally of the most banal, Kate had soothed the irate stable crew, turned Hades over to them, escorted the raging Roger outside and insisted her grandmother be part of any discussions.

"Mr. Hawks promised to do me a favor," she now continued with a puzzled frown as her eyes followed her neighbor's restless pacing.

"And just what might this favor be a London rake is willing to do for a country girl of no particular family or wealth?" Roger demanded, whirling on her.

"Believe me, it's not in the least out of the way or shocking," she insisted. "I'm most grateful to him, though he has been rather lackadaisical about it so far, speaking primarily of developing a certain air, but I'm not completely comfortable regarding the reward he intends to exact for doing that favor, and perhaps it's not something which can be taught in any case."

"Hades?"

"How ever did you come to learn of that?"

"I, ah, heard him mention it."

"What gall! You were listening at doors?"

"In a manner of speaking, I suppose," Roger mumbled, shuffling his feet and flushing as Mrs. Watford watched with amusement from her chair by the fire. "Let's just say I was where I shouldn't've been."

"Dear heaven, Roger! Did he catch you at it? I know you believe the sun rises and sets on our prestigious London visitor, but believe me, it doesn't. He's quite ordinary despite his elevated position in the *ton*."

"I know that only too well, to my sorrow."

"Why, there're moments I'd swear Mr. Hawks makes our prosy vicar appear the licentious reprobate," Kate continued with disgust. "Such a lecture I had of him this morning! And all as a favor to me, he claimed."

"You did?" Roger spluttered from the windows. "What a farce!"

"That's ever the way," the old lady threw in with a chuckle. "Take care our guest doesn't come the Calvinist where you're concerned, Kate, preaching prunes and prisms at every turn. He gives every evidence of coming to it."

"And totally uncalled-for, believe me," Kate fumed on. "I've never been trailed by a groom, and I certainly don't intend to begin the practice now. Totally unnecessary, and demeaning into the bargain. I, come to grief? Ha! Besides, not a one of 'em could keep the pace, and so I informed his high and mighty gentlemanship. My safety is Papa's concern, and no one else's."

"It's all balderdash, believe me," Roger agreed, ignoring Mrs. Watford's amusement and Kate's vexation. "I have reason to know. You'd best watch your step with that one. He's not to be trusted."

"On what basis do you say that, for heaven's sake?"

"A good one, believe me."

"How your song's changed! And just as I was coming to find him not so totally despicable despite his lamentable tendency to bore on forever about taking proper care. I can't believe such a turnabout in such a short time. Only two days ago you were worshipping at his altar."

"As for being accompanied by a groom," Roger scowled, "he's dead right there. You shouldn't be riding Hades in any case. Or gadding about with Hawks. Not at all the thing. And you shouldn't be riding astride. It was barely permissible when you were a girl, but you're a woman now—that'd be obvious to a blind man. Why, you're issuing a clear invitation to every lecher in England to track you down and do what he will."

"What!?" Kate exploded as Mrs. Watford broke into peals of laughter. "Why, even Mr. Hawks didn't have the temerity to suggest such a thing."

"Marry me, Kate," Roger pleaded. "I'll keep you safe. You know our families've expected it forever. I'll help your father with the stud and learn the business, and you can stay properly at the house and do the things married ladies're supposed to do."

"Such as what?"

"Oh, have children, I suppose, and pickle things and embroider fire screens, and gossip with the neighbors about the latest fashions. All that female nonsense."

"Like Mama, in fact? I thank you, no!"

"It's the only way I can see out of this bog in which you've mired yourself."

"Dear heaven, isn't that a bit drastic? Not that I'm insensible to the honor you do me in offering, feeling as you do about my reprehensible behavior."

"Oh, you'll come about once you're increasing. Least that's what my father's always said, though Mama's never been so sure."

"Listen to your mother," Kate spat, barely repressing her fury at having her future thus planned out with no regard to her own inclinations, and all because Papa had brought an undesirable guest to Twin Oaks. "I'd never come around! Aside from which, what of Portia?"

"Portia be hanged. Only played the fool with her because all the chaps were doing it," Roger shrugged. "Never meant a thing. We wanted to make sport of old Prohl, don't you see, and her as well. She's a silly ninnyhammer, what with all her airs and graces. Peahen of the worst order. At least you've some sense to you."

"Poor Portia," Kate murmured, then broke into giggles. Her exasperation at the limited choices even her oldest friend foresaw for her could wait. Hawks might prove some help there. He had a fine head on his shoulders, and she didn't mean just his handsome features, either. He'd think of a solution that wouldn't set the neighborhood on its ear, or land her in Bedlam or worse. "How devastating for her. What a farce this last week has proved. Why, I don't know how we ever survived without Mr. Hawks and his ladybird to entertain us."

"*Kate!*" Roger roared.

"Well, I do know about her," she countered, brows rising. "Hard not to, what with her parading the village twirling her sunshade and twitching her skirts to show the most ankle possible. On your arm, I might add. I saw you myself, just day before yesterday. She was in front of the inn, and you went up and doffed your hat and bowed like a caper merchant and offered her your arm. So, I asked Mick when I got home, and he told me exactly who she is."

"Blast it, Kate—"

"Enough, children." Mrs. Watford struck the floor with her stick to attract their attention, eyes twinkling at the look of derision on Kate's features and the embarrassed fury on Roger's. "This will all sort itself out without the least help from either of you.

"You've been squiring the London petticoat, Roger? I think the more of you for it. Time you were sowing your wild oats. Won't be ready for marriage until you have, so we'll hear no more of that nonsense. But remember: while bits of muslin are fine for entertainment, they're not for serious purposes. Just because Kate's turned you down doesn't mean you should leap into parson's mousetrap with the next available filly, though your current interest's more of a proven broodmare, and ready for the knacker."

"You wouldn't say that if you knew her story," Roger protested. "And now the blackguard's chased her away! I tried to call him out, but he wouldn't listen. She left this morning, cry-

ing buckets and saying she didn't know what she'd've done had
I not stood her friend."

"I do know her history, which is precisely why I feel a caution's necessary," the old lady snapped. "She's almost old enough
to be your mother, and's passed through more hands than a sheep
at shearing time, only you're the one's been fleeced."

"See here—"

"Did she wheedle you out of your allowance? I'll wager she
did, plus anything you managed to borrow. She's famous,
Roger," Mrs. Watford continued more gently. "Very famous,
only you're too green to've heard of her. Born with round heels.
Two of the royal dukes, among others, not that she saw any
brass from them. They say she started her career at fifteen,
running off with a highwayman. Wanted more than she could
earn at her father's inn. When her highwayman swung, she went
on to an entire militia regiment. Then, with a few pounds in her
stocking, she set up in London. I've always kept abreast of gossip. Not much else for an old lady to do most times."

"I don't believe it!"

"Oh, I'm certain she spun you a fine tale of betrayal and
deceit, and a promise of marriage from Hawks. She did, didn't
she? All a take-in. She's past her prime, my boy, and desperate.
Don't let her hoodwink you, or you'll regret it the rest of your
life. She's naught but a bit of muslin, and a frayed bit at that,
with hair as gray as mine if only she'd stop coloring it for all
she's kept her figure remarkably well. I've had reports. Probably
thinking of retiring, which is why she took you for every shilling
she could get."

"I'm not a boy," Roger protested, incensed.

"You all are, even Hawks, or he'd never've become entangled
with her. Now, we'll hear no more of Chloe deSaules. Yes, I'm
aware of her name, as well as the one with which she started
life: Peg Dorking. Chronicle subscribes to the London papers,
and they contain more than shipping news and military dis-
patches.

"Now, there'll be no more foolishness about your marrying

Kate, or Portia either. They'd both lead you a dog's life, Portia because she hasn't a thought to sully her mind and Kate because she has too many. Go home and take a cold bath, and see if you can talk your father out of a pound or two to last you 'til quarter day. Say the name 'Suzanne,' and he'll cough up whatever you require. Leave Kate and Mr. Hawks to me."

"I don't know what to do, and that's the truth," Kate confided to her new friend as they rode out the next morning. "They all want to turn me into just such another as Mama or Mrs. Appleby, even Gram and Papa. I won't stand for that. As for Roger, he's become impossible!"

Hawks raised his brows, but kept his thoughts to himself.

They'd made no pretense about it this time. Hawks had mounted Hades as if he'd been doing so all his life while the stableboys watched, grinning behind hands supposedly stifling coughs, eyes darting from their Miss Kate in her cherry red habit to the infamous London rake and the equally infamous rogue stallion. The great black hunter had made not the least demur at Hawks's presumption, nor his mistress either.

It was just past dawn now, long shadows streaking across the land, the air fresh and sweet and cool as they cantered down the lane leading to Chilton. Dew beaded each blade of grass, each wildflower budding on the verge. The countryside glistened and shimmered, magical, fairylike. They rounded a bend, slowed to a steady trot and turned onto a side trail leading into low hills that swelled like a frozen sea.

"You're dreadfully silent," Kate commented over the syncopated thud of the horses' hooves. "Customarily you have an opinion on every subject, especially when it concerns my deportment and future."

"I'm not quite certain what to say," Hawks responded as they entered a tract of beech and oak, the branches arching above them like benevolent arms, spangled with swollen buds. The world was waking, the silken mists of night shredding before the rising sun, the shadows rolling back even as he watched. "From all appearances, you had everything well in hand when your father and I arrived."

"I did, except for Mama and Mr. Prohl, which is what's so puzzling. It's as if you and Papa didn't just bring the spring. You changed everything. I'm even older somehow in ways I don't approve in the least—more than a mere nine days can account for."

"Ten."

"Ten? Ten what?"

"I arrived ten days ago this afternoon, if you're counting," he returned wryly. "I agree entirely: they've been an unaccountable ten days."

"Less than a fortnight, in any case. At least you've fulfilled your ambition."

"And what was that?"

"Why, to ride Hades of course, silly!"

"Yes," Hawks agreed, the ghost of a rueful smile quirking his lips, "I've achieved that one."

"You had others? Besides acquiring Hades, that is?"

"Not when I arrived. Now I believe I do. In fact, I know it."

"Must you be so enigmatic? One would think I was conversing on one subject, and you on a completely different one."

"Possibly, or possibly they're the same in the end. You were saying you'd metamorphosed?"

"It's these clothes Papa insisted upon, perhaps." Kate's eyes flew to the unforthcoming Hawks. "I actually like them. That's dreadful! Clothes should be no more than a cover for nakedness, not a matter of pleasure."

"How puritanical."

"Not really. Merely practical. But there's more to it than that. No one person should have so much power," she concluded bitterly, "and now you won't even offer any suggestions as to how I might extricate myself from this imbroglio, and you haven't taught me how to be a rake, even a ladylike one, and I'm deeper in the suds than ever, with ever blacker clouds looming on my horizon, and not the slightest touch of jollity or freedom in recompense, and still you get to ride Hades. I call it most unfair."

"Oh, I have a prime suggestion, but you wouldn't like it. Besides, it's too soon. You wouldn't believe me, even if I explained in the excruciating detail you seem to require. Or, perhaps you would. I'm really not certain, and I'm not willing to risk it. One thing I will say: Don't ever sell Hades. He's your champion, a *chevalier noble et preux,* and will keep you safe when all else fails until the time's right."

"My gallant knight errant? That's a novel concept."

"Or your pet dragon," Hawks said with a whimsical smile, "shielding you from the world's frenetic and often tawdry dance."

"You are fanciful! I'd never realized that. What's your idea? At this point I'd consider most anything, and there's no time better than the present. You wouldn't believe—well, yes, perhaps you might: Roger Appleby paid me his addresses yesterday. He always promised he never would, no matter how our parents pressed him. We swore a pact when he was twelve and I was eight. I suppose ten years isn't a bad run for a treaty, given how our continental allies view their pledges."

"And how did you respond?" he asked, the slightest pucker between his brows.

"I refused, of course. I've already told you I'd never marry Roger. He was most relieved at first, for he only did it because he felt he must. Out of friendship, you understand? He said I wanted protection from you, of all things. Then Gram said it wouldn't do, and he became incensed."

"Young Appleby made you his offer in your grandmother's presence?"

"Why ever shouldn't he've?"

"Dear Lord, what a cawker! Perhaps someday I'll explain the solecism, but believe me, that's not how one goes about it if one desires a positive response."

"You suggest moonlit gardens and plashing fountains and masses of roses and nightingales singing in the trees? And a violin screeching somewhere in the distance, I suppose. Fustian!"

"Fustian, indeed," he chuckled. They came into a shadowed hollow, walked their mounts to the brook tumbling through it over worn, moss-covered rocks. Hawks glanced around him absently, brows rising. "No, there's more to it than that."

"I should hope so. Only a peahen would be impressed by warbling birds. Still, I don't see how you can know so much. You've never offered for a lady, have you?"

"No, for my sins—not that I wouldn't go about it in a far more efficacious manner than your young neighbor. He needs instruction in more than how to tie a neckcloth."

"Oh, really? And I thought his offer most efficient."

"Efficiency isn't what one would seek."

"What would one seek, then? I thought marriage was primarily a business transaction among the *ton*, like the buying and selling of breeding stock, only it's fortunes and estates and people on the block instead of horses and sheep and cattle."

"Not always."

Hawks smiled, noting the wildflowers poking through the moss at the brook's edge, the chuckle of water over stone, the clear liquid light, the air of almost breathless anticipation, as if everything awaited the sun.

"A place such as this," he said softly, "and at precisely this time of day. The present, not to put too fine a point upon it, and the devil take the hindmost." He swung from the saddle, dropped to the ground, led the great black to a sapling and looped the reins over a low branch. While his back was still turned he pulled off his gloves and tucked them in his pocket, his lips twisted by a slight, rueful grimace. Then his features cleared, and he strode back to Kate. "It's pretty here. We've no precise schedule to keep today, have we?"

"No, none. Papa intends to spend the morning closeted with Mick McReedy, and Gram's decided she requires a new gown or two and has appropriated Miss Timmins. They're the only ones who matter."

"Good. Let's tarry awhile. I believe I spotted a fawn across the brook. If we're very quiet, perhaps he and the doe will come down to drink."

"Oh, d'you think so?" Kate swung her leg over the cantle, beaming. "I always feel touched by magic when one sees them like this, almost as if one were being treated to the sight of a unicorn."

"Dragons and unicorns? How appropriate," Hawks murmured, catching her lightly about the waist as she kicked her left foot free and dropped to the ground in a single fluid motion.

"We're not at Astley's," he informed her as she stiffened at his touch. "Ladies are supposed to permit gentlemen to assist them in mounting and dismounting. Makes the gentlemen feel useful, you see. Gentlemen like to feel useful."

"Indeed?" she replied shakily. "I'll remember that, in case I've ever a desire to cater to a gentleman's whims."

His hands rose to her shoulders. He turned her toward the brook. The doe he'd prophesied watched them from across the tumbling water, a fawn at her side, his knob-kneed legs splayed, his delicate head bent to drink.

"Hush," Hawks whispered, his hands lingering on Kate's shoulders.

The girl shivered, her breath coming in shallow gulps, Folly's reins and her crop clenched in her gloved hand. Behind them Hades whickered. With a flick of her tail, the doe whirled and bounded into the woods, the fawn scrambling awkwardly after her.

"How lovely," Kate sighed, attempting to pull away from Hawks.

"That's how I would begin it," he whispered huskily, "at dawn, when things are beginning rather than ending, with a lovely young lady in a crimson habit who has no notion of what is coming next, though having the deer join us would be something I couldn't anticipate, and definitely a bonus."

"Begin what?"

"And then," Hawks continued, suiting actions to words, "I'd

turn that lovely young lady around in my dawn clearing, and I'd say her face was like the sunrise flaming the treetops with Midas's fingers, only it would be my heart she was flaming." His fingers trailed Kate's cheek, coming to rest on her lips. "And I'd say her mouth was a fountain from which I must drink or perish of thirst, and I definitely would not wish her grandmother to be present."

He bent his head slowly, smiling at Kate's wide-eyed confusion.

"D'you know why I wouldn't want her grandmother present?" he said. "Because then I would do this."

His mouth was gentle, tender, first against her forehead, then velvety and warm against her lips, like a newborn foal's muzzle.

"And then," he continued, pulling her fully into his arms and trailing his lips down her neck, "I'd offer her my solution to her problem. I'd tell her my world will be a bleak and cheerless place indeed unless she agrees to join me in it."

Kate gave a cry of disillusioned rage, sent a swift booted kick to his shin and wrenched free of his arms, tears of fury sparkling on her lashes.

"I trusted you," she stormed. Behind them the great black turned his head, watching them with wise eyes. "I thought you were different. Roger said not, but I was too stupid to listen. Oh, what a fool I was!"

"My darling girl, I—"

"I'm not your darling anything! Is this how a seduction's accomplished? Gram wasn't specific, you understand. Such honeyed words. You've mucked me up with an entire year's supply. What a waste!"

"Kate," he pleaded, hands spreading helplessly as he came toward her.

"Miss Watford, to you. You're offering me a carte blanche, of course. Gram's told me of those, too. Have you become so bored after chasing your mistress from the village that you must appropriate whatever's to hand for your pleasures?"

"Kate, I'm not offering—"

"The famous London rake! The great and wealthy gentleman of the *ton!* Oh, you're skilled, I'll grant you that. The words were so honeyed I almost believed them. You've ridden Hades for the last time, I can tell you that! And you've a long walk ahead of you. A very long walk! I pray you perish of thirst and bruised feet."

She struck Folly's rump with her crop, sending him cantering back down the trail. Then she tore across the clearing, freed Hades's reins and attempted to mount the great black hunter. Hades sidled, dancing just beyond her.

"Here you, sirrah," she sobbed, seizing the bridle and attempting to turn him so she could hoist herself into the saddle, "behave yourself."

"God bless all perspicacious dragons who understand when they've met their matches," Hawks murmured, standing where he was and watching Kate's futile attempts with a slight smile.

Hades's dancing was bringing Kate closer and closer to where Hawks waited. Suddenly the black reared, tearing the reins from her hands. He twisted in midair and came down stiff-legged, just as he had done when he schooled Hawks on the day of his arrival. Then he snorted, butted Kate's back with his broad forehead, and sent her stumbling into Hawks's waiting arms.

"I was serious, little Amazon," Hawks said, seizing her in a grip she couldn't break, "but not about a carte blanche. Stop leaping to erroneous conclusions. I want you to become my wife, with all the ceremony Chilton and Twin Oaks and Mr. Prohl, blast his constipated soul, can offer."

She ducked her head, face tear stained, as she emulated Hades and butted him in the chest, attempting to wrench away.

"Before you refuse me, take two things into consideration: I love you to distraction," Hawks said, gripping her chin and forcing her to meet eyes that burned into hers, "which is something I never thought I'd say to any woman. Why d'you think I sent Chloe packing? Why d'you think I sent for her in the first place, come to that? You terrified me. At first I wanted protection. Then I decided I didn't want it at all."

"Oh, I'm that dangerous to you, am I?"

"You are indeed," he grinned crookedly, "as I've just proved. And, there's no one else you'll ever find who'll understand or appreciate Hades half so well, or whom Hades will be likely to understand and appreciate. Why, the rogue sent you back to me, Kate! Trust your dragon. He and I belong together, and we belong together with you. I told you it was too soon, but you must believe me. I don't know what I'll do if you don't. And," he concluded, smile fading, "I believe you care for me, if only just a little, else you wouldn't've been so infuriated when you thought it was a carte blanche I was offering."

"The stud?" she gulped warily, biting her lip and blushing furiously at being caught out. "And I will ride astride, you know."

"In the country, do as you will. Town? Trust me—that's another matter. As for the stud, you have my word it's yours. If you don't consider that sufficient, I'll formally deed all rights to you. But, I hope that won't be for years, and when the time does come, perhaps you'll've learned to trust my judgment sufficiently that you'll consult me on occasion, just as I fully intend to consult you regarding my own breeding programs."

"Your breeding programs?"

"I, too, have a stud, albeit a small one. Nothing so grand as Twin Oaks, but respected by those who know of it nonetheless. How d'you think I persuaded your father to bring me here for an extended visit?"

With an impeccable sense of when to seize the moment, Hawks gave his little would-be female rake a gentle shake and a tender pleading smile, then bent his lips once more to hers. This time Kate made no attempt to escape, instead joining in the exercise at first timorously, then, as the sunlight flowed into the tiny glen in a golden benediction, with increasing enthusiasm.

And so it was that, some time later, the country girl and the fashionable rake returned to Twin Oaks, riding double on Hades and leading Folly, whom they'd found placidly cropping grass and wildflowers along the woodland trail.

Kate married her rake three months later, and gave him her

rogue as a wedding present. If the festivities were marred by a pouting and jealous Portia; if the bride's mother was more concerned with her own toilette and that of her older daughter than the bride's; if the vicar was most reluctant to perform the wedding service, considering both bride and groom unworthy of God's blessing, and paused for an inordinate amount of time when he came to the spot where those knowing of some impediment should speak or forever hold their peace, those things mattered not in the least to the principals.

In later years, Hades's colts became famous among the followers of the great hunts. And Kate's lessons in rakishness? To their private delight, Hawks taught his wife so well that he was forced to watch three sons descend on the *ton* with precisely the same goals of amusement and dissipation that had once been his, and to tremble for the two daughters who so resembled their mother when first he encountered her. "They'll all come about, given time," Kate whispered consolingly in Hawks's ear when he despaired over them, "just as we did." And come about they all did, given time.

Portia? She wed, eventually. Not Mr. Prohl, who ultimately concluded she was too vain and silly to make a proper vicar's wife, but a widowered solicitor from Bristol, untitled and not particularly wealthy, nor even particularly well-endowed mentally, whose first wife had given him only daughters.

And Hades? He survived to the age of twenty-two, a rogue to the end of his days, carrying Hawks in the Quorn, schooling his sons, and generally living a splendid life. Was he pleased with the fate he'd contrived for his independent-minded mistress? Horses can't speak, but there were those who said, watching the great black hunter and the former rake, that both were most pleased, though scarcely more so than she.

About the Author

Monique Ellis lives with her husband, popular watercolorist Jim Ellis, in Tempe, Arizona. She is the author of three Zebra Regency romances, THE FORTESQUE DIAMOND, De-LACEY'S ANGEL, and THE LADY AND THE SPY. She is currently working on her next Zebra Regency romance, which will be published in December 1996. Monique loves hearing from her readers; you may write to her c/o Zebra Books. Please include a self-addressed stamped envelope if you wish a response.

A Rogue's Honor

by
Valerie King

Look how the pale Queen of the silent night
Doth cause the Ocean to attend upon her,
And he, as long as she is in his sight,
With his full tide is ready her to honour.
—Charles Best

One

"Where is he, Thomas? Has he . . . ?" Winifred Childress could not bring herself to speak the words. She had thought of little else but her father's impending demise since having learned of the gravity of his illness three days earlier. But once arrived at Lord Burghfield's family seat in Berkshire, her throat grew tight with tears. The words wouldn't come. She simply couldn't believe such a strong, willful man could succumb— and that so quickly!—to a mere inflammation of the lungs.

"No," Thomas murmured, his gaze shifting nervously away from hers. "Not yet, that is . . . dash it all! Papa shouldn't have brought you here. I mean of course he had to, but, but . . ."

"I know," Winifred returned, deeply concerned by her brother's obvious discomfiture with the situation. She was standing in the middle of the entrance chamber where the butler, old Purley, had been preparing to show her to the drawing room when Thomas entered from the back hall to greet her.

She moved to stand next to Thomas and to look into his green eyes, hoping to allay his distress. She placed a hand on his arm. "Papa and I quarrelled. There is nothing you can do about that. He and I had such disparate views of life that how could it have been otherwise than that we would have one day parted company? I am only sorry that there has never been even the smallest opportunity for reconciliation. Though I did write to him often. Did he . . . did he never speak of my letters? Perhaps he never received them."

Thomas jerked his arm away from her, his cheeks red, his

brows snapped together in a deep frown. He seemed very angry. He ran an anxious hand through his long, curly blond locks.

"Hell and damnation!" he cried, again turning away from her. "You are making this devilishly hard, Winnie! Of course he got your letters, though I doubt he ever read them when you were forever prosing on about his *habits*. But that is all beside the point." His voice dropped to a whisper. "The fact is, *I* didn't want you here."

Winifred shook her head. *"You* didn't?" she asked, speaking to his back. "Thomas, I know we haven't always agreed on everything, especially on the fact that Papa has drawn you so fully into his wretched mode of living, but surely at this hour . . . when he is about to breathe his last—"

"That's just it," Thomas cried, whirling about to face her and extending his hands toward her in an imploring manner. "He's not . . . that is, I was not truthful. But there was nothing I could do, I had to do it. I . . . I'm sorry, Winnie!"

"What are you talking about?" she asked, a gnat of fear beginning to bother her heart. "You've lied to me about something?"

"There you are!" a familiar masculine voice called to her. "And precisely on the mark! But then I always could depend on my little Winnie. How are you, dearest daughter? A trifle dowdy, as usual . . . good God, you are wearing brown stuff! But then, you always were the most priggish chit! Though I must say those blue ribbons on your bonnet do bring out the green of your eyes. Isn't it amazing that both you and Thomas inherited your mother's eyes?"

"Papa," Winnie breathed, staring in utter stupefaction at Lord Burghfield's amazingly vibrant albeit ruddy countenance. Except for the scattered veins across his reddened nose and cheeks, he seemed to be enjoying every hallmark of excellent health. He walked straight and tall, his voice was firm, his blue eyes were clear. She continued, "You are not . . . that is, I cannot credit you could have recovered in only three days time, and that so completely! But I don't understand! Your letter, in a faltering scrawl . . ." She glanced at Thomas, but her brother's complexion was an even deeper shade of scarlet than before and his gaze now seemed fixed to something on the tall ceiling above.

Reality struck her in a sudden flurry of fear. She began to back away from her father and brother. Her father's illness had been a ruse.

The heavy door of the ancient manor house was behind her. She knew a sense of panic so profound that her senses began to reel and she felt ready to swoon. But she couldn't faint. She had to leave, immediately, before it was too late!

She stretched out a hand toward them, warding them off as they slowly advanced toward her. "I will not stay," she said. "You can't make me stay. I will not be drawn into your schemes no matter how desperate either of you are!" She began fluttering her hand toward them, like a farmer's wife shooing birds from her kitchen garden, yet still they came at her, ever more quickly.

She whirled toward the door but before she could open it and escape she heard brisk steps behind her as Lord Burghfield cried out, "Oh, no you don't, m'dear!" She then felt her father grip her left arm tightly and her brother her right.

"We need you," Thomas whispered. "I . . . I am sorry."

"Of course you're sorry," she retorted sharply. "You're always ever so apologetic after you've dislodged yet another paving stone of my life!"

"No fussing, Winnie," her father said firmly as his wine-embued breath flowed over her left cheek. He gripped her arm more tightly still. "We've a guest in the house and I'll not have you flying into the boughs and caterwauling. You only need to be here for this one evening and then you may return at leisure to your employer."

For a long moment she felt a powerful urge to scream and kick and wrench herself from each of their grasps. How could they have done this to her? How could they have behaved so unconscionably as to have lured her to Lambourn with the prospect of her father's death? The whole of it was beyond belief, beyond bearing, beyond comprehension!

"Only tonight," Thomas promised, squeezing her arm gently. "We're in the basket, Winnie. You've got to help just this once or it will be all hallow with us."

Lord Burghfield did not bother trying to plead with her. "The fact is, I won't permit you to leave. And don't consider trying to escape out the old oak behind your bedroom window. I had it chopped down this morning. Permit me to offer this warning, instead . . . if you don't comply with our schemes, I intend personally to pay a call upon Mrs. Stanmore and inform her of a certain personage you entertained in the heart of Mrs. Beenham's yew maze last summer. You remember the yew maze, don't you Winifred? And a certain Mr. Shaw?"

Winifred drew in a sharp breath. "But how did you know of that?"

"Miss Amelia Beenham, your most excellent friend, was so intrigued by Gentleman Shaw's interest in you that I doubt there isn't a member of the beau monde uninformed regarding your amorous adventure with him. Imagine my daughter falling under the spell of one of London's most notorious rogues!"

"But it was innocent . . . innocent, I tell you! Mrs. Stanmore won't believe you—"

"Won't she? You underestimate the depravity of Gabriel Shaw's reputation. I daresay most of it's a hum, the concoction of a great deal of unchecked gossip, but it won't matter." Lord Burghfield pressed home his advantage. "And how can I really be sure of your innocence? By Miss Beenham's recollections, she found you locked in an amazingly passionate embrace with Mr. Shaw after you had been with the man for more than two hours in utter seclusion. No, no, Winifred. Doing it a bit too brown to protest your innocence!"

"You must believe me! Mr. Shaw and I were talking of, of so many things. And then he kissed me, but that's all. I promise you Papa, nothing happened! You may ask him. He will tell you the truth!"

Both Lord Burghfield and Thomas laughed outright.

"Imagine Gentleman Shaw telling the truth," Thomas said.

"He's a damned rogue!" Lord Burghfield intoned. "But whether you are as innocent as you profess, Winnie, it really doesn't matter. The truth is, I'll do whatever I need to do to garner your assistance tonight. As Thomas has said, our pockets are to let and without your help we'll be all to flinders . . . and a little more if we don't come round tonight."

Winifred couldn't credit this was happening to her. It was all so ironic since not only had her father failed to see her established in society so that she might have married well and not only had his excesses forced her to take up an occupation in order to earn her keep, but now he meant to rob her of even that much. And all because it had become known that she had permitted Gabriel Shaw to kiss her.

She felt the fight go out of her and she sighed deeply. Lord Burghfield consequently released her arm.

She was employed as governess to Mrs. Stanmore's three young daughters and had been so for nearly two years. Last summer, she had accepted Amelia Beenham's invitation to spend a brief holiday at her parents' home in Kent. Gabriel Shaw was a particular friend of Mrs. Beenham and had also been in attendance. An odd camaraderie had formed between herself and Mr. Shaw resulting in a tête-à-tête in the yew maze and a subsequent kiss. Should her father choose to expose this event to Mrs. Stanmore, hinting as he would at other scandalous possibilities, not only would her employer turn her off without a reference but she would be fortunate to find another post anywhere in the kingdom. Mrs. Stanmore was her fourth post in five years.

Since she was one-and-twenty she had been supporting herself as a governess but from nearly the first she had found her path as an instructress of young girls fraught with an unexpected difficulty. The trouble lay in her own person, a flaw which had been carefully explained to her by her third employer, the very sensible Mrs. Ash who had smiled in sweet concern, taken her hand gently in hers, pressed it and began, "You are far too pretty to be a governess, Miss Childress. I know you never encouraged my Geoffrey to kiss you and I do lay the blame on the fact that he is just returned quite full of himself from his first year at Oxford. But the fact is, I can't have him, or his brothers, tumbling in love with his sister's governess. Yes, I know it is amazingly unfair and perhaps if you did not have such a sweet temperament and such engaging manners to enhance your beauty, your presence in my home might not be as dangerous as it has proved to be. As it is, the boys stare at you from morning til night, they make excuses to follow you and Jennifer on your daily walks through the park, and Harry who is but thirteen ogles you and sighs in the most ridiculous manner until I am ready to box his ears. No, no don't repine, though I do fear this may be your cross to bear. Please, don't try to argue me out of my decision. The fact is, I must release you from this post and I will. Jennifer will be cast into despair for she dotes on you, so for her sake I trust you will send a letter now and again. I only wonder how it is someone so very pretty did not find a husband, but then that is none of my concern." She had then picked up a sheet of paper which had been sitting beside her through the whole of the interview and handed it to her. "A fine reference which you most certainly deserve. Good luck to you Miss Childress and goodbye."

So far, she had acquired three *fine letters of reference,* and didn't want another. She had wanted to suggest to Mrs. Ash with great facetiousness that she could become as sour and unappealing as any governess alive if she would only give her a chance, but she had remained silent and had wisely sought a post where there were no elder sons in the house to confuse the matter.

As for a husband, her father and brother had made success on that score fairly impossible to attain. Their reputations had from the beginning assured her ineligibility on the Marriage Mart and, of course, her dowry, which had once been a handsome seven thousand pounds, had long since been eaten up in the payment of Lord Burghfield's gaming debts. Her personal charms, such as Mrs. Ash had indicated, had simply not been able to compensate for her familial disadvantages. After all, more than one confirmed gamester had been known to attach himself to the purse strings of an unsuspecting son-in-law.

So it was little surprise that her first and only Season had been cut short by nearly four weeks. Winifred had been *aux anges* at the prospect of enjoying her first Season. Her father at least had had enough sense to hire a distant, widowed cousin, Mrs. Vale, to chaperon her to the various soirées and balls. She had been courted for a time, since she was speedily acknowledged as a diamond of the first stare, but before long her beaux began to drift away and to find other more promising thrones about which to cluster. Her reign had been brief and in the end wholly unsuccessful.

So it was that at six-and-twenty, she was a confirmed apeleader with no prospects, and her hopes of even a tidy life was now pinned squarely upon her success in Mrs. Stanmore's employ.

There was nothing she could do for the present, therefore, but submit to her father's wishes. "What is it you require of me?" she asked quietly, pulling on the ribbons of her bonnet. The blue satin bow fell apart and she resignedly lifted the simple straw poke bonnet from her flattened, dark brown curls.

Thomas finally released her arm and she turned around to face her father. Her brother remained standing slightly behind her.

Lord Burghfield withdrew a gold snuffbox from the pocket of his coat and flipped open the lid. Taking a pinch of the light brown snuff, he drew the pulverized tobacco into each nostril with sharp sniffs. "We've a guest in the house, one who you will be intrigued to know has specifically requested your presence here tonight. Your task will be to entertain him."

"A friend of yours asked for me?" she queried, startled. "How is that possible?"

Her father and brother moved within a large circle of men who were addicted to every form of gaming. They frequented the east end hells and horse races and were known to lose and gain and lose again entire fortunes. Over the years her father

had won and lost some hundred thousand pounds by her esti-
mation. That he was currently bankrupt was neither a surprise
nor the first time he had been in such a sorry state.

Two years ago, she had broken with them both at a time when
she was between teaching posts. They had almost succeeded in
tricking her into becoming entangled in some gaming scheme
or other when she became aware of their full intentions. The
quarrel which had ensued had been horrendous and the only
contact she had had with either of them since had occurred nine
months ago when her father had landed in debtor's prison and
had needed five hundred pounds in order to escape his imprison-
onment.

She had been shocked to receive his request for financial assistance since she couldn't imagine what her father expected her
to do. As a governess her earnings had yet to exceed a mere sixty
pounds per annum. Out of a sense of duty, she had sent him five
pounds—her savings of three months—and a letter begging both
her father and brother to give up their wicked occupations.

She had received no response from either of them after that,
though a friend did convey to her the information that somehow
her father had escaped his difficulties since he had been seen
tooling a natty Stanhope gig down Piccadilly some time in Janu-
ary.

Having had so little contact with her father or her brother,
therefore, to learn now that someone of their acquaintance had
actually requested her presence tonight was baffling in the extreme.

She heard Thomas clear his throat behind her and when she
turned to glance at him, she saw that he was directing his anxious gaze up the staircase.

The entrance chamber of Lambourn Hall was perhaps its best
feature. The ancient, massive front door opened onto a square
hall paneled with a beautiful oak wood from the floor and rising
halfway to the ceiling. A vivid royal blue wallcovering filled the
remaining space up to just a few inches below the meeting of
wall and ceiling where the paneling resumed again extending to,

then spreading over, the high ceiling as well. The stairs were right angle and of the same heavily grained pleasing oak as the wainscoting.

The decor of the entrance hall was less pleasing since the blue wallcovering was scarred. It had been intended to serve as a background display for several grand paintings by Joshua Reynolds. All that remained now, as Winifred's eye drifted in the direction of the halfway landing, were the rectangular stains where dust and chimney smoke had marked the area about the frames. The paintings had of course been gone for many years, sold for paltry sums to pay for either Thomas's or her father's debts. Since neither gentleman had the smallest interest in housekeeping, and the staff at Lambourn was skeletal at best, the walls remained stained.

As her eye followed the line of the stairwell and drifted to the top of the stairs, she received a shock upon discovering the object of Thomas's rather horrified gaze. For there, standing at the top of the staircase was a man she had supposed she would never see again, *Gentleman Shaw,* the man who had last summer nearly stolen her heart.

"*Gentleman,*" she murmured, feeling her knees grow weak and nearly useless. She could not help but wonder just how much of the exchange he had overheard.

"Our guest," Thomas whispered into her ear.

So many thoughts rampaged through Winifred's mind that she again felt near to swooning. For one thing, she could not help but recall the last time they had met and how soft his lips had been when he had kissed her, and how ever since her dreams had been full of him. For another, he was known to be as rich as Croesus, therefore, she couldn't help but believe he was the object of her father's gaming lust. But lastly, and this thought brought a rather numbing fear into her heart, she felt there could be only one reason as to why he would have requested her presence here tonight. If he was to be fleeced, perhaps he felt she would be his prize. The wicked smile on his face as he bowed to her, rather confirmed her suspicions.

"I wasn't certain of your hours, here, Burghfield," he called down to his host as he slowly began his descent, "whether you reverted to earlier country hours or not. I see that I am mistaken," here, a half-smile played on his lips. "But I also see that I am now in time to welcome home your beautiful daughter. Well met, Miss Childress, how do you go on?"

"Very well, Mr. Shaw," she responded politely. Given the wretched nature of her circumstances, she could only wonder she was able to find her voice, but even in the midst of tribulation it would seem her manners would run to support her. "And are you in good health?"

"I have never been better," he responded, continuing to descend the stairs.

He was dressed impeccably, as always, wearing a black evening coat of elegant superfine which fit his broad shoulders to perfection, a white silk waistcoat, black pantaloons, and black silk slippers. His shirtpoints were of a medium height which touched the firm line of his jaw to a nicety and his white neckcloth was tied in neat folds in a style known as *à la Gabriel* or *The Angel,* appellations honoring his name if not his reputation.

He was remarkably handsome and sported an almost military appearance with his thick black hair cut *à la Brutus*. His black brows were arched nicely over perceptive, clear blue eyes, and his nose, though slightly aquiline, was of just the right proportion to give the sense that here was beauty from Olympus. His lips were neither full nor thin and when he had kissed her—oh, Lord she did not want to think of the kiss he had placed on her willing lips!—she had never felt anything so soft nor so sensual in her entire existence.

It was little wonder given his handsome good looks and his wealth, that his reputation among the fairer sex was one of utter devastation. That she, a woman of good sense and firm morals, could have been so easily kissed by Mr. Shaw, bespoke his abilities on that score.

And he had requested her to be present at Lambourn.

She shuddered slightly.

He could want only one thing of her just as her father and brother were quite specific in their intentions toward Mr. Shaw.

He reached the bottom of the stairs and ignoring his host, moved to stand before her, never once taking his gaze from hers. She became aware of her own appearance for the first time and felt a blush creep up her cheeks at her dull, indifferent gown, pelisse, bonnet, and crushed curls. Her gown and her pelisse were both of plain brown stuff and her straw bonnet dangled from hands clothed in worn York tan gloves. Her dark brown hair, which had not seen the skilled hands of a servant in over five years, was dressed in what was now a flattened chignon and certainly could have done little more than give her a travel-stained appearance.

He scrutinized her face as he looked down at her. "You are as pretty as I remember. My God, you've the complexion of an angel."

He had begun just as she would have expected him to—with a ridiculous compliment. Did he suppose she would fall into his arms again so easily?

"Mr. Shaw," she returned, with a slight lift of her brow. "And just how can you, of all men, know how the angels look?"

His lips twitched. "Ah. You refer to my scandalous reputation?" He clucked his tongue at her. Something in the sudden shifting of his expression as his eyes became harder and more piercing, made her think that had they been alone he would have ignored the proprieties and simply taken her in his arms. "You mustn't try to spar with me, Miss Childress. You are woefully inexperienced. But, to answer your question, since I know you to be an angel, I therefore know how they must look."

Something within her rose sharply in rebellion against the horrific nature of her circumstances. "I find your logic faulty and your compliments absurd." She turned to her father. "I should like to retire to my bedchamber now. I am unsuitably attired for the grandeur of your guest."

She ignored the flaring of her father's nostrils as she slipped past Mr. Shaw without casting another glance or word his direction. A low chuckling greeted these efforts, portending an evening fraught with difficulties.

Winifred stood on the threshhold of her old bedchamber and stared in mounting anger at an exquisite dark pink gown laid out on her bed. The pink of the gown contrasted sharply with the worn, red velvet counterpane. A short, heavily freckled maid, who she had never seen before, stood beside the four-poster bed of cherry wood and dropped a nervous curtsy.

"His lordship brought it from London," the maid explained with a frown between her brows. "He said I was to tell you he expected you to wear it tonight. I am sorry for I can see that you don't like it."

Winifred shifted her gaze to stare at the maid and repressed a strong desire to come the crab with her, but she had enough sense to know that the servant was only doing as she was bid. "I will not wear this gown, but don't fret yourself. For the present, I would have you tidy my hair. It is crushed from my bonnet." She moved into the chamber and began unbuttoning her pelisse.

"Of course, miss," the maid said, again dropping a curtsy and moving quickly to receive the hat from Winifred.

As Winifred sat before her old dressing table, she looked at her reflection and saw not the complexion of an angel, but the distress of a young woman who was being forced down a path entirely at odds with the precepts of her life. She wanted to cry out from frustration since it would seem she could neither change nor control what was happening to her.

But as the maid, whose name she learned was Olivia, began to slowly and quite tenderly brush her brown locks, her spirits grew calmer and less pricklish. She looked at the high neck of her brown stuff gown and the long sleeves and a smile made its way to her lips. She might have been brought to Lambourn for dishonorable purposes but she did not have to play them out.

So it was, that fifteen minutes later, with her hair drawn into a proper chignon, she emerged from her bedchamber.

However, her father was waiting for her and she could see by the expression in his eye as his gaze swept over her brown traveling gown that he was displeased. "I thought you might try to play off one of your tricks, Winifred," he said, his arms crossed over his chest and his ruddy nostrils again flaring. He then lifted an arm and pointed at her door. "You will wear the gown I purchased for you in London. I paid a fortune for it in New Bond Street and I insist you put it on. Mr. Shaw is used to the company of ladies of fashion. He will not be in the least content or pleased to be attended at dinner by a spinster in a dull brown dress."

"And will I be in the least content, Papa?" she queried, angrily. "What of my contentment or my pleasure? Do you never consider my happiness?"

He narrowed his eyes at her again crossing his arms over his chest. "You always were a selfish girl," he retorted, his face turning red. "Have I once in the past two years trespassed on you or asked for your help?" She wondered if he had forgotten the five pounds she had sent him while he was in gaol. He continued, "No, I have not, have I? Well, it would seem to me that since I am in desperate straits you might at least show a speck of familial duty and affection and offer your assistance without complaint. But I knew how it would be. Your concerns have always been uppermost in your mind. Do you wonder then why I had long since decided not to show you a bit of sympathy? Now do as you are bid and put on that gown!"

Winifred could not credit the distorted line of his reasonings and concluded as she had earlier that of the moment she truly had no choice but to acquiesce, particularly since her father seemed to have no awareness of her except in how she affected him.

She returned to her bedchamber and after a few minutes decided that if she must dress to please Mr. Shaw then she would at least make herself comfortable in the process. She bid Olivia prepare her a hot bath, build a fire in the hearth, heat up the curling tongs and secure as many colorful ribbons as she could find.

Olivia was both efficient and resourceful so that by the time Winifred was ready to greet the infamous rogue, the effect she had hoped to achieve had been all but surpassed.

She stood before the long gilt looking glass in the corner of her bedchamber and addressed her maid. "So tell me, Olivia," she queried, "do I look like a courtesan?"

Olivia stood just to the side of her and met her gaze in the mirror. Her large brown eyes were opened wide in astonishment. "I think you look just like a princess," she breathed.

This was not the answer she had been looking for nor did she think the maid's response was entirely accurate. But as she gazed into the mirror she thought there might be a little truth in Olivia's observation.

Her long, dark hair was dressed in a mass of ringlets which trailed down her back and which was laced with ribbons of green, pink, white, lavender, and blue silk. Though the overall effect was similar to those achieved by theatre actresses, she noted that the general arrangement of her curls enhanced her oval face, the arch of her brows, the almond shape of her green eyes and the slight retroussé of her nose.

The gown was of a beautiful deep rose silk, with puffed sleeves of tulle embroidered with seed pearls and a hem adorned by several rows of tulle ruffles. A stand of lace encircled the bodice and rose to a high rufflike collar at the back of her neck. In the Empire fashion, the waist was high, though gathered fully in the back and flowing to the floor in a demi-train, which would undoubtedly move beautifully when she walked. The effect was rather more like a fairy tale than she could have wished, but as she turned to the right then to the left, she still believed she appeared very much a courtesan especially since the neckline of her gown was quite décolleté and the swell of her bosom was displayed in a manner most likely to appeal to Gentleman Shaw. If he wasn't pleased, then he was a simpleton of no mean order!

Sighing deeply, she turned away from the mirror and headed

for the door. She couldn't remain closeted in her chamber much longer or her father might just return and drag her downstairs. Besides, she wanted to get the evening over with and the only way she could do that was to begin.

Two

Gabriel Shaw ignored his host. Lord Burghfield in his opinion did not deserve his conversation nor any other form of courtesy normally found in polite society. He therefore kept his nose pinned to a book of Shakespeare's play, *All's Well That Ends Well,* sipped a watery glass of sherry, and strove to keep his temper in check.

He sat in a tattered winged chair in the grand drawing room on the ground floor of Burghfield's country house. He was having great difficulty keeping the disgust from his voice, from his choice of words, and probably from the features of his face. The estate was clearly in a state of decay, the gardens were overgrown and disorderly, the avenue leading to the front door was full of pits and nearly caused his coach and four to break a pole, and the house was unkempt and full of dust. He had sneezed twice upon entering his bedchamber and one swipe of his glove across the window sill overlooking a tangled garden below, found the tip of his finger lined with black grit.

The drawing room certainly had been handsome at one time. But since the sky-blue silk damask walls were bare of art yet showed the faded outlines of paintings and sculptures long since gone, the effect of hominess was considerably diminished. The sherry he was sipping was bitter, the chimney smoked, and his nose was pink from the cold. In March, the wind frequently blustered through the downs as it did now, rattling the windows and promising a cold night.

Burghfield could have at least made the appearance of having invited him to a cozy weekend party instead of the fleecing to which he obviously aspired. Yet what else could he have expected from a confirmed gamester? What Burghfield didn't know, however, was that he had no intention of losing even a tuppence to his host and that the only reason he had accepted his invitation was in the hope that he might see Winifred Childress again.

He smiled to himself as he read another line of Shakespeare's lively play. As he considered Miss Childress, he wondered if his bed would be empty tonight. His thoughts took a delicious turn, one that he had been encouraging since last summer, and he found that the chill of the drawing room was not as oppressive as it had been.

Last July, Miss Childress had been a delight in his arms and he had found himself wanting more. That she had proved to be the daughter of Lord Burghfield had supported his hope that he might be able to partake of her fruits outside the bounds of matrimony. Surely the stable from which she sprang could not have sired any significant degree of virtue. Surely not! At least he hoped not. And if the little drama to which he had been partial witness and which had played itself out earlier in the entrance hall was any indication, he thought it possible Miss Childress had come to Lambourn under duress.

Or perhaps that was all part of the charade—the unwilling, virtuous daughter. Whatever the case, he meant to make the most of the weekend and to further, just as far as he could, his acquaintance with Miss Childress.

Thomas Childress sat opposite him on a sofa of tattered, blue silk damask. Burghfield's only son coughed every now and then as a puff of coal dust emerged to float his direction each time a gust of wind afflicted the chimneys. He had already imbibed a third glass of sherry and looked miserable as he stared into the weak glow of coals on the hearth, his elbow on the arm of the sofa and his chin settled deeply into the palm of his hand.

Lord Burghfield paced behind the sofa and made the same

comment over and over. "Where is that child! How the devil could it take a woman two hours to dress for dinner!"

Mr. Shaw ignored him until now when in addition to the usual complaining he added, "There you are, at last! And pretty as a, a, dear God, what have you done to your hair? Where did you find so many ribbons?"

Gabriel looked up from his book and for a fleeting moment did not recognize the lady who appeared in the doorway. Gone were both the poke bonnet of cheap straw and the pelisse of sturdy brown stuff. Instead a vision had appeared, one he had seen in his dreams many times, one that for a brief whisper of time drove straight into his heart. In just looking at Miss Childress, he had the curious sensation that he was falling from a great height and for a moment he forgot his purposes in coming to Lambourn.

Some of their shared conversation of the summer prior returned to him, of how easily he had been able to tell her so much about his past and about his home in Derbeyshire, of how sweetly and forthrightly she had encouraged him to speak his mind and heart and to not be afraid that she would judge him. And she hadn't. Instead, she had laughed at his jokes, she had been tender when he had expressed his concerns, and she had been careful in every sense not to wound his pride. More importantly, she had not flattered him. He couldn't have borne flattery. Had she sensed as much or was it merely not within her scope of abilities to gain his attention through such devices?

Whatever the case, he found strange sentiments running rampant through his mind as he set aside his bitter sherry and Shakespeare's play and rose to his feet.

"Good God, Winnie!" Thomas cried. "Whatever have you done to yourself?" He then glanced guiltily at Mr. Shaw and added, "That is, you look quite pretty."

Gabriel's lips twitched. His musings diminished and the sensation of falling ceased. The truth was, Miss Childress did look very pretty, but she also looked as though she had just stepped from the stage at Drury Lane!

Without missing a beat he moved quickly forward and took her arm.

"La!" she cried, taking strong hold of his arm in return, wrapping it tightly about his. "I was ever so distraught when I saw you coming down the stairs earlier. I weren't quite myself. Forgive me, *Gentleman,* if I did not welcome you at that time properly. But, la, I do mean to make it up to you now, if you will let me." She leaned into him as they moved toward the threadbare sofa and smiled up into his face.

His lips twitched again. "I will most certainly let you make it up to me," he responded taking her chin in hand and pinching it. He did not mistake the dropping of her eyes or the tense shot of anger which ran from her shoulder to the tips of her fingers which resulted in a lively pinch with which she afflicted him. So the chit was angry!

He didn't care. He was with her again and he could do anything he wanted if he was of a mind. In fact, the more he looked at her and took pleasure in the soft roundness of her breasts and the smoothness of her complexion, the more he thought it might behoove him to drop a few hundred pounds tonight after all. Who would then challenge his actions? Her protests—if indeed she had any—would be meaningless. Her father certainly wouldn't complain so long as he found himself richer and not poorer by Sunday night. He then began to speculate on just how much he would have to lose in order to take his prize without the smallest reproach from any of them.

Winifred played her part through dinner and saw to her great satisfaction that she had given her brother and her father a severe shock. Thomas consistently refused to meet her gaze, but drank steadily through the entire meal. Her father merely glared at her and occasionally frowned. She wondered just what they had been thinking anyway—that Mr. Shaw would leave her an innocent maiden once they had fleeced him? She wanted them to know precisely what the truth of the situation was since she strongly suspected neither of them had considered as much before.

Mr. Shaw, on the other hand, seemed to know exactly what he was doing and was enjoying the evening immensely. He maintained a steady flow of banter with her throughout the meal and countered every purposefully provocative remark of hers with one equally provocative. She might have blushed a little now and again but she was too angry to feel much of anything toward the whole situation other than a profound disgust.

After dinner, her father recommended she take Mr. Shaw to the library while they prepared the billiard room for a lively game of hazard.

Was this where the seduction was to take place? Did Mr. Shaw mean to offer her a carte blanche?

"La, Gentleman, you will like the library . . . so many books, and all!" she cried in her best, most vulgar voice.

She again attacked his arm and held tightly onto it. She led him up the stairs, smiling and pretending to be giddy from wine and laughing at his stupid remarks and clever sallies.

The library, to Winifred's surprise and delight, however, was still in Holland covers and each laden with so much dust that immediately her nose began to itch.

"La, but look at the furniture. Whatevuh was Papa thinking? How am I to entertain you in here?" She turned and smiled widely and stupidly upon Mr. Shaw.

To her great surprise, however, Gentleman did not seem to care about the state of the room, only that for the first time since her arrival he was alone with her. He wasted no time in taking her quite roughly into his arms.

Anger swelled up in her heart so fully that she lost complete control of her senses. She kicked his shins and beat at his back and his shoulders, she screamed hotly beneath his kisses until he suddenly released her in utter surprise.

She was trembling with rage and for some reason made the object of her anger the numerous ribbons tucked into all her curls. She began to pluck and pull at her curls and the ribbons until her dark brown hair was dangling in a mass about her shoulders, the ribbons in disarray.

Mr. Shaw watched her first in amazement, then settled himself on the edge of a nearby desk which she supposed would leave a fine trail of dust along his backside, in order to better observe her hysterics.

She held nothing back as she continued removing the ribbons from her hair, tossing them to the floor one by one. "Of all the scoundrels I have ever heard of," she cried, "or ever known, you must be the worst! What manner of parentage did you have that you must grow up to be such a monster! What would your mother say if she knew what you were about?"

"She had nothing to say to me between lovers," he responded coldly.

She plucked a blue ribbon from a displaced curl. "Is that an excuse for debauchery! Mr. Shaw," here she completely set aside her silly theatrics, and with tears in her eyes said, "You nearly won my heart last summer in only a few hours in a yew maze. You were gentle and respectful and I could not remember having enjoyed a man's company so much in my whole life. Why must you come here tonight to . . . to seduce me?"

A frown began to settle on his brow. She brushed away an errant tear that had seeped from her eye and rolled down her right cheek. "How could you have requested my presence at a gaming party?"

"I wouldn't have supposed you would have disliked it," he ventured.

"Do you know why I came here in the first place?" she said, drawing a pink ribbon from another curl and letting it drop beside the others.

He lifted a brow. "To share in the fruits of your father's labors this evening?"

She lifted her hands in sheer exasperation, shook her head, then sank into a chair next to the desk. A puff of dust rose up about her and she covered her mouth and nose with her hand but to little avail. She sneezed three times, then sighed heavily. She couldn't believe he thought her so bad.

"I have not seen my father for two years. During that time, Thomas only wrote me once when Papa was in debtor's prison and needed funds. I sent him my savings from my employment . . . five pounds!"

"Your employment?" he queried.

She looked up at him and blinked. "I am governess to Mrs. Stanmore's three young daughters in Hampshire. I have been in her employ for two years. Last summer, when I first met you, I was enjoying a holiday . . . that's all. Perhaps, I should have told you and Miss Beenham just how I was situated, but I think for just a little while I wanted to pretend that my life was as I had always dreamed it would be and not as it was."

"Good God," he breathed.

"I didn't know you were going to be here. Thomas wrote me a sennight past and said that Papa was . . . well, that he was dying. I shouldn't have come for any other reason and well they knew it. I suppose you are aware they intend to somehow steal some of your fortune tonight?"

Her arm was resting on the desk near his knee. He slipped his hand over hers and pressed it gently. "Do you like being a governess?" he queried, ignoring her revelation concerning her father and brother.

She looked up into his face and saw an expression of sympathy in his blue eyes which nearly undid her. She knew a brief impulse to rise from her chair and to slide into his arms, just as she had last summer.

Instead, she answered his question. "I suppose the job is like any other. There is a certain amount of tedium which is not pleasing, I only have two afternoons per week to myself, and for the most part I am at the whims of my employer and subject to the numerous ploys of my charges in their attempts to avoid their lessons. But on the whole, yes, I do enjoy being an instructress."

"And are the girls well behaved?"

She laughed and smiled a little. "They are horridly spoiled but I believe they are loved."

He did not remove his hand and she found the warmth of his touch comforting. To her surprise, he then slid from the desk and dropped to his knees beside her. He let his hands drift through her curls and he began to kiss her gently on the forehead, on the eyes, beside her nose. "Poor Miss Childress," he murmured, a lilt of laughter riding his voice. "Poor little Winifred."

How it was he did not offend her, she wasn't certain. Perhaps because she sensed that though he was being silly and even a little seductive, he did not lack true sympathy.

Thoughts of the prior summer began to run riot through her mind. She had been with him in the yew maze far longer than her friend, Miss Beenham, could have known. For nearly seven hours, in fact. They had talked, laughed, talked a great deal more and in the end his lips had found hers and he had kissed her and kissed her until she had found herself deeply within his arms. They had been seated on a stone bench, then he had lifted her to her feet and held her so tightly she could scarcely breathe. His kisses had been neither swift nor innocent. He had possessed her mouth in a way that had left her trembling and wishful of things she should never have wished for. Had an unexpected summer shower not interrupted the heady tête-à-tête, she was not certain what would have happened next.

The weeks following, when she had resumed her post at Mrs. Stanmore's, night after night she had fallen asleep dreaming of his kisses, longing to be kissed again, wishing that her life wasn't as it was. He had crept into her dreams, he had tormented her now for nine months, and he was here now torturing her, albeit willingly, all over again.

How odd that his lips were on her cheek now. How odd that she wasn't repulsing him. She shifted her face slightly and he responded to her invitation by drifting his lips over hers and teasing her. She parted her lips and caught the faint bouquet of Madeira. His lips parted, his tongue, so soft, touched hers. She moaned, wanting him to kiss her as he had last summer.

She lifted her arm to embrace him, amazed at how heavy and lethargic she felt. She touched his shoulder with her hand.

"Winnie," he whispered, her breath catching up the sound of .ıer name as she gasped lightly. His lips touched hers fully, his tongue touched hers again. She moved her hand and arm across his back, she embraced him as he drove his tongue into her. Memories of past kisses flooded the present one. She wrapped her arms about his neck and while he plundered her he lifted her to her feet and drew her tightly against him—just as before! She felt his hips and muscled thighs flexed hard against her. With one arm, he held her tightly about the waist. With his free hand, he explored the mass of her curls.

She spoke his name. "Gabriel," she whispered as he kissed her over and over. "Gabriel, where are your wings? Do you mean to lift me out of this house forever?" She heard him moan as he kissed her harder still.

After a moment, he drew back slightly and she looked into blue eyes heavy with passion. "Become my mistress, Winnie," he whispered. "Accept my protection. You will never suffer again, never work again. I will see that your future is made secure forever."

Why wasn't she offended that he was offering her the carte blanche? She didn't know. She simply wasn't. Strange as it seemed, she believed his motives, albeit immoral, were kindly meant.

"I can't," she whispered, disengaging her arms from about him and reluctantly stepping away from him. "I know my circumstances seem to you to be unacceptable, but I am able to earn a living and for that I have willed myself to be content as well as grateful."

He took a step toward her, closing the distance, and again took her in his arms. "This is no life for you. You've more passion than any woman I've ever known. Come with me. I'll settle an amount on your father and on you. We'll go to Europe. No one need know. Later, I can return you to London and you can say you received an inheritance and live however you please.

Only say you will come with me." She moaned faintly as he kissed her cheek and again found her lips and again took possession of her.

She responded to the depths of her soul to the sweetness found in the warmth and strength of his arms and to the rich resonance of his voice. She felt tears biting her eyes. She was tempted. She thought of all the weeks and months she had spent dreaming of being in his arms again, but to what purpose? There could be no purpose. Now, ever. He would want her only for a time, then he would cast her aside.

She could never live in such a manner. Never. "I cannot," she said at last.

Having made her decision, her desire for him seemed to melt away and disappear. His kisses no longer burned. She closed her soul to him and her passion dissipated like steam from a bubbling copper kettle into cold air.

He seemed to sense as much and pulled back from her again. He looked at her, searching her eyes. "You will not relent?"

She shook her head.

"You do realize this current situation would permit me to take you anyway? Your father would never press charges once I had given him a few hundred pounds, all in a strictly honorable game of whist or hazard, of course."

She laughed, brushing away another errant tear. "You are not so bad as that."

"You are mistaken," he said. "I am as bad as that, and a little more. Something I mean to show you. Now, come to the billiard room and see what I intend to do next. I have thought of little else but your kisses of summer last. Your father may have believed he could bribe me with your attendance tonight, but what he doesn't know is that I will have you without losing even a shilling."

Winifred looked at him, startled by the hard edge to his voice and by the mulish line of his jaw.

"What do you mean to do?"

He merely smiled quite wickedly as he walked to the door,

opened it, then indicated she was to come with him to the billiard room.

The truth was, she did not possess a profound knowledge of his character. Would he ravish an innocent? His reputation was very bad. His past was riddled with broken hearts, jealous mistresses, arguments between women in ballrooms over his favors, and many other terrible, terrible reports. But never before had she heard he had deliberately seduced and wounded an innocent. Was it possible this was how he succeeded in his more unsavory seductions, by bribing avaricious parents, or tricking them somehow?

The billiard room was as the others. Not a print, painting, miniature, or even a lady's sampler adorned the walls. The wainscoting was chipped, even the green baize on the table was ripped in three places.

But her father and brother, though a trifle bleary-eyed from too much wine, were ready to play at hazard. The dice were in the box. Pound notes were settled in neat stacks in front of each player. Several branches of candles were scattered about the chamber to illumine the table.

Thomas held the box in his hand, stared blindly at one of the rents in the fabric and rolled the dice about in unsteady circles.

When Winnie cleared her throat and finally caught his eye, Thomas frowned at the sight of her hair and she realized from her disorderly locks he immediately began to suspect the worst. He glared at Mr. Shaw and Winifred found herself disgusted that her brother would at this eleventh hour show even a mite of dislike for the very situation he had helped promote.

Lord Burghfield as well seemed daunted by her disheveled appearance. She ignored him, however, and took up a seat in a shiny, horsehair winged chair at the far end of the chamber, near the window which rattled from the March wind. She found the noise strangely comforting and settled her gaze out the window. The candlelight within the billiard room was sufficiently dim to allow a clear view of the east hills and the night sky beyond. The wind was keeping any nearby clouds at bay and a beautiful starry expanse reigned over a sleepy countryside. She let her mind escape into the beech-laden home wood. She didn't want to think about Shaw just now, or anything else for the present. She wanted to forget, if but for a half hour or so that her peaceful life had been interrupted by three men bent on mischief.

An hour of play passed. The men forgot her presence and became thoroughly engulfed in the pleasure of gaming. Every once in awhile, she would hear the word "crabs" called out, but otherwise, her mind became fixed on the stars and the wind and the dark sky.

Until, that is, her father cried out, "I won't do it! I can't believe you would even ask such a thing!"

Her attention became suddenly riveted back to the billiard table as she turned to face the players. Shaw was standing on the right, his hand clutching several scraps of paper. Candles guttering low in their sockets beyond him, cast his shadow over the skirts of her rose evening gown.

He shook the papers angrily at her father. "These are your vowels, Burghfield," he snapped. "You will settle them now, in this fashion, or by God I'll ruin you even from attending the east end hells."

Winifred was suddenly overcome with panic. She shifted her gaze to her father, then to her brother. Thomas was staring at her horrified. What had she missed? What was going forward? Instinctively, she knew the exchange involved her somehow, but in what way?

She rose to her feet.

"I won't do it," her father said, unconvincingly, his tone wavering. He, too, looked at her, his eyes red-rimmed and agitated. "I . . . I can't do it. She's my daughter. I have no power over her. She attained her majority too many years ago."

"A father can always manipulate or force his children to do whatever he wishes them to do . . . especially a daughter, as you very well know."

Burghfield gasped and took a menacing step into the rail of the billiard table as though to challenge Gentleman Shaw.

"Come, come," Mr. Shaw said, taking a slightly different approach. "I ask only for a fortnight . . . a small price to pay in any event. Besides, you're bound to win and I'll tell you what, I'll make it easier for you. Forget hazard . . . if you roll the dice and come up with a sum equaling any odd number, I'll give you two thousand pounds in addition to your vouchers, and your daughter may keep her innocence. That's like a cut of the cards, one chance in two of winning."

Winifred finally understood it all. She rose from the horsehair chair and moved to the table until the edge of it pressed into her hips. "Father," she breathed, her heart racing. "Don't do this, I beg of you. What if you lose? You can't do this to me."

He stared at her in return, his face white. His gaze did not precisely meet hers. It was as though he was looking into her and past her, weighing his life, his value for her. He shifted his gaze and stared at the vowels in Shaw's hand. Shaw let them drop to the table. "Three thousand pounds," he offered, upping the stakes.

"Done," her father stated suddenly, his eyes brightening to a plane of madness. He picked up the box and let them fly.

"Four," Shaw said with a laugh. "You lose." He then turned to Winifred and issued a string of simple commands. "You are coming with me. I've won you on a roll of the dice. You are mine for two weeks. If you do not come, I will have your father and brother stripped of the last vestiges of their honor, and I will inform Mrs. Stanmore of your family's history and vices."

Winifred stared at him, feeling as though he had taken a sword and was flaying her alive with it. He was as bad as her father. How could she have ever thought him any different?

"You cur," Thomas cried. "I'll call you out for this! How dare you treat my sister in this manner!" He rounded the table and lunged at Shaw with his fists.

But Thomas was half-foxed and Shaw was not. Shaw caught him easily with a facer, and knocked him nearly senseless to the shabby carpet at Winifred's feet. He moved to stand over Thomas, his complexion high.

"You dare to accuse me of misusing your sister?" he asked sardonically. "You are a fool, Mr. Childress. You no more deserve to call Winifred, 'sister,' than you deserve to live. That you are permitted in our society to do both is as much a farce as it is a crime."

Winifred saw the anger in Mr. Shaw's face and did not understand him in this moment. He was taking her to become his mistress, yet he clearly loathed Thomas for what he was doing. Rather like the pot calling the kettle black.

Winifred turned away from them both. She felt numb and frightened all at once. She was leaving her home to spend a fortnight with a monstrous rogue who had just defended her against her brother. She was confused and distraught.

"You will want to go upstairs, now, Miss Childress," Mr. Shaw said in a remarkably calm voice.

"Yes," she mumbled. "I need to change my gown and tidy my hair. You will not like my bonnet but it is the only one I have."

As she started toward the door, she looked at her father, but he would not meet her gaze. But before she moved past him, he caught her arm and murmured, "I'm sorry, Winnie. I've never done right by you. I . . . I truly am sorry."

A half hour later, Winifred found herself seated beside Gentleman Shaw in his town chariot. She was still numb, and unable to think clearly. She couldn't credit what was happening to her. Not eight hours earlier she had been a respectable governess, earning her keep and living a quiet life. Now she was to lose her innocence to a rogue among rogues because her father was a gamester. Her life would never be the same and whatever hopes she might have cherished a day earlier, a week earlier, a month earlier about a reasonably happy future, were utterly gone.

She closed her eyes and listened to the crunch of the gravel as the postilion guided the coach onto the King's Highway. She took a deep breath and concentrated for probably a mile on simply breathing until some of the numbness and shock of her circumstances began to dissipate. She opened her eyes and looked out the window. The stars were still shining brightly but not nearly so prettily as before. She glanced at the man on her right. Why did he seem so content, she wondered. His hat was settled firmly on his head and he wore a three-caped black woolen greatcoat against the early spring chill. His shirtpoints had wilted slightly but otherwise he was as elegant in appearance as he had been when he first descended the stairs at Lambourn. The dim light of the carriage lamp inside his expensive coach cast his features in a soft, warm glow. Was this man to be the one who would take her as a man takes his wife?

She couldn't believe it was true. "I wonder if you will be pleased with me as your mistress," she mused aloud.

"I have no doubts on that head," he stated baldly. He turned to look at her. Did his lips twitch? "Particularly since you kiss like an angel."

"And how do you know how angels kiss?" she queried with a bitter laugh, reminded of their earlier bantering. She didn't expect an answer.

But as she turned away from him, he caught her chin and her face toward him. "Because I have kissed you," he said, his voice warm and beckoning.

She caught her breath. Why did he have to look at her in just that way as though he was sincere and sincere again.

"I wish you hadn't done this," she whispered. "I have no desire to be any man's mistress."

"I know that," he said. "But you will like being mine." And then he smiled.

Perhaps it was the smile or the lateness of the hour or her fatigue. But whatever the case, she flew into the boughs. "Of all the arrogance, the high-handedness! You have gone beyond the pale, returned, then gone back again! How can you be so unconscionable? Have you no sense of propriety? Dignity? Shame?"

He shook his head, the smile now crookedly upon his lips. "None," he said, clearly amused and perhaps even pleased.

She growled. "I shan't stay. I shall run away the moment I am able."

"I consider myself warned."

She growled again.

"But let me give you a warning." He then turned to her and placed one arm behind her and one hand bracing himself against the carriage wall so that she was pinned almost beneath him. "Should you leave me, I will spend every waking hour hunting you down til I have found you again. By rights, you are mine for a fortnight and I intend to have my fortnight."

He then began to kiss her face as he had done in the library. "I will love you as no man could ever love you, Winifred," he whispered into her ear. Suddenly he was kissing her ear very deeply. She caught her breath as a ruffle of gooseflesh traveled in a spark down her neck and side. A strange, quite physical desire suddenly swept over her. Why was he able to make her feel such reckless, improper things?

He slipped his arm behind her and about her waist. She simply could not keep her arms from sliding up his chest and about his neck. He left her ear, found her mouth and plundered her with a kiss that left her breathless and aching. As much as she loathed the idea of becoming his mistress, she understood in this moment the awful truth that there was nothing she wanted more than to be with him.

After a time, he drew back and looked into her eyes. His expression seemed strange to her. It was loving and concerned yet full of desire. He slipped his hand to the buttons of her pelisse and began to undo them one by one until he was able to push the pelisse away. He looked down at her breasts, now safe behind the brown stuff gown. He lowered his head and began to kiss the hidden swell of her bosom. She felt his hand on her thigh and she realized that there was nothing at all to stop him from taking right now what he had won on a toss of the dice.

She stopped breathing and waited. She had no fight left in

her to mount a defense. Indeed, in this moment, with her body
still aching from his kisses, she didn't even have an inclination
to oppose him. He had won both the battle and the war.

She waited, tense. He let his forehead rest on her chest. She
felt his lips tenderly kiss her. For a long moment he remained
there, breathing unevenly, his fingers gently kneading the soft
skin of her thigh, yet he said nothing and did nothing more.

Then he lifted his head, removed his hand from her leg, drew
each side of her pelisse over her chest, and sat up. He did not
speak to her but directed his gaze out the window beyond her.
His expression was wholly inscrutable. She sensed that something had changed, but she didn't know in what way or why.

After a moment, she queried, "Where are we going tonight?"

"The George Inn. A small village past Newbury."

"Newbury? We won't arrive before dawn then."

"No, I suppose we will not. You may sleep if you like."

"How very kind of you," she responded facetiously.

He chuckled, but did not attempt to give her an answer.

Three

Sometime later, Winifred awoke to the sensation of Shaw's coach coming to a halt. She was curled into his shoulder and he was supporting her easily with his arm. The pungent smell of his shaving soap was one of the first sensations to greet her as sleep began to drift away from her brain. She rubbed her cheek against the lapel of his smooth greatcoat. When had her bonnet come off?

Now, she remembered.

She had drowsed and slid into his shoulder and he had complained about the brim of her bonnet, a nuisance he had quickly rectified by removing her hat for her. She was so worn out that she didn't give a fig at present what he was doing or even what he might do. That morning, she had traveled from Mrs. Stanmore's home in Hampshire to Lambourn in Berkshire, then she had experienced the worst night of her entire existence, and afterward had been whisked away in a coach and four heading again toward Hampshire. All she wanted to do now was sleep.

She thought perhaps they were changing horses yet again, but she didn't hear the usual sounds of a coaching inn—the call of the ostler, the sounds of the traces jingling as the horses were unharnessed and exchanged, the kind offers of tea and ale through the open door of the carriage.

In fact, it was too quiet.

With this realization, sleep began to desert her sufficiently to permit her to bring herself upright. She opened her eyes and rubbing them gazed out first her window and then the window next to Mr. Shaw. What she saw startled her.

This was no posting inn. Where on earth were they?

She glanced at Mr. Shaw. "I don't understand. This can't be an inn."

"No it is not," he responded unhelpfully.

"Shaw, don't be so elusive at this hour. Where are we?"

"My sister's home in Bedfordshire."

At that, sleep bolted from her brain. "What?" she cried, taking in a deep breath. "Lady Aldworth's home? Dear God, you've gone mad! What is she going to say? How will she receive me? How . . . how could you be so cruel, to her, to me?"

"Stop the theatrics, Miss Childress. My sister will not be in the least offended or even surprised. She is sufficiently well acquainted with me that she will not think it at all odd that I have brought you home to meet her. But you'll see for yourself soon enough."

Winifred was shocked. She had little knowledge of Lady Aldworth but from what she had heard, her reputation and her conduct was considered quite above reproach and as much unlike her notorious brother as snowfall was from sunshine. How was it possible, then, that a lady with such unexceptional morals could possibly condone, accept, or otherwise tolerate the introduction of a man's fancy-piece into her home!

"No, you can't do this," she murmured, shaking her head wildly. "You've gone mad! Pray, reconsider before it is too late."

He only laughed and when a footman emerged from the fine Elizabethan mansion to cross the drive and open the door for them both, Mr. Shaw handed her down with every care he would have given the finest lady of his acquaintance.

A moment later, a woman emerged at the portal, her hair tucked up beneath a mobcap, a dressing gown tied firmly about her waist and an oil lamp held high. "It is you, Gabriel!" she cried enthusiastically. "Aldworth said you had arrived, but I told him it was just a hum. But then it is so like you to surprise me. And who is this? Who have you brought home to meet me?"

Winifred looked into kind hazel eyes. Lady Aldworth was perhaps two or three years older than herself and was the mother of seven young children. "Why, if it isn't Winifred Childress?" she exclaimed before she received an answer to her query. "You probably don't remember me, Miss Childress, but we were at Mrs. Hungerford's Select Seminary for Young Ladies together . . . goodness it has been too many years to count. But I would know you anywhere. Oh, do come in. Forgive my poor manners, I am just so pleased to see my brother and truly delighted to meet you again."

She led the way into a lofty entrance hall and settled her oil lamp on a round, inlaid table in the center of the chamber. An arrangement of what seemed like a hundred yellow daffodils greeted Winifred's eyes. Lady Aldworth continued, addressing her brother. "I know Miss Childress does not remember me because I am such a plain Jane, but we used to stare at her, my friends and I, whenever she but entered a room." She turned toward Winifred. "You were so very beautiful what with your large green eyes and skin like porcelain."

"You're . . . you're very kind," Winifred responded.

"There, now I've made you blush and it is so very late, too late I think to be hearing compliments. I imagine you are longing for your bed."

"Indeed I am, ma'am, if you please."

"Miss Childress and I are to be married," Mr. Shaw interjected bluntly as Lady Aldworth picked up the oil lamp and took Winifred's arm.

Winifred drew in a sharp breath and glanced at Shaw in utter astonishment. Why on earth had he said that!

"Well, of course you are," Lady Aldworth responded sweetly. Since she had already turned Winifred toward the stairs, she looked back at her brother and smiled. "Why else would you have brought a lady to Upton Hall in the middle of the night?"

Some odd exchange then occurred between brother and sister.

Winifred watched the rather piercing communication, hazel eye to blue eye and wondered what either of them meant by it. Perhaps it was some sort of signal they had prearranged so that Lady Aldworth would comprehend the true relationship between Mr. Shaw and whatever lady might be on his arm.

When Mr. Shaw made no comment but to smile at his sister in return, Lady Aldworth slid her gaze back to Winifred. She immediately began guiding her to the stairs. "You shall have the chamber next to mine and then we can share secrets, if you like. So tell me, how long have you and Gabriel been betrothed?"

Oh, dear! What manner of secrets did Lady Aldworth expect to hear? Was she perchance as bad as her brother? As for answering her question about the betrothal, she blushed as she spoke. "Only . . . only since this evening," Winifred lied.

"Well, that would certainly explain why I know nothing about it. Of course, Gabriel always was secretive and unpredictable." She again glanced back at her brother and shot him a wide, rather happy smile.

Winifred slowly ascended the stairs beside her hostess. Her legs were heavy with fatigue as was her voice. After she had responded in a series of rather inarticulate mumbles to several of the viscountess's queries about the journey to Upton Hall and what she had accomplished since her education at Mrs. Hungerford's Seminary, Lady Aldworth reproached herself for her stupidity in not holding her tongue in the face of Winifred's exhaustion. She fell silent, and after seeing Winifred tucked between the sheets, she blew out the candle and quit the chamber.

Winifred was beyond grateful the kind woman was gone. She was more tired than she could ever remember. Yet one fear remained to keep sleep far from her as she clutched the sheets to her chin. Mr. Shaw knew to which room she had been led and would undoubtedly be joining her very soon to take advantage of his winnings at hazard. Her heart thumped loudly in her ears as she strained minute after minute to hear his footfall outside her door.

But no sound came. Several minutes passed, five then ten,

perhaps more. The dark of night, her fatigue, her fears all began to swim together in her head.

She felt her eyes droop. She was beyond drowsy. Just as she was dropping off to sleep a noise in the hallway awakened her. Again her heart set to thumping. Surely Mr. Shaw was coming to her now. But she must have been mistaken, or heard a sound from some other bedchamber because the hall emitted no further noises.

Though she tried very hard to keep awake, expecting Shaw at any moment, she knew she was slipping into her dreams.

More noises came to her as sleep dove into her brain then retreated. This time she heard giggling, then nothing, then more giggling.

Why would Mr. Shaw be giggling? How absurd! He sounded just like a child. She could barely open her eyes. "One moment, if you please," she murmured. "Couldn't this wait? I'm so very tired."

The giggling resounded again—how was it possible Mr. Shaw could sound like a little girl? Curiosity began to dig at her and only then did her sleepiness begin to recede.

More giggling, but this time several voices greeted her ears. Children's voices!

Her eyes popped open. Sunlight streamed through a window opposite her bed and beside her the giggles resumed. She looked to her right and there standing over her bed and staring directly at her were three, no four children.

"Goodness!" she cried, blinking back at them. Her bedchamber was decorated in dark blues and golds and the entire chamber was lit with a warm, late morning light. She then realized she must have fallen asleep for several hours, especially given the brightness of the light coming through the window.

The eldest child, a girl of perhaps eight years, stepped forward. She had Lady Aldworth's lovely freckles and soft hazel eyes. "We couldn't wait to see Uncle Gabriel's bride," she cried. "How do you do? I am Meg."

"H . . . how do you do, Meg? I am Miss Childress."

The other children stepped forward and in turn announced their names. "I am Stephen. I am seven."

"George."

"You must be six," Winifred said.

George nodded.

"And I am *little* Gabriel," the third boy announced. He seemed inordinately proud of his name and nickname. He had a tooth missing, was sturdy in appearance and gave every evidence that he would not be so very *little* after all when he grew up.

"Hallo, Gabriel," she said, turning on her side and tucking her hand beneath her cheek.

All the children stepped closer and leaned their elbows and forearms on the tall bed to observe her better still. Besides the missing tooth, she saw that little Gabriel's chin was bruised and his lip was swollen.

"Have you been sparring with your elder brothers?" she queried, amused.

He broke into a ravishing grin. "No!" he exclaimed. "Papa would pull me hard by the ear if he thought I had been boxing with George or Stephen." He then whispered, "I fell out of one of the peach trees."

Winifred laughed.

George, a solemn fellow, asked, "Are you betrothed to our uncle?"

In spite of herself, Winifred felt a blush touch her cheeks. "So it would seem," she responded, trying to sound light-hearted. At least that wasn't precisely telling a whisker since she was merely repeating what Mr. Shaw had already said to their mother.

George nodded. "Well, I like you. I hope you wish to be our aunt for there are seven of us, though Mama still keeps the twin girls beside her bed. They are not yet two months old."

The picture of the children before her and the one of Lady Aldworth tending to her infants brought such a longing rushing through Winifred's soul that she suddenly felt tears sting her eyes. "I have a brother," she said, "but he has no children and I have been wanting to be an aunt for a very long time. So I consider myself immensely fortunate that there are so many of you."

Since at that moment, little Gabriel seemed to have taken some exception to Stephen having pulled his hair, a quarrel was primed to commence when a large woman with a booming voice entered her bedchamber. "What will your mother say if she should discover you have trespassed her guest's bedchamber? Out with you now, all of you, *at once!*" She then smiled not unkindly and turned her attention to Winifred. "Miss, I do beg your pardon! Usually the children are far better behaved. But then it is not every day Mr. Shaw brings home his bride-to-be."

She then ushered the children out and left Winifred to the enjoyment of her prickled conscience.

A bride, betrothed, Uncle Gabriel to be married.

She pulled the sheet over her head and groaned. It was bad enough to have been thrust into the veritable bosom of Lady Aldworth's family, but to have her relationship to Mr. Shaw so thoroughly misunderstood was nearly beyond bearing. Why had he thought it at all proper to bring her here and why had he said she was his betrothed? He ought to have told Lady Aldworth that he had found her in distress and knew that he could count on his sister for assistance—oh, anything but that she was his bride-to-be!

"But I don't understand?" she whispered, some two hours later to Mr. Shaw. "Why did you have to tell her we were to be married? Why couldn't you have said you found me stranded at an inn, that we were old acquaintances, and that you simply couldn't leave me to fend for myself when I was utterly destitute?"

"Why were you destitute?" he asked, being nonsensical.

"I don't know," she responded, huffing out her frustration with an impatient sigh. "Perhaps I had been accosted by footpads or . . . or highwaymen and I had been robbed of my savings while traveling back to Mrs. Stanmore's. Surely you could have used a little more imagination than to have presented me to your sister as your betrothed!"

"What?" he asked, his lips twitching. "And *lie* to my sister about an imagined encounter with thieves? She would have found me out in a trice. No, it wouldn't have fadged. Better to have told her I mean to marry you. After we're gone, I'll explain it all in a letter."

Winifred tilted her head, her eyes widening and her hands finding themselves planted firmly upon her hips. "You are a master at self-deception, Mr. Shaw. I don't make you out! Why isn't it a lie to tell Lady Aldworth that we are betrothed? And how can you say you will simply write to her and *explain* my presence at Upton Hall to her? How did you think to phrase it? *Oh, by the by, my dearest sister, but that lady who you supposed was my betrothed was really just a lightskirt I found at one of my cronies' home.*"

He lifted his brows. "Lightskirt?" he queried. "If we are to be married, Miss Childress, I hope you don't mean to begin speaking vulgar cant. What a terrible example for the children!"

Winifred closed her eyes and tried to calm the rising agitation and fury which threatened to engulf her. "Oh," she breathed angrily. "But you are the most insufferable, odious, arrogant, boorish man I have ever met—"

"Hush! Here come the children."

They appeared at the doorway of the morning room, having escaped their nurse again. Catching sight of their uncle they fairly ran into his arms. He was besieged with gestures of affection which quite knocked Winifred out of stride. Shaw's reputation was completely at odds with the homey scene before her.

Since the youngest child was a little girl of about two or three—a child who had not been in her bedchamber that morning—and could not find her way to Uncle Gabriel's arm, Winifred rescued her, lifting her up so that she could see her uncle.

"Uncle Gabe," she pleaded in her little girl's voice, holding her arms out to him. "Uncle Gabe."

"Madeleine!" he cried, drawing her easily from Winifred's

arms while the other children pelted him with questions and begged to know if he had brought presents with him from London.

Winifred watched Madeleine catch her arms about his neck. She was utterly astonished by the sight of so much enthusiastic affection. She could not credit that a man with such a burning reputation as Gabriel Shaw should be able to command the affections of anyone, nonetheless a passel of children.

He led his flock toward the fireplace where a small log fire kept the chill from the room. He seated himself on a winged chair of forest green velvet and the children wasted no time in clustering about him. He appeared to have forgotten all about his *betrothed* as he attended fully to his nieces and nephews. His eyes, his hands, his mind, his kisses were all for the children.

She watched and wondered, and wondered again.

She did not know Lady Aldworth had arrived until her voice appeared over her shoulder. "I hope you don't mind, but my babies are exceedingly fond of Gabriel."

"How could I mind," she murmured. "I find the whole of it charming beyond words."

She felt Lady Aldworth's arm slip about her waist. "I thought you might. You were always wont to take the younger girls under your wing at the seminary. Anyone who was frightened or lonely could find succor at your side." She released her and said, "Now let me look at you." She rounded Winifred and continued, "I thought that gown might be just the thing. With your complexion, your green eyes and the deep brown of your hair, blue suits you to perfection."

She was wearing one of several gowns Lady Aldworth had loaned to her. "Thank you ever so much," she said.

"Gabriel said he had stupidly lost your portmanteaus coming from an inn in Berkshire." A curious frown touched the viscountess's brow.

Again a blush touched Winifred's cheeks. "Y . . . yes. Quite stupid of him, wasn't it? I was so fatigued from the journey I fear I was fast asleep or it wouldn't have happened."

Lady Aldworth merely smiled then begged the children to come to table where a tidy nuncheon was soon served and devoured by her active offspring.

Later that afternoon in the center of the yew maze, while playing at Blind Man's Bluff with the children, Winifred was removing a pretty pink lace kerchief from about her eyes when Mr. Shaw came to join them. He had unhappy news, however, for he was dressed in traveling garb and told the children much to their dismay that he would be leaving them. "But only for as long as it takes me to get to London and back again, I promise you." He was greeted with groans and complaints.

Winifred, however, received his news with trembling knees. Why had she not thought he would have insisted on continuing their journey immediately? She supposed then that the reason he had not come to her bed last night was from fear of discovery. Once away from Upton Hall there would be nothing to stop him from taking his prize.

"I suppose I should be fetching my bonnet, then," she said, trying to smile but feeling as though her cheeks had become frozen in place. When she saw his lifted brow, she continued, "And . . . and my pelisse. I won't be a moment. Have my bandboxes been sent down?" When the children realized they would be losing both their uncle and his bride-to-be their caterwauling increased until Shaw silenced them.

"Enough!" he barked. "What manners are these?"

The children begged pardon, but their faces showed their disappointment.

"As it happens," and here he turned to Winifred, "You are not to accompany me at this time. I hope to be back by your birthday Saturday next." A loud cheer rose up about her. He added, "I expect you to stay here and entertain my nieces and nephews."

His smile was crooked and his lips twitched. Who was this man, she wondered yet again. After he had bid farewell to each child, she insisted on accompanying him to his traveling chariot.

The children, however, only permitted her to go when she had promised to return to the center of the maze as soon as the horses were pounding down the avenue.

Once out of earshot of the children, Winifred addressed his decision. "I had thought you would want me with you. I am only obligated . . . if even that . . . to stay with you a fortnight? I don't understand?"

"I have matters of business to attend to in London and when I return . . . in a scant few days . . . then we shall settle the matter of 'our wedding' and, er, go on our honeymoon. But it is adorable of you to be so anxious to be with me."

"I am not anxious to be with you," she cried, astonished that he would say such a thing. "I am merely extremely uncomfortable with this charade at your sister's home."

He was unimpressed. "Then you will have to become more comfortable with it since I mean to go to London and I mean to leave you here. Don't fret yourself. Hetty is famous company and will tend to your every need."

"But that is precisely what I am trying to tell you. She will be extending her kindnesses toward me because she believes I am to become your wife."

"Now that is ungenerous," he reproved her. "Hetty would be so with you whether you were to be my wife or not."

She opened her mouth to debate the point, but she didn't know how. For some reason he consistently proffered arguments which she couldn't answer.

Since the postilion who awaited him would soon be able to overhear their conversation, Winifred whispered, "You are being nonsensical. Have you no shame? No sense of decency? Common courtesy?"

"None, as I told you before," he returned, looking down at her with a twitch of his lips and a lift of his brows.

She growled. "I wish you would reconsider and permit me to go with you."

"Well, I shan't. Goodbye, then." With that he hurried forward, leaped into the open door of his traveling coach and shouted his order to the postilion.

There was nothing for it, Winifred realized as Shaw's four black horses picked up speed and headed for the King's Highway. She would have to carry herself with dignity over the coming sennight, fortify her failing courage and bear Lady Aldworth's numerous kindnesses with all the bravery she could summon.

Four

A week later, the day of her birthday, Winifred sat with Lady Aldworth in the library of Upton Hall which had become a second nursery of sorts. The older children, ranging from the age of three—Madeleine had been incensed that Winifred had thought her only two years old—to the age of eight, were permitted the use of the long ancient room so long as they played quietly, read books, practiced their letters or stitches, and conversed in hushed tones. Of course, two maids were in constant attendance to keep their busy hands properly occupied, but the whole of the experience was warm, full of life and curiosity, and enhanced by Lady Aldworth's obvious involvement and affection for her children.

Winifred would never have believed that a home could be so happy or enlivened as this one. Her own experience had been quite, quite different. Her elder brother, from earliest memory, had always been away at school, her father had been absent more days than present, and her mother, though sincere in her love for her children and wish that she could have taken a more leading maternal role, suffered from ill-health only to perish of a decline when Winifred was but sixteen.

She counted the year of the death of her beloved mama as the changing time, when her father's predilection for gambling in any form began running to excess. Ultimately she was forced to make a decision at the age of one-and-twenty—to remain with her father and endure the resulting instability of his mode of living or to become a governess, earn her keep, and find solace if not joy in a more peaceful existence.

With little Madeleine on her lap, she awaited Shaw's return, albeit a trifle anxiously, since he was expected to arrive sometime today. When Madeleine asked her to sketch another doggy but this time one with curly fur, she could not help but somehow think she had stumbled onto paradise.

"You mustn't place too much emphasis on the on-dits," Lady Aldworth said, startling Winifred from her musings.

"I beg your pardon?" she responded.

Lady Aldworth drew a practiced needle through a fine white linen kerchief trapped within the frame of her round embroidery hoop and with three careful jerks of her wrist pulled the light green silk floss taut. The viscountess lifted her gaze from her work and met Winifred's questioning stare. She smiled, a very knowing, wise smile. "Gabriel is a good man and with the right wife will become a great man. His wealth and properties have made him too much an object of feminine wiles to have afforded him the leisure of believing any woman capable of loving him for merely his character. It is no wonder he stumbled on the very bride for him outside his usual London haunts. I just hope you are not overwhelmed by his reputation. Many an ambitious female has suffered disappointment in her schemes which I believe must account for a goodly proportion of the rumors."

"I hadn't considered as much," Winifred answered truthfully.

"I believe you haven't," Lady Aldworth responded with an odd frown between her brows, almost as though she wanted to say more but didn't feel she could.

"What are *wiles*, Mama?" Madeleine asked.

Lady Aldworth chuckled. "Something you shall never have, my darling."

Madeleine's attention turned suddenly to George who had found a spider near the corner of one of the bookshelves lining the walls. "What have you got, Georgie?" she called, sliding off Winifred's lap and landing with a plop on the wooden floor.

Winifred found that her legs were a little numb. Madeleine

was a plump child and had been settled on her lap for nearly three quarters of an hour. She rose and shook out her skirts. She was wearing another of Lady Aldworth's gowns, this one a patterned calico in blues and browns with just a touch of peach. It was made high to the waist, quite full in back, modest across the bodice and long in the sleeve.

Glancing down at her hostess, she addressed Lady Aldworth's concerns. "I believe it is fortunate I came to know Shaw apart from his London acquaintances. He is clearly a most beloved uncle, for instance."

"He will make an excellent father as well."

Winifred had become used to such hints, for both Lord and Lady Aldworth were anxious to encourage their future sister-in-law. After a week she had learned to smile politely and to keep her cheeks from turning a pretty crimson each time the subject was introduced. "I have little doubt on that score," she murmured as she walked toward the window.

The library was situated on the first floor of the mansion and overlooked a fine avenue lined with stately beech trees. A wind was whipping the leaves about and sweeping the grasses into an undulating sea of green. In the heart of Bedfordshire and nestled in gentle hills, Upton Hall was a dignified yet welcoming retreat from London and from the cares of life in general.

The first two days after Shaw left, Winifred had been nervous and fearful, frightened that one or the other of her hosts would guess the truth of her situation. But because she was accepted so fully as Mr. Shaw's intended, and she had to some degree learned to play that part, she had finally relaxed sufficiently to enjoy the family, the house, and the many walks she took with the children when the capricious March weather permitted.

She looked down at the avenue and saw that only a few puddles were scattered about the long drive giving evidence of an early deluge. The storm had broken up and the afternoon sun was actually shining through a remnant of tenacious clouds, blue sky and puffs of gray reflected in the puddles.

Suddenly, a curricle, proceeding remarkably slowly, appeared at the entrance of the avenue. The lane was completely cloaked by a hedge in front of which rhododendrons bloomed in pink abundance. Her heart leapt in her breast. There was no mistaking the man driving the glossy vehicle—Mr. Shaw had returned from London. A moment later, a large town coach and four appeared and followed the curricle up the drive.

The sounds of the horses's hooves and the wheels of the coaches on the gravel soon brought the children clustering about her skirts. As recognition traveled from child to child, affectionate shrieking followed, along with a scrambling of boots and shoes on the wooden floors of the library. One by one the children ran from the chamber to greet their uncle. The maids went with them, quietly adjuring them to walk, to behave, to stop squealing, but all to little effect. Uncle Gabriel almost always brought presents with him when he returned from London.

Winifred remained by the window and watched the inevitable occur. Mr. Shaw drew his curricle to the front door and jumped lightly to the ground. As the children poured from the mansion, he began catching each one up to him in quick succession. How her heart swelled at the sight of him, at his love for his sister's offspring, at the way he carried Madeleine in his arms as he moved toward the doors, at the way, when Madeleine pointed up to the library windows, he directed his gaze toward her, smiled, and waved.

He was a good man, a very good man. How strange, however, that such a man would also be intent on forcing her to become his mistress.

The crowd then disappeared from sight into the entrance hall.

"Are you in love with him?" Lady Aldworth's question flowed quietly and unexpectedly over her shoulder.

She looked quickly back at the viscountess who watched her carefully. Returning her gaze to the window, she gave the simple answer which rose clearly to her mind. "Yes," she responded, speaking from her heart, without wondering if it was true, without questioning whether she ought to say such a thing to her or not. "I think I have loved him since we were together last summer."

"When did you first meet him?"

"At Mrs. Beenham's in July."

"Ah," Lady Aldworth nodded. "Mrs. Beenham has always been a good friend to Gabriel."

"Her daughter, Amelia, was always a good friend to me. Dare I reveal your brother kissed me after having led me to the center of Mrs. Beenham's yew maze?"

Lady Aldworth chuckled. "So very much like him."

"Indeed." The word was barely a whisper.

"Goodness!" Lady Aldworth cried, her attention diverted by the sight below. The door of the traveling coach had been opened and a string of footmen were hauling a vast number of bandboxes and packages from the belly of the maroon and black vehicle. "Your bridesclothes! Of course that is why Gabriel went to London!" Lady Aldworth then quit the room on a quick, excited tread.

She turned back at the doorway and said, "Do come! Gabriel is nothing if not an arbiter of female fashion. He will have clothed you to perfection. What is it? Oh, now I hope you don't mean to quibble over his generosity? He has already explained to me precisely where your dowry went, though I would have suspected as much from, well from all the on-dits regarding your father. Please believe me when I say that neither Aldworth nor I give a fig for any of it. Your character speaks exclusively for itself." Her expression was motherly and commanding and she might as well have been fifteen years older than Winifred in that moment, rather than the mere three she really was.

Winifred cringed inwardly at Lady Aldworth's kindness. If only the clothes Mr. Shaw had purportedly purchased for her in London had actually been her bridesclothes, she would undoubtedly have been as excited as the viscountess. But the true reason for his purchases—to rig her out in style because she was to be his mistress—brought a chill to her heart.

She shuddered as she descended the stairs, hoping that perhaps Lady Aldworth had misjudged the nature of the bounty heaped on the floor of the entrance hall. But her hopes were quickly dispelled and a veritable sea of packages awaited her inspection. He greeted her by placing a kiss on her cheek but said nothing to her of his purchases except to beg permission to have them sent to her bedchamber. The several remaining boxes, wrapped in brown paper and string, he shook, rattled, mused over, then handed to each breathless child in turn.

Fortunately for her nerves, the return celebration of Uncle Gabriel completely overshadowed her own confused and unhappy feelings.

Only later, as she fingered the fine silks, cambrics, muslins, and satins of the gowns he had provided for her, did the true horror of her situation tumble over her. She loved him. Yet she was just his mistress, and that is all she would ever be to him. She could not stop the tears once they began to flow, nor did she try. She found she was no longer angry, just desolate. For not only did she despise the thought of being any man's fancy-piece, but she had been shown paradise and knew that paradise was denied her. Marriage did not await her at the end of this adventure with Mr. Shaw. From the start he had made his intentions clear. He would take her to London where he would display her beauty for all his acquaintances to observe and envy, he would take her innocence and when he was done, he would endow her with an annuity.

But she didn't want an annuity. She wanted Mr. Shaw.

When her tears ceased to flow, she remained in her bedchamber for a very long time, thinking and pondering her circumstances. She reviewed the whole of the extraordinary train of events which had brought her to Upton Hall. She realized that at any time over the past sennight she could easily have unburdened her soul to Lady Aldworth, explaining the truth of her relationship to her brother, and perhaps even asked for her help. Or at any time she could have left the mansion and simply disappeared. Why she had not done so was something of a mystery to her except that until this moment she had not been thinking very clearly.

For the first time since the game of hazard at Lambourn, she considered taking one or the other of these paths now. She knew Shaw well enough to presume that if she left to return to her governess duties, he would follow her back to Mrs. Stanmore's home and probably create a scandal just as he had said he would. But he couldn't follow her if she took on a new identity and using her savings, made her way to the west to Bristol and booked passage to the Colonies.

As these thoughts circulated through her brain, over and over, she knew at last what she must do. She would flee to America and begin again. She might be in love with Mr. Shaw, but she could not be his mistress, not even for one night.

Once the decision was made, she was surprised to find how peaceful she quickly became. For that reason, she had no difficulty in wearing one of the new gowns Mr. Shaw had bought her since her sole purpose now was to keep him from becoming suspicious.

The gown was of a deep forest green silk, covered in a shimmering, sheer tulle and flounced about the hem with three rows of narrow green silk ruffles. She wore her hair in a simple chignon fringed with wispy curls across her forehead. A rope of seed pearls was wound through her curls and a fine string of matched pearls adorned by an ivory cameo graced her neck. The pearls had belonged to her mother, the only jewelry to have escaped her father's gaming habits.

When she began to descend the stairs, she was surprised to find Mr. Shaw waiting for her, quite alone. He stood next to the banister, one arm draped negligently over the oak rail and looked up at her with a warm almost affectionate smile on his lips.

"Oh," she murmured inarticulately, caught off guard by the tenderness of his expression as he awaited her. If only he was not so handsome, she thought for the hundredth time, then she could be easy and content in her decisions. But the mere sight of him, a strong reminder of what she would lose the moment she quit Upton Hall, brought such a sadness to her heart that even breathing became difficult.

She saw a frown creep over his brow. When she reached him he whispered, "Why are you so sad? Are you not happy here? Do you not like the gowns and fripperies I purchased for you?"

"How can you speak so as though our situation is perfectly normal or in any manner agreeable to me?" she asked. "You know very well that I cannot be content in such a circumstance nor take a true pleasure in the fineness of the gowns you purchased for me. You are deceiving yourself again."

"You are right of course," he breathed, his expression solemn. On a whisper, he continued, "Then tell me, could you be content to become my wife instead of my mistress?" He watched her closely, his blue eyes scrutinizing her face.

She blinked once then twice. She didn't know how to answer him. Did he mean to torture her further by posing such a hopeless question? Why couldn't he be considerate of her feelings? Did he think she had no pride? "How can you ask such a thing of me?" she retorted at last.

"Because, I wish to know," was his childlike response.

She shook her head. "You may wish to know but I do not wish to answer you."

He seemed impatient as he offered his arm to her in order to escort her to the dining room. But he did not permit her to move away from the stairs quite yet. As he looked down at her, he pressed her again. "Miss Childress, will you not even give me a hint? I would be most grateful for even a hint as to what your sentiments might be?"

She looked into blue eyes and felt tears rim her lashes again. "Sir," she responded. "I have had a most trying week which began with my arrival at Lambourn Hall. For you to ask for hints is to be cruel beyond reason. I beg you will not do so."

He turned her toward him and appeared quite distraught. He released her hands then took her shoulders gently in hand. "I have not meant to be cruel. Indeed, I intended only kindness by asking you as much."

She laughed and lowered her gaze to stare blindly at a small emerald tucked into the folds of his neckcloth. "I believe you erred when you chose to make a governess the object of your attentions and not an opera-dancer."

"If I erred, it was because I could not put you out of my mind. You have haunted me, Miss Childress, since last summer. You have floated teasingly through my dreams and awakened me a score of times before dawn. The sweetness of your kisses have stayed on my lips and made every kiss since taste of bitterness. I had to see you again, to know you. Will you not now give me even the smallest hint as to what your sentiments toward me might be?"

At that she looked up at him. She could feel the pinch of a frown settled between her brows. "I don't understand you or what you want from me. I only know that had I the choice I would leave here on the instant."

Her words struck him hard, changing the hue of his skin to a chalky white and dimming the light in his eyes to a strange deadness. How surprising! But what did it mean? She truly did not understand him yet had he been anyone other than the infamous *Gentleman Shaw*, she would have supposed she had wounded him. That of course was quite impossible.

He released her shoulders, again offered her his arm and led her to the formal dining room where a surprise awaited her.

"Happy birthday, Miss Childress!" The events of the day had so disturbed her that she had quite forgotten that today was her birthday. Wishes flowed from every member of the Aldworth family, all of whom were present for dinner—even the twin baby girls, Annabel and Sophia, for a few minutes—in order that her birthday might be celebrated in a joyous fashion.

When Lord Aldworth seated her at the top of the table in honor of her birthday, and as the family party commenced, she knew never before in her life had she been so happy nor so miserable at one and the same time. Paradise had again been teasingly displayed before her but as before there was no doubt in her mind that Eden was and would always be completely out of reach.

By the end of the evening, with much of her attention focused upon first the children until they retired for the evening and then Lord Aldworth who insisted she play at piquet with him, her spirits were restored. Mr. Shaw had treated her with consideration during and after dinner and she had again resumed her intention of leaving Upton Hall quite early on the morrow, before the house was awake.

When the hour chimed ten o'clock and Lady Aldworth directed a number of meaningful looks, nods, and winks toward her husband, and when Lord Aldworth finally sighed and acquiesced to her not-so-subtle hints that the betrothed couple ought to be left alone for a while, Winifred again found herself tête-à-tête with Mr. Shaw.

She tried to excuse herself at once and feigned great fatigue hoping to avoid any conversation with him. But he begged her to remain with him for a few minutes since he had something of a particular nature he wished to say to her. When he closed the door and made certain it would not pop open unassisted, she began to realize other intentions of his were clearly paramount in his mind.

Oh, dear, she mused. Would he rob her of her innocence tonight, the very night she meant to make her escape! What a great irony that would be.

She moved toward the fireplace and steeled herself against the inevitable, intending all the while to find some manner of taking flight if even the smallest opportunity presented itself. She took a deep breath and tried to still her quickly beating heart, but she could not. When he drew near her and took her in his arms and kissed her, she could take no pleasure in his kiss. She placed her hands on his chest and after a moment she attempted to push him away, but unsuccessfully. Though he drew back from her, he still held her arms, searching her face all the while. "How have I erred?" he asked.

"I can't!" she cried. "I can't! As soon as I am able I shall run away from you but I beg you Mr. Shaw, please don't take my innocence. Please. But it won't matter. I shall escape you anyway. I promise you I shall!"

He squeezed his eyes shut as though her words had again wounded him, or perhaps he was merely angry. Her heart beat more quickly still. Would he bind her up and closet her in one of the attics? Would he take her to his home in Derbyshire and chain her in a secret Priest's Hole?

"Dear God," he murmured. "I've been such a fool."

These were not the words she had expected to hear. "I just want you to know that I think it very odd of you to invoke *God's* name in this moment." She was stiff in his arms, stiff with fear.

He chuckled at last and released her, but he remained standing on the wide brick hearth beside her. "Miss Childress," he began quietly. "I've made a mull of it. I should not have teased you so sorely for the past sennight. You see, from the moment I took you to the billiard room at Lambourn I had determined not to harm a hair on your head. Don't you realize that when I was *invited* so generously to your father's house and that he had particularly stressed that you would be the chief amusement at his home that I had believed you were in league with your parent and your brother?"

"How could you have thought such a thing?"

"Did I have reason to believe otherwise? You must remember, I had only met you once and you had succumbed to my kisses most delightfully. Indeed, quite thoroughly. In fact, I have had the impression that had it not commenced raining . . ."

"Please, don't speak of it," she cried.

He took a step closer to her. "Why are you so frightened? Are you telling me you would have . . . ?"

She took a deep breath and said, "Well, who would not have though I've little doubt you would have blamed me. But don't you understand, you kissed me as though summer resided in your whole being and you were pouring a bountiful harvest all over me. I had never known anything so wondrous in all my life as being held in your arms especially when you had been so kind and spoken to me so openly and with such attentiveness.

Of course, I realize now it all happened because you are a practiced libertine."

He started, his eyes opening wide. She was surprised she had shocked him, but clearly she had. "I shall try to ignore that last bit," he said, "at least for the present. What I will say is that I think you've misgauged the kiss we shared. It was you who was playing the part of seductress. You were summer, sunshine, and rich earth rolled into one. No," he shook his head in disagreement. "You were the one, not I. It was your kisses that convinced me you were in league with your father."

"Well, you *were* and *are* heartily mistaken," she stated firmly.

"I know that now. Indeed, I have known it since before I played at hazard with your father."

"I don't believe you," she said. "Had you not been mistaken I would not be here, now, pleading with you to let me go."

"There you are out. Once I saw that I could bring both your father and brother low by pretending to require you in a stake against their losses, and pretending that I meant to make you my mistress, I could not resist doing so. It promised too much fun and gig to be denied. Whether or not either of them have learned a mite of sense I can have no way of knowing though I sincerely doubt any good will come of my efforts. The truth is they are both so deeply in the clutches of the gaming vice that I hold little hope for either of them.

"As for you," and here he lifted his hand and stroked her cheek lightly with his forefinger. "You rose so easily to the fly that I couldn't resist teasing you and pretending a little more. The fact is, I never intended to take you to London. Never."

She was completely stunned. "Never?" she asked. Her mouth fell unattractively agape and she gasped. When he shook his head, she cried, "Mr. Shaw, how could you!"

"Please, if we are to brangle, will you not at least call me Gabriel as you have done so delightfully before? I am far too fond of you to wish to keep on such formal terms."

She lifted her chin. *"Mr. Shaw,* you have behaved reprehensibly and I think at the very least you ought to beg my forgiveness. And what of your sister? Do you not have the smallest idea what you have done to this poor family, for instance? They think we are to be married. I have been living here under the most heinous of deceptions. What of them?"

"Well," he pondered. Oh, dear, his lips were twitching. She feared what would come next. "We could get married," he suggested, "if you wish for it? I do love my sister and her family. And they are fully persuaded we are to be wed. I shouldn't like to disappoint them. What do you say?"

"Of all the absurdities I have heard you utter in my brief acquaintance with you, this is the most absurd. You? Married? It is unthinkable."

"Why?" he asked.

How odd that his blue eyes seemed hurt, yet again. She didn't understand him. She didn't. He couldn't possibly wish to marry her, or any female for that matter. "I would never think of marrying a man, who, by his nature, would always prefer not to be married. That's all."

"So you will not marry me?" he asked. His brows became creased.

"No, I will not. But you aren't really asking me, are you?" This was undoubtedly the strangest conversation she had ever had with him.

He looked away from her and leaned his elbow on the mantel. He placed his hand on his forehead and sighed. "This is the damndest thing," he murmured. He remained silent for a long moment and then slid his elbow off the mantel and dropped his hand to his side. "Because of my reprehensible conduct this past sennight, I wish you to know that I will give you two choices, my hand in marriage or I shall gladly escort you back to Mrs. Stanmore's house . . . tomorrow if you wish for it."

She stared up at him in disbelief. Then his questions hadn't truly been rhetorical. "You would marry me," she stated, completely dumbfounded.

He nodded. "Yes, of course I would."

"How very chivalrous," she said, stunned.

"Am I so very bad," he snapped, "that now you must mock me?"

"No," she replied sincerely. "I am simply and utterly amazed. I didn't expect you to behave chivalrously."

"Worse and worse. You have no great opinion of my character then, do you?"

She opened her mouth to speak, to say of course she did not, but then she stopped. She looked away from him, letting her gaze fall into the past. What did she know of him? What was the truth about the infamous Gentleman Shaw? He had been angry with her father and brother for the way they had treated her and he had punished them both while at the same time protecting her reputation all the while. He was clearly a beloved brother and uncle. And in the end, though he certainly had no need of doing so, he had offered her his hand in marriage if that is what she felt the situation required in order for him to redeem his conduct toward her.

She looked back at him. "Since having come to know you better this past week, I can with honesty say that I do esteem your character . . . at least as much as I know of it. You've a terrible reputation, otherwise. What else would you have expected a lady to think?"

"You are quite different from most of the ladies I know. In fact," here his eyes grew hard, "I know not one who would have failed to jump at my offer had they been in your shoes."

"Surely you underestimate the ladies of your acquaintance."

He grimaced. "I don't think that I do."

She didn't know what else she could say to him. She certainly had no power to defend her sex against his opinions, only herself and she had no need to defend herself. Finally she said, "I thank you very much for your kind offer, but seeing that it was a chivalrous gesture I shall respond in a like manner and beg that on the morrow you will return me to Mrs. Stanmore."

"And this is what you truly wish? You have no desire to become my wife?"

She wished he would not look at her in just that manner as

though he indeed wanted her to become his wife. He must not realize how he appeared. "Don't be silly," she responded with a smile. "I would not subject you to such tedium."

"To such tedium?" he queried. "I should not consider marriage to you in the least tedious."

She laughed. "Mr. Shaw, you would be bored to tears within a fortnight. No, keep your life as it is and let me return to the Misses Stanmore."

She reached up and kissed his cheek, then moved past him and quit the chamber.

Five

The next morning, Winifred awoke feeling rested after having slept the best she had in over a sennight. Her future was settled and in a few hours she would return to her post, with none the wiser, and her life as a governess would recommence. As she sipped her hot chocolate, she began to plan her day and to recall precisely what her life had been before she had crossed paths with Mr. Shaw at Lambourn. She sighed and a prickling of sadness began to weigh down her heart.

But she refused to be sad. She would not be sad. She sipped her chocolate again. She looked out at the morning spring sky which unfortunately was rather leaden, gray, and dull, not unlike Mrs. Stanmore's disapproving face when she expressed her dislike of the walks Winifred would take with her charges in the pine grove to the south of her estate. Mrs. Stanmore disapproved of excessive exercise for her daughters. There were a lot of things of which Mrs. Stanmore disapproved.

Another prickle of sadness and regret tugged at her heart. She lifted the cup of chocolate to her lips and took another sip. She would not be sad. Not today. Mr. Shaw had been kind and generous and had returned her life to her when he had no true moral obligation—given her father's horrid intentions toward him—to do so. No, she refused to be sad. She had her life back and it was a good life, she could earn her living and continue doing so year after year, teaching the Misses Stanmore, reprimanding them for taunting each other, for pinching at each other, and for pouting every time they didn't get their way.

Suddenly her heart simply plummeted, a sense of desolation overwhelmed her and she found she could hardly breathe.

The truth was, she wanted more than life itself to be married to Gabriel Shaw. There, she had let the thought rise to take preeminence in her mind even though she knew it was a hopeless matter. Last night and this morning she had been suppressing this thought, hoping to make her departure easy and uncomplicated. But she couldn't any longer. The truth in all its painful aspects wouldn't be denied.

If only Mr. Shaw loved her, how differently her answer might have been last night. But he didn't. He had offered for her from a strange sense of chivalry and for no other reason. Her heart kept begging her to believe otherwise, but she ignored its clamorings. After all, if Mr. Shaw had truly been in love with her and had offered for her from such a motive, he would have professed that love—but last night he had said nothing except to offer her two matter-of-fact choices—his hand in marriage or Mrs. Stanmore's employ.

She had made the only choice she could given the circumstances.

She slipped her legs over the edge of the bed, rose to her feet, and moved slowly toward the window. Her bedchamber overlooked the back gardens. She had an exquisite view of a landscape managed to perfection, one that had been originally designed in the picturesque by Capability Brown. No formal French gardens here, only a lake which looked as though nature had created it of its own volition along with an easy vista of scattered clumps of trees and shrubs which appeared arranged as though the clouds and the earth had decided precisely where each would be placed to be most pleasing to the eye.

The one marring aspect of the view, over which Lord and Lady Aldworth had disagreed tenaciously, had been the introduction of the yew maze. In the end, Lady Aldworth had won the argument saying that the purpose of the maze would be to provide a place for the children to run, play, and hide, where they would be safe and where for small pieces of time they could believe they had effected an escape from Nurse.

As though having heard her musings, George and Stephen suddenly came into view and bolted toward the maze. Madeleine toddled after, then little Gabriel and finally Meg.

But Meg wasn't alone. She was holding Uncle Gabriel's arm.

Winifred lifted her hand as though to reach out to him and let her fingers touch the window. The glass was cold.

A knock on the door interrupted her unhappy thoughts. Lady Aldworth's abigail then entered her bedchamber in order to help her dress and to brush her hair. She seated herself at the dressing table and without a word, permitted the maid to perform her tasks.

Twenty minutes later, standing before the long looking glass near the windows, the abigail buttoned the very last button of Winifred's old traveling gown of brown stuff. As she shook out the dull skirts, a scratching sounded on the door and afterward Lady Aldworth begged admittance.

Winifred welcomed her into the bedchamber.

"I was hoping—" the viscountess began when she entered the room, but broke off at the sight of Winifred's gown. She lifted a brow, then continued, "That is, I was hoping to have a few words with you before you left."

Of all the encounters Winifred was likely to have had this morning, she had been dreading this one the most. Lady Aldworth signaled for the maid to depart and when the door was closed upon her, she spoke quickly before the viscountess could speak. "Did he tell you all?"

"All that I had not guessed."

Winifred could hardly bear to meet her gaze. The whole of it was such a slight to Lady Aldworth's goodness and her kindness in having her as a guest in her home that she was sick with misery. "I should never have come. I am so ashamed." She turned back to the window and again looked the direction of the maze. She could see no one, but the sounds of the children playing and squealing rose to the windows.

"Of what can you possibly be ashamed?" Lady Aldworth cried, sounding incredulous.

Winifred glanced at her over shoulder. "Of what should I not be ashamed? I have trespassed on your every kindness with only deception—"

"Not of your making or doing and from what I understand Gabriel coerced you."

"I should have effected some sort of escape. I should have laid my case before you the day after my arrival. But I failed to do anything and now I can only beg your forgiveness and your pardon."

"Your conscience is too fine," she said, shaking her head. "As for Gabriel, I scrutinized his history quite carefully this morning. From what I perceive he threatened you quite forcefully."

"Yes, he did, but I should have run away. In fact, last night I had quite made up my mind to go to the Colonies."

She lifted a brow. "I don't recommend you do so. Have you ever traveled on a ship?"

Winifred shook her head.

"It is horrible. I was on a ship once, during our honeymoon. The tossing and pitching every time a wave meandered by! You would be ill, in this you must trust me. Much better to stay in England." She paused for a moment as certain memories clearly rose to her mind and apparently served to turn her stomach completely over. She gave herself a strong mental shake and after taking a deep breath, she addressed the former concern, "As for blaming yourself about all that has transpired this past sennight, I will have none of it. All that I wish to know is whether or not you lied to me yesterday."

"Well, yes, all of it was a lie, a terrible lie."

"So," she said, slowly folding her hands in front of her, "you are then *not* in love with Gabriel?"

"Oh, that," Winifred responded. "I thought you meant the betrothal and such."

"Then you didn't lie to me? You do love him?"

Winifred looked into oddly hopeful eyes. "I don't understand,

Lady Aldworth, what it is you hope to achieve? I would only ask that you forgive me and let me go in peace. Your brother doesn't wish to be married."

"Is that truly what you think, what you believe?"

"Well, of course."

"I see. What a coil, for not half an hour ago he was telling me he was certain you were the one who had no interest in marriage. Is that true? Do you not wish to be married, to have family of your own, your own children to love and instruct instead of the offspring of some other woman?"

Her crooked smile wrenched Winifred's heart. "Of course I wish to be married and I didn't know precisely how much until I came to your house. I didn't know that a family could be such a joy. My mother was always ill, you see."

"And my mother was never at home. If it weren't for the fact that I had gone to live with my aunt in Sussex I daresay I would not have fared much better than my brother. But my aunt's home was a place of real love and familial devotion. She was a most excellent mother to me. Everything I know I learned from her. But Gabriel has always been so confused about women . . . until now. Now I think he understands what he wants, but if I am not much mistaken, he bungled it last night, didn't he?"

Winifred felt a little butterfly begin to flutter in the very center of her heart, a butterfly which carried something like *hope* on its wings. "Whatever do you mean?" she breathed. She was afraid she might misunderstand Lady Aldworth and hope things she should not hope.

"When he was proposing to you last night, he forgot to take you madly in his arms and profess the depth of his love to you, didn't he? Instead, I think he supposed that you would understand he was saying he loved you by offering you his hand in marriage. Men can be such simpletons."

Winifred uttered a small noise which sounded like a cross between a gasp and a sigh. "He loves me?" she queried, wanting to believe her but afraid to.

"Let me see, his words were something like, '*I shan't know how to live without her. She was everything I have ever wanted and so pure of heart. Have you noticed as much, Hetty, that she has no designs on me? None."*

"He said as much," Winifred whispered, a film of tears distorting her vision.

Through her tears she saw Lady Aldworth smile and nod.

The viscountess moved to stand next to Winifred at the window. She embraced her fully. "I know it must seem hen-hearted of him to have sent me to you, but he is after all just a man. I don't think he could have borne another rejection since according to him, he proposed to you twice yesterday."

"Twice?" Winifred cried, astonished.

Lady Aldworth laughed outright. "It would seem the first time was at the foot of the stairs."

"But he didn't. He . . ." Winifred recalled his words, his query, *Would she be content to be his wife.* She continued, "Oh, dear. He is something of a simpleton, isn't he?"

"Very much so."

"Then I misunderstood him, completely."

"Yes. And what I wish you to do, to atone for your utter wickedness in having carried out such a dreadful deception beneath my nose, is to go to him now and lay your heart before him."

Since Lady Aldworth then promised that once all was settled they would plan a wedding breakfast together, there was nothing for her to do but to obey her hostess.

Winifred's knees were trembling when she reached the opening to the center of the yew maze. She peeked around the edge of the neatly trimmed yews and saw that Gabriel was blindfolded and performing his part in Blind Man's Bluff to a nicety. Meg, George, Stephen, little Gabriel, and even Madeleine were all racing about him, ducking, and pulling on the tails of his blue coat as he in turn called out to them and reached ineffectually for them by grasping at the air a good two feet above any of their little heads.

"There you are!" he would cry. "I've got you now! You won't escape me this time." He would then embrace the air much to the continued pleasure and amusement of all the children.

Winifred kept herself hidden from view, then one by one surreptitiously began drawing the children away from Gentleman Shaw, hoping to keep her presence a secret until she could attack him herself. She had the greatest fear that Madeleine would be unable to restrain herself once she discovered that "Aunt Winnie" had come to play, but George solved that dilemma by capturing Madeleine himself and by placing a hand over her mouth as he dragged her behind the screen of yew. Her protests at having been thusly handled by George were quickly subdued when she understood that Winifred meant to play a trick on Uncle Gabriel.

The moment the children were all out of the center of the maze and hidden behind the yew hedge, she quickly stole toward Mr. Shaw as he turned about in a circle.

"Now where have all of you gone?" he cried. "I can't hear a sound. Ah, I hear someone."

The gravel crunched beneath Winifred's half-boots. He turned and advanced toward her and she slipped beneath his arms as he lunged at her. Again the gravel gave away her location, again he approached and again she escaped. The children by now were peeking about the edge of the yews and giggling. Every time they giggled and he turned toward them, Winifred would catch Shaw's coattails and give them a hard tug.

Finally, she stole up to him and with a quick jerk, pulled the blindfold from his eyes. He was startled, surprised but not displeased. "Winifred," he breathed. "Then you've spoken with Hetty?"

"What a silly man you are," she whispered, her heart racing as hope began to glitter in his blue eyes.

She didn't pull away from him when he caught her suddenly in his arms and drew her roughly to him. "I bungled it last night," he explained, his eyes alive with fear and relief all at once.

"You most certainly did," she responded slipping her arms about his neck.

"Are you saying you will reconsider—"

"I will not go down that path again," she stated firmly, holding him more tightly still.

"My God, I love you so much. Winifred, don't go. Be my wife. Be the mother of my children."

"I'm not going anywhere and I want nothing more than to be your wife, truly. I love you, Gabriel! Since last summer. I just never thought . . . but none of that matters any more. Only that I will always love you."

"My darling," he whispered, his gaze drifting hungrily over her face. He touched her lips with his fingers, then her cheek, drifting down to the soft line of her chin. "I was so afraid you would leave. I was at a loss as to how to stop you. Hetty said I should have kissed you last night instead of arguing the point, or letting you choose your future."

Winifred let her hand rest on his cheek as she lovingly placed a kiss on his lips. "Yes, you most certainly should have," she agreed.

"Perhaps I ought to do so now," he whispered, his lips but a breath away. Ever so slowly he drew her more tightly to him and at the same time began a teasing, delicate assault on her lips. Closing her eyes, she gasped faintly as she felt the barest butterfly of a sensation, which disappeared then returned, again and again as her barely touched his lips to hers.

He whispered her name. She sighed and again the butterfly touched her lips.

"Gabriel," she murmured.

"I love you," he said. The butterfly metamorphosed as he placed his lips fully upon hers. She felt herself disappearing, feeling only his lips and the length of his body pressed firmly against hers. His love was surrounding her, flowing over her, invading her mind and heart, causing every fear to take flight.

She loved and she was loved.

"I will be with you always, Winifred."

Again he kissed her, causing summer to again sweep through her soul even though March was still blustering about the yews. Joy flooded her, hope drenched her with pleasure. Her whole being became lit from within at the knowledge that she would indeed become the wife of the man she loved.

"He's biting her!" Madeleine cried.

"No he's not," George returned, indignant. "But I wish he would stop such nonsense. I'm about to cast up my accounts!"

Meg's older and wiser voice of eight intruded. "But that is what all married people do. Mama said so. We ought to leave them alone!"

Stephen said, "I think one of the grooms repaired my hoop. I mean to go to the stables and fetch it. Who wants to come with me?"

A general enthusiastic cry went up among the children followed by the scurrying of little feet, the sound of which disappeared in quick stages.

Gabriel drew back from her slightly and looked down into her face. "Do you know, you look just like an angel."

She smiled, her heart full to overflowing. "How would you know what an angel looks like?"

"Because I've seen you my dearest, most adorable Winifred."

This time she didn't argue with him, but rather gave herself completely to the enjoyment of his love, of his kisses, and of his promises that theirs would be a marriage made in heaven.

About the Author

Valerie King lives with her family in Glendale, Arizona. She is the author of thirteen Regency romances and one historical Regency romance (VANQUISHED), all published by Zebra Books. Valerie's newest Regency romance, a SUMMER COURTSHIP, will be on sale in July 1996. Valerie loves hearing from her readers and you may write to her c/o Zebra Books. Please include a self-addressed stamped envelope if you wish a response.

The Rake and the Lacemaker

by
Isobel Linton

One

Is it only my fevered imagination, Lord Daltrey wondered idly, draining yet another glass of wine, or is Cordelia Wynter-Wynbourne really trying to put lemon ice down the gown of that tall ginger-haired girl?

His lordship first squinted and then raised his quizzing glass trying to make out just what was happening at the far end of the grand ballroom at Barcourt Manor. Then, with the swift decisiveness characteristic of him, Lord Daltrey resolved it was certainly not due to his imagination, nor due to the off-deceptive effect of intoxicants, but that indeed, Miss Cordelia Wynter-Wynbourne was on the verge of some sort of social misbehavior.

Quite deeply foxed already at this early hour of the evening, but certainly not yet entirely out of the running, Daltrey, who disliked boredom above all things, decided to take it upon himself to look into this unusual and interesting matter.

Before Lord Daltrey, a dark young man broad of shoulder, elegantly dressed, was able to cross the polished pinewood floor and more directly confront the suspected assailant, a stifled shriek from the red-headed girl confirmed for Daltrey that his reading of the situation had been correct.

His lordship, letting his quizzing glass drop with a snap, found himself seriously displeased. Cordelia really should *not* be conducting herself in such a manner. She should certainly not be doing so in the middle of his great-uncle's Dunnington's ballroom during a grand country weekend at Barcourt Manor.

In particular, Cordelia Wynter-Wynbourne should not be going out of her way to play such a childish, mean-spirited trick on that foreign girl with the unfortunate red hair who was here as his great-uncle's guest, and soon to become Lord Dunnington's legal ward. Cordelia's behavior simply would not do, and he would not scruple to tell her so.

Though it was all too true that Lord Daltrey's own private life was filled to overflowing with late nights and ladybirds, not to mention duels, drunkenness, wagering, and questionable escapades of all sorts, he was, unaccountably, widely known as a high stickler for proper comportment during the hours spent in parlor and ballroom. Oddly enough, with regard to all formal aspects of *ton* life, Daltrey was the pattern-card of a perfect conservative.

In fact, Daltrey's obsession with propriety in public was, his beleaguered mother often sighed, his only virtue. All the rest of him, she used to sniff to her husband, was vice.

His young lordship's vices were, to be sure, utterly fashionable vices, but they had been persistent ones, worrisome to his family and—not to put too fine a point on it—costly in the extreme.

But by Easter of 1811, both of Daltrey's parents had long gone on to their rewards in Heaven, he had acceded to title and fortune, and was free to behave just as he pleased.

On this particular weekend, it had pleased his lordship to go down to the country to pay a visit to Lord Dunnington, his maternal great-uncle. It was a mark of his affection for this elder gentleman that he had acceded to his relative's request that he attend the ball at which he witnessed the scene described.

By the time Viscount Daltrey arrived at the scene of the crime, the red-haired girl, publicly humiliated, had fled the room. Miss Wynter-Wynbourne was looking wickedly pleased with herself and was making light jokes about her victim, while the Duke of Evert's three horse-faced daughters stood in an admiring circle around her, laughing too loud and gesturing with their arms as they did so, their silken shawls flapping around them 'til they looked like a dancing pack of crows.

Daltrey frowned and shook his head. Why should Cordelia have behaved in such an unseemly fashion? If it was a ploy to attract *his* attention, it would not work. Daltrey vowed that, if need be, he would see to it himself that things were put right with that reclusive chit, what *was* her name? Something French, of course.

Elise, yes; that was it. The girl was called Elise de Bourget.

Lord Daltrey vowed he would see to it himself that Mademoiselle de Bourget received from Miss Wynter-Wynbourne a complete and abject apology—as well as her personal promise never to repeat this humiliating story among society. It was the least he could do for a young girl come so suddenly into his great-uncle's care.

"Cordelia!" he said sternly to the young lady who, apparently still amused, was still giggling. "What can you be thinking of to behave in this manner? How can you ill-treat a girl who has done you no harm?"

The grave look in his lordship's eyes went unnoticed by Miss Wynter-Wynbourne. Rather, she faced the young gentleman very closely, and, entirely avoiding answering his question, favored the handsome brown-eyed gentleman with her thrilling smile.

"Freddy!" she called, tapping him coyly with her fan. "Freddy Daltrey! What a surprise to see you here! I vow, I thought not to see you again until later in the Season. What brings you all the way out here in the country? You *can't* have been rusticated! Perhaps you merely wish to keep a low profile? Ah! I know . . . you've lost a packet on the horses, have you? You can't bear to show your face around Town, is that it? I see I am correct. Naughty, naughty Freddy!"

Lord Daltrey, unamused, took her arm rather strongly, and steered her into an antechamber.

"I wish to have speech with you, Miss Wynter-Wynbourne."

"Oh, dear, Freddy! You do sound cross! I hate it when you don't call me Cordelia. I'm sure you are about to give me a terrible scold, though I know of no reason that you should, for

I'm not your younger sister, or any relation at all in fact, so you really should be minding your own business. I want to return to the ballroom."

She made as if to go past him, but Lord Daltrey blocked her way, and he said, in a meaningful voice, "I particularly wish to be private with you."

"Oh, poppycock! The only reason one 'wishes to be private' with a girl is if a gentleman wishes to propose, and I know by that dark, tantruming look in your eye that you do *not* wish to propose to me."

"Or do you?" she asked in mock innocence. "Perhaps you wish to settle down at last, Lord Daltrey. Well, I won't accept, you know. Your predilections are much too shocking for *my* taste. You drink too much; you gamble too much; and, worst of it, you do all those other things one may not mention. No, I'm sure you would always be in a terrible temper, from lack of sleep and excess of alcohol, and irritability is unacceptable in a husband. Do you not agree?"

"I'm certainly in a terrible temper right now. I've not come to cross swords with you, Cordelia, nor to exchange pleasantries; rather, I mean to find out what in God's name you meant by treating that poor girl so shabbily."

He waited just a moment.

"Well, Cordelia? What did you mean by your shabby treatment of that girl?"

"What girl? Can you mean that *French* creature? You quite misunderstand. It was that girl's *dress* that was shabby, Freddy, not my treatment of her. She should not have been freely mingling amongst her betters in the ballroom, but, as a foreigner, should rather have been hiding over in the far corner, with the companions and the governesses and the rest of the hoi polloi. The girl was clearly out of place, so I merely depressed her pretensions by giving her the set-down she richly deserved.

"Set-down? Since when is putting ice down a lady's dress deemed a 'set-down'?"

"Yes, it was a nice touch, the lemon ice, was it not? Dear

me! What a shame! Such a careless accident! I'm sure her dress is ruined forever. That at least will serve to keep her in her place . . . if that horrid rag was her best dress, and I feel sure that it was, she will be quite unable to find suitable raiment in the future, and will stay safely upstairs doing tatting or weaving or knitting, or whatever it is that poor relations do in order to while away their miserable existences."

"I'm shocked, truly. I had no idea you could be so malicious, Cordelia."

"Malice? You call that malice, do you? I, for one, do not. I was not acting according to malice, but according to patriotism. You should have heard me when I called her a simpering little Frog spy. *That* was the set-down, calling her a Frog within hearing of anyone who is anyone. It was a most delicious moment, I assure you. The lemon ice slipping down the back of her gown was merely the coup de grâce, shall I say?"

Daltrey looked at the girl with wonder. She was a magnificent-looking creature: glossy chestnut hair, finely defined features, perfect skin, high brow, large, lovely eyes. She had a thin necklet of diamonds and a pair of long diamond earrings to match that seemed somehow to magnify her long, aristocratic neck. Her pale-orange gown, made of the finest silk with an overskirt of thin gauze and decorated with silk ribands, had come from the hands of London's finest couturier.

Cordelia Wynter-Wynbourne—she had everything a girl could wish for. She had beauty, breeding, and wealth, but none of this could ever compensate for her shallow, mean-spirited heart.

He looked at her grimly, hoping to shock her, and thus somehow break through her defenses.

"I will not hesitate to put this story about, Cordelia. You will not appear to advantage when seen in such an uncharitable light."

"To the contrary, society will understand perfectly well my zeal in defending its interests and defining its boundaries. One *must* punish those who cross them without leave."

"May I remind you, "said Lord Daltrey coldly, "that Mademoiselle de Bourget is a guest of my great-uncle Matthew, who is also your host?" He turned to indicate an elderly man on the other side of the room, whose dress, though costly, was that of an earlier generation who marked elegance in terms of wigs, lace, and powder.

The girl looked in the same direction and nodded her head in agreement.

"Sadly true . . . she *does* seem to be his guest! I intend to take issue up with Lord Dunnington at his earliest convenience."

"I trust you are joking, Cordelia."

"Oh, by no means. I have known Lord Dunnington since I was in leading-strings, and have no qualms about discussing such matters with him. Any friend of the family would do as much, I am persuaded. My papa, in particular, thinks it's *scandalous* for your great-uncle to have taken in a French foreigner, at a time like this, when the heinous monster Napoleon is threatening our nation and our allies."

"I had no idea you took such an interest in matters political," he said with unmistakable sarcasm.

Cordelia, noting his tone, colored hotly.

"Well, sir, even females may opine on matters relating to the safety of hearth and home, I do believe. Everyone knows the French to be evil and deceitful. Why must I meet such persons in society? Why should I not express my very reasonable views upon this subject? I do not wish to know such persons as the French, or even the *half*-French. I do not wish to make their acquaintance. I despise such persons."

"One may despise whomever one wishes, of course," said Lord Daltrey in a deceptively smooth voice. "If that is one's character. However, to display one's emotional weaknesses in public, for all to see, is execrable behavior that demonstrates poor taste, bad judgment, and ill-breeding."

Cordelia gasped at this set-down, and fanned her face with desperation, but Lord Daltrey continued.

"Your display this evening of rank prejudice toward Mlle. de

Bourget, your show of meanness of spirit, was, in my view, quite disgusting."

"How can you say so?" cried Miss Wynter-Wynbourne, furious.

"Because it is the case, Cordelia."

"I am sorry to think so, Lord Daltrey, for I had *thought* we were friends," she snapped back at him.

"If you were sorry enough to have apologized for your behavior, I would be more impressed."

"Apologize? Certainly not! No, I shall *not* do so."

"As you wish," he said coldly, bowing himself out from her presence, leaving her there on the floor to fend for herself.

A man powerfully built, and with a determined stride, Daltrey made his way quickly from the ballroom up into the family's quarters, resolved to find the half-French girl himself and offer his own apologies to her, at least, for Cordelia's abhorrent behavior.

The rather loud interview between Lord Daltrey and Miss Wynter-Wynbourne had not passed unnoticed among the *ton*. Whispers began to pass around the room as he left, wondering what had caused an obvious schism between two young persons who had previously been on perfectly good terms.

It was Lady Dalhousie who was the first to point out to wealthy Mrs. Edward Simms, who had recently arrived in the country, that Miss Wynter-Wynbourne had thrown a furious glance at Lord Daltrey after he left the ballroom.

"That glance of Cordelia's," her ladyship announced to whoever was paying her attention, "bodes ill for that tall girl, does it not?"

"Pooh!" opined Lady Stilton. "Who cares what becomes of that silly girl Dunnington had foisted on him? I'm sure *I* do not." Lady Stilton was a childless widow, and as such, could not be expected to take an active role in the affairs of young persons of marriageable age, much less in the affairs of one not entirely of English blood.

"Is that ginger-haired girl who ran out earlier Dunnington's ward? Extraordinary!" said Mrs. Simms. "I had heard there was some remote relation of his that was recently discovered in France, and brought back to Mother England. I wonder if that is she?"

"Indeed it is," said Lady Dalhousie conspiratorially. "I know *all* about the affair. She was found under most peculiar circumstances, I was given to understand. I believe she is the granddaughter of Matthew Dunnington's father's second wife."

"A distant relation if ever I heard of one!" said Lady Stilton. "I shouldn't think Lord Dunnington would be required to acknowledge her at all, really."

"To be sure. After all, her father *must* have been a Frenchman . . . the girl calls herself 'Mademoiselle de Bourget.' "

"That's asking for trouble to begin with, if you ask me. Why can't she be known as 'Miss de Bourget,' like a civilized human being? Why must she veritably *parade* her foreignness around? Why does Dunnington permit it?" chimed in Viscountess Stilton. "It's bad enough that she's part French."

"She's not only half-French, she was *raised* in France," pointed out Mrs. Simms, who was fond of precision.

"So much the worse. No doubt the girl has been corrupted by foreign ways. Most unsuitable among company," said Lady Dalhousie. "Young people being so easily swayed, you understand."

"No wonder Miss Wynter-Wynbourne was so cutting to her. One cannot say one blames Miss Wynter-Wynbourne," said Lady Stilton with a sniff. "Can one? We all know how girls like Cordelia treat persons who are attempting to rise above their station."

"I don't know that that was what she was trying to do, really. This is her guardian's home, her new home. She had a perfect right to attend the party. I think Miss Wynter-Wynbourne's behavior was not very good, and it all makes me feel rather sad for the foreign girl," said Mrs. Simms bravely.

"Certainly she may live here if Dunnington lets her do so, but why should she expect to be accepted by society? She won't be, you know. Why, the girl had better retire from the lists at once, for she will never fit in anywhere."

"Cordelia Wynter-Wynbourne will see to it that, far from gaining acceptance in society, the French girl will be anathema," said Lady Stilton, who was thinking it would be nice to find a gentleman to bring her some refreshment.

Lady Dalhousie nodded in agreement.

"No, the girl will never find a husband, if that's what Dunnington has his heart set on. Someone should take pity on him, and tell him so . . . tell him to stop wasting his time and his money. I shall tell him just that the next time I see him: that girl might as well be sent back to wherever it is she came from, straightaway."

Two

Lord Dunnington had given Elise de Bourget a suite in the west tower, one which she found perfect for her needs. She was able to work there, undisturbed, for hours at a time; this life quite suited her, and helped make the adjustment from her old situation in France to living in England, under the aegis of kind Lord Dunnington, who had discovered his familial connection to her and plucked her out from her reduced state, just like the heroine in a fairy tale.

It was, therefore, to her tower room that Mademoiselle de Bourget retired after the ballroom contretemps caused by Miss Wynter-Wynbourne. Elise did not call for her maid to assist her in removing the ruined dress; she removed it herself, and put on something more somber. She removed her earrings and bracelets; she removed the carefully preserved pearls that had belonged to her mother, and placed them in their velvet box.

She left her bedroom, and her dressing room, and went into the personal sitting room that formed part of the tower suite. She removed a linen cover from a wooden frame, and began to search for the set of bobbins she wanted to rewind.

Elise de Bourget went over to a cedar box in which her finished pieces were kept: she took a moment to look over them with love. Even the slightest glance of an outsider would have revealed the intricate treasures within, treasures which Elise guarded, jealously, and rarely had shown to any human being. Within the box was the most delicate stuff in the world, made painstakingly by hand; there were figures of cupids and angels and roses and lilies, all magically created in thread. It was the same sort of work with which Mary Queen of Scots had whiled away her lifetime of imprisonment.

There was a knock on the door, and Elise de Bourget hastily closed the lid on her cedar box. She ran her hand lovingly across it, then turned to throw the linen cover over the wooden frame, her needles, and several long strips of paper with holes in them. She took up some white thread, and the bobbins, and sat herself down in a comfortable chair.

The knock was repeated, and Elise responded, "You may enter."

It was in the tower room that Lord Daltrey finally caught up to her, as the girl sat quietly, working away at what Daltrey took to be embroidery, or some such female occupation. Mademoiselle de Bourget was sitting near the window with one foot tucked up beneath her, winding thread onto some marvelously carved ivory bobbins quickly and methodically while she looked out the glass window into the night, perfectly composed, serene, and self-possessed. As he took some time to study her demeanor, it struck Lord Daltrey with some force that Elise de Bourget must surely be the most composed female he had ever known.

She sat winding her bobbins with thread, sitting there with perfect dignity, with nothing in her manner to suggest that only recently she had been the butt of a cruel joke, precisely designed to demean her in the eyes of society. She sat there as if nothing of an embarrassing nature had occurred to her, but that she was happy to leave the ball, come upstairs, and stare out of a window into the night.

Searching his mind, Daltrey vaguely remembered having been introduced to Mademoiselle de Bourget by his great-uncle, some weeks past, but had taken little notice of her beyond recalling an air of shy self-control. In fact, the moment after they had been introduced, he had put her entirely out of his mind, never thinking once of her until he saw her at the ball with Miss Wynter-Wynbourne.

Her red hair, although unfashionable in the extreme, very much became her, Daltrey thought, as he watched her, waiting for a good moment to speak. She would by no means be considered a London beauty, certainly not the flamboyant, blonde kind of beauty that would take society by storm, season after season, in boring regularity.

No, from her white skin to her gray eyes, or her unfashionable height, she could not be said to be precisely beautiful, and yet Daltrey found something very arresting about her dignity and her composure, her long neck that she held up not from pride, but from what seemed to him to be an attractive kind of inner strength.

"Mademoiselle de Bourget?" he ventured at length. She turned to him, reading his face with those solemn gray eyes of hers, and he felt as if she were testing him, trying him, measuring his character.

"Lord Daltrey," she replied, rising at once, and extending her hand. Her voice was soft, but straightforward, with only the slightest hint of an accent. "How do you do? Your great-uncle Matthew mentioned that he expected your presence at the ball this evening."

She sat again, and motioned Lord Daltrey to a chair opposite hers.

"I arrived later than I thought I would. Mademoiselle de Bourget, I . . . saw what happened on the dance floor," he began, with some trepidation. "Just now. I saw what happened to you."

"What?" she said blankly. "What happened?"

Reluctant to bring up what must certainly be a painful subject, he nonetheless said, in a gentle tone, "I saw what Miss Wynter-Wynbourne did to you."

Mademoiselle de Bourget looked almost puzzled for a moment, then replied, shaking her head, "Oh, *that. Ce n'est rien.*"

"Nothing? You were not greatly offended, then?"

The auburn-haired girl shrugged slightly, saying, "How should I be? Hers was a silly child's trick, nothing more."

"Your dress is ruined, I am sure."

"Yes," she said regretfully. *"That* is true enough. It was even one of the very few I liked to wear. It's so difficult to find a color that suits my hair and my complexion."

"I apologize profoundly for Miss Wynter-Wynbourne's behavior, mademoiselle. Her rudeness should not be seen to typify English hospitality."

"Thank you, Lord Daltrey. But, please, should not Miss Wynter-Wynbourne herself be the one to make me an apology, if one is required?" she asked him, with a slight raise of an eyebrow. "Or are the making of apologies by well-bred young ladies, perhaps, not the English fashion?"

Lord Daltrey colored faintly.

"Of course they are the English fashion. Out of simple civility Miss Wynter-Wynbourne should apologize to you, and should do so at once. She *should* do so at once, but she is, unfortunately, of a proud and obstinate nature."

"And refuses to make me an apology? That is hardly surprising. Indeed, if her character were *not* just as you describe, she would hardly have seen fit to behave toward me as she did, would she?"

Her logic was impeccable, and Daltrey could not respond at once, but merely looked quizzically at her, rather amazed at the tone of this female. She ought most likely to be facing him while choking back tears, a girl who was humiliated in such a way in front of society, and yet she was not.

"Please, mademoiselle, do not take her rudeness to heart."

"I do not, I assure you. The incident was nothing."

Lord Daltrey just looked at her for a long moment.

"I see you think I am making light of the event, my lord. You must understand, Lord Daltrey," she said cryptically, "that I am used to being a survivor of far worse injustices. That girl's ill-conduct toward me meant no more to me . . ." and here her voice trailed off, and her gray eyes misted over very slightly.

"Than what, Mlle. Bourget?"

"It caused me no more pain than would a dry leaf falling upon me in a forest."

It was obvious that the girl was speaking the truth. Logically speaking, she should, like any other girl wishing to make her way amongst society, have been devastated when snubbed and sneered at in public by a girl who was one of the belles of the Season. Yet she was not devastated, not at all. She appeared to be utterly untouched.

Remarkable, Daltrey thought to himself.

"May I see you to your room so you may change your attire? Once you have done so, may I escort you back to the ballroom?"

"No, thank you, Lord Daltrey. I do not believe I will return."

"Please, mademoiselle, do so. Lord Dunnington will be most upset if you do not."

"How kind your great-uncle has been to me!" she sighed, shaking her head. "Lord Dunnington wishes me only well. He believes that if I can only spend some time going about in your English society, that I will make my place in it. He hopes that I will find myself a husband and thus obtain a place for myself in the world!"

"Why should you not?" asked Lord Daltrey. "It is something done by dozens of girls, Season after Season."

"I think your Season will not do for one such as I," she said, raising her gray eyes toward him. "Certainly what passed between that young lady and myself this very night is proof enough. No, I wish with all my might that I might lighten Lord Dunnington's burden by removing myself from his care, but his wish for me to do well in society will not, I fear, be granted."

"Please, Mademoiselle de Bourget. Do favor us with your company, and put this incident behind. Come down again, and join us: Lord Dunnington will wish it."

"Kind as he is, and kind as you have been, I cannot do so. Lord Dunnington is all too well aware of my retiring disposition. Besides, I have work to do."

"Work?" said Lord Daltrey, puzzled. "What work have you?"

The tall, gray-eyed girl looked at him for the first time quite directly, favoring him with an enigmatic smile he found deeply affecting.

"Lace, Lord Daltrey," she whispering softly, unaccountably, as if her words held some great secret. "I make lace."

Three

"I shall be returning to town this morning," Lord Daltrey said to Lord Dunnington, who was mending his quill pen, and not doing a marvelous job of it. "Is there anything I might do on your behalf while I am there, Great-uncle Matthew?"

The white-haired man stopped, put down his quill and his knife, and turned to face his favorite relative.

"No, my boy, there is nothing you need do for me . . . unless you can fix this pen *and* contrive to find me a husband for Elise de Bourget. Do you think you might, Frederick?"

Lord Daltrey laughed lightly, put down his hat and whip, and took a seat. "The pen I will happily repair for you," he said, picking up the pen and deftly cutting a new point. "As to your other problem, I cannot help, I'm afraid. However, I think Mademoiselle de Bourget hardly needs *my* help to make a match for her, Great-uncle Matthew. She appears a sensible girl, and is neither an antidote nor an ape-leader."

"No, certainly she is not. It is a matter of concern to me, however. As a carefree bachelor, you know too little of the ways of women in the world, and the machinations of marriage. How little *I* know of all this is being daily brought home to me, and pounded into my head until I am well tired of it. I must find a husband for her, this very Season, or the next at the latest. I truly wish my Alice were alive still; she could have the thing done in an instant, I am persuaded.

"I am staying up nights, worrying myself white about it. Are you sure that, among your friends, you could not find a suitable candidate? Some quiet, well-bred lad, perhaps? Someone as reclusive as she is, but dependable?"

"Among *my* friends?" he replied, laughing out loud. "Dear Great-uncle Matthew, you must know that I cannot."

The old man sighed and shifted in his seat.

"No, my boy, I suppose not."

Lord Dunnington said nothing for a few minutes and, then suddenly, turned back and gave his grand-nephew a sly look.

"I suppose *you* still have not thrown your hat into the matrimonial ring as yet?"

"Me? God save me, no, I have not, Great-uncle Matthew, nor shall I do so, ever. I'm a confirmed bachelor, and a famous flirt."

"You could lift from me a great burden if you took her off my hands," he said meaningfully. "I would be very grateful."

Lord Daltrey gave a nervous chuckle.

"I am ready to do you any service but that, Great-uncle Matthew. Pray do not ask me. In the first place, I am not the marrying kind, as all London knows by the long history of my, er, exploits. Second, Mademoiselle de Bourget seems a most respectable girl, and on that account alone, I feel sure she wouldn't have me."

"Your address, Freddy, is impeccable."

"But my tastes are hardly what a woman wants in a spouse."

Lord Dunnington laughed out loud at this.

"Sometimes I wish you weren't quite so wild, Freddy, but your taste in women is certainly faultless. Who was that blonde beauty I saw on your arm last year? Wasn't she the outside of enough? Fancy-piece, indeed!"

"Great-uncle Matthew, you hardly came to town at all last year. How could you have seen me with Carolette?"

"I came to town often enough to hear all there was to hear about you, and about her, and about the quarrel that caused you to, er, retire her from your protection. But tell me, was she as fabulous as rumor had it? Or not quite?"

Lord Daltrey almost blushed.

"I feel shy to discuss this with someone so much my senior, but, yes, Great-uncle Matthew, Carolette was truly a . . . a *memorable* mistress. I was almost sorry to part with her."

"Almost?" inquired Lord Dunnington.

"When she *demanded* that I lavish upon her a frightfully expensive diamond necklace set, complete with earrings and bracelets to match, we were every night at dagger's-drawn."

"Why did you not give the girl the baubles? You are famous for wasting the ready on your ladybirds!"

"It wasn't the money that bothered me . . . it was the dreadful whining tone in her voice when she was trying to wangle it out of me! The sound began to haunt me in my sleep! A most frightening, shocking sound, I promise you!"

Lord Dunnington began to laugh again, and Lord Daltrey continued his story in a spirited way.

"And then, to make matters even worse, the silly wench had the audacity to send me a series of wheedling missives, drenched in the most nauseating kind of perfume. Faugh!" Lord Daltrey shuddered. *"That* was beyond bearing, and, of course, that was the end of the affair. Straightaway, I gave her her *congé."*

Lord Dunnington brought his chair closer, and leaned toward his grand-nephew.

"Listen, Frederick. You can rest assured that Elise de Bourget has been well brought up. She's just a quiet thing who spends most of her time reading, or up in her room with some sort of intricate embroidery project she works on for hour after hour.

"She's the nearest thing to invisible! She's a good girl. Elise would scorn to wheedle, or whine, or to interfere with your life in any way. If you were to agree to marry her, you could go on living just as you have done and then she would have a home and could live quietly out at Devonhurst. If you didn't come to really fancy her, you need never see the girl except at Christmas."

"An arranged marriage with an unreformed rake? She deserves better than that, Great-uncle Matthew."

"True enough. I just thought it would be an easy solution, as I am fond of both of you. Two birds with one stone, don't you know?"

"Great-uncle Matthew, from what I have seen of her good character, Mademoiselle de Bourget is not just in the common way. She deserves a better man than me, wouldn't you say?"

Lord Dunnington looked serious for a moment, and then said, "Well, yes, I suppose she does, Freddy."

Hearing this, Lord Daltrey found his pride stung by his relative's expressed opinion of him, but said nothing more about it. He merely bowed to Lord Dunnington in a gentleman-like manner, picked up his hat and whip, and exited the room, ready to take up his notorious London life once again.

Four

That spring, Lord Daltrey's wild exploits were the talk of the town, just as they always were, every year. Tongues wagged when, after a long siege, he finally succeeding in winning the heart of the fascinating new opera-singer, Anna Celestina, seducing her away from her previous protector, the Earl of Forbent. The young earl became distraught, following the girl around day and night, and finally challenging Lord Daltrey to a duel. The duel was carried out at Garwood Forest, just on the outskirts of London; the earl, to the surprise of no one, was wounded.

The Earl of Forbent recovered from the wound to his body, but not from the wound to his heart, and Forbent's faithfulness in love was finally rewarded when, after a brief, meaningless quarrel, Daltrey cut his ties to Anna Celestina, and abandoned her to the waiting arms of the still-amorous earl.

Daltrey and his bosom friend Sir Jeremy Stanton made a twenty-thousand-pound wager as to whose horsemanship was superior at taking one's hunter over fences. The two were to ride at dusk, when it is most difficult to see obstacles exactly. They agreed to ride at full tilt over a series of high fences especially constructed for the event, and then were to switch horses and do the fences, in reverse order, all over again.

Public sentiment was on Daltrey's side when, after a dazzling run, Daltrey's horse Pacer stumbled in a rabbit hole, allowing Sir Jeremy to pull ahead, but the brave-hearted Pacer was able to make up the time, and win the whole pot for Lord Daltrey.

Daltrey and his faithful valet, Simpson, became famed during that Season for their having discovered, or rather invented, a fascinating drink concocted of elderberry wine, Spanish hot peppers, olives, anchovies, pepper, and salt as a sure cure for the morning after megrims following a long night of drink and debauchery. Known as "Freddy's Fizz," it became all the rage among young men cutting a dash in society: even young ladies approaching their first seasons begged to be given "just a taste" of it, for it was all the crack.

Elise de Bourget, out at Barcourt Manor, heard some of his exploits, and thought very kindly of the man who had sought her out to offer her his apologies.

Lord Daltrey heard nothing at all about Mademoiselle de Bourget; he hadn't the time or even the inclination. He had quite forgotten her existence.

After much soul-searching, Lord Dunnington finally prevailed upon his old flame, Lady Southward, to come to him and take Elaine de Bourget under her wing, with the thought of getting her ready to make her way in London society.

In April, Lady Southward descended upon Barcourt Manor in fantastic fashion, accompanied by a vast retinue of dressers and hairdressers and mantuamakers and maids, lorded over by Mlle. Mathilde, her chief dresser, and M. Olivier, her personal chef, whose decoctions of rose water and whose dish of pheasant under glass Lady Southward swore by as the only ways to maintain, respectively, a perfect complexion and a perfect figure.

By May, Lady Southward pronounced herself very well satisfied with the results of all her labor. The girl's manners, happily, were already impeccable, though there was a kind of reserved quality to her that Lady Southward rather wished Elise had not had. Perhaps, she hoped, she might pass it off as a regal demeanor.

After the sending back and forth between London and Barcourt Manor of numberless ells of the finest silks and satins and muslins, Elise's new wardrobe was declared to be perfection itself though accomplished at a very pretty price. (When Lord Dunnington, at one point, complained about the outlay, Lady Southward assured him it was absolutely necessary to acquire just the right hued fabrics, in order to balance out and modulate the impossible red color of that girl's hair.)

It was late May when Lady Southward, without introduction, marched into Lord Dunnington's study and announced that she had done all she could do. It remained only for them to enter her in the Season, late as it was, and see whether or not Mademoiselle de Bourget "took."

"She has the looks for it," said Lady Southward. "No mystery about that. And no matter about that wild red hair of hers, she certainly has the dignity and taste to pull it off."

"Then, Mary, what opinion do you have? Will she be offered for or not?" asked Lord Dunnington.

"She has no particular fortune, so she won't be pursued for her money, which really is a mercy, when you think of it. The problem that I see, Matthew, is that the girl's heart isn't in it."

"How do you mean?"

"I mean precisely what I said. I declare, I was always precise in my understanding of things . . . why did you never take what I said seriously when I was young? I always wished I had married you rather than Donald, you must know."

Lord Dunnington suddenly colored, saying, "No, I hadn't known that."

"Well, I had," said the widow. "But that's water under the dam. I married Donald, and I had five exquisite daughters, and I buried Donald young, and I had five daughters left without great dowries. But despite that, I managed the most fabulous marriages for all of them: one duke, three earls, a viscount, and for Eliza, the prettiest, I found a well-bred commoner wealthier than all the rest. None of them were arranged marriages, mind you. They were love marriages all. That's what I had hoped to do for your Elise."

"Do you now think that you cannot?"

"I don't know, Matthew. As I said, although she's perfectly civil, and does whatever I tell her, and behaves however I tell her to, and wears whatever I tell her, her heart is not really in the business . . . which makes it difficult.

"You have to have a girl with her own interests at heart. Look at that Wynter-Wynbourne girl. Certainly good-looking, but her dowry was only just acceptable. However, she knew what she wanted in a marriage . . . a high title, and vast estates, and plenty of money. She knew just what she wanted, and she went out and got it, and now she's 'Her Grace, the Duchess of Anderleigh.' "

"Ho! She paid a high price for *that* title!"

"What price?" she asked. "Anderleigh himself, you mean?"

The two old friends broke into laughter.

"Good heavens, yes, Matthew, that's true enough. The old duke is a certifiable slow-top, but I'm sure the new duchess doesn't care a fig for that, so long as Anderleigh still has wit enough to sign bank drafts. At any rate, you must see my point with regard to Elise. Cordelia Wynter-Wynbourne knew she wanted to become 'Duchess of Something or Other,' and that's what made it occur. She had a goal, an intention, a desire to make a brilliant marriage. But this Elise of ours is another thing altogether, no matter how smartly we fit her out. It's her attitude that is problematic. It's almost as if the girl just doesn't really wish to wed.

"But what girl would *not* wish to wed?" wondered Lady Southward. "That's what puzzles me."

"Perhaps it's not so much a reluctance to marry as it is a reluctance to enter into the fray of high society," mused Lord Dunnington. "Do you recall how cruel that Wynter-Wynbourne girl was to Elise before she married Anderleigh? The story became common knowledge: she humiliated the girl at a ball, in my own house."

"Very ill-bred of her, I must say."

"Just so. But, what can one do? Girls will be girls, and some of them can be devilish catty."

"Elise has a good head on her shoulders. She'll survive the rigors of the *ton*."

"It's settled, then. We shall repair to the London house in a week or two, whenever you're ready, and then we'll fire her off!"

Five

It was the first week in June when Lord Daltrey was making his way down Bond Street, late to meet his friend Sir Jeremy Stanton, and there was a commotion in the crowd up ahead. A loud cry was just audible above the noise of hooves on cobblestones and the general bustling.

"Thief!" someone said. "Cutpurse!"

Everyone immediately checked his or her belongings, looking for the perpetrator. Lord Daltrey noted a slight figure running at full tilt heading in his direction, dodging pedestrians, dogs, sellers, and sweepers alike.

As the child approached, his Lordship stepped deftly to the right, and the figure barreled straight into him, and was there incarcerated by two strong arms.

"It wasn't me, guv'nor! Lemme go!" cried the urchin, grabbing at Lord Daltrey's immaculate coat with two grubby hands. "Honest, guv'nor! It weren't me what done it, it were Chipper Sue, I saw 'er with me own eyes! Don't let 'em take me away, please, guv'nor!"

A flustered lady's maid then joined the fray, and began squawking over the boy, threatening him with corporal punishment and worse if he didn't hand over her good young lady's purse straightaway.

"Give it up, boy! Give it up, now, I say! I know you have it! I saw you take it!" she shrieked.

Next, threading her way through the growing crowd, came a tall young lady with splendid auburn hair, wearing a most fashionable bonnet and gown. It took Lord Daltrey just a moment to realize that he was already acquainted with this modish lady.

She inclined her head toward him and smiled.

Immediately, he bowed over her gloved hand, which wasn't easy, as he still kept one hand tightly holding of the collar of the squirming boy.

"Mademoiselle de Bourget! How very nice to see you again! Is there any way I can assist you? What seems to be the problem?" he asked, indicating the child he held.

"How do you do, Lord Daltrey? You always seem ready to render me assistance whenever I encounter unusual circumstances. Do you suppose this child is the one who took my purse?"

"It's him alright, who took mademoiselle's purse!" said the maid. "I saw him do it with my own eyes. You'll pay for this, you little beast!"

"I didn't, I didn't I swear it! Her what took the miss's purse be hidin' right back there! Look sharp, guv'nor! Over there!" cried the boy.

Lord Daltrey turned his head just in time to catch a glimpse of a guilty, frightened face disappearing into an alley. Immediately Daltrey let go of the boy, and dashed down the alley after the miscreant.

In a moment, he emerged with a filthy young girl held in one hand, and holding up Mlle. de Bourget's reticule with the other, which he handed to her.

"Oh! Thank you so much, Lord Daltrey! I don't know what I would have done without your help. You are too kind."

"My pleasure, Mlle. de Bourget. What shall we do with this young rascal?"

Elise looked at the dirty, ragged little girl and her heart was touched. "Don't turn her over to the authorities, please. Here, take this," said she, giving the urchin a coin from her purse. "You mustn't do such a thing again, you know."

The girl snatched the coin out of her hand without a word of thanks, and was off in an instant.

"You are staying with Great-uncle Matthew, I presume? I had

not realized he was come to town. My apologies . . . I have been out of town myself, and am behindhand with affairs. I should surely have called upon you had I known."

"We are only just arrived yesterday, and have not had time yet to take our cards about. I came with your Great-uncle Matthew, accompanied by his friend, Lady Southward, who has kindly undertaken the onerous task of making me presentable to society."

"That sounds intriguing. How is that done?"

"Making a girl presentable to society? It is a very intricate business; at least, I am finding it so. I am so glad that you are interested enough to inquire."

"I am; you must tell me all. May I escort you back to your carriage?"

"By all means. It is just over there."

Mademoiselle de Bourget indicated to her maid that she should follow them at a safe distance, and Lord Daltrey placed her arm in his, walking to the outside, as a gentleman must on a dangerous, dirty London street.

"Becoming presentable, I have discovered," said Elise de Bourget, "has mainly to do with learning how to spend a great deal of money. That is the first and most essential rule of society. Whatever one's taste in clothes may be, it must be indulged at the very greatest expense.

"For example, Lord Daltrey, if two ribands look precisely the same, it is the *dearer* riband which is the *better* one, and it is *that* which must be purchased. Even if an outsider cannot tell the difference, the effect of wearing the richest clothing upon the wearer will be to induce a sensation of pride and self-confidence that will dazzle all onlookers, and prove useful in heightening one's reputation.

"Do you follow me, Lord Daltrey?" she said with a raise of the eyebrow. "For I am persuaded I am correct."

"I do follow you, mademoiselle. Pray, go on."

"That's the first point . . . one *must* engage in financial profligacy in the service of high fashion. I have been practicing that, just today, on Bond Street, and I can reveal to you that I am doing *very* well at it. I have spent a small fortune, with little to show for it, and that is just as it should be."

Lord Daltrey stifled a laugh, trying manfully to keep a straight face.

"Now, the second point of making a girl presentable to society," Elise went on, "requires that she cultivate a brilliant, lively disposition. This is, of course, my weakest point, for I am not naturally of a sociable nature.

"My talents as a conversationalist, I have been advised, are *sadly* lacking. To make up for this, my mentor, Lady Southward, has taught me that in my case, due to my unfortunate natural tendency toward silence and reclusiveness, that I must try with all my might to cultivate a 'trilling laugh.' "

She paused as if lost in thought, asking, "Or was it the 'laughing trill'?"

Lord Daltrey maintained his composure with difficulty.

"You see what a poor student I am, Lord Daltrey! Since Lady Southward has found me unable to make light conversation when needed, I have been told I must just laugh sweetly, every now and then, when I am in a social situation, and that I am to try to *look* intrigued."

"Very interesting," he said, smiling broadly, deeply appreciating the humor of her approach.

"It is interesting, I assure you! May I practice upon you, kind Lord Daltrey?"

"By all means."

"Please make several comments about something inconsequential, and I shall demonstrate my trill."

"Very well. 'The negus is sadly lacking this evening, mademoiselle. Don't you agree?' "

Elise gave a small, meaningless little laugh, and put on an intentionally vapid look. She smiled slightly and batted her eyes, giving a little simper.

Lord Daltrey went into whoops of laughter, and said, admiringly, "Well done, mademoiselle! A breathtaking performance! One worthy of Mrs. Siddons!"

"Thank you so very much. Oh, and perhaps I should take this time to inform you that I am no longer Mademoiselle de Bourget, but have been transmogrified to 'Miss de Bourget.' So much more suitable, don't you think?"

"Whose idea was that?" asked Lord Daltrey, beginning to wish he might prolong their conversation.

"My mentor's, of course. Oh, perhaps you were thinking that it might be a result of Miss Wynter-Wynbourne's witchery, but it is not. Actually, she is married now, I understand, rather suddenly, and married into a very favorable position."

"Poor Cordelia. She'll live to regret that marriage. I should rather have a steak pasty as a spouse than old Anderleigh. Shocking simpleton, you know."

"I did not know anything about him. I am still learning all the ways of London. The burden of having to master so many new notions and new London manners has quite overcome me, as you can see. There is very little left of the quiet person who came to visit your great-uncle so long ago. I feel that I am becoming improved despite myself. I believe that I shall never be quite the same girl again!"

They reached Lord Dunnington's carriage. The maid put the bandboxes inside, and Lord Daltrey handed Miss de Bourget up into the carriage.

Miss de Bourget gave Lord Daltrey her hand.

"It was a pleasure seeing you again, and very kind of you to let me show off all my new propensities to you at such lengths."

"The pleasure was all mine, I assure you," said Lord Daltrey, bowing.

The carriage took off down Bond Street, and Lord Daltrey took off in the opposite direction. As he walked down the street with a lightened step, he realized that what he had said to Miss de Bourget about the pleasure of her company was very true. He had found the company of the tall young lady with arresting gray eyes to be pleasant in the extreme, and a far cry from his long succession of costly ladybirds.

Six

Lord Daltrey paid his morning call upon his great-uncle promptly the next day, and offered to take Lady Southward and Miss de Bourget out for a ride in the park. With the proceeds of his wager with Sir Jeremy Stanton, Daltrey he had recently bought, among other things, a splendid new pair of match bays; and he wanted to show them off.

Lady Southward declined the invitation, but indicated that Elise was free to accept, so long as her maid rode beside her.

He picked them up at the hour of the grant strut. Elise de Bourget was wearing a delicate green walking dress, with a full ruched bonnet and a ruffled parasol to match. He thought her looks perfectly charming, and told her so.

He handed her up into his carriage, and his driver, John Coachman, showed off his considerable skills by threading his way deftly and swiftly through the busy London traffic. Elise was still so unused to the city that she made no attempt at conversation for some time, as she was fully occupied looking around her at all the extraordinary sights and sounds.

As they turned the corner to enter Hyde Park, Elise said to him, "I hope you know that I am very appreciative of your condescending to invite a green girl for a turn about the park, Lord Daltrey. Your compassion toward me is very much appreciated."

"It's the least I can do. Besides, I enjoy your company very much."

"Oh, my! Very prettily said! I can see I shall learn a lot from you, about how one carries on flirtations, Lord Daltrey."

Lord Daltrey laughed and said nothing, but Elise responded, "From your evident amusement, you are probably thinking that the things about which you are most expert are topics unsuited to my ears."

Lord Daltrey colored faintly, looked taken aback, and replied, "Indeed, those topics you bring up are so unsuited to your ears that I am most displeased that you are even *aware* of their unsuitability."

"But you must be aware that people talk."

"I am," he said, giving her a puzzled look.

"And that they talk about you. And your many wagers. And your . . . how shall I put it?"

"Don't put it at all," he said warningly.

"Your escapades, shall we say?"

"As a fond relative of your guardian, I must tell you that this line of discussion is completely improper, even between friends, such as ourselves."

"Are we friends, then? That is very reassuring. I am trying so hard, out of respect for Lord Dunnington, to present myself in a more *outgoing* way, but I fear it is not really natural in me.

"I am gabbling away today, but it is because I am really very nervous to be in a new country and a new situation with so many people expecting me to behave and think in a certain way. Such discussion as we have just had, for example, would not at all have been seen as improper in France, for example, where I was brought up. There, whether or not a man had a particular mistress would be common knowledge. Even young girls could know about it and speak their minds."

Lord Daltrey blushed hotly.

"Yes, but this is not France, Miss de Bourget!"

"No," she said with a sad sigh, suddenly turning her head away from his, and pressing her lips together. "Thankfully, it is not."

A silence fell upon them for a few minutes, each person lost in individual thoughts.

Then, as they began passing friends and acquaintances, Lord Daltrey would nod his head in acknowledgment, Elise would smile shyly, and then he would explain to her precisely where this or that person fit within the universe of the London *ton*. He pointed out a royal duke, and the arbiter of fashion, Beau Brummell, and Elise was very much impressed.

Lord Daltrey had just told John to turn back the barouche toward Lord Dunnington's house, when a shining, brand-new maroon carriage came into view.

The magnificent crest on its sides proclaimed for the world that this equipage belonged to the Duke of Anderleigh. In it was the duchess, dressed in all the splendor she could afford and that Mlle. D'Aubert's salon could provide. She was accompanied by Lady Angela Evert, whose horsy laugh could be heard at a distance.

When the duchess identified the occupants of the carriage approaching hers, her face paled, and afterward became flushed red and angry. She lifted her nose high into the air, indicating to Lady Angela to do likewise, and in this manner the two ladies passed by, violently projecting the cold and haughty indifference that was the cut direct.

It was too much.

The two had not yet fully passed, when Lord Daltrey and Elise de Bourget burst out in immoderate laughter.

"We mustn't laugh so loud, I'm sure we mustn't! She can hear us!" said Elise in a choked voice, tears forming at the sides of her pretty gray eyes.

"What if she did hear us? Her behavior was outrageous! Each time I meet her, her folly increases exponentially! Believe me, I shall call upon her and explain to her my precise opinion of her conduct. Should she have the effrontery to attempt to cause you any unease, Miss de Bourget, you must tell me at once, and I shall repair the damage."

"You mustn't call on her, Lord Daltrey. If you did, you

would be censured. At any rate, as I once told you, long ago, I am not afraid of her at all, and give no consequence to her ill-considered actions.

"Although I know only too well what folly, and even what unmentionable deeds, are done in this world, I know that such actions spring from ignorance. That is the case here, as in all cases."

"But, Miss de Bourget—"

"Please, let me finish. You must know, the arena in which the Duchess of Anderleigh is attempting to injure me is itself so shallow, and so superficial, and so entirely meaningless, seen in the light of what is truly important in life, that it is the easiest thing in the world to disregard it . . . not giving it a second thought."

"You underestimate the power of ill-rumor in London society. The girl has taken a dislike to you, and, I fear, will try to break you."

Elise gave a rueful laugh.

"Let her break me, then. You are my superior with regard to the rules, regulations, and ways of high society. However, I must humbly point out that there are things I have seen that even you, for all your experience, have *not* seen. In the light of what is truly important, the current height . . . or depth . . . of one's social reputation is not worth thinking of."

"To what do you refer, Miss de Bourget?" he said, turning toward her, as he felt for the first time in his life a stirring within his being, a strong wish to protect this person from all harm, and to defend her above all things.

"I refer, Lord Daltrey, to matters of life . . . and death. Matters of the heart. Forgive me, I fear I have said too much already. Some things do not bear speaking of, and I beg you will allow me to change what can only be a painful subject for me. Pray, do not take what I said amiss. I did not mean to be presumptuous."

"Certainly not," said Lord Daltrey, who was both puzzled and captivated by hearing her point of view.

He grew silent, and, to the accompaniment of the rhythmic sound of hoofs on cobblestones, drove the young lady home, without pursuing the matter further.

As he handed her down from his carriage, and walked her to her door, he began to be aware that the very presence of the unique and reclusive Elise de Bourget had a powerful effect on his being, and that he did not fully understand the reason this was so.

Seven

After this auspicious start, it was observed about London that Viscount Daltrey was making quite a point of seeking out the company of the once-reclusive Miss de Bourget, who now found her social schedule so full she barely had time to work her lace at all.

Lord Daltrey's friends observed him going in to Almack's, of all dreary places, with the evident intention of dancing with Miss de Bourget; he escorted her to the theater and to the opera and to the park. He took her on picnics and even (Heaven forfend!) took her sightseeing at the Tower of London.

His cronies teased him about it, but he tossed it off as merely paying a kindness to his great-uncle's ward as a matter of family propriety. Biddies and tale-mongers, however, were not persuaded by such an obvious smoke screen, and it became an on-dit of some consequence that perhaps the French girl might change Lord Daltrey's bachelor ways.

It was at a musicale given later in the Season by Lady Easton, that the paths of Elise de Bourget and Frederick, Lord Daltrey, crossed in a particularly fateful manner. Lady Southward was there, sporting a fabulous purple turban with white plumes, acting as chaperon for Elise. The new Duchess of Anderleigh was in attendance as well, over in a corner, dressed in a thin gown of dampened light gold silk which clung to her figure; Her Grace was thronged by a noisy crowd of admirers and cicisbeos.

The duchess paid no attention whatsoever when Elise's name was announced, nor did she turn toward her to see the girl enter.

Miss de Bourget was dressed in a handsome white muslin creation that was the very essence of innocence and simplicity. Her
auburn hair had been swept up high, leaving but a few soft
tendrils toward the side of her face; her ornaments were simple
perfection itself: a diamond necklace, diamond drop earrings,
and a diamond bracelet on each white-gloved wrist.

When the arrival of the viscount was announced, Her Grace
of Anderleigh raised her head toward the door and favored him
with the coldest of stares. If the duchess noticed how elegant
he looked, his powerful shoulders filling out his tight-cut black
coat, his hair brushed back into a Brutus, his cravat tied in a
way that would put others to shame, she did not allow her admiration of his dress and figure to show at all.

Preoccupied with her own affairs, the duchess failed to note
that, despite his elegant appearance, Lord Daltrey was in the
very blackest of moods. It took Elise de Bourget, however, only
the time of a glance at him to understand that something was
very wrong indeed with her friend and advisor.

As soon as she was able to extricate herself from a particularly boring account of the progression of symptoms of her
stomach ailments by the Countess of DeVere, Miss de Bourget
chose to fly in the face of convention and go directly to the part
of the room where Lord Daltrey was standing, next to a pillar,
in order to speak with him.

When she approached him, he bowed to her, saying, "How
do you do, Miss de Bourget? I hope you are well."

"Yes, thank you. I am," she replied.

Elise noted that Lord Daltrey's face was ashen, and that his
lips were pressed tightly together. There was no hint of either
warmth or humor in his countenance, and she began to be afraid
that, for some reason, he might be angry with her.

"Forgive me for my directness, but you seem upset, Lord
Daltrey. Are you upset with me? Have I done something I ought
not?"

"No, not at all. I have had some hard news."

"I am sorry to hear that. I did not mean to intrude."

"As it happens, I should like to have someone to talk with. If you are not engaged for this dance, let me fetch some refreshments for you, and then let us step aside to the outer room, where we can speak without the eyes of all society upon us. I have a particular dislike of revealing my private business in public."

"Of course, Lord Daltrey." Elise picked up her skirts, and hurried, in a ladylike manner, through a side door to a small room; she seated herself on a small, satin-striped chair, and began fanning herself with her fan not due to heat, but due to the anxiety she felt for her friend.

After a few minutes, Lord Daltrey returned, handed her a glass of ratafia, and seated himself at a chair by her side. For some minutes, nothing at all was said; Lord Daltrey seemed at a loss for words.

Finally, he began, saying, "I learned today of the death of Sir Jeremy Stanton, who was my dear friend."

Elise said sympathetically, "Of course, that would be a great blow to you. I had heard that Sir Jeremy had had some sort of accident. I understand that he died by drowning, in a small lake on his father's property, having become tangled in some weeds."

"How quickly bad news travels through the *ton!*" said Lord Daltrey bitterly.

"The death of someone young and vital is shocking, and I think that, rather than mere sensationalism, is why the story came round so quickly."

"Perhaps," he replied with a grim look.

"From my own experience, I know that such a loss is painful."

"It is painful beyond belief," said Lord Daltrey, putting his head in his hands.

After a few moments, he appeared to try to shake off his depression, raised himself up to his full height, and began to pace round the anteroom.

Elise waited patiently for him to reveal whatever was the true

source of his unhappiness, for she knew intuitively there must
be more there than met the eye.

Finally, he turned to her, his dark eyes filled with sorrow and
self-doubt.

"The thing is, Miss de Bourget, that I firmly believe the
responsibility for Jeremy's death is on *my* hands."

Elise knew enough not to display the confusion she felt. Remembering what Lady Southward had taught her, she took command of her feelings and her tone of voice.

She kept her tone neutral and even as she said, "I do not
precisely understand. Why ever would you feel *yourself* responsible? You weren't even with him at the time of his
death."

"Was I *not* there?" cried Lord Daltrey, slamming his fist
suddenly onto a mahogany table.

The force of the blow sent some bric-a-brac flying, attracting
the attention of a footman, who came in, pretended he had heard
nothing out of the ordinary, picked up the pieces silently, and
disappeared.

They waited until the door was fully closed behind the servant.

Lord Daltrey sat down near her once again, and took her hand,
speaking in a very soft voice, saying, "Please excuse my unforgivable loss of temper. I was not present at his estate, and yet I
was with Jeremy at his death, just as surely as if I had tied him
to a rock and had pushed him into the waters with my own
hands."

Elise looked at him. Her eyes were so full of compassion
toward him that he could hardly breathe. All of a sudden he had
a desperate sense that if he could only take this woman up into
his arms forever, everything in the world would suddenly be
healed again.

"The death of a loved one," she began to say, "is so painfully
distressing one can hardly speak of it in words, and yet, I cannot
help but think—"

Lord Daltrey cut her off abruptly.

"No, Miss de Bourget. You still do not perfectly understand the circumstances of his death, nor his state of mind. I had recently won from Jeremy, on the very stupidest of bets, a fortune of twenty thousand pounds."

Elise gasped, in spite of herself; Lord Daltrey saw her reaction, winced at it, and then, looking even more depressed, continued on.

"Jeremy had pledged to me some lands his family held in order to cover the bet. When he went home, his father told him that there were debts by other family members which his father had intended to settle by selling these lands. There was a tremendous quarrel, for, in order to settle Jeremy's outrageous debts, either his mother's jewels would have to be sold, or there would have to be an invasion of the holdings of the main estate. His father berated Jeremy for acting in such a heedless, profligate way."

"One can feel sympathy for his father's point of view, surely."

"Certainly. That is why I am so ashamed of myself. I have no family to look out for, and am sufficiently well-heeled to be able to wager just as I wish, even quite outrageously, and there is no one who suffers for my actions save myself. But to lead Jeremy into debt, just to carry on some stupid, foolish, boyish nonsense, is unforgivable, and to help put him in a position where he undermined the stability of his family, is equally unforgivable."

He paused for a moment, unable to speak, barely able to contain himself, and took two deep breaths.

In the softest tone possible, he added, "To have acted in a heedless way that led to my dear friend taking his own life, is not only unforgivable, but unbearable."

"Take his own life? But he did not take his own life. The drowning was an accident!" said Elise.

"It was not. It is not a thing generally known, but among his close friends and family, there is no doubt of it. He took his own life."

"No!" she said weakly, now able to comprehend his state of mind.

"There was a note, you see. Under the double burden of shame at his actions and fear he would continue to be a burden to his family, Jeremy took his own life."

What could be said after that? For many minutes, a horrid silence passed between them, till finally, Elise managed to say, in a small voice, "Oh, Lord Daltrey, I am *so* very sorry."

He looked at her with gratitude, and again took her hand, pressing it in his.

"Thank you. Thank you as well for letting me confide in you. I feel this is an experience from which I shall never recover."

She sighed suddenly, and looked at the floor.

When she brought her gray eyes up again to meet his, Lord Daltrey was once again struck by the look of profound compassion in them, and he was moved.

"In some sense, what you say is true . . . such a loss cannot be resolved," Elise said in a whisper.

"That is why I feel so responsible, and quite miserable," said Daltrey. "Now, I can see all too clearly what a wasteland I have made of my life, spending my time on vain pleasures . . . which are worthless, completely worthless in the face of such news."

There was another long, uncomfortable silence.

"It *is* important," Elise said carefully, "to know what things in life are only of temporary importance, and what are of lasting value."

At first he made no reply, but looked at her with a glance so filled with admiration that she had to look away.

"You are wise, Elise," he said softly, touching her soft, rose-red cheek with his hand.

She started when he used her given name; it sounded so intimate on his lips. When he touched her hand, she felt desire arise, then felt a sudden fear that perplexed her.

Elise listened to his strong, soft voice, as if she were in a trance; it sounded like a voice she once heard long ago, a mas-

culine voice that was a portent of love, security, and promise.
It sounded like her father's voice.

"I can only hope to turn this tragedy around by using it as
a warning. Elise, I must change my life," he said to her. "Somehow, I must make something of myself. Whatever that might
mean. I have thought, in these past few days, that perhaps I
should begin thinking of starting again and settling down."

Elise withdrew her hand, blushed furiously red, and turned
away to hide her reactions from him. She felt attraction, she felt
desire, but there was more to it than that: in all her life, she had
never felt such fear.

She then gave a little nervous laugh, and tried to hide her
nervousness in a joking remark, saying, with a lightness she
knew to be false, "Settling down? What? No more bachelor
escapades for Lord Daltrey? Dear me! What shall society do?
London will lose its primary source for tales of the *ton.*"

Lord Daltrey looked at her deeply, with a look of perfect
seriousness, and she felt ashamed by her own cowardice.

He shook his head, and continued speaking in a rueful tone,
"See what a mull I have made of my life? I am nothing more
than a buffoon for high society. A provider of scandalous tales
to amuse the idle rich."

"Then, perhaps you will find a good woman," Elise sighed,
thinking of the beauties of the *ton* who regularly set their caps
at Lord Daltrey.

Lord Daltrey drew closer to her and picked up her right hand,
and held it in both of his. Her heart began beating at an un-
imaginable pace. She could feel his breathing, close to her, close
enough that she could hear the quickening pace of it.

"Perhaps I *have* found one," he said, coming still closer to
her, flicking a tendril of hair away from her forehead.

She tried to draw away, but his enveloping hand remained
tight around her wrist.

"Please," Elise said desperately. "Please don't say such
things to me."

"Why not, Elise? Why should I not make love to you? To

win your love would be a worthy goal. Let me try to win you for my wife."

She made her hand break free, and turned away from him.

When, after some time, she finally turned her face toward him again, tears were glistening on her face as she said, sadly, "Lord Daltrey, if you knew the truth about me, you would not approach me on that subject. Please, you must not speak of such things to me again."

He went to her, took her hand, and kissed it.

"Very well. I shall say no more for now."

Eight

A man whose offer of marriage has been rejected by a female has been ceded, historically speaking, a perfect right to seek solace in intoxicants, but that is not what Lord Daltrey chose to do. A life filled with wine, women, and song had been his predilection always, such that "drowning his sorrows" in wine meant less than nothing. Rather than turn to drink, Lord Daltrey let Elise's rejection of his suit turn him to thoughtful contemplation of his predicament.

The fact was that Lord Daltrey's proposal at the musicale had come to his mind spontaneously; it had been the inspiration of the moment, coming as much of a surprise to Lord Daltrey as it had been to Elise herself.

However, Daltrey was by no means unhappy at the way in which his feelings had, for once, overcome him. The more thought he gave the matter afterward, the more his mind was utterly determined upon making the tall girl with the grave but sparkling eyes his own lady, for all time. It seemed so obvious an answer, he wondered why it had not occurred to him long before.

Lord Daltrey set about the matter with energy and thoroughness. He wrote a series of letters to his various paramours, thanking each one, offering each a generous gift, and giving each her *congé*.

He withdrew from all society, both high and low, and left for his country house at Devonhurst. He reduced his consumption of alcohol to a single bottle of wine with meals. He ceased to receive his former companions for two months, telling them that he was hard at work on a project for his family, and would see them again when he returned to London life.

As to gambling, he simply ceased to place wagers. The death of Sir Jeremy had made that sort of entertainment anathema to him, and it was, of all his rakish habits, the easiest to break.

His goal was clear; his mind was certain.

Lord Daltrey thought that, if he could demonstrate his worthiness, Elise de Bourget would accept him. He felt that she had not even allowed him to begin to pay court to her because she detested his reputation as a rake.

He wanted to show her he had changed, and that those ways that had led to such suffering were things he had now abandoned, with all of his heart.

He believed that if she would give him the chance to do so, he would be able to win her heart.

Lord Daltrey, however, was not in a position to know that he had won the heart of Elise de Bourget long ago. Nor was he aware of the odd fact that Elise, though painfully aware of her feelings for Daltrey, had not the slightest intention of giving in to them.

Nine

The soggy heat of August had long passed, and the fox-hunting season had not yet arrived. Many of the upper ten thousand were gathering on country estates to enjoy the grouse-hunting season. However, that society was no longer concentrated in London did not lessen the swift passage of gossip from country house to country house. Rumors, especially juicy ones, traveled faster than the London Mail.

The talk of the town and country set was of the Duke of Evert, who had separated from his wife of many years and taken up openly with his mistress, Jane Swift, who now presided over his immense estate, Pemberton. This event, while sad for the rest of the duke's family (his three horse-faced daughters had fled to their aunt's house in Dartmouth), was a source of censure of the duke, since the woman he had chosen to preside over his table was not even remotely acceptable to society. The fact was, the woman was not only vulgar, she was homely, and society found such a combination appalling.

This topic was the greatest on-dit of the time.

Second to it, however, was the unaccountable transformation of Viscount Daltrey from rake to respectable peer. Speculation as to his motives were rife: some said it was caused by his break with Cordelia, Duchess of Anderleigh; some said it was due to the death of Sir Jeremy Stanton; some said it was due to Lord Daltrey's marked attentions toward Lord Dunnington's ward, Elise de Bourget. Daltrey's inexplicable preference for Miss de Bourget had not gone unnoticed: nothing ever went unnoticed among the upper ten thousand. Indeed, how could it be otherwise?

The Duchess of Anderleigh had noticed this preference, and it made her wild with jealousy. The fact that she was now the wife of another man made no difference to her. She regarded any man who had ever shown attention to her as being quite naturally part of her court, and she had hoped to convert Daltrey, despite their foolish quarrel, into her main cicisbeo. It would add to her esteem, for Daltrey was a dashing, wealthy figure.

To be deprived of Daltrey, and deprived of him by that French creature, was inexpressibly painful for her, and it made her angry in the extreme. Therefore, any time she had a chance to say an unfavorable thing about Miss de Bourget, she did so; any time she had the chance to start a cruel story about the girl, this she did as well. Poor Lady Southward had a terrible time keeping track of all the rumors, countering them as best she could.

Freddy Daltrey had become a famous figure once again, but now he was famed for his sobriety and propriety, and these good qualities extended throughout all aspects of his life. He hadn't gambled in ages; he'd given up ladybirds and hard drinking; his old friends found him rather a dead bore.

He spent time with the managers of his estates, trying to devise ways to improve their productivity and improve the standards of life for his tenants as well, which many persons criticized as being radical beyond need.

Hopeful mothers, instead of warning their daughters about Lord Daltrey, invited him to whatever they could; though many young girls had set their caps at him before, now that he was such a respectable young man, such a model of decorum, the number quadrupled. His heart, of course, was touched by none of them, though he was unfailingly polite.

It was the last week in September when Frederick, Lord Daltrey, looked into his mirror and considered what he saw reflected within: a man who at long last knew what he wanted in life, and why he wanted it. He saw a man who had succeeded in making the definite changes he had sworn he would make, and who was now ready to try his hand with Elise de Bourget once more.

He was staying at Devonhurst at the time, and so ordered his bay stallion Pacer to be saddled and made ready for the journey to Barcourt Manor. He set out early, after a light breakfast of coffee and scones, a man confident that his offer would now meet with Elise's acceptance.

Elise de Bourget saw Lord Daltrey approach from an upstairs window. To her mind, no other gentleman was his equal on horseback: his dark, powerful figure was somehow set off by his obvious mastery of the great animal he rode upon. His attire was perfection itself: his broad shoulders beneath his hunting jacket, tall beaver hat, white cravat, his beige breeches that clung to his legs like a second skin, his shining top-boots.

Elise had not seen Daltrey once in the time since he had virtually retired from society, and she was well aware that some said he had changed his ways on her behalf, to win her respect and affection.

As high as her heart surged when she set eyes upon the man she loved, it sank to equal depths when she realized that she must inevitably speak to Lord Daltrey, and that she must find words to give him the answer she knew she must.

She opened the door to the bedchamber, and heard Lewis, taking Lord Daltrey's hat and coat, assuring him that Lord Dunnington would receive him. She watched as Lewis showed him up to her guardian's bookroom, and then sighed as she saw Daltrey go within.

It was only a matter of time before they would send for her, no more.

* * *

"How do you do, my boy?" said Lord Dunnington, putting his arm around his visitor, and shaking his hand warmly. "I have been hearing a lot about you lately. I'm sure the London inamoratas are desolated by your sudden about-face.

"You know, you have become quite the most respectable young man of my acquaintance."

"Yes, Great-uncle Matthew, I knew you must have heard of my surprising ascent into virtue. It seems to matter not a whit whether my reputation is very good or very bad; I attract people's attention whatever way I follow."

There was a short silence.

"I expect you know why I have come, Great-uncle Matthew."

"Yes, my boy, I believe I do."

"I should like your formal permission to pay my addresses to Elise de Bourget, your ward."

"Very good, my boy. You have my blessing. It seems odd that the last time we met in this book-room, we spoke about the very same subject . . . your offering for Elise de Bourget."

"Yes, Great-uncle," he replied. "Wasn't I a fool not to do so at once?"

"Who knows? Things can change, as I perceive they have, and persons can change, as I perceive you have. I would have given my blessing at that time to any union between yourself and Elise, but I do so now with a far greater pleasure, for I see the sacrifices you have made in your own habits to make yourself acceptable to Elise as a husband. I commend you for that."

"Do you think this time she will accept me?" he asked anxiously.

Lord Dunnington looked warmly upon Lord Daltrey, for whom he had always felt a special affection.

"That, my boy, I cannot say. She has returned to her old, reclusive ways since she came back from Town; she does little else here besides read and work on her lace.

"She works her lace with such a passion that sometimes I wonder whether it's quite a wise thing for her to do. She seems quite possessed by it . . . the angels and the unicorns, everything so delicately made, that it is as if Elise has planned out and fashioned for herself a miniature paradise.

"Her mind is on her work, and so I cannot say precisely what her mood toward you may be; whether it is the same as it was, or whether it has changed.

"I wish you all success, but you'll simply have to try your luck."

Ten

When asked, she agreed to see him. What else could she do? Turn away an ardent suitor without giving him even the common courtesy of meeting him in person? It just was not done.

Elise de Bourget received Frederick, Lord Daltrey, in her private sitting-room in the west tower. She felt that she would better be able to endure the inevitable scene surrounded by her own chosen space and objects, in particular, the lace frame she had brought with her from France.

She motioned him to a seat, able to see his nervousness that showed in the slight play of his hands. He had dressed very properly in a coat by Weston, dark green, with biscuit-colored breeches, and shining boots. He looked the pattern-card of a perfect gentleman: elegant, in command of himself.

Elise had selected a demure dress of light-yellow muslin, with puffed sleeves and scalloping at the neckline. A thin gold locket ornamented her tall neck; a few wildflowers adorned her hair. She looked lovely, and every time Daltrey stole a glance at her, his pleasure at being in her company deepened.

They waited quietly together, neither one wishing to be the first to utter a word.

Finally, Lord Daltrey spoke.

"We have not seen each other for some time, Miss de Bourget," he ventured.

"No, we have not," she replied in a soft voice.

"I have been spending most of my time at my country house, Devonhurst, which you must know is not far from here."

"I see. Has it been pleasant?"

"Yes, very. How have you been?"

"I have been living here most of the time, with Lord Dunnington, very quietly, as you can see. Lady Southward had to go off to care for her daughter, who is being confined, so my tutorials in the ways of English ladies have ended for the moment."

"Do you miss them?"

"At the beginning, I found it all rather amusing, but it soon began to pall, and I had just as soon remained in my room, weaving and making my lace."

"I see," he said, clearing his throat. "Miss de Bourget, the last time we met . . ."

Elise colored hotly, knowing what was to come.

"Please, Lord Daltrey—"

"Let me finish. I have just finished speaking with your guardian, and with his kind permission, indeed, with what he told me was his *blessing,* he has allowed me to pay my addresses to you."

"Lord Daltrey, I cannot . . ."

He walked to her, and put his hand to her lips to silence her. Tears began welling in her gray eyes.

"Elise, give me a chance; just give me a chance, I beg of you. I ask no more than that . . . a chance. I ask for no promises; I do not ask for any return of feelings. I simply ask that you allow me to spend time with you so that we may both come to know one another better. Can you not oblige me in this?"

"Lord Daltrey, I know you well enough already," she said.

Stung, Daltrey colored hotly.

"I admit I have wasted my life up till now," he said bitterly. "I regret that. But believe me, I have changed."

"I do believe you. I know what you have done. I am happy for you; I salute your courage," Elise said.

He looked at her in an uncomprehending fashion.

"Then why will you not at least give me the chance I ask for?"

"It has nothing to do with you, Lord Daltrey. I have my reasons."

"If you have reasons," he said insistently, losing his patience, "why may I not be permitted to know what they are?"

Her eyes flashed with anger suddenly.

"Not all reasons revolve around *you,* Lord Daltrey, as does the earth around the sun!" she said sharply. "As I said, I have reasons of my own which are very compelling, very private, and which I do not wish to share with you . . . or with anyone. Not even Lord Dunnington."

"Don't be ridiculous!"

"I do not wish to cause you pain, but you must realize that nothing you can do or say can change my mind, nothing."

"What am I to understand? That you have no regard for me at all? That the friendship we once shared was a false one? That my history makes you despise me?"

Her gray eyes melted into inexpressible pain, and she cried, "Despise you? On the contrary, I have always held you in my highest esteem. No, Lord Daltrey, it is myself I despise, and *that* is why I will not marry you."

"Ecod, my good girl! This is the sheerest nonsense!"

Lord Daltrey took Elise into his arms, and kissed her with a passion of which she had never dreamed, and a passion which she returned with equal ardor. They remained enveloped in each other for what seemed like a lifetime, till Lord Daltrey whispered, in a low, husky voice, "Can feelings such as this be denied?"

As if being sharply brought back to her senses, Elise de Bourget backed away from him, suddenly looking at him as if he were her mortal enemy.

In a hard, frightened voice, she said, "Yes, such feelings *can* be denied, Lord Daltrey." I thank you for your offer, but I cannot marry you. Not now. Not ever."

"Damn and blast! What are you, mad?" he said, banging his fist hard on the side table.

"Perhaps so," she said angrily, gesturing toward the door.

"Perhaps I am. At any rate, I wish you a good day, Lord Daltrey."

A look of rage on his face, Lord Daltrey made no reply. He favored Elise de Bourget with a frigid, formal bow.

The slam of the door as he left the room resounded throughout the house.

Everyone in the household, from the master to the scullery maid, knew by that sound precisely what had been the outcome of their interview.

Eleven

If the winter passed in a passionate renewal of Lord Daltrey's wild ways, it passed in a new return to solitary ways for Elise de Bourget. She kept up her constant lacemaking, and was once again the quiet, thoughtful girl Daltrey had rescued at his great-uncle's ball. Lord Daltrey, on his part, took up with a vengeance a new set of *petites amies,* including the gorgeous and hot-headed redhead who called herself Jeannette d'Abry, and was known for a tell-all diary of her exploits which had brought several prominent politicians to their knees.

It was early spring before they met again, in London, at a ball held by the Duke and Duchess of Evert, in celebration of their Lady Alice Evert's coming-out, and in secret celebration of the end of some family difficulties. The duke's vulgar mistress, Jane Swift, had died suddenly (some said suspiciously), and so all the problems between them were immediately resolved. It was very odd, and some persons said rather undignified to hold a party to celebrate the end to such a scandalous affair, but since they knew the duke to be ready and willing to spend a fortune on entertainments, no one who was invited thought to decline.

Elise de Bourget had not wanted to attend the ball, but as Lady Southward and Lord Dunnington particularly wished that she attend it, she acceded to their wishes. Elise, of course, was desperately afraid she might encounter Lord Daltrey at such an affair, and she was standing around in the great crush fanning herself, wishing she were home when the a footman announced in stentorian tones the arrival of Viscount Daltrey.

So flustered was she that, although she had promised herself she would dance not at all, when Captain Sir John Hunt asked her to dance with him, she surprised herself and accepted him. She was desperate to know just how to conduct herself, she could feel the hot spread of a blush on her face already, even though Lord Daltrey was on the far side of the ballroom.

Lord Daltrey watched Elise de Bourget and Captain Sir John Hunt dance from the other side of the floor, and felt every step as if it were a blade driven deep into his heart. Elise was looking particularly lovely in light green silk dress; the low neckline was lined with small silk roses, and was cut so as to show off her shoulders and her swanlike neck. Her hair was piled high atop her head; she wore a necklet of pearls and a matching pearl tiara. He thought she looked like a goddess on a Greek frieze.

As he watched her gracefully perform the steps of the dance, Daltrey tried to smother his jealousy. He told himself that Elise would surely toy with Sir John Hunt's feelings just as she had toyed with his; in his mind, he repeated against her a long negative litany. He told himself that Elise was just another heartless woman, just another woman without feelings, like the most greedy of his ladybirds. He told himself she was no better than Cordelia, who had married for a title, ignoring love.

Elise had said she would never marry him, but he had felt her desire for him in that first breathless kiss. What kind of woman would kiss with such passion, and not wish to marry? Was her reputation not what it should be? Or was he too poor to suit her needs? Was she of a Puritan turn of mind, and his notorious reputation still an obstacle?"

It was maddening. *She* was maddening. He wished he had never met the heartless jade.

He would stay well away from Miss de Bourget this evening. He would make an appearance, speak with his friends, and take his leave.

* * *

Elise de Bourget very prettily thanked Sir John for the dance, and moved as far away from Lord Daltrey as she could manage, which unfortunately put her in a corner of the room near to where Cordelia, Duchess of Anderleigh, was holding court. Elise hoped the duchess would take no notice of her, but this was not to be. She had stood there for only a few seconds when the duchess's false-honeyed tones could be heard above the music.

"Look! I declare, it's that French creature! I had thought she was not invited out among society any longer!" said the duchess. "Charles, do bring her over here and let us see what is behind this shocking story I have heard about Freddy Daltrey!"

Charles Wright, a vapid young man quite at the mercy of the duchess, actually tried to bring Elise over to their circle, but Elise wisely refused to come.

This refusal only made Cordelia more angry. Her voice became louder and more shrill. Elise winced as she heard it, and looked around to find Lady Southward, so she might make her escape before the duchess made another scene in public.

"What, Charles? She won't come and be sociable? Isn't that just the way of *peasants!*"

A little gasp passed from person to person when she said this. The smell of scandal was certainly in the air. Elise knew it was time to leave, and began to do so, when the duchess's next sally froze her in her footsteps.

"Yes, my dears, I call this girl nothing more than a *peasant,* for I have learned something more about her background . . . if you can call it that. This creature whom Lord Dunnington unwittingly tried to foist upon society is nothing more than a . . . a *lacemaker!* It is no different from being a dressmaker, or a hatmaker! A seamstress, a mantuamaker, a milliner!"

"How shocking!" cried her apparent cicisbeo, Charles.

"You there!" the duchess cried out to Elise, gesturing toward her haughtily with her fan. "Tell them! Isn't it true, what I've said?"

Elise summoned all of her considerable store of dignity, and walked toward the duchess with her head held high. The other guests gave way before her, making a path she walked down till she stood directly before Cordelia, looking her straight in the eye.

"Yes," replied Elise defiantly. "I do make lace."

"I told you so," said the duchess to her rapt audience, who began murmuring and whispering to one another.

"My mother taught me!" said Elise, not without pride.

"Oh, so there it is! You see?" said Cordelia in a nasty tone. "Her *mother* taught her. This Elise de Bourget, or whoever she is, must come from a long line of lacemakers, members of that underclass that is given the task of creating things for their betters.

"Well, Elise, do tell us: why are you trying to fob yourself off as a lady? Why didn't you tell Lord Daltrey where you really come from?"

Elise said nothing, but began to redden with shame.

"Why didn't you tell Lord Daltrey that the real reason you rejected his suit and broke his heart is that you spent the past seventeen years living in poverty, raised by a family of farmers?" crowed the duchess.

Elise looked for an escape route, but the crowd had now closed in around her. They were all whispering at her and pointed toward her, and weighing her worth with their callous eyes. She began to feel ill; she couldn't breathe. A mist of perspiration began to cover her brow.

The duchess went on, relentless, *"Why* didn't you tell Lord Daltrey that you are an ape-leader of twenty-four? *Why* would a vulgar old jade like you try to pass herself off as a young lady in her first Season? *Why* didn't you tell Lord Daltrey about what I noticed upon first meeting you . . . that your hands, when you arrived here, were *callused* from those years of hard labor? You're just a *peasant!"*

Elise was listening as if in a trance. She felt only the weight of the woman's irrational anger passing through her like the heat of fire. She turned white, and began to breathe rapidly. She put her hand to her heart, and heard the duchess say, "Why did

Lord Daltrey ask you to marry him? Because he did not know what I know, and what all London shall now know . . . that you are nothing but a nameless orphan, lacking distinction, lacking breeding, lacking family!

"Tell me at once! Is it true, or isn't?"

Elise replied in a small, strained voice, "I am twenty-five. I am an orphan. I lived with poor farmers. Worst of all, most true of all . . . I have no family."

Then, in the middle of the grand ballroom, Elise slipped to the ground in a dead faint.

On the other side of the ballroom, as he stood in the doorway of the cardroom, Lord Daltrey could make out the Duchess of Anderleigh's voice ringing out over the music. He could not make out the words precisely, but he heard her tone of voice very well: high-pitched and contemptuous.

He put his wineglass down on a sideboard, and began to thread his way through the crowd. Over the tops of turbaned heads, he made out the motionless form of Elise de Bourget, lying senseless on the ballroom floor. The crowd had all withdrawn a few feet around her, and were offering her no aid whatsoever; they were merely staring at her with a look of disgust on their faces, as if observing the corpse of an animal killed on a road.

Lord Daltrey growled at the crowd in general, saying, "Move farther back! Give the girl some air!"

Then he saw Cordelia standing there with a look of smug self-satisfaction on her face, and he shouted, "I might have known you would be behind this. What mischief have you done Elise de Bourget this time, madam?"

"I?" she said smoothly. "I have done nothing but speak the truth about this vulgar girl. The girl admitted in front of everyone what I said about her was quite correct. If I were you, Lord Daltrey, I'd know her for what she is, and have done with her."

"If I were you, Cordelia," said Daltrey very loudly, with deep undisguised contempt, "I would be ashamed of my contemptible conduct. If I were you, for the rest of the London Season I should never show my face in public again."

Cordelia then slapped Lord Daltrey full across the face.

"I see that I have struck a nerve, madam," he said to her scornfully, bowing to her with extreme hauteur. "Your conduct, Your Grace, is *not* that of a lady."

The duchess struck him once again, and then, with tears of humiliation burning down her cheeks, she turned and ran out of the ballroom.

Lord Daltrey swept up into his arms the prostrate body of Elise de Bourget, and, carrying her, exited the ballroom.

Twelve

Lord Daltrey brought Elise de Bourget straight home, and at the time when he gave her over to Lord Dunnington's servants, she still had not regained consciousness. He spoke to his great-uncle only briefly, who assured him a doctor would be sent for at once and that Miss de Bourget would receive the very best of care. He returned to his rooms, and spent a fitful night, worrying about her.

He called first thing in the morning, hoping to be able to visit Elise, but instead was summoned by Lord Dunnington, who received him in his library. Dunnington looked as if he had not slept all night; his face was care-worn and weary.

"Sit down, Frederick. I have some things to tell you," said the elderly man, with a look of deep concern.

"Good God, sir! Tell me at once what is wrong! How is Miss de Bourget?"

"Not very well at all, I'm afraid. On the express orders of Dr. Stevens, this morning at dawn I sent Elise, along with several servants, up to Barcourt Manor. She in the charge of one Mrs. Wardrup, an associate of Dr. Stevens."

"But why?"

"Dr. Stevens firmly believes that Elise's malady is mental in origin, and that the tranquillity of the countryside will most quickly restore her to her senses."

"I see," said Lord Daltrey uncertainly. "I had thought she merely fainted under the stress of some unkind words spoken to her by the Duchess of Anderleigh. That is what persons present there last night gave me to understand."

"There is a bit more to it than that, I'm afraid. Elise has not been herself at all since the incident. She is refusing to speak to myself, to Dr. Stevens, or to anyone. You should know that Dr. Stevens is not entirely sure when a recovery will occur, or *if* it will occur."

"Why ever not?"

"Shortly after Elise informed me that she had rejected your suit, I began to make inquiries about the details of her early life, as best I could at such a distance from France. It was only yesterday that I received a reply, a very sad and depressing one, I must say, from the very family with whom she stayed for many years.

"In the letter, are details of her life I had not known. Elise is said to have suffered very much during the Terror in France, and it is most likely that which perhaps has affected her mind."

" 'Affected her mind'? What do you mean 'affected her mind'?"

Lord Daltrey looked very grave indeed, and commented, "It is not the first time I have heard of something like this happening. A distant cousin of one of my friends had family in Spain, and told me of a case in which everyone in that family had died during a plague; afterward there was only one young boy left. The doctors were able to save his life, but due to the mental shock of losing his family, he lost the capacity for speech. Later, he was taken to Scotland where he lived out his days, but never said a word again till the day he died."

"It is the opinion of Dr. Stevens, and of myself, that this illness of Elise's has as its basis some sort of profound shock. Indeed, Elise's refusal of your offer of marriage, and her generally reclusive behavior, might have some basis in some events of her past. Elise's habit of spending hours up in her room alone, lacemaking, is certainly out of the ordinary."

"That is so," said Lord Daltrey grimly.

"All the laces that she creates, however, are certainly exquisite. Odd that something so beautiful should be linked to her past sufferings. I've never seen anything quite so fine in all my life as what she does, have you?"

"I've never really seen it. She never showed me."

"It's a wonder, believe me: her patterns, the definition of the lace figures are enchanting, almost magical. Was it her mother who taught her, I wonder, or those peasant people in the Vendée with whom she was finally found?

"I never had the heart to question her, you see. I once made the error of asking her a little of what her life had been since she lost her parents, but her reaction to that inquiry alone was so swift and so unhappy that I dropped the subject at once, and never after mentioned it, or said anything again about her life before she came to me."

Lord Dunnington sighed, and shook his head.

"Poor child. How she must have suffered, a small child alone, torn from the parents and the world she knew before, taken in secret and hidden with a peasant family Elise's mother and father knew they could trust entirely to keep her safe, should they not survive. Mme. and M. Marcale were worthy people, certainly worthy of the trust the Comte de Bourget and his wife placed in them. I have sent them a reward, though nothing can ever repay their kindness to Elise, for they sheltered her at their own peril."

Lord Daltrey was speechless, hearing this tale.

"That is what I wished you to know, my boy. A little of what I have learned of Elise's past. I expect she will remain living at Barcourt Manor permanently; English society is too cruel for such a sensitive soul."

"May I visit her, great-uncle?"

"You may do as you wish, my boy, but I think you must face the fact, that if it is marriage with her that you still have in mind, you really must give up hope. I think such ideas are, at this point, useless."

"Why?" he asked. "Nothing has changed."

"When I arranged passage for Elise, I had thought she would

come to me here at Barcourt Manor, I would set her up, and marry her off, with no particular difficulty. Now, I see that she has many problems, ones of a sort that are not easily solved. It's sad, but you must resign yourself to finding someone else to wed."

"I don't want anyone else. No one else but Elise will do for me."

"I don't mean to be cruel, Frederick, but you must be reasonable. Think of the future, think of the children, think of the girl herself! How can you marry a girl who is mentally unstable?"

"When you say 'unstable,' you really mean you think she's mad! Well, she's not mad, Great-uncle!"

"If she's not, she's the closest thing to it."

"No, this cannot be. I *must* see her. I must talk to her myself."

"Do as you see fit, my boy, but you had best prepare yourself for the worst."

Thirteen

As Lord Daltrey's carriage rounded the bend at which one caught one's first glimpse of the imposing vista of Barcourt Manor, he was strongly reminded of the day, now long past, when he had first made the acquaintance of Elise de Bourget, in his great-uncle's book room.

At that time, Daltrey had not even wanted to go out to spend a few days at Barcourt Manor, for some of his particular friends were come down to London. Nevertheless, out of the respect and affection he felt toward his Great-uncle Matthew, he had gone to Barcourt Manor, and he had been presented to the girl with impossibly red hair, and disturbing, deep gray eyes.

He had thought little more of Elise de Bourget until the night of the ball, when he chose to intervene on her behalf, and rescue her, or so he thought, from the toils of Cordelia Wynter-Wynbourne.

Lord Daltrey could hardly comprehend how long ago that seemed, and how much he had changed in the meantime. He now felt that his whole happiness revolved around a girl about whom he, at first meeting, had not given a second thought.

His carriage reached the front portico, and he alit, at once anxious about what Lord Dunnington had told him, and hopeful, despite his great-uncle's cautionary advice, that everything could somehow be resolved. Daltrey approached Thomas, the porter, whom he had known since he was a child, and wondered why the fellow was not greeting him with his customary warmth and friendliness.

"Good day, your lordship," Thomas said.

"I'll be staying for just a few days," said Lord Daltrey. "My man has my things. I am here to visit Miss de Bourget. I presume Lady Southward is staying with her?"

"No, Your Lordship. There's another lady in charge just at the moment. She's Mrs. Wardrup, and she be sent from the London Hospital. I'm sure she'll not be letting you see Miss de Bourget, not for some days yet. Mrs. Wardrup says she's not fit, and has ordered the way barred to all visitors, including you, my lord, if you'll pardon my saying so."

"I must see Miss de Bourget. Kindly show me in to see this Mrs. Wardrup."

"Just as you like, Your Lordship."

The interview that passed between himself and Mrs. Wardrup was even less satisfying than had been his discussion with Thomas at the front entrance. Daltrey told her he had Lord Dunnington's specific permission to speak with his ward, but Mrs. Wardrup would not be moved. She told him that Elise had retired to her rooms for the foreseeable future, that she wished to see no visitors, and that even if she had wished to see someone, it would not be allowed, for reasons of Miss de Bourget's health. Mrs. Wardrup showed him a letter Lord Dunnington had written, placing Miss de Bourget's welfare in her hands, and giving her full run of the estate.

Unwilling to be dissuaded from his objective, Lord Daltrey tried his luck with all the staff, who knew him very well indeed, and who pitied him. Not the housekeeper, not the butler, not the groom of chambers—no one could be persuaded to act against Mrs. Wardrup's wishes.

That night, Lord Daltrey dined alone in the large dining hall, feeling more wretched than he had ever felt before. He was so close to speaking with Elise again, and yet was being prevented even from making his case to her by an interfering old woman who knew nothing of the real facts of the matter.

After dinner, he went for a walk in the garden. He walked out over the lawn at a furious pace, made a round of the man-made lake, and returned by way of the western wing. There, he looked up, and saw a light burning in the window.

It was a window in the tower room Elise de Bourget stayed in.

A thought occurred to him, and as the sunset light faded into twilight, Lord Daltrey went over to the base of the stone tower. With his strong hands he got a good grip on the thick English ivy vines that enveloped the west wing tower at Barcourt Manor.

Slowly, inexorably, he began his difficult climb to the top of the tower—and to Elise.

Elise was sitting where she always sat when her thoughts were discomposed. She was in her tower room, weaving her beautiful lace, trying to finish a particular figure before all the light of day was gone. She was plying the thin needles through their paper patterns, though by now Elise could just as well have woven her fine figures without using any paper pattern at all. This was because each and every pattern she worked was either one of her own making, or her mother's making, or that of Madame Marcale, the peasant lacemaker who had sheltered her and had brought her up.

Elise's mother, Diane de Bourget, had woven mainly in the Venetian *punto in aria* style brought to France by Catherine de Medici when she married the man soon to become Henry II of France. Noblewomen, impressed by Catherine's skills, began to follow her example; that was when the making of needle lace became an accomplishment necessary to a well-brought up French young lady.

Madame Marcale, who was originally from Flanders, had been a master of bobbin lace, which, during the time when she worked in service of the de Bourget family, she learned to combine with needle lace as well.

Both techniques became second nature to little Elise. Sometimes Elise wove needle lace; sometimes she wove bobbin lace, keeping perfect track of scores of hand-carved wooden or ivory bobbins, winding them around their base-strings deftly, purposefully, without error. Madame Marcale always complimented Elise, even when she was still a child, about the cleverness of her fingers and her mastery of these two forms of lacemaking.

In the days since her recent, sudden exit from London life, Elise had done little else than work on her lace, as she was doing as Lord Daltrey peered in at her from the window. She would hardly speak, hardly move, hardly do anything but make lace, sometimes furiously, sometimes doing so with a deep sadness, rarely stopping for sleep or for food.

Elise wove as would one possessed—and this was in fact, the case.

She was weaving all her feelings into the lace, just as she had done when she was a child, weaving until her deepest feelings became part and parcel of the lace pattern itself, and no longer a part of herself.

One could, if one knew the secret, learn the story of her life by reading the lace of Elise de Bourget that was still stored in her cedar box.

There was the first piece, the most important piece at the beginning, which she had completed under the tutelage of her lady mother, the Comtesse de Bourget.

One could see quite clearly the lines woven by the child's uneven fingers, and the corrections made, patiently, time after time, by her mother. Diane de Bourget, whose nimble fingers could work six hundred pins an hour, was able to complete less than a third of an inch per week, so that first piece, all in all, was not so very long.

One could still see how, with practice, the child's confidence and capacity had increased; as it did so, the patterns Diane set her daughter to make became more challenging and more intricate. As the lace went on and the girl's mastery became apparent, her mother would set her daughter Elise another task, which she would learn, have corrected, and then add to her repertoire.

And then, at a certain point, that first, somewhat childish, pattern of sampler lace came to an abrupt end. That piece, made by mother and daughter together, was the piece of lace Elise treasured most, and kept in her cedar box wrapped in a rich piece of blood-red velvet.

Lord Daltrey peered in the open tower window, and saw Elise de Bourget at last. Her auburn tresses were left loose, reaching down across her shoulders, her hands swiftly and deftly weaving her lace. With her swanlike neck, her perfect white skin, and her long fingers, he thought she looked like the most beautiful woman he had ever seen in his life. Then she turned toward him, and he knew that she was the most beautiful creature in the universe.

She was unsurprised by the manner of his entrance, simply saying, "You should not have come."

"Call me by my Christian name, Elise."

She obediently replied, "Frederick, you should not have come here."

Lord Daltrey swung himself onto the window sill, and jumped to the floor. He went over to Elise, took her hand, and knelt at her feet.

"They told me you would not speak to me, or to anyone," he said with a worried look, searching her face to see if she had undergone some obvious mental change.

"I had nothing to say," she said with a shrug. "There is nothing to say."

"You must marry me, Elise."

She bowed her head and sighed, saying, "No. I cannot."

"You must marry me."

"No. I cannot," she replied, more firmly. "I am not fit to be your wife, Frederick. The things the Duchess of Anderleigh said about me are true: I have no family; I was raised by peasants; I am nothing but a lacemaker.

"I am capable of being nothing more than what I am today."

"You are capable of being Lady Daltrey," he said tenderly, "if you would but consider it."

Lord Daltrey took her in her arms, and the kiss they exchanged was the sweetest he had ever tasted. He tried to keep her within his embrace, but she pushed him away, shaking her head.

"Frederick, I am a wounded person," she said, beseeching him. "I *must not* love again. I loved once, and they were all taken from me, and I will not endure that pain again."

She walked over to her cedar box, and lifted up its heavy lid, allowing its fresh smell to permeate the tower room.

"Look at this lace. Do you see it? Do you understand it? *This lace is my life.*"

She picked up one particular piece, filled with an intricate design of lilies and angels, saying, as she held it up to the light, "This lace is how I survived the Terror, and have survived these many years since. Do you see this part, right here?"

"It looks like a garden."

"Yes. That is where I have designed and portrayed what I call 'the garden of souls.' That is where I put everyone I loved who was taken from me. This figure stands for my mother, this one for Papa, and these angels for little Jean and Marguerite."

"You lost your family, Elise?"

"I did," she said simply, with a slight shrug of her shoulders. "You see, I had the misfortune to grow up in France at the very most dangerous of times. The *ancien régime* had fallen, for the most part, and all those citizens who were happy to see it go spent their time amusing themselves by tracking down and ridding themselves of anyone who reminded them of the excesses of the old order.

"Unfortunately, my parents were of the aristocracy. My father was the Comte de Bourget; my mother, the Comtesse Diane de Bourget. There was my little brother, Jean, who would have succeeded to Papa's title, had he lived, and there was my sweet baby sister, Marguerite.

"We were all at risk, of course, from the very beginning. My father was quite liberal, and at first he had approved of the new political changes being made, but he saw, early on, the bloodthirsty turn that events were taking, and he had us all sent deep into the countryside. We were split apart, my mother with the baby with a family in the village of Brielle, my brother Jean in a place called Valentins, and I was put in the custody of a servant of ours, called Madame Marcale.

"I remember so well the moment when we all parted and I had to say farewell. I said goodbye to my father, who scooped me up into his arms and hugged me and kissed me, and told me he would see me again as soon as he was able. I remember kissing and hugging my mother, and my brother and sister, and being led away, and put into a peasant's cart, filled with straw, to cover me and hide me.

"I never saw any one of them again."

Lord Daltrey could hardly bear listening to her story, but he held his tongue, giving Elise the strength to continue. Her eyes welled up with tears, as she said, "During the many years I lived in secret with Madame Marcale, I learned to spin my feelings into lace, and I began my work at once, after that last parting. I was only seven, and I was desperately lonely, and frightened. How could I not be?

"From the very first night, when I had just been brought into their country house, I overheard Madame Marcale talking with her husband about how they were putting their own lives in danger to shelter an aristocrat's child. That was the night I took out my needles and patterns, and I began in earnest: I wove the Marcales's fear and their courage into that lace. The very next night, when I hid in a closet, terrified, and I could hear horrible shouts outside and I realized that the village people were looking for me, in order to take my life, I wove my own fear into my lace.

"At night, when I missed my mother and father, I would make

my tears cease by weaving my love and my misery into my lace. Otherwise, you see, it would have been unbearable."

There was a moment of silence, and then Elise wearily began again.

"After the war, we tried to locate them, but there was no trace. They had vanished, totally. I knew they were lost to me forever. All that remained to me was my love for them, and my memories of them."

She put the lace down, and looked at him again with her beautiful gray eyes.

"That is how I have survived all these years. I wove every feeling I ever had into that lace, and through it I made for myself my own paradise, a universe in which nothing would ever go wrong."

For the first time, he saw her eyes blaze into anger.

"I have everything to lose by loving you!" she said. "Everything! Everyone I ever loved was taken from me . . . do you think I want to suffer that again?"

She picked up the lace, and put it back roughly into the cedar chest, slamming its lid.

"There is an ancient saying which goes: 'Sooner or later, whatever is high shall fall, and whoever comes together will be parted.' No, Lord Daltrey. I have had enough for one lifetime. Rather than having to bear again the pain of ultimate parting, I prefer to live my life alone."

"Now you are being foolish beyond permission. Elise, I will not let you sink into this melancholy state, so you may act out some Cheltenham tragedy. Remember, I have seen you when you were in London. I have seen you when you were gay, dancing and laughing till the small hours of the morning."

"I was trying to be like other people. *That* was foolishness. The Duchess of Anderleigh brought me to my senses. It all became too much for me: it was too painful. Once I began to know you, and then to love you—"

"You do love me?"

She nodded, wiping her moistened eyes, saying, "I do. Once

I began to love you, all my old pains began to surface once again, and I saw my past would never allow me to forget who I was and what I had become. I saw I could never escape my own history."

He took her hand, and led her to a soft chair. She seated herself, still holding his hand, and he knelt at her feet. He felt himself calling on all of his inner strength, willing Elise to attend to his words.

"Let me tell you a secret, one that I learned from you, Elise. It is this: one must know who it is one cherishes, and then one must be unafraid to cherish them, come what may.

"I cannot bring back your family. I cannot promise you the day will never come when we are parted, for it must come. That is all true enough, but I *can* promise you that I will love you faithfully throughout your life. I *can* promise you that I will cherish each and every instant I am vouchsafed the wonder of your company.

"When I lost Jeremy Stanton, my dear friend, I felt so lost that my pain became insensibility, for I wished to feel no more."

"That is how it is," replied Elise. "That is just how I feel."

Lord Daltrey rose, leaned over toward Elise, and tipped her chin up.

Looking into her pensive gray eyes, he whispered, "One must *savor* life, Elise."

Slowly, and with extreme tenderness, Lord Daltrey began to cover Elise with kisses. He kissed her lips, her eyes, her forehead; he kissed her hands, each one all over, methodically, carefully, poignantly. He kissed her long, swanlike neck, and she began weeping.

He held her around the waist in his strong embrace, and he waited until her shuddering tears had subsided. He waited, still holding her in his arms, until they ceased.

He noticed a slight change in her breathing. He inhaled the rose fragrance that always enveloped her, and began to kiss her once again.

Then, at first shyly, and then with a steadily heightening confidence, Elise began to kiss Lord Daltrey in return, returning his ardor with an equal strength and equal tenderness, as well as with the deep transforming gratitude of love.

Epilogue

The marriage of Elise de Bourget to Frederick, Lord Daltrey, was celebrated at St. George's, Hanover Square, with much pomp and circumstance; Lord Dunnington was well pleased with the union, which was a long and happy one that produced much progeny.

Cordelia, Duchess of Anderleigh, was not invited to the wedding, to the surprise of no one. Soon afterward Her Grace was declared persona non grata amongst the *ton,* even though she was the wife of a duke.

In the end the duchess was forced to take her silly, wealthy husband and retire to Ireland for, due to her past unkindness to the Viscountess Daltrey, no one at all would receive her.

About the Author

Isobel Linton lives with her family on Cape Cod. Ms. Linton's Zebra Regency romances include A GENTLEMAN'S DAUGHTER and FALSE PRETENSES. Her newest Zebra Regency romance, AN IMPROMPTU CHARADE, will be published in September 1996. She loves hearing from her readers and you may write to her c/o Zebra Books. Please include a self-addressed stamped envelope if you wish a response.

ZEBRA REGENCIES
ARE THE
TALK OF THE TON!

A REFORMED RAKE (4499, $3.99)

by Jeanne Savery

After governess Harriet Cole helped her young charge flee to France—and the designs of a despicable suitor, more trouble soon arrived in the person of a London rake. Sir Frederick Carrington insisted on providing safe escort back to England. Harriet deemed Carrington more dangerous than any band of brigands, but secretly relished matching wits with him. But after being taken in his arms for a tender kiss, she found herself wondering—*could* a lady find love with an irresistible rogue?

A SCANDALOUS PROPOSAL (4504, $4.99)

by Teresa DesJardien

After only two weeks into the London season, Lady Pamela Premington has already received her first offer of marriage. If only it hadn't come from the *ton's* most notorious rake, Lord Marchmont. Pamela had already set her sights on the distinguished Lieutenant Penford, who had the heroism and honor that made him the ideal match. Now she had to keep from falling under the spell of the seductive Lord so she could pursue the man more worthy of her love. Or was he?

A LADY'S CHAMPION (4535, $3.99)

by Janice Bennett

Miss Daphne, art mistress of the Selwood Academy for Young Ladies, greeted the notion of ghosts haunting the academy with skepticism. However, to avoid rumors frightening off students, she found herself turning to Mr. Adrian Carstairs, sent by her uncle to be her "protector" against the "ghosts." Although, Daphne would accept no interference in her life, she *would* accept aid in exposing any spectral spirits. What she never expected was for Adrian to expose the secret wishes of her hidden heart . . .

CHARITY'S GAMBIT (4537, $3.99)

by Marcy Stewart

Charity Abercrombie reluctantly embarks on a London season in hopes of making a suitable match. However she cannot forget the mysterious Dominic Castille—and the kiss they shared—when he fell from a tree as she strolled through the woods. Charity does not know that the dark and dashing captain harbors a dangerous secret that will ensnare them both in its web—leaving Charity to risk certain ruin and losing the man she so passionately loves . . .

Available wherever paperbacks are sold, or order direct from the Publisher. Send cover price plus 50¢ per copy for mailing and handling to Penguin USA, P.O. Box 999, c/o Dept. 17109, Bergenfield, NJ 07621. Residents of New York and Tennessee must include sales tax. DO NOT SEND CASH.

ELEGANT LOVE STILL FLOURISHES —
Wrap yourself in a Zebra Regency Romance.

A MATCHMAKER'S MATCH (3783, $3.50/$4.50)
by Nina Porter
To save herself from a loveless marriage, Lady Psyche Veringham pretends to be a bluestocking. Resigned to spinsterhood at twenty-three, Psyche sets her keen mind to snaring a husband for her young charge, Amanda. She sets her cap for long-time bachelor, Justin St. James. This man of the world has had his fill of frothy-headed debutantes and turns the tables on Psyche. Can a bluestocking and a man about town find true love?

FIRES IN THE SNOW (3809, $3.99/$4.99)
by Janis Laden
Because of an unhappy occurrence, Diana Ruskin knew that a secure marriage was not in her future. She was content to assist her physician father and follow in his footsteps . . . until now. After meeting Adam, Duke of Marchmaine, Diana's precise world is shattered. She would simply have to avoid the temptation of his gentle touch and stunning physique — and by doing so break her own heart!

FIRST SEASON (3810, $3.50/$4.50)
by Anne Baldwin
When country heiress Laetitia Biddle arrives in London for the Season, she harbors dreams of triumph and applause. Instead, she becomes the laughingstock of drawing rooms and ballrooms, alike. This headstrong miss blames the rakish Lord Wakeford for her miserable debut, and she vows to rise above her many faux pas. Vowing to become an Original, Letty proves that she's more than a match for this eligible, seasoned Lord.

AN UNCOMMON INTRIGUE (3701, $3.99/$4.99)
by Georgina Devon
Miss Mary Elizabeth Sinclair was rather startled when the British Home Office employed her as a spy. Posing as "Tasha," an exotic fortune-teller, she expected to encounter unforeseen dangers. However, nothing could have prepared her for Lord Eric Stewart, her dashing and infuriating partner. Giving her heart to this haughty rogue would be the most reckless hazard of all.

A MADDENING MINX (3702, $3.50/$4.50)
by Mary Kingsley
After a curricle accident, Miss Sarah Chadwick is literally thrust into the arms of Philip Thornton. While other women shy away from Thornton's eyepatch and aloof exterior, Sarah finds herself drawn to discover why this man is physically and emotionally scarred.

Taylor—made Romance From Zebra Books

WHISPERED KISSES   (3830, $4.99/5.99)
Beautiful Texas heiress Laura Leigh Webster never imagined that her biggest worry on her African safari would be the handsome Jace Elliot, her tour guide. Laura's guardian, Lord Chadwick Hamilton, warns her of Jace's dangerous past; she simply cannot resist the lure of his strong arms and the passion of his *Whispered Kisses*.

KISS OF THE NIGHT WIND   (3831, $4.99/$5.99)
Carrie Sue Strover thought she was leaving trouble behind her when she deserted her brother's outlaw gang to live her life as schoolmarm Carolyn Starns. On her journey, her stagecoach was attacked and she was rescued by handsome T.J. Rogue. T.J. plots to have Carrie lead him to her brother's cohorts who murdered his family. T.J., however, soon succumbs to the beautiful runaway's charms and loving caresses.

FORTUNE'S FLAMES   (3825, $4.99/$5.99)
Impatient to begin her journey back home to New Orleans, beautiful Maren James was furious when Captain Hawk delayed the voyage by searching for stowaways. Impatience gave way to uncontrollable desire once the handsome captain searched *her* cabin. He was looking for illegal passengers; what he found was wild passion with a woman he knew was unlike all those he had known before!

PASSIONS WILD AND FREE   (3828, $4.99/$5.99)
After seeing her family and home destroyed by the cruel and hateful Epson gang, Randee Hollis swore revenge. She knew she found the perfect man to help her—gunslinger Marsh Logan. Not only strong and brave, Marsh had the ebony hair and light blue eyes to make Randee forget her hate and seek the love and passion that only he could give her.

Available wherever paperbacks are sold, or order direct from the Publisher. Send cover price plus 50¢ per copy for mailing and handling to Penguin USA, P.O. Box 999, c/o Dept. 17109, Bergenfield, NJ 07621. Residents of New York and Tennessee must include sales tax. DO NOT SEND CASH.

COMING SOON: ROMANCES THAT
WILL MAKE YOUR HEART POUND

WHISPERS   (0-8217-5360-6, \$5.99)
by Lisa Jackson
The last thing Claire Holland St. John wants is anyone digging into her life. But her father's decision to run for governor of Oregon is awakening old ghosts and new scandals. Investigative journalist Kane Moran is proving the biggest threat of all. A man with a mysterious grudge against her family, the handsome, virile writer is asking too many questions for comfort, and arousing feelings Claire would prefer dormant. As long-buried secrets surface, Claire is drawn into Kane's embrace—unable to resist a passion that could destroy her . . . or save her life.

NIGHT, SEA, AND STARS   (0-8217-5325-8, \$5.99)
by *New York Times* best-selling author Heather Graham
It was fate that helped fashion executive Skye Delaney survive the crash of a Lear jet. It was also fate that stranded her on a Pacific island with Kyle Jagger, a seductive pilot who was both domineering and unexpectedly tender. In a sultry eden, where a man's passion and a woman's love were their only hope for survival, she succumbed to his caresses. Would a love born in paradise bring a lifetime of joy and happiness to two yearning hearts?

PRECIOUS AMBER   (0-8217-5328-2, \$4.99)
by Kathleen Drymon
Terror fills Amber Dawson when she realizes that her stepfather intends to sell her to the first fur trapper who can pay the price. When a surly woodsman claims her, there is nowhere for the flame-haired Missouri beauty to run— except into the arms of a magnificent Indian warrior. Spirit Walker is enchanted by the maiden with hair of golden fire and takes her to his mountain home. There he brands his precious Amber with his body and heart.

RIVER MOON   (0-8217-5327-4, \$4.99)
by Carol Finch
After a lifetime of being dominated, first by her father, then by her conniving husband, recently divorced Crista Delaney takes control: she becomes head of physical therapy in a far-off Oklahoma hospital. Nash Griffin, a former king of the rodeo, meets this spirited woman and finds only she can comfort his bitter soul. Can Crista trust Nash when all she's ever known of men is manipulation? Will she be left with heartache—or with precious love.

Available wherever paperbacks are sold, or order direct from the Publisher. Send cover price plus 50¢ per copy for mailing and handling to Penguin USA, P.O. Box 999, c/o Dept. 17109, Bergenfield, NJ 07621. Residents of New York and Tennessee must include sales tax. DO NOT SEND CASH.